Windy City RWA Presents:

A Lovely Meal

From Thanksgiving to New Year's:
A Collection of Romance Stories with Recipes

Acknowledgements

Profits from this publication will be donated to the Ovarian Cancer National Alliance. We appreciate the efforts of many professionals who donated and offered discounts on turnaround time and services:

This book was edited and coordinated by authors Ann Macela, Amy Alessio, Savannah Reynard, Mary Welk (http://www.marywelk.com) and editor Carla Ralston (Carla.ralston@lrsc.edu).

The cover for both the print and online versions was designed by the talented Karen McQuary at KMcQ Designs: https://kmcqdesigns.wordpress.com

It was formatted for both print and online publication by the exceptional professionals at Polgarus Studio http://www.polgarusstudio.com/ .

Dedication

This book is dedicated to the memory of author Cathie Linz, a founding member of the Windy City Chapter of Romance Writers of America. Cathie passed away in 2015 and was a treasured friend, mentor, librarian and author. She and her trademark red boots inspired us to write for this anthology and readers will enjoy catching our references to our beloved friend. For many, it is their first publication, something she would have cheered.

A Dedication to Cathie Linz

Early in 2015 we lost one of the romance genre's most passionate authors and advocates—a woman who has been a dear friend to so many of us. In addition to being a wonderful writer—both under the Cathie Linz and Cat Devon names—she was a vigorous and articulate spokeswoman for the genre. She was also a pioneer in an effort that led to a seismic shift in the way America's public libraries viewed the romance novel. In large part due to Cathie's vision and hard work, readers can walk into almost any public library in America and find a robust collection of romance novels cataloged and on the shelves.

It wasn't until after Cathie's death that I discovered how many writers, published and aspiring, she cheered on. If a writer were having a difficult time or unsure about her talents, Cathie was always there with encouraging words. Her personal need for a supportive writing community inspired her, to be one of the founders of the Windy City Chapter of Romance Writers of America, a vigorous group that has spawned many published writers.

Cathie was an avid reader and also one with a hugely generous heart. Nothing thrilled her as much as sharing her discovery of a new romance author with other readers. She read widely within the genre—loving any book that was well-written and delivered a great, happy-ending love story. She did have a quirk, however. As a reader, she preferred dark-haired heroes, and she confessed that, if she read a book where the hero had blond hair, she simply switched the hair color in her head. How is that for being adaptable?!

I admit I still talk to Cathie—and not always just in my head. I have to resist sending her emails at the end of my writing day to report on my progress with a particular chapter, plot line, or character. I know I'm not the only one.

Cathie, we miss you so much—your smiles, your words of encouragement, and most of all your passion for the books we care so deeply about. We dedicate this volume, with love, to you.

Susan Elizabeth Phillips

Contents

A Christmas I Do
By Katrina A. Bauer

Katrina Bauer is a storyteller turned writer. For the last few years she has been writing Contemporary Romances about Knights and Cowboys, learning her craft, making new amazing friends, and loving every minute. Thanks to the Chicago weather she gets a lot of time to write while cooped up with her daughters and husband. Learn more about her at www.katrinaabauer.com.

"Why does baking take so many ingredients?" Linda O'Brien-Fatoni huffed while shivering. She struggled to keep all her grocery bags from touching the elevator floor.

December in New York sucked with its cold and snow. That was the number one reason Linda spent Thanksgiving until after New Year's in a warmer climate. Her second reason was to avoid seeing her father.

"Because, my clueless friend, baking requires a dash of this and a smidgen of that," a bored Polly answered, checking her nails. "Unfortunately for you, ingredients aren't sold by the dash or the smidgen."

Linda glanced over at her BFF since birth with gratitude for not letting her linger in unhappy memories. Polly had not changed a bit; her long blonde hair and sun-kissed skin glistened in any light. Of course, her thin long frame had helped Polly become a trophy wife, first to a young jet setter, and when that marriage ended in a divorce, to an older husband who passed away a year ago.

Even though Linda came from the same Boston high society as Polly, she wanted to make a name for herself in a career she loved, not make a career of changing her name.

"When do you think the rest of the cooking supplies will be delivered?"

Polly lowered her hand with a smirk. "I'm sure within the hour."

The elevator door opened. Linda heaved up the bags, trying not to fall over from the weight, while Polly walked beside her, not offering any assistance. Polly was unwilling to sacrifice her French manicure to help a friend.

One of the best features of Linda's penthouse was the back entrance to the kitchen. It looked like a service closet door. Linda had found it to be her secret to a happy marriage for the past three weeks.

The two women walked past an apron belonging to Linda's housekeeper, Maria, before entering the spacious kitchen. Linda dropped the bags on the black granite counter top before fishing out her list and Paul's mother's cookie recipe.

"Why are you doing this again?" Polly asked, making herself at home on the barstool next to Linda's papers.

"I told you, Paul's mother hates me for marrying her son after knowing him for only ten days." She sighed. "And, the biggest sin of all, not getting married in a Catholic church."

Polly rolled her eyes, "In a church, on a beach, what's the difference? A marriage either lasts or it goes down in flames." Her lips kicked up. "With a hefty alimony check."

"I want her to like me, so Paul doesn't feel like he disappointed his whole family." Paul never said those words, but she saw it in his beautiful blue eyes. A ping of guilt struck her gut. She'd always wanted a close-knit family, similar to the one Paul described as his when they first met; a family with a rich history of funny stories and laughter.

Polly read the recipe over her shoulder. "What is a ring of fig?"

With a long suffering breath, Linda rested her head in her hands. "I don't know. It's for the filling. I bought bags of figs. The whole recipe is in pounds and cups. I guess in Italy way back when, they baked for the masses. Paul told me how he would make the dough with his dad while his mother and sister did the filling."

"According to the recipe, you need to grind all the filling ingredients together. How are you going to do that?"

"Grind?" She grabbed the recipe from Polly. Scanning down to the second paragraph, she read, "Combine all dried fruit and add slowly into grinder. A grinder? Oh my God, Polly." Panic started to build within Linda. "I don't even know how to use a mixer. How am I going to work a grinder? Did I buy one?"

Polly's hand rested on Linda's shoulder. "When Maria comes in tomorrow, show her the recipe. I am sure she can help."

Linda shook her head. "You don't understand. Paul wants to do this together on Saturday. These cookies are a family Christmas tradition, along with midnight Mass. Plus, his parents are coming over Sunday after church for coffee."

"Cookies are a Christmas tradition?"

"Yes." Hopelessness caused her voice to rise. "Apparently, there is more to it than going down to the kitchen while the staff makes Christmas cookies."

"Does Paul know you hate the holiday?"

Hate wasn't a strong enough word. Christmas brought back painful memories from her childhood. Thankfully, her phone alarm went off, pulling her from the thoughts of her last disastrous Christmas with her parents.

"Time to order dinner." She scrolled through her list of menus on her phone. "What restaurant haven't we had in a while?"

"Tell me the man hasn't figured out yet that you don't know how to cook?" Her friend still frowned down at the recipe.

"Nope. Mama's Kitchen it is." She called and ordered two dinners of meatloaf, macaroni and cheese, asparagus, and a side salad.

"Linda, I really think you need to come clean with Paul. It's not a good idea to start a marriage with a lie."

She flinched. "It's not a lie, it's a secret. You can't tell me you told either of your husbands everything in the beginning."

Polly glanced away for a moment. "With Warren, I waited until the end, which did not save our marriage." She brightened a bit. "And with Teddy, I was up front from the start with my flaws. He accepted them, and me, until he passed away. I realized being honest made our marriage stronger. I will not settle for anything less the next time around."

This, Linda hoped, would be her only marriage. She began to put the groceries away. Opening cabinet after cabinet, she noticed boxes and bags of foods she hadn't ordered. Maria must have signed for the wrong Peapod order. Hurrying to get the counter cleaned off, she pulled out dishes to place the take-out on before Paul got home.

Home.

For the first time in years, her heart felt complete in a home of her own. Well, theirs. Paul loved the penthouse the moment he walked in. He thought the view over Central Park put his Bronx apartment to shame. He marveled at the clean white oak and gleaming dark wood floors. Linda recalled him "oohing" as he continued further into her space.

Her father held a different opinion the one and only time he visited. He'd said in his condescending way, "This penthouse resembles a hospital ward. As an interior designer, you would think you'd know how to use color."

Simplicity gave her life control and order. Paul told her the same thing the day they met. She fell in love with him in a moment. Well, sort of. His gorgeous dark hair, striking blue eyes... She'd first noticed him coming out of the water on the beach, water dripping down his tan, well-muscled chest to his six-pack abs. His strong thighs made her mouth water and her mind go blank as he passed her and Polly.

"What qualities make a perfect husband?"

Polly had repeated her question three times before it sunk in.

"A perfect husband would support my career and its crazy hours. He would, of course, do the cooking, and keep me sexually exhausted in bed every night."

"If that's a proposal, I accept." A deep husky voice sent shivers down her spine. Turning, she faced a set of smoldering indigo eyes.

Her heart crashed against her chest in tidal waves. "Uh..."

A devilish smile crossed his seductive lips. "Hi, I'm Paul."

"Linda," Polly called from the door, "your deliveries are here."

She pulled herself back from the memory of the best and craziest day of her life.

Her best friend helped unbox the mixer, cutting board, mixing bowls, measuring things, and a rolling pin. Linda found places in her cabinets for all of it. She then put the take-out dinner on serving dishes and placed them in the warmer before setting her small glass table in the breakfast nook.

Quickly, they gathered up all the garbage and ran down the hall to the trash chute.

"Please, remember what I said." Polly gave her a tight hug. "Life is too short." Stepping back, she wiped away a tear.

"I will." Giving her friend a kiss on the cheek, Linda ran back into her penthouse.

Not many people understood Polly's relationship with Teddy. He was thirty years her senior, but when they looked at each other, Linda saw the love in their eyes. Teddy accepted all of Polly's little hang ups on not having children and why. His first wife gave him four children. He was content just being with Polly.

A twinge of guilt swam into her gut. Would Paul understand her reasons for hiding a few of her flaws? She glanced at the clock on the stove. "Five thirty, just enough time to do a little work until Paul arrives at six."

Her office was a safe haven for creativity. A large window took up one wall, illuminating her glass desk with pink hues from the sunset. Reaching into the top drawer of her white-oak file cabinet, she pulled out her appointment book. Sitting in her over stuffed black suede chair in the corner, she opened the book to December. She turned on the light and picked out a pen from the metal holder on another glass-top table.

"Cancun is where I should be working. I have never rescheduled a job in five years. I need to switch some jobs around to be here for Christmas." Bleakness crept into her chest. "How am I going bluff my way through this holiday? I don't even own a nice winter coat. I'll add those things to the list of things to buy." She scribbled the items in the back of her book.

She needed to contend with one more problem. She needed to avoid her father, who was also in town.

Honesty. Really.

Snow crunched under Paul Fatoni's boots as he walked along the cement ramp at the top of the parking garage. He muttered to himself, "This is sweet, our own parking spot. This is so much better than blocking out a spot on the street in the Bronx." His breath filled the crisp air.

He continued to the elevator that would take him to the building's lobby. Heat assaulted him the second he left the elevator and walked into the corridor. "Have Yourself a Merry Little Christmas" played from the speaker system above his head. A smile crept across his lips. How his life had changed in the last three weeks.

Paul had met the most amazing woman in Cozumel over Thanksgiving. He found himself totally transfixed by the beautiful strawberry blonde with sparkling green eyes and perfectly winged brows. Thinking of her small shapely frame made him hard. His fingers tingled at the thought of caressing Linda's soft, creamy skin. Images of the cute freckles across her nose and the way her nostrils flared when she laughed danced in his mind. God, he loved to make her laugh. When he thought of how her face lit up, the sound of little crystal bells rang deep in his chest.

His wife… *Wow, I have a wife.* In one crazy and insane moment he'd accepted a proposal. Well, more of a description of a husband. The woman wanted to be her own person, and didn't need a man to provide for her, but wanted one to warm her bed.

Perfect. How could he pass up such a great offer? Owning his own construction firm, he understood it took long hours and dedication to keep it afloat.

At first, he accepted her proposal as an ice breaker. With a simple touch of her hand, he felt intense immediate chemistry. He found himself wanting Linda like no other woman he'd ever met.

Right now, his sexy little wife would be in her office, working until the last moment.

Lightness seeped into his chest. He was home. Linda being there at the end of the day made him work faster and harder. Her sweet smile and the way her eyes sparkled when he talked about his work rendered him completely head over heels for her. Her simple touch inflamed him to new heights of passion he never knew existed.

The women he'd known before Linda only wanted to be taken care of, have babies, and spend his money.

Leaving the Bronx and the old neighborhood was the best decision they'd made as a couple so far. Since Linda worked from home, living in her penthouse really did make sense. Plus everything was taken care of, and when they wanted fresh air, they could walk across the street to the park.

Arriving at the door to their place, Paul inhaled deeply. Ah! Mama's meatloaf. He imagined by now his darling wife might have figured out you need pots and pans to cook dinner. A big smile formed on his face as he opened the door.

"Sweetie, I'm home," he called, but got no response. He proceeded through their spacious living room to the south corner of the penthouse.

Hands on hips, his wife stood in front of an oversized closet containing shelves, drawers, and bins filled with fabric and foo-foo things. An explosion of color and textures covered her desk, illuminating the white rug beneath it with a kaleidoscope of jewel tones.

"Which hue of cerulean do you think would go in a summer cottage in Maine?" she asked, not even turning.

Unable to resist, he crossed the room in purposeful strides and put his arms around her hourglass curves. "Hello, my Irish queen," he murmured, dropping kisses down her neck to where her pulse beat just for him. When she rested back against his chest with a moan, he resisted the urge to ease her down to the floor.

"Hello, my Italian virtuoso," she teased, holding tight to his arms for support. "You didn't answer my question."

She turned in his hold and her green eyes gleamed up at him before he devoured her parted lips. He'd spent most of the day dreaming of this moment. In his job, a loss of concentration at a thousand feet up ended in death.

Right now, all his thoughts focused on the hot sweet taste of her mouth. Their tongues mingled, and each swipe ignited a passion so hot it burned down to his soul. Tingling fingers ached to hold her lush breasts and firm round bottom.

Reaching his goal, she whimpered. God, he needed her so badly, it scared him to cardiac arrest proportions. Did a passion this strong last?

Small hands tangled into his hair, sending a lightning bolt down to his strained crotch. She gently pushed him away. "Paul," she uttered breathlessly. "I want you."

"I..." He rested his forehead on hers to catch his own breath. "I thought it was obvious I wanted you."

She backed away when he went to kiss her lips again. "No, I meant we can't do it in here."

He arched a brow. "Why not? We've done it in every other room."

Pink tinted her skin from the buttons of her white blouse to the tip of her brows. "I know, but I work in here, and I cannot be distracted by memories of our...adventures."

He fought back a grin to no success. He understood having a private space to work free of distraction. This was her place. Letting out a sigh, he released his Irish queen. "We can continue this later, after we get some nourishment to keep us going all night."

"I'm holding you to it." She laced her fingers with his, leading him to the kitchen. "You never answered my question."

He racked his brain.

"Which hue of cerulean do you think would go in a summer cottage in Maine?"

"May I remind you I'm a guy and have no idea what cerulean is?"

Her laughter echoed in the hall. "Oh, honey, I know you are a guy. Cerulean is a shade of blue."

Even her sassy tone and endearment touched him instead of annoying him. Maybe because the way she said it, it didn't have a Bronx accent.

He carried the two plates to the table and she brought the salad. Across from him, her glorious smile kept him from mentioning there was no salad dressing.

"Well?" she blurted out.

"Dinner looks good."

"No, silly. Would you like blue or not?" She held his stare, waiting.

"What color are your eyes?"

Her fork stopped inches from her mouth. "Green."

"No, I mean what shade." The crinkle between her brows made him chuckle.

"Just green, why?"

"They are not just green. They remind me of the grass covered hills in Ireland, and the way waves crash on the white sand beaches of Cozumel." Pulling out his phone, he looked up shades of green. "Here, I think they're a combination of sea foam and spring green. No… Here, harlequin." Even though he was sure she knew what he meant, he still slid the image across the table.

Tears clung to her lashes before one flowed down her cheek. Oh God, what happened?

"You said harlequin to describe my eyes." She wiped away the tears with a frustrated hand. "No man has ever taken the time to learn the different terms used to describe color. You understand me."

Tears of happiness he understood. His chest puffed up, wanting to make her cry like this always. Another part of him wanted to kill the other men she'd dated who didn't take the time to get to know his lovely wife.

Covering her hand, he spoke from his heart. "Of course I do. Your career is part of who you are. I get that you keep everything around here white so no other color impinges on your thoughts when inspiration strikes."

Now the tears flowed. "Paul, I love you more and more every day." She picked up her napkin with her other hand, not breaking their connection. Her pulse beat a heavy rhythm under his fingertips. "Your understanding and honesty make me want you right now."

Guilt crashed into his chest, the word *honesty* cooling any flames about to be ignited. He thought he loved her, and he told her he did in the heat of the moment to get her to marry him on the spot. Some days he believed in love, like now.

But, if he truly wanted her love, he needed to be completely honest about his family's feelings about their marriage.

Giving her hand a gentle squeeze, he released it. "We need nourishment first, remember?" Her eyes lowered with such disappointment it almost brought him to his knees. "Sweetie, we really should try and finish one meal you've made since we've been home," he teased.

She brightened then blushed. "Maybe we should try today."

"We can enjoy the view of the snow falling and talk while we eat." Her features fell again as he continued, "I thought after dinner I could go down to the storage area and bring up your Christmas decorations."

A loud clatter from the other side of the table made his Spidey senses go on alert. Her deer-in-the-headlights expression did not help his feeling of dread.

Linda stared at Paul, unable to speak, yet agonizing over how to explain. Agreeing to make cookies for Christmas after his visit with his mother was one thing. Decorating and buying into the season was a whole different escapade.

"Sweetie, is there something wrong?"

His concern and beautiful words touched her to her very soul. No man ever took time to understand her quirks. The man before her did it effortlessly in less than a month.

Honesty.

Damn Polly.

"I don't have any Christmas decorations." Picking up her fork, she stabbed into her meatloaf while waiting for the gasp she knew would come from Paul.

"Not even a wreath for your door?"

"No, I don't celebrate holidays, especially Christmas," she answered, not looking up so she wouldn't have to see his regret for marrying a Christmas dud.

"Sweetie." His soft voice wrapped around her like a warm security blanket. "Can you tell me what happened to make you so anti-holiday?" No hint of judgement tinted his words.

She met his stare, gaining her courage in his blue depths.

Honesty.

Taking a deep breath, she mustered every reserve to confess her flaw to the saint of a man sitting across from her.

"The Christmas I turned nine, from all outward appearances, looked like a child's Christmas dreams come true. I received everything I asked for, including a pony."

"Wow! I—"

Her hand went up to stop him before she lost her nerve. "After I opened all my gifts and I rode my pony in the ballroom, we sat down for breakfast. Again, everything I loved to eat covered the table. Once I'd filled my plate and taken my first bite, my father announced he and my mother were getting divorced. I remember the tears sparkling in my mother's eyes. My father got up and kissed my head, murmuring 'Merry Christmas, Baby.' We both watched him leave without looking back.

"My mother and I held each other and cried for a long time. Mrs. Parker, our housekeeper, came and hugged us both. She told us to be strong, that when God closes one door, he opens another. Together we would have to have faith in the new path God laid before us. Can you guess what our first steps were?"

Sadness, or maybe pity, covered his features and he slowly shook his head.

"We never spent Christmas in Boston or with my father ever again. We went to some place warm and adventurous instead."

"When was the last time you saw your father?"

Of course, let's keep asking questions about something she doesn't want to linger on. His strong loving hand covered hers. She welcomed the reassurance.

"My graduation. No, when I moved into this penthouse." His brow rose and she hurried to explain. "I didn't know he owned the building until I'd already signed the lease. My father happened to be in town for some sporting event with his sons."

"You have brothers?"

The old hurt rang in her chest at how her father started a new family, not once looking back, except with a check, because her father was a good provider, according to her mother. "I have never met them, and I do not plan to."

"Sweetie, I'm so sorry. I had no idea. Maybe we should forget about Christmas this year. Do you want to go back to Cozumel?"

Did this man fall from heaven? He loved his family and they were important to him, especially his grandparents. She would do anything to make him happy. He wanted her to meet them. After hearing all the wonderful stories about their holiday dinner, she wanted to meet everyone, too. Well, before this talk she'd wanted to.

"This is our first Christmas together. I want to make new memories with you." Even if it meant staying in the cold bleakness of New York; she kept the thought to herself.

His eyes glowed as he tugged her up from her chair and onto his lap. "I promise this will be the best first Christmas, with great new memories to wash away all the bad ones."

She got caught up in his hopefulness for a fresh start together. "Okay, but I make no promises."

Brushing a lock of her hair behind her ear, he kissed her temple. "All I ask is, if this gets to be too much for you, you'll tell me, and we'll be on the first plane to Cozumel."

This was his way of giving her an out. Grateful, she wrapped her arms around his neck. "I promise, but—"

He placed a finger to her lips. "Linda, I mean it, no buts about it. I want our marriage to be one of trust and honesty."

Something flashed behind his lashes, then disappeared in an instant. The next thing she knew he lifted her into his arms.

"Wait! I thought we were going to eat dinner first!" she shrieked.

He halted steps from the doorway. "You're right." He carried her back to her seat. "We'll finish dinner and then plot out our plans for the rest of the week." Sitting down, excitement radiated from him. "First thing tomorrow, I'll pick you up a winter coat and gloves."

Her mouth gaped. How did he know?

He tipped up her chin with his finger. "I noticed you don't own a winter coat when I hung up mine in the closet our first night. Plus, you didn't bring one to wear home from the airport." His lips kicked up on one side. "Even though I did enjoy carrying you wrapped inside my parka."

She shivered at the memory of being in his strong arms, the warmth of his body heating her in all the right places. The second they crossed over the threshold, the door clicked shut behind them. They'd shed every item of clothing into a careless pile in the foyer. Then he'd sprawled out on her white rug like a sacrifice for a pagan goddess before obliging every one of her demands. Afterwards, he'd covered the two of them with the cashmere throw from the couch. They'd slept on the floor until noon the next day, only waking up to indulge again in pleasure.

"If you keep daydreaming about our escapade, we're never going to get through this wonderful meal."

Heat shot from her toes to the top of her head. "Sorry. Can you pick me up a Northface coat like yours?"

His sexy smile returned, letting her know they were going to be okay for now. "It would be my honor, sweetie."

"Make sur—"

"I get a white one, with gloves to match."

Her heart melted even more at his understanding. "Yes. Oh, I almost forgot, I got all the things we need for the cookies today."

"Really?" His brow rose. "Did Polly help you?"

"Well, she came with. You know with Polly, anything remotely resembling work she doesn't do. Plus, she met me after her nail appointment."

"Nothing is worth sacrificing a manicure. Trust me, with three sisters, I know. Every Friday when my mom came home from the grocery store, their nails were always conveniently wet or not quite dry." She laughed at how he shook his hand and admired his own nails, imitating his sisters. "So I had to bring all the bags in by myself. Mind you, up two flights of stairs."

"Oh, you poor thing," Patting his arm, she sympathized.

"When we're out tomorrow shopping for Christmas decorations, maybe you should pick up a parka and gloves."

"Why?"

"Because, my sweet, we're going to have to get a tree and carry it home."

Before panic consumed her body, he picked her up, molding his lips to hers. Walking to the bedroom, he awakened their hunger from earlier in her office. She tumbled onto the bed. Paul followed, covering her with his wonderfully warm hard body. Greedily she pulled up his black, long-sleeved Henley to run her palms over his chest.

A loud groan vibrated at her neck where he kissed and nipped his way down. Eagerness for more raced through her. She let her hand lower to his tight abs, and then to the top of his jeans.

"You are killing me, my Irish seductress."

She giggled at his wicked names for her until his hot mouth covered her breast. Her long moan made him chuckle.

Paul knew how to distract her from her issues, at least for now. Tomorrow, she'd obsess over all the changes in her life in the past few weeks and hours.

Paul's new bride slept curled up next to him. Her hair flowed over his chest like a layer of silk. He enjoyed the feel of her naked skin against his. Her lush lips inches from his neck drove him mad. It was a good kind of mad, one he wanted to indulge in every night.

Her confession earlier weighed heavily on his mind. If his dad had left like hers did, his mom, he, and his sisters might not have recovered.

I want our marriage to be one of trust and honesty. God, I'm such an idiot. A marriage based on trust and honesty?

He couldn't even bring himself to tell Linda about how poorly his visit went with his mother. He gave her the recipe for the cookies with a lame excuse about wanting to start their own Christmas tradition. He did add later that his mother was a little disappointed they didn't get married in a church.

His mother's screams and sobs still echoed in his mind.

"Paul Mathew Fatoni Junior, how could you get married without your family and not in a church? A wedding on a beach does not count in the eyes of the Lord. You are living in sin! Is this woman even Catholic?"

His loud mouth cousin George had spilled the news before he could introduce his parents to Linda, in his own way. He thought of ways to get back at his cousin, but killing him in the slowest, most painful way didn't seem a good enough punishment. He'd never take George on vacation again. "I'm not sure it ever came up," he mumbled.

"What!" she yelled.

He ducked when the pot from the stove flew past him and hit the kitchen wall. Boy, his mother hadn't been this mad since he and George *borrowed* his dad's car. They would have gotten away with it if they'd known at the time that the gas gauge was stuck on full. They'd barely made it out of the kitchen alive when the pots and pans started flying.

Despite being small in stature, the dark-haired Italian woman had a large voice that carried throughout the neighborhood. He just didn't want everyone to know he'd gotten married.

She continued to yell. "You listen to me, young man. You will bring that hussy of a wife over here, and the two of you will be married at St. Andrews."

He never yelled back at his mother. His father said, "For harmony sake, keep your mouth shut and agree with your mother." But today he couldn't. Linda was his wife, the woman he cared deeply for. "Mother, you will not call my wife a hussy. I convinced her to *marry me*."

"Why in God's name would you convince a woman you hardly know to marry you?" Her voice hit a new pitch.

"Have you ever heard of love at first sight?" he questioned, knowing he wanted Linda because she was different.

"Oh, for Pete's sake, that only happens in the movies. This is the real world, Paul. You date a woman for a while, and then get married in a church. Not on some beach in a foreign country. Certainly, not to some strange woman who makes your dick hard."

Wow. His mother had lost it.

"Mother," he started in a lethal tone. "Do you remember the saying '*a daughter is a daughter all her life; a son is a son until he finds a wife*'? You will not say one more callous word about my wife, or you will never see me again."

She flinched as if he'd struck her.

"Okay, this is over." His father came in from reading his paper. Paul found himself being lifted by the collar from his chair at the kitchen table. His dad was called Big Paulie in the neighborhood for obvious reasons. He never yelled; he didn't have to. Just the thought of him raising a hand was enough of a threat. His dad pushed him into his recliner before getting nose to nose with him. "Listen to me well, because I will only say this once. I fell in love with your mother the moment I laid eyes on her in P.E. class." A small smirk formed. "Your mother filled out a gym uniform like no other."

"Ew, Dad." He cringed at the image.

"Sorry, I want you to know I understand. I also agree with your mother."

"Dad—"

"I agree you need to be married in a church. Uncle Phil can marry you before New Year. I don't care if we are there, just as long as it's in a church." He got closer. "If you ever talk back to your mother again, I will knock you into next week. Go in there and apologize." He backed away far enough to still be able to give a backhanded slap for good measure.

Slowly Paul walked back into the kitchen. His mother sat at the table with her cook books open to the old family recipes.

"Ma, I'm sorry. Linda's my wife and we are very happy together. We understand each other. I know you will love her."

"I don't even know what my daughter-in-law looks like." She sniffled.

Pulling out his phone, Paul scrolled through his photos for one suitable for his mother to see. Perfect, their wedding on the beach at sunset. Linda looked so beautiful standing next to him in a long white sun dress, her red hair blowing in the breeze, her green eyes sparkling up at him, so full of love. "Here." He held it up for her.

"Is she's Irish?"

"Yes, mother, but only a quarter."

"Well, at least she will have a good solid Italian last name." That was something his mother took pride in since all of his sisters married Italians.

He grimaced. "Sort of, she is going by Linda O'Brien–Fatoni."

"What, Fatoni isn't good enough for her?" she uttered in disgust.

"Ma, Linda has her own company. You wouldn't like it if I changed the name P&F Construction because I got married. Her clients know her by her maiden name."

"I'm not going to say anything else." Her voice lowered to a deadly calm, which meant this wasn't finished, but for now no judgement would be made. She walked over to the counter and pulled out an old piece of paper, one he recognized as his great-grandmother's Cuicidata cookie recipe. "Have your wife bring this to Christmas."

Great. Linda didn't know how to cook, so she obviously didn't bake either. This was his mother's way of testing his wife's ability to take care of him.

Taking the paper, he kissed his mother on the cheek. "Thank you. How about you and Dad come over Sunday after church for coffee? We can talk and get to know each other without all the interruptions of the whole family."

She clasped his hand tight, digging her rings into his fingers. "Please, tell me she loves you for you."

His mother knew him so well; all his frustration floated to the floor. "Ma, we love each other. Trust me, you will love her."

She patted his cheek. "I made a tray of lasagna for you. It's in the freezer. If I were you, I'd grab it and go before your sisters get a hold of you."

"Thanks, Ma."

Warm breath tickled his neck, bringing him back to the present and his lovely wife. In the next four days he wanted to bring Christmas back into her life. His mission was to make happy memories for Linda to erase all the devastating ones from her past. To do it, he would go back to his childhood and all their family traditions.

He also needed to find a way to ask his wife to let his Uncle Phil marry them in a church and un-hyphenate her name to appease his mother. He really didn't care about either of his mother's issues, but Linda being welcomed into the family on good terms meant making his mother happy.

"Honey, why are you still awake?" Linda asked sleepily.

Her sweet voice soothed some of his apprehension. "I'm trying to work something out."

Linda rested her chin on his chest. "I can help, if you want to talk about it."

He brushed away the hair from her face. "How hard would it be to change your name?"

Her beautiful smile appeared. "What would you like to change it to?"

"Oh, I don't know, Linda the Seductress."

Musical laughter filled his ears.

"Or… Linda Fatoni."

Silence followed.

"How about you make love to your wife," she purred, straddling him.

Pearl white skin shimmered in the moonlight coming through the blinds. Her perfect breasts stood ripe and puckered inches from his mouth. Strands of red silk surrounded him in a veil of mutual desire. He took one of her nipples in his mouth as she rubbed her heated core against his erection.

Small hands caressed up and down his chest causing sensual havoc to his already ragging hunger to be inside her. Unable to wait, he grabbed her hips, raising her up and then thrusting into her hot wet body.

He liked her way of distracting him and not answering his question.

Avoiding her father did not happen. Somehow he found out she was home and summoned her to lunch. Since her mother and father never spoke, someone else must have informed him.

She stood in the dining room at The Plaza where she was to meet him. Lighted Christmas trees and wreathes were displayed all around the hotel. Her heart rate elevated at the thought of shopping with Paul, decorations, and his question about changing her name. She remembered how her father always emphasized the importance of the O'Brien name.

A soft cough from the maître d' caught her attention. She followed him slowly, making sure her emerald coat dress remained wrinkle free, and her black boots were still shiny. Her father sat a table to the right of a huge tree. More gray peppered his auburn hair since she last saw him. He stood holding out her chair. His green eyes that matched hers were cold and distant.

"Hello, Father." She sat, waiting for a greeting.

He dismissed the maître d' with a wave of his hand before saying, "You married without informing me?"

The reprimand implicit in his tone stunned her. "I was unaware you cared what I do. I've not seen or heard from you in five years."

"You are my daughter and an O'Brien. Your actions affect my family."

What the hell?

"Excuse me? You left me and my mother when I was nine. How dare you…"

"Keep your voice down." He glanced around the room. "You and your mother could never keep your emotions in check."

The abandonment and hurt he'd caused came crashing to the surface in a tsunami of rage. "Are you serious?" she hissed. "You selfish bastard! You broke my mother's heart. Then you married some foreign model and started a new family. You never once thought how your actions affected us."

Twitches in the small muscles adjoining his eyes gave away his efforts to stay in control. "I left because I needed an heir to carry on the O'Brien name, damn you."

Her fingers curled into fists under the table. "Damn me? Did you forget I *am* an heir?"

"I needed a son, and your mother couldn't have any more children after you. I had no choice." His jaw clenched. "Don't act as if my name hasn't helped your career."

"Well, Father, I have a choice." She stood up. "You don't have to worry about your precious name any longer where I'm concerned. My last name is now Fatoni. Good bye, Father."

Turning, head held high, she walked away, never looking back even when her father muttered something about her marrying below her station.

Walking home helped Linda burn off some of her irritation. Anger still coursed through her veins at his accusations. At the same time, excitement pounded in her chest at telling him off for all the pain he'd caused.

Weightlessness spread through her limbs and up to her lips, where a huge smile formed. Passing one of the many Christmas windows displays, she found herself laughing. Her father chose to leave them years before. Now she chose to leave him in her past.

A Santa on the corner sang "Jingle Bells" while he rang his bell. "Now there's a beautiful happy smile," he said as she neared him.

"Thank you, Santa." She reached in her pocket and put her cab money in the red bucket.

"Merry Christmas, Miss."

"Merry Christmas to you, Santa." Laughing, she continued home.

Home. Her heart swelled. *Yes, home to Paul.*

Adventure awaited.

Paul met her at the door when she got off the elevator. "Are you ready?"

"Yes!" She launched herself into his open arms. Finding his mouth, she kissed him and let all of her emotions flow.

He stumbled back against the door matching her excitement with each swipe of his tongue. He broke their kiss. "Sweetie," he said, his voice sounding strained. "We will never get started if we continue this."

A giggle escaped her lips as her feet touched the floor. "Sorry."

Reaching inside the door, Paul held out her new coat. He helped her into it, adjusting the matching scarf under the hood, and handed her gloves. "Your first Christmas present."

Exhilaration flowed through her. "I have a present for you too."

He glanced around her, and she laughed again. "It's not one you wrap." He frowned as she continued. "I've decided from now on I shall be Mrs. Paul Fatoni, Jr."

In an instant, she was engulfed in two strong arms and being spun around. "Really? Oh, Linda, this is the best gift I have ever received."

"Well, we *are* married."

A shadow crossed over his features then disappeared. "Yes, we are." He held out his arm to her. "Shall we go on our Christmas adventure, Mrs. Fatoni?"

Putting her hand through his arm, she squeezed it. "Yes."

22

He picked up a tan work bag and locked their door. Minutes later, she sat in the front seat of his company truck as he drove out of the city. "Where are we going?"

Glancing over, he flashed a silly grin. "To my old high school, St. Thomas."

"Why."

"We need a tree, do we not?"

During their drive, he told her how his school had planted a tree farm. The students learned about enterprise by selling the trees to help support the school. They also raised pumpkins and sponsored a pumpkin patch they could visit in the fall.

Abbot Vince met them at the gate. He spoke highly of her husband and how he sponsored some of the students and gave them jobs after they graduated. She noticed the Fatoni name on one of the buildings.

Paul led her down rows and rows of trees. "I know where all the biggest and best Christmas trees are located."

She followed, shaking her head. The sun broke through the branches in larger gaps until they stopped in an open field where three full Scotch pine trees stood. She only knew the name because he told her the kind of tree his family picked every year. "I think that one will be perfect in the living room." She pointed to the one in the center and then paused for a moment, getting caught up in his enthusiasm. "This one will go great in the corner of our bedroom." Hurrying forward past another row, she said, "Oh, Paul, I can put this one in my office."

He remained rooted in the snow, his eyes wide and mouth open.

"Paul."

"I thought…" He shook his head. "Sweetie, we can start slow with one tree this year."

Linda inhaled the scent of pine with every crisp breath as her heart pounded with the Christmas magic. Wrapping her arms around Paul's neck, she gazed up into his eyes. "I want our first and every Christmas to be filled with all the joys of Christmas."

"Does that mean three trees? They're ten dollars a foot." He brushed a lock of her hair behind her ear. "You realize we have to get these home ourselves."

"Come on, Mr. Fatoni. Where is your sense of adventure? We can do it."

Giving her a quick kiss, he bent down and pulled a hand saw from his bag. "Come on, Mrs. Fatoni, let me show you how to cut down a tree."

By the time they cut down all three trees, their sides hurt from laughing, and the sun had set. Linda didn't mind dragging her little tree through the snow. She felt bad, though, watching her husband struggle with two huge ones. Nevertheless, he carried them with a big smile that matched hers.

After buying some wreathes and garland, they donated a few hundred dollars to St. Thomas and tipped several of the boys for all their work carrying and tying everything down. Even though the evening temperature had dropped, Linda didn't want to leave yet. She bought hot chocolate and freshly baked donuts for everyone who helped them.

When Paul got into the truck, he noticed the boys had opened the back window to fit two tree trunks through it. With a shake of his head, he chuckled. "Sweetie, let's not let a tree come between us."

Crossing her finger across her chest, she teased back, "I promise."

When she'd awaken this morning, she'd thought she would dread everything about today. Instead, Paul had made it wonderful. Every day Linda fell more and more in love him.

Maybe being honest was best. Only one more flaw still needed to be revealed.

Paul spent most of the night putting up all the trees, wreaths, and garland. Thankfully, over the years, St. Thomas had expanded to carry everything he needed to complete the Christmas set up.

He'd thought for sure he'd be dragging Linda from shop to shop for Christmas decorations when she'd arrived home earlier that afternoon. He knew she'd met with her father for lunch. She didn't mention it, though, and he didn't ask. He figured when she wanted to talk, she would. Now she floated around the penthouse singing John Lennon's "So This is Christmas" a little out of tune. This new attitude gave Paul hope. Changing her name might make his next step easier

"Mr. Fatoni," she called from the kitchen. "The Chinese is getting cold."

"I will be right there, Mrs. Fatoni." Cleaning up all his tools, he put his bag in the hall closet and went to meet her. He took his seat at the table and filled his plate.

"I forgot how wonderful Christmas smelled," she said, taking a bite of her food. "I'm starved from all this decorating."

He'd had a few concerns about bringing all these things into the penthouse. Linda chose all clear lights and ivory and gold ornaments. He worried all of it might affect her work. "Linda, are you sure about all these accents in the penthouse?"

Her glorious smile returned, filled with gratitude. "Paul," she said as she reached across the table and squeezed his hand, "I am fine. This..."—she waved around the room—"is perfect. I might have to work more in my office during the day. Honestly, I should since all my stuff is there."

"I don't want you to be overwhelmed." Tomorrow might be her breaking point.

"I'm not. Have I ever told you how glad I am I married you?"

Oh, he prayed she still felt that way after Sunday.

"Me too, sweetie. We better finish and get to bed early so we have energy to make cookies in the morning."

Her features fell. "Oh, I forgot."

"Have no fear, my wife, we will do this together. We're a team, remember?"

"You're right, we are team Fatoni."

They finished dinner and he carried her off to bed. Christmas lights twinkled from the tree in the corner of their bedroom, allowing him to watch the desire grow in his wife eyes.

Morning sunlight filtered into their bedroom. Paul rolled over, feeling for his wife's warm, soft body. Cold sheets filled his palm. Banging from the other room startled him awake.

Oh God, Linda was starting without him. Jumping from bed, he threw on a pair of sweats and headed for the kitchen.

His wife stood in a shamrock blouse and jeans at the island surrounded by an explosion of cookware, gadgets, and a black KitchenAid food processor. Cookie sheets lined the back counter. Apprehension shadowed her beautiful features as she glanced down at all the ingredients arranged around her.

"Wow, you are up early." Paul turned to look at the clock; five a.m. "Did you have breakfast?"

She shook her head silently.

"Do you want me to run down to Panera?" Her only response was another shake of her head. Panic began to build in his chest. "Linda…"

Silken strands of red hair thrashed from side to side. "I don't know where to start." Tears glistened in her lashes.

He rushed over, wrapping an arm around her shoulders. "This I know." His memory flashed back to his mother's kitchen. All the girls and the filling stuff were at one side of the room. "Alright. Let's get all the ingredients for the fruit filling over here." He swiped aside the bowls, measuring cups and spoons. "Read them off to me."

A whisper of "fig" came from Linda's lips, followed by the names of the rest of the fruits. Paul faltered at blanched almonds and almond paste. "Sweetie, we can do this. We need to do one step at a time."

Hope sprang up in his heart when she finally let out a breath and said, "Okay, you gather the things for the dough, and I'll start putting the fruit in the food processor."

A glimmer of the self-assured woman he fell in love with showed behind her beautiful green eyes. "That's the spirit," he said, smiling at her.

"We need music." She ran out of the room then back in with her phone. "Simply Having A Wonderful Christmas Time" echoed through the room. Her hips swayed to the rhythm while she sang as she added dates to the fruit mixture. Securing the top of the processor, she started it.

The biggest smile lit her face. Paul had no choice. He swept her up in his arms and kissed her.

She pulled back as merriment danced in her eyes. "I'm cooking. This"—she waved around the room—"is amazing. Thank you."

This woman fascinated and excited Paul to a whole new level. Right now he fought the urge to clear off the whole counter and take her right there. Instead, he lowered his head, taking her sweet mouth.

Linda added more fuel to his fire by putting her greedy little hands over his chest. He needed her now. Picking her up, she wrapped her legs around his waist.

A grinding metallic sound broke their merry tryst.

His wife disappeared in a flash, running to the food processor and screaming. Smoke billowed from the machine. Paul leaped into action and unplugged the KitchenAid.

"No no no!" she cried. "I… ruined it." Linda collapsed into a heap on the floor. "I'm a failure of a wife. I should have told you… I can't cook. Your mother will know I can't take care of you, and never accept me."

Sobs shuddered through her body, every one of them digging deep into Paul's gut. He crouched down next to her and scooped her up into his lap. "Oh, sweetie, I know." He caressed her back while she confessed all her secrets.

"My love, I know about Maria and the take-out every night."

Glassy-eyed, she gazed up at him. "How?"

"Cooking takes ingredients and things to cook them in." He kissed the top of her nose. "I noticed Maria brings her own."

Her head shook as more sobs followed. "I'm sorry. Your family is going to hate me." She scrambled up and ran out of the room.

Paul raced after her only to have the bedroom door slam in his face.

"Linda."

"No, Paul… You have a poor excuse of a wife."

"Sweetheart, I don't care if you can cook."

Loud cries followed.

Going back into the kitchen, he did the only thing he could think of. He reached for his phone and dialed.

"Mom?"

Less than an hour later, his parents and sisters were at his door. Instead of a hug from his mother, he got a smack to the back of the head.

"Ow!"

"Do you ever listen to me when I speak? I gave you your grandmother's recipe to welcome your wife to the family, not to make. Sometimes I wonder where you grew up."

His father walked by him without a word, shaking his head. Unfortunately, his sisters oohed and squealed their way through the penthouse.

"Paul," his mother said, pausing by the tree, "what a beautiful angel." Tears filled her eyes. "It reminds me of my great-grandmother back in Italy."

"Linda saw it in a little shop yesterday and had to have it."

"This is a sign."

With that, they all disappeared into the kitchen.

Linda woke from her worst nightmare. Her husband knew she was a total fraud. Loud voices came from the other room. How could Paul watch TV at a time like this?

Pulling herself together, she went to face her doom. His family would never accept her now. Seeing the truth in his eyes would kill her. She wanted this marriage to work. He loved his family. Now he would always have to choose between her and them.

The voices got louder as she neared. It wasn't the TV, people were in her house. When she entered the kitchen, the talking stopped. Four women with dark hair resembling Paul turned to her with big weary smiles.

The oldest woman came forward with the warmest expression and open arms. "Linda!" She hugged her. "I'm Paul's mother, Rose. Welcome to the family."

Welcome?

Scanning the room, she found her husband standing next to his dad.

They came forward and his dad hugged her. "I'm Paul Senior. Welcome to our family. Bless you for marrying our son."

Linda thought her heart might explode. His parents didn't hate her.

Tears clogged her throat, rendering her speechless. Thankfully, his sisters rushed her, pulling her into one big hug and introducing themselves. Julianna was the oldest, Giovanna the middle, and Stefani was the youngest sister. They were all talking at once, and all she could do was smile.

This was a real family, and they were all accepting her flaws.

"Alright, stop man-handling my wife." Paul wrapped his arm around her waist, anchoring her to him. "I forgot something about making these cookies."

"Yes, he did." His mother tugged her free from the security of her husband's arms. "This cookie recipe takes a village to make them."

"Because they feed a village," Julianna said as she went back to the counter.

"You see, Paul is the baby, so he doesn't remember all the grandmothers and aunts coming over to the house before Christmas to make them the old fashion way," Giovanna added while chopping up some figs.

"Junior over there"—Stefani rolled her eyes Paul's way—"helped get the dough started until the kneading got too hard. Then he went to play his video games while the rest of us worked in the kitchen."

His father kneaded a ball of dough at the end of the breakfast bar. "Now, now, girls. Stop giving your brother a hard time."

"Stop giving your baby brother a hard time," Stefani said, imitating her father. "All he ever did was put the sprinkles on the cookies after I slaved over the icing."

"We did all the work, and grandma would praise her little man for his help." Giovanna did not hide her annoyance with her brother. "Then the little brat would get the first cookie."

Paul stuck by his father, taking his turn kneading the dough.

"The best part of this tradition is spending time together and making something sweet from the old country." His mother attempted to change the subject.

"We're sorry your husband is such an idiot," Julianna continued, ignoring Paul's protest. "Ma gave him the recipe to welcome you to the family, not to have you make them alone."

Stefani admired the stove and the view of the park. "I vote we make a new tradition to do the Cuicidata's at Linda and Paul's."

"Linda, you do have a beautiful home." Rose smiled while handing her a bowl.

"We're a rowdy bunch," his father added.

Meeting her husband's gaze, Linda's heart filled with joy. Christmas from now on would be spent in New York, with snow, trees, and family.

"I would be honored to have everyone over to make cookies. I would love to invite you over for dinner…" She lowered her lashes. "But I only know how to order a meal."

His mother patted her hand. "You don't have to cook. Paul knows how to cook."

Giovanna interrupted. "It's the cleaning part he sucks at. You might have to give Maria a raise."

Linda glared at Paul. "You told them about Maria."

"No." Stefani held up the apron with Maria's name on it.

Linda found herself laughing with them all.

"Seriously, Linda, my son is a slob," said Rose.

"More like a filthy pig. Oh, and he smells, and never puts the toilet seat down," his sisters added all at once.

"Hey, in the room," Paul said defensively.

"Girls, stop picking on your brother," his dad said, half agreeing with them.

Paul made his way to her. "Don't listen to them." His voice held a bit of uneasiness.

Reaching up, she cupped his cheek. "Honey, it's nice to know you have some flaws too."

"Oh, he has flaws," Stefani agreed.

Paul brought her palm to his lip. "Welcome to my family." With a wink, he added, "I told you they would love you."

Everyone worked together, including Linda. Rose showed her how to chop up all the fruit first and then put it in the processor. She also learned how to boil sugar and cinnamon in water to add to the fruit filling.

By the time the last batch of cookies was frosted, it was almost ten o'clock. Exhausted, Paul and Linda said good bye to his family. Well, her family now.

Lacing her fingers with his, they walked to the bedroom. Before they reached the door, Paul stopped, trepidation flashing in his eyes. He must have known she loved his family. "Linda," he said, getting down on one knee and holding her hand, "will you marry me in front of God and my family on Christmas eve?"

She stepped back surprised, not expecting the question. Seeing Paul at St. Thomas, she knew his faith ran deep. When she saw the angel in the window on their way home, it reminded her of a statue in an old church she visited once in Italy. She thought an angel held more of the meaning of Christmas than a star.

Christmas was the season of new life. Why not start their new life together on the same day? Lowering down to look into his eyes, she kissed his cheek. "I will marry you, again."

Paul jumped up, bringing her with him. "I love you more than you will ever know."

"Oh, I know, because I love you just as much." She covered his lips with hers and let him carry her off to bed.

Avoiding Christmas would never be an issue again. She realized Polly was right. Honesty did make a marriage stronger.

Cuicidata Original Recipe

2 ½ lbs. flour – 8 cups

¾ lb. shortening = (1 stick butter- ½ lbs shortening)

1 lb. sugar – 2 cups

5 eggs – well beaten

10 teaspoons baking powder

2 tsps. Vanilla

1 tsp. lemon extract

¾ cup milk

½ tsp. salt

Mix flour, baking powder, salt, and shortening as for pie crust; add sugar, mix well. Add eggs, vanilla, lemon extract, and milk. Knead until smooth and shiny. Place in refrigerator – Roll thin into rectangle (about 1/8"). Place filling across and roll edge of dough over and seal. Cut about 2" apiece.

Cuicidata Fruit Filling

1 lb. fig (in the ring)

1 cup light raisins

1 cup dates

1 cup mixed fruits

½ lb. blanched almonds

Grind in food chopper

Mix ½ can of almond paste with above.

Boil together 2 minutes:

½ cup water

½ cup sugar

¼ tsp. cinnamon

Mix together in fruit mixture.

Bake at 350. 6 to 12 minutes checking bottoms to be golden brown.

Icing

1 cup powdered sugar

½ tsp vanilla

1-2 tablespoons milk

Mix powdered sugar, vanilla, and milk 1 tablespoon at a time until spreadable.

Sprinkle with rainbow nonpareils before icing sets.

Thankful for Pie

by Julia Curtin

Julia Curtin

Julia Curtin is an adventurous but perhaps not skilled baker. She was an award winning teen and adult readers' advisory for many years and now helps authors connect their books with happy readers and giving talks on food history. She has an Amazon bestselling adult mystery series with recipes under a different name and a young adult adventure. Learn more about her and her passion for vintage recipes at www.amyalessio.com.

The pumpkin pie definitely looked raw in the middle. Estelle turned off the light in the oven and pretended she wasn't witnessing the collapse of PP trial #4. When the timer finally dinged, she cracked the oven door again, hoping to see a change.

The pie had been baking for ninety minutes, and she was afraid the crust would burn. She put on her vintage cherry-covered oven mitts and slid it out of the oven, managing not to burn her arm on the rack this time.

Wet pie filling still shone in the center. "This would never happen to Grandma Star," she said to herself. "What would she do?"

The only phrase she remembered her grandma and namesake saying regularly was "il matrimonio fa un cuore felice", which she was pretty sure meant something about her need to find a husband. Estelle said it aloud anyway, but it took her three tries to get the accent right from her memories of her Grandma.

Switching off the oven, she grabbed her phone and took a photo of the pie. After adding a few notes to this version of the recipe, she examined the picture. The pie looked fine. Whirling around, she checked the pie again. The top was dry and the crust even when a minute ago it was raw in the middle. Did invoking her Grandma's catch phrase help?

Or maybe that extra teaspoon of nutmeg she put in by accident worked after all.

Estelle just pulled on a turquoise sweater when she heard her sister Marianne in the kitchen. She knew it was Marianne and not Rosalyn, because she heard the tapping of heels on her hardwood kitchen floor. Rosalyn was more of a clog wearer; she'd scared Estelle more than once when Estelle hadn't heard her youngest sister come in.

"Star, this pie looks fantastic." More tapping, drawer opening.

"Wait, don't cut it!" Estelle yelled. She was afraid to mess with the perfect pie, her first ever. Her sisters and brother had called her Star since she was little, just as they called their Grandma Estelle 'Grandma Star.' Estelle sounded like Star to her older sister Rosalyn when she was a baby, so the nickname stuck for their grandma, then for her granddaughter Estelle. As Estelle meant star in more than one language, it seemed like a good fit all the way around.

"Why? Roz won't mind."

Star finished yanking a brush through her hair, tossing it on her bed in her hurry to leave the room and head downstairs. "Just don't."

Mari glanced at her sister, and then cut a slice with their grandma's silver pie server.

"Wow, it's great. Have you been going through Grandma Star's old cookbooks again?"

When Star moved into the house, she couldn't bear to get rid of a single volume of her grandma's 500-volume collection. She often read through them like novels. "I did get this pumpkin chiffon recipe from one of them, but it's the first time it worked."

"We need grandma's dessert plates for this one. Then I'm taking a picture." Star tried to pull open a drawer on the antique buffet. After a tug or two, the drawer finally opened a few inches. Inside, she could see the milky white cake plates with scalloped edges.

Mari came over and pulled on the drawer, opening it smoothly the rest of the way. "You need to work out, girl."

"Wow, you're so strong. Six months of karate, and you're a champion drawer puller. We should all be so lucky."

Mari took the doilies and plate into the kitchen. "You know you're jealous of my moves."

"So you like the class?" Star rummaged around in a cabinet for powdered sugar.

"Yeah. I mean, I took it so I could defend myself better, but somehow now I look forward to classes. I miss them if I have to work late and can't go."

Mari signed up for the class after a date got uncomfortably aggressive before she was able to escape. Star would never forget the hysterical call she'd gotten from a bar at 2 a.m., or how her bubbly sister was so dejected for weeks after the event.

"You know, Star, it wouldn't hurt you to come with me sometime, at least to kickboxing."

"I really should." Star nodded in agreement while centering the slice of pie.

Mari laughed and let it go. "Let me get my phone and send Roz a picture. You're right. It's a notable occasion."

Twenty minutes later, both ladies leaned back in their chairs, having polished off half the pie between them. Mari's phone buzzed with a text.

"Roz wants us to come to the bakery. She's working late again."

Star had just refilled their mugs with tea. "What? I thought she was meeting us here after the commuters left."

Roz was trying to help save the family's failing bakery by staying open until 6 p.m. and offering sandwiches for the commuter crowd that passed by the storefront. So far her efforts were keeping the bakery out of the red, but her sisters didn't think they could keep going.

Star helped with the books for the business, and knew firsthand about the precarious bakery finances. She kept her job at a local CPA firm, but she tried to help with customers some mornings and Saturdays.

"How is Enrique working out?" she asked. The girls had advertised for a baker intern at the local community college. They were surprised when six foot four inch Enrique, with his huge muscular arms and bold swirling tattoos, arrived in person to ask for the job.

"Charlie loves him. He's learning all kinds of things from him."

Star pretended she didn't see her sister take another sliver of pie. "Like new cakes and stuff?"

Their eighteen-year-old brother thought he was the next Top Baker for the country and couldn't understand why his sisters worried about the business so much. The three sisters tried to step in and keep an eye on him, as their mother was mostly lost in depression after losing her husband and business partner to a heart attack two years ago.

"Some of that, sure. But when I went back there last week and both were working, Enrique was giving Charlie advice about how to kiss girls."

Star set her mug of tea down with a clang. "Why?" She thought through the line of girls she'd seen Charlie with over the last couple of months, usually just some in a group of friends.

"Then there's the elephant toes."

"Excuse me?" Star set down the tea she had just picked up again. "What are elephant toes?"

"Charlie's new bakery invention. Roz nixed it, but he put them out when she wasn't there. They all sold." Mari laughed. "I mean, the name is pretty repulsive, but I tried one, and they're delicious. Like a delicately light doughnut with a praline glaze and chocolate filling."

"I'll have to try one. Isn't Charlie there today? Think he's making them?" Star stood up and began gathering the dishes.

"Maybe. I'll come with you. That hottie Enrique should be there tonight too. Let's bring them the rest of this pie and see what they think. We can take separate cars so I can get to karate later."

The smell in the bakery always gave Star a sense of home. She practically grew up in the small storefront bakery, first when her father took it over from his mom, then as her parents ran it together. Her mother had tried to run it by herself since their father died. If only they'd realized how bad things were, she thought to herself. After their father's death, Charlie was the only one helping their mother with the bakery while Star was busy with her new professional accounting job. Mari was in graduate veterinary school then, and Roz was finishing her culinary degree and working in a restaurant in downtown Chicago. Star had known business was down, but when she examined her mother's tax files in the last year, she realized her mom was losing track of things. Luckily, they talked her into getting counseling to help with her devastating grief, and Roz returned to help run the bakery.

"Hey, Star!" Charlie waved from behind the counter. Two pretty girls with long straight hair looked up from where he was helping them select desserts from the case. "My elephant toes are selling out again."

The girls pointed to the remaining toes, and he quickly boxed them up.

"He's so cute."

Hearing the giggling teen girls as they made their way out of the shop, Star's thoughts returned to the bakery. "Stop flirting with the customers." She ruffled Charlie's hair as she stepped behind the counter.

"At this rate, you'll have to give me a raise. My zombie cookies are hot also."

Star faced Charlie. "Did you say zombie cookies? As in monsters?"

He pointed proudly to a tray holding some headless gingerbread men decorated liberally with red paint. Only three remained.

"It's after Halloween, Charlie. I'm not sure."

"Look. Roz had extra gingerbread cookies and was going to toss them, but I made them into zombies. Enrique said it was okay. They are kind of like holiday cookies."

The door opened again as Star picked up the tray of zombie cookies and turned to get Mari's help in convincing her brother that they were gross. But it wasn't Mari entering the shop.

A man in a navy suit with a gray shirt and matching silk tie walked in, a frown on his olive toned face. "I'm looking for Henry." He glanced at Star. "Could you go get him?"

She bristled. "There is no Henry here. You must have the wrong address."

"I got it, sis. Enrique!" People down the block likely heard Charlie yell.

"Yo!" The tall, dark haired baker leaned his head out, smiling at Star before looking at the man. "I'll be out in a minute, Steve."

The man sighed and ran a hand through his wavy brown hair before looking at his gold watch. "He was supposed to be done half an hour ago. You know he's just an intern, right? He shouldn't be working night and day around this place."

The bell over the door rang as Mari came in. "Steve! I didn't recognize you in that suit. Usually I see you in a karate gi. And who works night and day around this place?"

"I just help out with some of the karate classes," the man grumbled. "I'm a finance manager during the day. And I meant my brother, Henry. This is just training until he gets a real job."

"Can I get you a sample? Enrique made some lovely, um…" Star quickly looked down, but she was still holding the tray of zombie cookies in her hand.

The man shook his head. "I don't think so."

Enrique came out, wiping his hands on his jeans. "Steve, did you meet Star and Mari? They own this place. This is my brother, Steve."

"Come on, let's go."

"Sorry, he's pretty uptight." Enrique's grin brought out one in Star, too. He vaulted over the order counter with one muscled arm holding his weight. Steve was already heading out the door.

"See you, Rico," Charlie called after his new hero.

"Where's Roz? I thought she was working late." Mari snagged a zombie cookie from Star's tray.

Charlie shrugged. "She went to get some more coffee a while ago. That book group is coming tonight. Plus she had that order for 500 holiday cookies. She worked on that all day, and all the cakes are nearly sold out. Luckily I came up with my zombie cookie idea."

"An order for 500 cookies sounds good, though, right?" Mari looked at the racks that were filled with cookies.

"It would be, except they never showed. Roz called them, but the number they gave her had been disconnected."

"She didn't get a deposit?" Star closed her eyes for a second, thinking of the cost of supplies.

"Well, she didn't want to turn away business."

"Maybe we can make a few things." Star looked at the empty bakers' racks.

"No way, Star. We don't want to get sued." Charlie nearly doubled over laughing at his own joke.

"Hey, Charlie, Star actually made something good today. We brought you a piece." Mari pulled out the wrapped container. "Save some for Roz!" she called as he tore it out of her hands and broke off a piece.

"Hey, this isn't bad. Who helped you?"

Mari hit Charlie lightly on the back of the head.

"Come on," he grumbled. "We all know her stuff usually turns out awful."

"Just like we know everything that comes out of your mouth usually turns out awful," Mari said in return.

"It is good, isn't it?" Star broke off a corner of the pie. It was still moist, and the flavors blended perfectly, even in that small bite.

"Hey, are you two gonna help me set up for the book group before Roz comes back? I got homework."

"Homework, Charlie? Is that what they're calling it these days? I think we used to call it flirting, though you likely do it via text or Skype now."

"No, for real. I have a ton of English reading to do. We have to stop by the library or bookstore and get a copy of a book, too." His voice became muffled as he went back to look up what he needed.

"Think it's due tomorrow?" Star sighed as pulled out the tablecloths Roz liked to use with groups.

Mari started pulling racks from the cases to wrap up the last few items for the local homeless shelter. "I'm sure. Otherwise, why would he be doing it?"

"We just have to pick a classic. It has to be 200 pages." Charlie stared at the assignment on his iPad as if he'd never seen it before.

"Exactly 200 pages? Or at least 200 pages?" Star muttered as she printed the closing receipt.

"You know. How do we find one that's 200 pages?" A buzzing sound came from Charlie's pocket. He started typing in a response. "Hey, can I go out later?"

Both sisters stopped what they were doing and glared at him. "You mean before or after we buy the 200 page book, you read it, and write up whatever you need to do?" Mari blasted him with her response .

"Yeah. So can I?"

The door chimed and a tall redhead walked in. The customer looked familiar. "Hi, Star, right? And Mari?" The woman smiled as she approached the cookie display. "Those look good. You all are getting a start on the holidays with all these fancy cookies. We're still concentrating on pumpkin treats at the Break Room. I'm so tired of making the pumpkin mini muffins. How much are the Linzers?"

Star remembered the woman from the local coffee shop. Their muffins were delicious. "We're having a special. Buy six, get six free."

"Wow. A sale, really? I'll take eighteen then, for a total of three dozen."

As Charlie boxed them up, Star took the woman's credit card. *Karen, that's right*, she thought. "Karen, I didn't realize you did the baking over there. Those muffins are wonderful."

Karen laughed loudly. "It's not as big an operation as this, but we do pretty well."

"Sure, we're a huge operation." Mari commented after the door closed behind Karen. "So big we can't afford to stay open."

The discount used bookstore was filled with teens. Apparently, Charlie wasn't the only one who had left the assignment until the last minute. Star had called the library about a few titles, but they were cleaned out already.

"There should still be a *Lord of the Flies* here somewhere," she said while tugging Charlie's jacket as he glanced at his phone again.

"How many pages is that one?"

"Do you mean, what is it about? Will I like it?" Star wondered again how she let Charlie talk her into this.

"Excuse me." An arm reached right in front of Star's face.

"Anna, just wait for her to finish."

The tight voice sounded familiar. Star took a step back and bumped into a man. Turning around, her eyes landed onSteve's loosened tie. "Sorry," she muttered.

His hands covered her shoulders. "Sorry. My sister pretty much knocked you out of the way. I mean, I'm happy to see teens so eager for books, but..."

She smiled. "Eager to avoid late grades, you mean. Charlie is here doing the same thing."

"We didn't get to talk before. I'm Steve Fernandez. Henry and Anna's brother."

"Star."

His hand was rough, but warm when he grasped hers. He held it a beat longer than she expected, but it wasn't unpleasant. This was the same rude man she had met in the bakery?

"I was late picking up Anna before, which is why I was annoyed with Henry."

"I understand perfectly." She laughed.

"Hey, stop flirting. I think I got my book. Look, it's 201 pages." Charlie elbowed her, breaking her hand connection with Steve. The cover of the book he presented to her featured a pirate complete with shirt opened to the waist, long black hair, and an eye patch. She'd never heard of the title or author.

"Do you have a list or something, Charlie?" She could feel her face getting hotter due to his flirting comment. "I don't think that's a classic."

Steve's bright white teeth stood out from his five o'clock shadow as he grinned. "You don't think *Sea Man's Revenge* is a classic? Do you judge all books by their cover?"

The cover is pretty hot, she thought. Her cheeks kept burning. "No, just a hunch."

"Come on, Star, help me." Charlie stepped close to the bookshelves again. "These all look so boring. And long."

"Star? I thought your name was Star."

She looked at the shelves next to Charlie. "*Lord of the Flies* is right there,

Charlie —grab it." Several teens turned but Charlie was fast. She had to duck three outstretched arms before she could reply, "My name is Star. Star is a family nickname." Another teen jostled her, shoving her closer to Steve. "Sorry."

Steve grabbed her elbow and pulled her out of the crowd of teens. "It reminds me of *Lord of the Flies* in here. Let's wait for them here, where we are out of the way, Star."

"You said you're a finance manager, right? Which firm? I know Enrique wants to be a baker." She tried to fill dead air as she always did, but her words brought a frown to his face.

"Henry is unrealistic about his ability to make a living in that profession. From what I can tell, there aren't many jobs open, and the available ones are overnight six days a week." He paused and shrugged. "No offense."

She took offense. "My parents worked that schedule for years. My mom made sure we got off to school and were fed, and then she'd go back. But they loved it. It worked for them. Maybe your brother will find his way."

"I've been supporting my sister and brother for a while now. I don't know if I can just let him find his way."

"He is a really talented baker, and great with customers. Maybe he'll have his own business."

"Who would fund that?" Steve grimaced and ran a hand through his hair. "Look, I know he has talent. But talent is not a ticket to wealth. Surely as an accountant, you realize that. Look, I've gotta go."

"Is wealth the goal?"

But he had turned back to his sister. Star tried to process the conversation and mood change, but couldn't. She saw Steve and Anna walk to the register.

Star's long black skirt swirled against her favorite red cowboy boots as she hurried into the bakery the next morning. Her mind was on her accounting job and the meeting she had at ten o'clock.

Only a handful of customers waited for coffee and baked goods.

"Want to try some holiday cookies? We get in the spirit early here." Enrique winked at an attractive elderly woman in a red coat.

"At that sale price, I will take a couple dozen for my church group meeting."

Star smiled as she washed her hands to help the next customer. "Hi, Enrique."

"Hey, Star. I can handle this. Roz wants to see you."

Roz should have been elbow deep in bread baking by now, but Star found her in her tiny office, looking at a computer screen. "Roz? You're done baking already?"

"There's no point!" She didn't turn from the screen. "We have no customers. I think it's because of these reviews."

Star leaned in and scanned the reviews on the popular website. Phrases like "bad service," "dirty," and "worse than store bought" jumped out at her.

"What on earth? These were all posted within the last week?" Her stomach dropped.

"Our numbers have been dropping all week, and Enrique mentioned one of his friends saw these. His friend put up a good one, but there's like fifty of these. What are we going to do?"

Star slid into her office at 9:45, her mind full of marketing ideas she, Enrique, and Roz had brainstormed. They were good ideas, but she didn't see how it would be enough to help the bakery.

"Focus," she told herself as she pulled out her tablet for the meeting. *"Maybe hearing about tax incentives for small businesses will help me with the bakery too."*

After the end of the three hour training, her cubicle mate Evan stopped her. "Hey, Star, can you look at this report for a second? I've gone over it twice, and I still don't understand how this business got so successful so quickly."

She sat down in his chair and scanned the quarterly tax report for this quarter versus the one from two quarters ago. The cost of supplies went up a little, but the profits seemed to have doubled and even tripled in some areas.

"Business is good there. Where is this?"

"The Break Room. You know, the little coffee shop? It does look like they're doing well, but then they should be ordering more supplies, right? So I thought maybe they raised their prices. I went in there this morning, and the muffins cost less than they used to. There weren't that many people in there."

Star scrolled up to the top again. "Karen is the owner?"

"Yes, it's owned by Karen Trenton. She only has a couple of employees, too." He pointed to the staffing expenses. "Yet wages didn't go up either."

"Hmm, this is odd. Show it to Alice." Alice was the audit expert in the firm.

Later that evening Star stopped outside of the karate studio where she'd arranged to meet Mari. Somehow she'd let her own sister talk her into taking a beginner class. She rubbed the back of her neck. For sure, she had to stop sitting at her computer looking at numbers for such long stretches. The training session at work had been tiring, and then she'd had client calls for three hours, but she'd formed a few ideas for the bakery.

"Hey, there you are. Come on, get your uniform!" Mari pulled her into the studio.

"Uniform?"

"You have to wear a gi for beginning karate."

She groaned. "You said it was mainly self-defense techniques."

Ten minutes later, Star was trying to do a second pushup. "You can do it!" yelled the gorgeous, fit young woman in the red uniform with a black belt from the front of the room. Star felt the opposite of all those things in her loose fitting white gi. She wished she hadn't worn her purple satin underwear, which seemed to glow through the thin white fabric. She stayed in the back of the room in case she had to bend over.

At least a couple other ladies seemed to be struggling. One was a mom who looked to be in her late twenties. Her four year old waited in the doorway to the studio, munching on goldfish crackers and watching the class.

"Twenty." Mari finished a series of pushups and started on the sit-ups. Star gave up on the pushups and joined her. With nothing to hold her feet down, the sit-ups were even harder than the pushups.

Gabriela, the instructor/torturer, came up next to her. "It will get easier, I promise. Just keep trying."

Star wanted to hate her, but managed to make it through ten sit-ups and even the twenty jumping jacks.

"Okay, they're all warmed up," she heard Gabriela say to someone as she exited the room.

"Great. You ladies ready to work out?" Star closed, and then opened her eyes as she recognized the voice. It was Steve, wearing a black uniform and black belt with several embroidered strips at one end.

She looked at Mari, who grinned at her and shrugged.

"Everyone grab a spot on the bar and I'll give you one of the slingshots o'fun."

Star felt his eyes on her. When he handed her the yellow rubber apparatus, he nodded at her.

"Up and pivot for slow round kicks. I'll help those of you who are new."

Star noticed that everyone else seemed to know what to do. She was the only new one there, so he came and stood beside her. She tried to kick at the bar like her sister in front of her, but she could not kick much higher than her knee while Mari kicked up to the height of her head.

"I want to hear yells," he called out as he put his hands on her leg.

Star tried to remember if she shaved that morning as the pant leg of the gi rode up her calf. For an uncomfortable moment he moved her leg into the right position. She was pretty sure her leg had never bent that way before today. But she didn't want to let him know it hurt.

"Hurts, doesn't it? That means you're doing it right." He smiled at her, and she was struck again by his light green eyes. Not struck enough to ignore the pain, though.

"Then I must be a natural," she muttered through gritted teeth.

The class did not improve, but Star was determined to make it through one session, anyway. She certainly wasn't coming back for more.

Forty-five going on forty-five hundred minutes later, Star wiped another bead of sweat off the side of her face. The folks around her smiled at her as they calmly went about kicks, blocks, yells, and burpees. She knew they were trying to be encouraging.

She thought Steve was trying to be encouraging too, as he kept yelling, "Come on, almost there, Star," no matter where he was in the room..

Her sister wore a fancy uniform with her name on the back—M. Tenalia—in black lettering over the studio's logo. She also wore a red belt. Star saw a red belt like it in the middle of a display of belts one the wall. The white belt was the first, and the black was the last.

When the class finally ended, Star thought about changing back into the skirt and sweater she'd worn at work, but realized that would involve bending. It was hard enough to put her red boots back on. She put her coat on right over the gi, grabbed her bag, and headed home.

Enrique was late arriving at the bakery the next morning.

"Chill, Star. He'll be here. He probably had something due for school. See, there is he is."

She and Charlie looked out the front window and saw Enrique arguing with his brother. They could make out raised voices but no words.

Enrique looked at his watch and pointed into the bakery. Steve put a hand on his shoulder and shook his head. Enrique shook off the hand and threw open the door. The bells clanged loudly as the door banged against the brick façade.

Star noted Steve's look of disgust and saw red. She hurried past Enrique and out the door, where she confronted Steve.

"What's your problem?"

"This is none of your business." He took a step closer to her. "I'm protecting my family."

"From what?" She resisted the urge to step back as another thought occurred to her. "Just how far would you go? Putting in a big order, and then cancelling it? Posting bad reviews?"

She put a hand on his chest to push him back, but he grabbed it and twisted, forcing her to lean down awkwardly.

"Calm down. Stop struggling." His voice was close to her ear as he kept up the pressure on her arm. It didn't hurt, but she couldn't move. "What are you even talking about? I just want my brother to get a real job so he can have a secure future."

"Let go!"

He did, and she rubbed her shoulder, though it didn't really hurt, while trying to decide if hitting him was worth it.

"If you came back to class, you'd know how to get out of that hold."

Star's hands remained clenched until well after Steve crossed the street.

The bakery saw more traffic that morning, possibly due to the Yule Get Through Thanksgiving sandwiches Charlie designed. Similar to a vintage sandwich loaf, the horizontally cut loaves held layers of turkey salad and cranberry dressing made with corn bread. The top layer consisted of thick cream cheese.

A quiet word with Roz inspired the sisters to offer Enrique a small raise and commissions on wedding or special order cakes. It was part of their marketing strategy, thinking Enrique might have friends who'd book cakes he made.

At 6:32 p.m., Star closed her last accounting file. The double shifts between the bakery and the office were catching up to her. She stretched as her phone buzzed.

"Aren't you coming to class?" It was Mari.

"I'm beat, Mari. Not this time." She rubbed her shoulder absently, remembering Steve's hold, even though it hadn't hurt.

"Come on. He's not teaching tonight. I checked. I never get to see you anymore."

With a sigh, Star grabbed her purse.

Tonight's class was easier. Star managed eight pushups and fifteen sit-ups. She remembered the round kicks and even got some praise for her boxing combinations. That was worth the red knuckles.

She was still wiped out after class and sat trying to catch her breath as she waited for Mari when Steve sat down next to her.

"I'm sorry about this morning." He was wearing his uniform again. So Mari had it wrong.

She just nodded, still breathing hard from the class.

"Henry said you gave him a raise. It isn't enough for him to live on, but it will cover his car insurance and some of his textbooks. I still want him to think about other careers, but I'm willing to let this go for a while."

"Big of you," she bit out.

"Are you ok? You'll get used to classes soon. Leah said you did well today."

She tried to stand up and was unsteady. He put his hand on her arm.

"Would you be interested in some coffee at the Break Room? I'd like to talk more to you about the bakery business. I promise not to put you in any holds."

"Who wouldn't be tempted by that?"

Mari walked over and joined them. "Hi, Steve, we missed you at class."

"Star and I were just going for coffee. Want to join us?"

Mari winked at her sister. "No, I have to get going."

Star held back a sigh, as she knew Steve—and everyone else still in the studio—saw that wink.

"Ok, let's go. You getting changed, Star?"

She knew she couldn't bend over to do it until she got home and had a free hour. "Nah, I'm good."

The Break Room was empty except for a couple of high schoolers typing at laptops.

"Hi, Karen, got any of those wonderful pumpkin muffins?" Star headed up to the display case and looked at the shelves. Her gaze caught on the

Linzer cookies that looked very similar to the ones Karen bought from the bakery two days ago.

"So I like Linzer cookies, so what? After I ate the ones I bought, I thought why not make some for here? I mean, it's not like you had all that many people buying yours."

Surprised at the woman's hostility, Star took a step back right into Steve. He put a hand on her elbow to steady her; the warmth felt good. She didn't move away. Maybe she misunderstood Karen. "What?"

"Come on, can't you stand a little competition?"

"Let's go somewhere else." Steve pulled her out of the coffee shop.

"I don't understand. She's always been so friendly."

"What did she mean, no one was buying your cookies? Does this have something to do with those reviews you mentioned to me?"

She touched her shoulder absently and he grinned. She ignored it. "Probably. But I don't get it. She was friendly enough when she bought the cookies the other night. She came in late and commented on how many holiday cookies we had." She paused as an unwelcome thought suddenly struck her.

"Oh, no." She closed her eyes, and Steve grabbed her elbow again. He smelled good, she decided, better than she did after that karate class for sure. Thrusting that thought aside, she glared at Steve and said, "It's her. Posting the bad reviews, canceling the big order. She's the one having trouble with her business. I can't believe it."

She turned to storm back into the store, but couldn't move as Steve held on to her.

"Hang on. What are you going to do?"

Pulling on her arm did no good, so, Steve pulled her closer and trapped her arm between them.

"Do you use karate moves on all your dates?" She blushed as she realized she'd called this a date.

"Only the ones I really like. But you have to calm down before you do anything rash. You don't know for sure it's her."

She tried again to pull away, but Steve stopped her by leaning down to kiss her.

Both were breathing hard a minute later when he lifted his head. When he let go of her, her heart was racing. "Well," she muttered in embarrassment, "I should get going."

"Hang on." He grabbed her hand. "Rain check on coffee? Or better yet, let's make it dinner. After class tomorrow night? I'm teaching."

"Ah, well, could I meet you afterwards?"

"Am I that bad?" He cupped her face with his hand and she got goosebumps.

"I don't think I can handle your classes." *Or you*, she thought.

"You can handle it." He gave her another kiss, and then another at her car that made her want to invite him back to her place for a moment of insanity.

After ignoring Mari's teasing texts, Star was almost afraid to go to the bakery in the morning. Charlie was boxing a strange looking cake for the same elderly woman in a red coat when she arrived.

"Hello, Star." The woman smiled. "Your brother let me have one of his new creations, the Turkey Day Delight. I think you have another hit on your hands, Charlie. You two have a good day now.

"How does she know us?" Star whispered to her brother as she put on her apron. "And what the heck is Turkey Delight?"

"She's come in here like every day for the past few weeks. She's a friend of Grandma's. She's tried some of everything, and is always encouraging me to try new things. Like my awesome new cake!"

In between helping customers, Star learned that Turkey Day Delight was a variation on the Chicago classic Atomic cake, which was three layers of cake, fruit, and pudding fillings topped with whipped cream. Charlie's version featured pumpkin, chocolate, and vanilla cake layers with a thin cranberry-strawberry filling and pumpkin flavored pudding, all topped with nutmeg sprinkled whipped cream.

It was the busiest morning she could ever remember. Not only did the

Turkey Day Delight fly off the shelves, but she also sold several Corny Breads, which were corn bread muffins made in turkey molds Charlie found on eBay.

Before she left for her office, she told Roz what she suspected about the Break Room owner. She suspicions were heightened when Roz showed her a review of "terrible Linzer cookies" posted the night before.

"Luckily, that cute little old lady with the red coat bought them all yesterday."

Four men in dark suits prowled the waiting room of the accounting firm when Star arrived for work. She hurried back to her cubicle to confront her co-worker, Evan.

"Who are those guys? They look like Feds." She handed Evan a coffee and cookie from the bakery.

"Shh!" He stood up and glanced around the room before leaning over to her. "I think they might be. Alice called me early this morning at home about the Break Room audit and said she had to report some things from it. She wouldn't explain, but said I should dress nicely today in case the authorities needed to talk to me."

"No! Really?" Star took her water bottle and pushed herself away from her desk. "Let me see if I can find out anything."

As she walked towards the bottle refill station, she heard shouting from Mr. Maveson's office. The head partner had a deep gravelly voice, so she knew it wasn't him yelling. The door opened, and as she heard the voice wish the elderly partner ill in several swear words, Star realized it was Karen.

"Are you being reported, too?" Karen's voice made it clear that Star's attempt to sidle away unnoticed didn't work She moved in front of Star.

Behind the woman's back, she could see Mr. Maveson quickly walk down the other hallway towards the waiting room.

"Um, no, I work here."

"So you have lots of money. That's awesome. Of course your family is rich, and you don't have to worry about the bakery you all play in. I work hard—I put my soul into that coffee shop. But I don't have lots of help like you. And you're all so stuck up over there. That intern laughed when I asked him to come work for me. And your freaky brother with his ridiculous desserts. Plus that Enrique with his perfect pies! Everything you do over there comes up roses. Some of us have to work for everything we get!"

By now Karen's shrill voice had alerted several of Star's colleagues, who quietly moved into place behind her.

"You have no idea what's it like to worry if you can even stay open. And you are all so patronizing about my muffins. Guess what? I buy them at Costco. That's right! And you were too dumb to notice!" She reached out to grab Star's arm.

Star grabbed Karen's arm with one hand and her elbow with her other and twisted downward. The sudden move surprised the woman into silence for one second before she started shouting and trying to hit Star.

Two of the suited men had her on the floor in seconds. "You can let go, ma'am." One man placed his hand on Star's, which was still gripping Karen's elbow.

Star spent the rest of the day in interviews with the federal agents and the staff who worked on Karen's files. Trying to alter her tax records was the last in a line of illegal activities the woman had tried to keep her business going. While her marijuana-laced brownies were actually making a profit, growing and selling the plants online over several states had already attracted the attention of the FBI.

Star had no time to text her sisters and let them know what happened. At 5:45 she decided to try and catch up with Mari at the karate studio. It had nothing to do with seeing Steve there. Neither did her stop to add lipstick.

She slipped into the end of the line for bowing in. Steve smiled at her, but didn't ease up for the next forty-five minutes of character building. Each time she thought about slipping out the door again, he seemed to be right there, urging her on.

"Seriously? I can spit harder than that."

And it worked. She kicked harder, and at the end, she could actually bend and put on her socks and shoes without screaming.

She found Mari and Steve chatting in the waiting area.

"So Enrique wants me to help him buy the coffee shop," he was saying. "Once the place is cleared out and all the evidence collected."

She stopped and stared.

"What?" he asked. "I'm trying to be more supportive. I guess I'm falling in love with the bakery business."

"You guys know about Karen and the Break Room?"

"It was on the news. How do you know?" Mari turned to face her after lacing up her shoes.

The rest of the room cleared out as she told them about her day. When she got to the part about how she twisted Karen's arm, she grinned. "I'm sure you'd have a lot to say about my technique, but it actually worked."

Steve kissed her cheek. "I'm glad she didn't hurt you. I'm going to show you some more moves next time."

"And that's my cue to go," said Mari. "I want to help Roz box up Charlie's new Not-So-Dumpy-Lings. We have an order for a hundred. And it's knitting night."

"I should go help. I don't know what those are, but that's a big order." Star turned to Steve. "Can I call you when I'm done?"

He pulled her towards him by her new white belt. "Why don't I go with you? I have to see those. I loved the Corny Bread muffins."

The bakery still held some of the commuter crowd, and the charity knitting group Roz had started filled all the seats.

Star pulled Steve into the back room, but he started washing his hands. "Do I get a free treat if I help?"

"Is that a euphemism?" Charlie looked up from the dough he was rolling. "ACT word, right?"

She just shook her head as Steve followed her out to the store.

"There you are, Star. I'd love to have those chocolate pumpkin tarts with the chocolate turkeys on top in the case there." The woman's red coat sported a rhinestone cake pin today.

Another new dessert. "Charlie's?" she asked Roz, who was helping another customer.

"No, Enrique's. He's practicing what he learned in his candy making class."

"All of them?" Star saw about thirty in the case.

"Yes, dear. Another Bible Study group. And we're coming here next week to help with the charity knitting. I want the last of your Grandma's kolackies, too."

Star examined the cookie case and spotted about twenty of the folded kolackies her family had now made for a few generations. There was nothing fancy about them, but they always had some in the bakery to remind them of their grandmother.

Mystified by this strange woman and everything she'd said, Star replied, "We'll get more chairs; that's great."

She showed Steve how to box the tarts and stack them with paper. Then she turned and asked the lady, "What's your name? This might take a few minutes and you could sit down with some complimentary hot chocolate. Charlie can bring you a chair."

"Estrella Baggio. Your grandma used to babysit me when I was a child in Italy. She sent me the money to come over to this country years ago. I didn't see her more than a couple of times before I moved to be near my daughter when her husband got a job here."

Steve proved to be good at boxing tarts. "Henry could at least make us some candy at home," he grumbled. He seemed to put his hand on Star's waist or stand behind her more than necessary as they worked, and she knew she was blushing.

A few minutes later, Estrella finished her hot chocolate .She returned to the counter just as the last of the tarts were boxed. She smiled at Star.

"Have a good night, dear. And il matrimonio fa un cuore felice."

Charlie's Not-So Dumpylings

Pie Crust: mix together 1 1/2 cups flour, sifted and 3/4 tsp salt. Cut in 1/2 cup shortening and sprinkle with 3 tbsp. water. Roll out to 1/8″ thick.

Divide dough and cover two large cored apples in a 9x13 baking dish.

Boil together for 3 minutes: 2/3 cup sugar, 1 ½ cups water, 2 Tbsp butter and ½ tsp cinnamon.

Pour the hot liquid over the dough covered apples. Bake at 425 for 30 minutes.

Makes 2 enormous dumplings that can be divided to eat!

FLIGHT 22
by Dyanne Davis

Dyanne Davis is a Multi-Published, Award Winning author of 22 novels, several novellas and anthologies. Dyanne lives in a Chicago suburb with her husband of 45 years, William Sr.

She has been a presenter of numerous workshops. She hosts a local cable television show in her hometown on Bolingbrook Community Channel, on channel 6 "*The Art of Writing*," to give writing tips to aspiring writers. Interviewing many of her favorite authors has been the highlight of doing the show. You can catch some of the clips on Youtube. https://www.youtube.com/results?search_query=Dyanne+davis

Dyanne also writes a vampire series under the name of F. D. Davis. You can reach her at davisdyanne@aol.com. www.dyannedavis.com www.adamomega.com

"Is this seat taken?"

Sela smiled as the now familiar heat traveled along her spine. She'd have to ask Nick how he managed to do that. Raising her gaze to meet his, she decided against it. He was already far too cocky where she was concerned.

"The seat is taken," she said sternly, trying her best not to melt from the heated glance he was bestowing on her.

"Was your plane late?" she asked. "You should have been here over an hour ago."

"I missed the earlier one and was forced to take the next flight."

Sela thought for a moment before pulling out her phone and tapping on it. "You could have called."

Nick grinned and took the phone from her hand. Raising a brow, he looked at the phone, touched a couple of buttons, and handed it back to her. "If you'd had it on or bothered to check, you would have seen I'd called." He waited, knowing she wouldn't just take his word for it but would indeed check the message. When she'd listened to it, she barely glanced at him, as though she were not in the wrong.

"Did you get me coffee?" he asked, sliding into the seat alongside her instead of the one across. As she moved away, he advanced on her.

"Why are you moving away from me? This is our first real date, Sela. After three months of meeting like this in airports, it's the first one we've planned instead of meeting accidentally."

"But still we're in an airport."

"To be more precise, we're in a Starbucks in an airport in Vegas. I kind of think of this as our connection now. Don't you?"

In spite of her intention, Sela smiled back. This was the first step toward something that could be more than a chance meeting. They'd both decided they wanted that. No storm stranding them, nothing of the sort.

"Starbucks is our connection?" she asked.

"No, Starbucks in airports. So why are you moving away from me? It's not as though we've never kissed. And you do know I want to kiss you, right?"

"That's why I'm moving."

Before she could protest, his arms were around her and he was pulling her to him. She slid toward him. Maybe it was the slick material of the seat, or maybe it was because she wanted to be in his arms. Whatever it was, she was moving, hypnotized by this bronze Adonis sitting next to her.

"I like the taste of you," he murmured, placing soft kisses on her lips. "Let me see if I can tell what kind of coffee you had."

His tongue slid between her lips and his hand splayed against her spine. She knew she should stop him but she didn't want to. His lips were doing things to her that she'd wanted since the last time they'd been together. The man filled her with lust. Breathing deeply, she took his scent into her lungs and sighed. He grinned at her and moved his hand downward just a little. She was trying her best to remember they were in an airport.

To her surprise, another small sigh of satisfaction escaped her lips, causing Nick to pull back and smile at her before deepening the kiss. God, he tasted good, peppermint and chocolate. Sela wanted to laugh. He'd already had coffee. She almost drew back from the kiss to ask, but the feel of the oral assault stopped her. She didn't care at the moment if he'd had an entire carafe of coffee. She just hoped he would continue kissing her.

"Just what I wanted," he whispered into her mouth before returning to gently sucking on her tongue.

"Just what I wanted also," she admitted, half breathless because of his kisses. Sela closed her eyes and gave herself over to him, needing his kiss to fill the empty crevices she'd not known needed filling. For a nano second she wondered if they had an audience. If they did, she only hoped they were aware how giddy she was feeling.

"Are you ready to leave?" he asked at last while holding her face between his hands, caressing her jaw line with the pad of his finger. "We finally have three full days. It could be two weeks if you would consent to be with me through Christmas."

"You know I can't. I have to be with my family. Family is very important to me."

At the mention of family, Nick stopped abruptly. He stared down at Sela. "Family's not all it's cracked up to be, Sela." He shrugged. "I don't see one in my future."

There it was, out in the open between them. He'd punctured her core without even knowing it. How could he? It wasn't even something Sela allowed to surface, but it had always been there, gnawing at her bit by bit. She wanted to belong to someone totally and completely. She wanted family. Tilting her head a bit, she gave Nick a smile determined not to let him know his remark had hurt her in any way. "I think it's time we left, like you said," Sela said and began walking toward the door.

With just a few words, Nick had wounded her. No, she hadn't been thinking wedding bells, but she'd have to admit some infinitesimal part of her soul had whispered, '*maybe.*' She brought her gaze up to meet his, chastising herself.

How could he work so closely with children and not want a family? She'd always wanted to have her own family. Sure, she loved her mom and dad, but there'd always been something missing, some disconnect that she firmly believed was the result of blood. She didn't have theirs. She wanted that connection someday that a family tie was supposed to give. Sela sighed softly, knowing she'd never be able to let go of that dream. She wanted children someday, and she wanted to give a sense of belonging to them.

"What do you see in your future, Nick?"

Sela continued out the doors of the airport, waiting for him to catch up with her, waiting for him to answer.

"I'm not sure." He shrugged his shoulders. "I don't want to start this off by lying to you. I'm not a big believer in marriage." He shrugged again. "My parents married and divorced each other twice."

His hand snaked out and he allowed his fingers to travel down her face, caressing her satiny skin, pausing at her chin and tilting it upward so she could look into his eyes.

"I know I'd like to see more of you in my future. I want this first weekend with us to lead to a second and a third. I wouldn't be averse to meeting you in airports for a very long time."

His words carried a warning, and Sela should have been listening. In fact she was, but he was staring into her eyes, his look of desire for her blazing a path of want along her spine. Her heart screamed for her to take a chance. Nick Winters didn't have to be 'the one,' but she definitely didn't have to discard him for telling her the truth, either.

As he continued smiling seductively at her, she could feel much more than she wanted, knowing what she now knew. With his touch, his looks, and his kisses, he was claiming bits and pieces of her. She had to say something to stop him from gazing at her like he wanted to devour her then and there.

"Listen, I wanted to thank you for getting the ticket."

"That was necessary," Nick countered. "How else would you be allowed to go through the gates to wait for me at Starbucks if you didn't have a ticket?"

Sela couldn't stop the smile if she'd tried. Nick was beginning to grow on her big-time, and that she didn't need. But....he grinned. And she sighed. Her heart was leading her on this because her head had apparently taken its own vacation. Sure, spending a couple of hundred bucks for a ticket just so she could wait for him at the Starbucks was not a major amount of cash. But it was the thought that he'd wanted to do it that had her heart thumping. She could have paid for the ticket herself, she thought and frowned, wishing for a few years in the past. A past when a ticket hadn't been necessary to go past the gates to the Starbucks and wait for a friend.

Sela's hand swinging back and forth while entwined with Nick's made her stare down. He was behaving like...like a little kid caught in some mischievous act. She looked at the shy smile that played around the corners of his mouth. *Hmm*, she thought, *that was a first.* She'd seen his smiles, flirtatious, teasing, sweet, seductive, but not this, not shy.

"Nick, are you embarrassed?" she asked. "You shouldn't be. It was romantic. You could have just come to the Mandarin. I told you I have a room." It was Sela's turn to smile. "My company paid for it for the entire week. They're so pleased I got the job done in half the time."

"I'm not embarrassed." Nick grinned. "I don't know… I've just gotten used to seeing you at the airport."

"What about the time we spent at the hotel in Atlanta, during the storm?" she teased, remembering how much she'd wanted him to make love to her, knowing she didn't know nearly enough about him to go for it. Every meeting until today had been a chance encounter. If she was going to go to bed with the guy, the least they could do was have a for-real-honest-to-God-date. This was it, this one they'd planned; it was one where they were not worrying about rushing off to meet family or working. Sela had double checked three times. No emergencies with the family or her job, she was good to go.

Suddenly she found herself spinning. Nick had taken her hand and twirled her about, making her laugh, making her feel like a silly teenager. It felt good.

"This is our first date, Sela. I think we're worth it. I think we need to see what fate has in store for us. I can't believe our constantly running into each other at airports in different cities is an accident. I didn't want to mess with that formula."

"You're superstitious?"

"Not usually," Nick said, turning her to face him. "But I don't want to tempt fate by changing things." He stopped and stared at her. "Can't you feel it?" he asked and pulled her to him. "I've felt it. Every time I've kissed you I can hardly wait for the next one." He kissed her lightly on the lips, pulling back as she glanced around.

"Are you worried about kissing me in public," he asked, "or just kissing me period?"

"I don't do public displays of anything, Nick. I'm a market analyst. You're an actor, you're in the public eye, and that's old news for you, but not for me. I don't want to have my life invaded with paparazzi that might be following you for a story. I hope you understand."

"I understand if you think because I'm an actor I'm always looking over my shoulder for the camera that we need this date more than I thought. My job is a job, same as yours." He narrowed his gaze. "You shouldn't believe everything you read. I haven't found one woman yet who's intrigued me the way you have. Besides, have you ever noticed the paparazzi following me? I live under the radar, and I don't notify anyone of my schedule in order for them to make a fuss over me. That's not what I'm about." He shook his head. You didn't even know who I was when we met. That was one of the things that intrigued me about you. Now it's everything."

His voice turned soft and he stopped his half glare. "When I kiss you, I feel this rush of warmth." She hit him lightly on his arm and he grinned. "Not there, although that too. But in here," he said, using his finger to tap his chest. "I feel something stirring here. I've never had this feeling before, so I don't know what it is. I just know I want to find out more about you. I want to kiss you until you're as dizzy as I am, and then we'll see."

Darn, but he was good. He had her right then and there. Her bronze Adonis was making her melt and she knew they needed to get to the hotel quickly and take a nice cool dip in the Garden of the Gods' pool. Her Adonis would be right at home there.

Several hours and two mojitos later, Sela was falling even more under Nick's spell. She'd suggested a swim in the hotel pool for more than one reason. True, she'd had a couple of fantasies picturing Nick in a swimsuit alongside all the plaster gods that lounged in decadent poses along the entire length of the pool. It was an appropriate name, Garden of the Gods. But she'd wanted something more, a sure fire jerk test. She'd covered her eyes with her wrap around sunglasses, wanting to hide somewhat from Nick, wanting him not to be able to tell what she didn't want him to know.

So far, Nick was passing the jerk test with admirable colors. She'd watched as tall slinky blondes, brunettes and redheads had sauntered by, some doing a double take when they recognized Nick. And she'd watched one give him a come hither look or two. Sela was grinning like a Cheshire cat. He'd barely glanced at the banquet of scantily clad women. His attention remained focused on her as he told her about his family.

Just when she should have been preening, another thought took root. A stray thought, *why wasn't he looking?* Could he be... Nooo, he wasn't. But then again one never knew. He was perfect for it, the business he was in was known for it. Look at his body. Someone should mount him on one of those plaster statuettes.

Before she could stop herself, she blurted it out. "Nick, are you gay?"

For a moment he didn't answer her, just stared, then his face contorted into laugher. He quickly recovered and looked offended.

"Excuse me?"

"Are you gay?"

"Where did that come from?"

"Think about it." She waved her arm around. "Look at all of these beautiful women here, and you've barely glanced at them. That's not natural, my friend."

"Not natural for whom?"

"It's not natural for men to be surrounded by this much naked flesh and not look," she insisted.

"Forgive me if I'm wrong, but I thought we were here on a date."

"We are. But what does that have to do with the fact that you've not ogled any of these women. I know you're not blind."

He was staring at her like she was crazy, and all she was doing was trying to protect herself. "What?" she asked. "I just want to know what I'm dealing with."

"Sela, where is this coming from? I'm not sure if your words are aimed at yourself or me. Either way, I don't like it." He stopped her with a hard look. "Why would I be focused on other women, half naked or otherwise, when I'm with you? That remark offends us both. Did you think because you've been ogling the beefcakes around here I would do likewise?"

He gently lifted her huge sunglasses from her face. "Women in bikinis don't make me come unglued. There is only one woman at this pool who interests me, and that's you."

He smiled down at her, sweeping his eyes across her body, making her melt. She could almost feel the straps loosening and sliding off her shoulders from the heat.

"You still didn't answer the question," she said softly.

"Do you really think I'm gay?"

"No, but...come on, look around you." Sela swallowed as he did so, taking his time, *his slow time,* allowing his gaze to land on each woman at the pool before returning his gaze to her.

"I must admit," he said at last, "this place does have an overabundance of beautiful women. But you're the only woman here who pulled my attention in a crowded airport, who had me stalking her just so I could say hello. There is something very special happening between us. It's been happening for three months now. I thought you knew that."

"But that night in the hotel, in the storm, you didn't do anything."

"You said no."

"What about now? You didn't argue when I told you to take the other bed."

"Why argue? If you said no, I would respect your wishes, though personally I don't think this will end with us sleeping in separate beds. Do you?"

Nick paused for a moment but didn't give her time to answer. "Tell me something, Sela. What kind of men have you been involved with who've made you place so little value on your worth? You're worthy of any man's full attention. I hope you've never settled for less. I hope you never expect less from me."

He trailed his fingers slowly over her torso. "I know I expect to give you my undivided attention. Unlike you," he teased, grinning at her, "I have no need to check out the buffet. I already have what I want." He trailed his fingers over her again, then leaned down and kissed her.

Her words hadn't been a ploy for another kiss, but now Sela was glad she'd said them. He was making her tingle all the way to her toes. When he pulled up, his look had become serious. She knew he was about to ask her a

70

question she didn't want to answer.

"Who hurt you, Sela? Who made you feel unworthy? Tell me and I'll find him and kick his behind."

Her already melting, soft and squishy heart melted even more. "I'm adopted. You're going to have a hard time finding 'him', since I don't know who he is." She ran the tip of her tongue over her lips, biding her time, trying hard to not allow her eyes to pool with tears.

"Then I'll find your mother," Nick said softly.

"Unfortunately, my birth mother is beyond your reach, Nick," Sela whispered, interrupting him. "She died giving birth to me."

"I'm sorry."

"No, I am, for unloading on you like this. I've had a very good life filled with love. I have nothing to complain about." She sighed, turned away, then turned back to face Nick. "I was born on Christmas. I can't help but become a bit melancholy around the holidays. I wonder about my biological family. I find myself looking into the faces of strangers and wondering if we could be related."

"I'm assuming you've done a search through birth records."

"I tried. There wasn't any information. It was a closed adoption, no family stepped forward to claim me. That's all the information I have."

Nick was killing her with the way he was looking at her as though he wanted to rewrite her beginning, as though she was someone he cherished, as though he cared. She couldn't stop the lone tear that fell. She'd never told any man she'd ever dated that she was adopted. Why the heck was she telling Nick? She barely knew him.

His finger was brushing away the tear, and then he was kissing the path it had taken, pulling her to him, holding her against his heart. She had to get this out quickly then get them back where she'd meant for them to be, carefree, happy, no problems, no worries, and no family. At that thought another tear fell and another and she was where she wanted to be, in Nick's arms with him kissing away her tears. She'd had no idea it felt so good to cry.

"My adoptive parents love me," she rushed to explain. "That's why I have to go home for the holidays."

Sela was babbling and couldn't help it. She never lost control. What the heck was wrong with her? She was finding a connection with a man who wasn't looking for one, who didn't believe in family.

"You poor baby," he crooned.

His words were what she needed to stop her tears. She never had accepted pity and she wouldn't now, no matter how connected she felt to him.

"Don't pity me, Nick. When the holidays are over, so is my melancholy."

"Pity is the last thing I have for you, Sela. I said 'poor baby' because you have no idea how I plan to get rid of all your doubts. I plan on worshiping your body for the next three days, so much so that you won't have a spare thought for anything or anyone else. In fact, when I'm through, you'll never look at another man."

He narrowed his gaze and glanced around the pool at the men who had on even less clothing than the women. He brought his attention back to Sela and smiled. "Naked or otherwise." He grinned. "I plan on leaving you tired and breathless. I said poor baby because like it or not you've just about captured my heart, and I'm not an easy guy to lov...I mean...I'm not...well...you know...I'm not an easy guy to get close to. You poor baby," he whispered in her mouth. "I'm going to enjoy showing you how much you deserve to be adored."

Mercy, Sela thought. Maybe it was the decadence, the pool, the men, the women, Nick. It was definitely Nick. She found herself spilling her guts to him, telling him things she'd never shared with another soul. When she finally took a breath, she could only stare at him and wait for him to run for the hills. No man liked a woman who talked too much about herself. Right?

"So that's why you're so involved with the adoption agency you told me about?"

"That's part of the reason."

"We both work with organizations that help disadvantaged kids, and you want to try and tell me fate didn't have a hand in this? We were meant to meet, Sela."

Nick studied her, his hands steepled, his index fingers worrying the bridge of his nose. Why was he getting involved in her life? he wondered. Sure, he wanted to make love to her, had from the moment he'd spotted her in the Chicago airport months before, but this …true confession time…this wasn't him. He'd meant it when he told her she didn't know her worth, but why was he telling her that? He'd never loved a woman. A body was a body was a body. He knew the seamier side of love and it wasn't for him. Any woman would do. They were interchangeable, so much so he'd stopped even bothering with names.

Sela, he thought and looked at her chocolate brown eyes. Her name was not interchangeable and neither was she. She was definitely different. She was piercing his reserve, making him want to protect her, making him care. But a woman with Sela's background would be looking for love and marriage. He couldn't offer that to her. Best for them to get that out of the way up front. No matter that his heart might be beating a little too hard whenever she was near.

"Sela, you're making me feel things I've never felt before. I don't want to hurt you."

"Nick, don't go there. I have no plans on getting serious with you or having you fall in love with me or anything. Back up and take this slow."

Whoa, what just happened here? That was going to be his line. In fact, he was in the middle of that same speech when she'd rudely cut him off.

"What," he asked, "are you talking about?"

"You. You're looking all misty eyed. I can tell you want to rush in and play the hero for me. I don't need a hero, Nick. I get along quite well on my own."

"You're hard on a man's ego." Nick tried for a smile then shrugged.

"I don't want to hurt you," Sela whispered.

And just like that she had him. He grinned at her, trying to make light of her rejection but saw her expression remained unchanged. So, she was serious. *Poor baby,* he thought, *I'm falling in love with you. It's too late for both of us.*

"I hate shopping," Nick complained as Sela dragged him from one store to the next. "You said we were going to get to know each other. How in the world is shopping going to do it? You're just using me for an extra pair of hands to carry your purchases."

Sela burst out laughing. She couldn't believe what a baby Nick was being. Men. Maybe it was time to stop the shopping, she thought, then spotted the Disney store right ahead. "Just one more store, Nick, please," she pleaded. She reached for his hand, stood on tiptoe and gave him a kiss, smiling when the look in his eyes showed his acquiescence. She'd make it up to him later.

Sela and Nick carried armload after armload of toys and clothing to the counter. After dumping her last batch of toys, she turned toward Nick, who was filling his arms with an array of sweaters. "I thought you didn't like shopping," she said as she waited while he dumped another load on the overcrowded counter.

"Just for kids."

The grin on his face was wider than any she'd seen thus far. Again her heart thumped. He loved helping disadvantage kids. "I want to buy you a Christmas present," she said without thinking.

"You don't have to do that."

"I know. But I want to."

"Sela, I already have everything I need. Seriously. I think Christmas is just a way for people to overspend and buy things the other person doesn't want."

He saw the look that crossed her face but didn't take back anything he'd said. Her words sounded too much like those of his parents, especially around the holidays when he'd briefly visit them. Always, the wanting to buy him a present, was followed by, *Can you help out? I need a loan. I'm in debt. I've spent a little more than I should have.* He didn't want to be rude to Sela, but his parents' way of celebrating Christmas was a sore spot for him.

He had no pleasant experiences with holidays. They'd all been spent with his parents, fighting. Even when they'd divorced, they'd fought over who Nick would spent the holiday with, who bought him the best present, who he'd given the most expensive gift. They'd always equated their gift giving with love, and he'd always equated it with excess, too many fights, too much misery, and too much pain.

The thought of a holiday meal was enough to give him hives. As far back as he could remember, it seemed that the start of the holiday meal was the predetermined signal to start fighting. Carving a turkey came with angry words. Slicing a ham caused insults. Even the water was a sore spot. No thank you. He no longer did holidays or holiday meals. And definitely no gifts for him. As rude as it seemed, he didn't want Sela to buy him any gifts; he wanted her to be his gift. And he wanted to be the gift that she wanted, not things. So much for not getting serious.

He'd hurt her feelings. She wore them on her sleeve whether she thought so or not. Right now wasn't the time to apologize, or to explain.

"Are you done?" he asked and pulled out his gold card, passing it to the clerk. "Can I get all of these packages delivered?"

"I'll pay for my own," Sela said, moving the piles she'd bought away from his purchases.

"Stop it, Sela. I wasn't trying to hurt your feelings. Just give me the address of the agency." When she refused, he pulled his phone out of his pocket and pushed the button for the operator. He wrote the information on a slip of paper and handed it to the clerk.

"I want all of the purchases delivered to this address," he ordered in a stern but friendly voice. "Please include a card that they're from Ms. Sela Adams."

If she didn't get out of the store, she'd deck him. He was arrogant, showy, and rude. Who did he think he was? He could pay for all of her purchases, but she couldn't buy him a gift. To hell with him, she thought and walked out of the store. To hell with the way her heart thumped in her chest, the way he made her feel, the way his kisses melted her resolved, or the fact that she'd told him her entire life story in one afternoon. To hell with all of that. The only bed Nick would be sleeping in would definitely be the one beside her; he would not be sleeping in her bed. No way! No dang way! He'd ticked her off big-time, and if he knew what was good for him, he'd stay a safe distance away from her.

She'd almost made it to the parking lot when she heard Nick calling her name. It didn't matter. She didn't answer, nor did she stop. Instead, she increased her pace.

"Sela, stop," Nick rushed up to the rental car out of breath. "I'm sorry."

"Don't be, you're right. You can afford to buy what you want; you don't need any gifts that I have."

"But I do, Sela. I do. I need the gift of your time."

She blinked. The big guy had done it again. He'd gotten to her, made her almost forget that she was ticked.

"What's going on, Nick? Why did you behave that way?"

"I should have shared this when you were sharing, Sela. Holidays mean nothing to me because they were always ruined. You think not knowing your blood made your childhood rough. Knowing mine made mine hell. I hate Christmas. I hate all holidays and families," he said and held her gaze. "I wasn't trying to hurt you, honest. Your wanting to buy something for me just brought back things I didn't want to think about. You already know I'm an only child. That's hard when dealing with dueling parents. Gifts and holidays always brought out the worst in us. And I'm afraid it's brought out the worst in me right now."

"But in there you bought all of my gifts for the kids, even though I didn't want you to. You were even picking up things for them."

"It was making you happy to buy those things for the kids. I wanted a piece of your happiness. I was fine with that. I wasn't having to worry that my mother's feelings would be hurt when she called the store to check on the price of her gift and found out my father's cost ten bucks more."

"Nick?"

"I'm serious, Sela."

"Poor baby."

"Are you saying you pity me?"

"No." Sela reached for his hand. "I'm saying you have no idea of your worth, and I'm going to show you." When he grinned at her, she rose on tiptoe, but was caught up in his arms.

"You're not ticked anymore?"

"Not anymore," Sela answered, waiting for his lips to close over hers. "Why don't we go back to the hotel and finish this conversation there?"

A grin met her for an answer. Then a butterfly soft kiss landed on her lips and an explosion began in her nether regions. Her heart had long abandoned its steady thumping and was marching double time. This man was doing something to her, and thank God she didn't have a plane to catch. She was falling in love.

"Will you have dinner with me and my family?" She almost whispered the words. When he gave her fingers a squeeze, she had hope.

"Sela."

"I promise you there will be no fighting. No one will expect a thing from you." He was staring at her, not answering. "It would mean that we can spend the entire holiday together rather than part while I go alone to visit my family."

"That sounds tempting. Will we have to stay with them?"

"No, we'll find a nice private hotel and make our own holiday…that is, if you want to."

Nick sighed and shook his head. He was a goner. Nothing could have ever prepared him for this, but he found himself willing to take a chance on Sela, on Christmas and on family, and on a hopefully stress free holiday meal. "Will you cook for me?"

"Definitely. What would you like?"

"Chocolate chip cookies with lots of nuts."

"You've got it. In fact, I'll make you my famous kitchen sink cookies."

"Kitchen sink!" Nick laughed. "What's in it?"

"Tons of nuts, chocolate chips, raisins and oatmeal."

"Yes, I'll go." Nick sighed again, knowing a lot in his life was going to change. He stared into Sela's eyes. "I'm falling in love with you. I hope you're ready for that."

"Ready or not, I'm falling in love with you also. Don't look so pained. We're going to take it nice and slow. First a holiday with family and a wonderful meal, then we'll see what the New Year brings."

When his lips moved over hers, she sighed in delight. She now had what she wanted most: Nick's love.

The Kitchen Sink Cookie

Recipe makes 4 dozen cookies
Chocolate chips with oatmeal, raisins and nuts.

1 cup butter, softened
1 cup packed light brown sugar
1/2 cup white sugar
2 large eggs
3 teaspoons vanilla extract
1 1/4 cups all-purpose flour
1/2 teaspoon baking soda
1 teaspoon salt
3 cups quick-cooking oats
1 cup semisweet chocolate chips
1 cup chopped walnuts
1 cup pecans (halved or chopped)
1/2 cup baking raisins
2 tablespoons water

Directions

Preheat the oven to 325 degrees.

In a large bowl, cream together the butter, brown sugar, and white sugar until smooth. Beat in eggs one at a time, then stir in vanilla. Combine the flour, baking soda, and salt; stir into the creamed mixture until just blended. Mix in the quick oats, walnuts, and chocolate chips. Drop by heaping spoonfuls onto ungreased baking sheets.

Bake for 12 minutes in the preheated oven. Allow cookies to cool on baking sheet for 5 minutes before transferring to a wire rack to cool completely.

Aluminum foil can be used to keep food moist, cook it evenly, and make clean-up easier.

Dream of Me
by J. C. DePaul

Dedication

In 2011 I had the pleasure and honor of sitting next to Cathie Linz for the first time at a Windy City RWA meeting. I will admit to having a small "Fan Girl" moment and gushed to her that I'd loved her books since I was a teenager. That night, and the one or two other times I was lucky enough to sit next to her, she was always gracious and kind.

I can honestly say she is one of my writing heroes. Sadly, she lost her battle with cancer earlier this year.

So I dedicate this to her and my fellow Windy City RWA writing sisters who won their battles with cancer and KICKED ITS ASS!!! You know who you are.

J. C. DePaul is a lifelong reader of romantic fiction. She started consuming them as a teenager and has not stopped since. After spending twenty-plus years in Customer Service, she took to the keyboard to fulfill her dream of writing romantic fiction. She is a firm believer that you should never put off your dreams until tomorrow.

J. C. DePaul is the mother of a beautiful, amazing and energetic tween girl. They make their home in the Midwest.

The End. Boy, did typing those words at the end of another manuscript make me both happy and sad. I always got a little melancholy after spending time with my favorite characters, Inara and Dex. After writing about them for the last two and a half years through half a dozen books, we were old friends. Never in my wildest dreams did I think that my books would be as successful as they had been.

Dex. My dream man. I looked over at the drawing of him a fan made for me recently. Fans! I had fans. How cool was that? Color me shocked when my mail box service called and told me they had a package (12" x 14") that was too big to fit in my small mail box. So now Dex's portrait holds a place of honor on my office wall.

"I wish you were real." I sighed to the picture. That wish was one I had made out loud and in my head countless times since his character came to me. Oddly enough, the picture bore a startling resemblance to my next door neighbor and good friend Samson Decker. Or "Dec", as he insisted I call him the first time I'd met him when I moved in three years ago.

The clock sitting on my desk chimed. Midnight. It was now officially Christmas Eve. Time for bed. I saved my document. Again. And shut down my computer. Picking up my coffee mug, I drained the last few swallows and grabbed my phone.

If I had bothered to look out the window before I'd left my office and killed the lights, I would have seen the stars briefly glow brighter. But I didn't. I just left the room.

Clang!

"*Dunmot!*"

The *Bellatorian* curse, a favorite of Dex's, made me smile. I settled in to dream a little dream of my favorite man.

Wait... Clang? That's not right. Unthinkingly, I turned on the lamp. And saw a man standing at the foot of my bed.

I wish I could say that I handled myself like the tough, smart, together woman I pretend to be and leaped out of bed and kicked major ass.

Instead, I screamed like the too-stupid-to-live chick from a horror flick.

"*Dunni,* cease screaming!"

I stopped screaming, but not because he told me to. I simply had no choice. I'd run out of breath to scream with. My eyes were totally glued to the massive man standing in front of me holding the long, really, *REALLY* sharp sword. The light from my lamp glinted off the metal.

Oh my God, I was going to die.

I opened my mouth to scream again.

"Nay, *dunni!*"

My mouth snapped shut. Some of what he'd said penetrated my fear-drenched brain. *Dunmot. Dunni.* Lady/female/woman. I stared hard at the man still standing at the foot of my bed.

Bald. Blue eyes. Black mustache and goatee. *MASSIVELY* built. Shirtless. Silver torc with dragons' heads at the end. Tattooed armbands on his biceps. Leather pants molded to his thighs and—erm...never mind. Knee-high boots. And a wicked sharp sword.

"*OH MY GOD!*"

My eyes rolled into the back of my head. Everything went black.

"*Dunni?* Awaken," the concerned male voice said.

Male voice? My eyes snapped open. Eyes bluer than Caribbean water on a sunny day stared into mine.

Holy. Holy. Shit!

"D-Dex?"

"Aye." The man leaned back, cautiously nodding.

Ohmygod! It's official. My brain broke. Because there was no way—NO WAY!—that the character, my dream man, was standing in front of me in the flesh. Things like that just didn't happen in real life. Right? Right?

I mean, when I was a little girl I used to wish my dolls would turn into real babies that I could take care of. Never happened. Obviously I, at forty-something, had jumped on the bullet train to crazy town.

"This isn't happening." I snatched my glasses off of the nightstand and practically vaulted out of bed, sprinting for my bedroom door.

"Okay, Chris, calm down." I hustled into the kitchen talking to myself. While I'd like to honestly say that was something I didn't do very often, I'd be lying if I did. Unfortunately, I talked to myself *all the freakin' time.*

"You're going to be alright. You're just having a nervous breakdown," I continued. Like *that* was going to make me feel better.

With jerky movements, I opened the cabinet where I kept my glasses. Glasses. My eyeglasses were still in my hand. I put them on. The contents of the cabinet came into focus. I grabbed a glass and sort of lurched to the fridge. My hand shook a little as I pressed my glass against the ice and water dispenser built into my refrigerator door.

"*Dunni?* Where ye go?"

Nope, didn't hear that.

I jerked sideways when a hand suddenly touched my shoulder. I half spun and ran into the bench that was part of my dining set. I sat with a thump and blinked at the apparition before me. Miraculously, I didn't break my glass or spill any water.

"You don't exist. You're not real." My voice shook.

"I beg ye different, *dunni.*" He put his sword back in its scabbard.

I blinked again. I just couldn't wrap my head around this.

"Impossible! I made you up. You're nothing more than a figment of my imagination." I pointed my finger at him…at it? Whatever.

Dex just stared at me and crossed his arms. I tried not to squirm in discomfort at the disappointment I saw in his eyes.

Great. Now I was going to placate my delusion. I took a sip of my water.

85

"Okay, let's say for the sake of argument that you're really here."

What could only be called a scoff came from Dex.

"Why are you here?" I asked. I mean I *was* curious.

He looked heavenward, almost like he was talking to someone. See! Even my delusions were mental.

"My *dea* said to tell you that your wish has been granted. I am to be here for twenty-four hours."

So I guess wishes really did come true. I had my very own *Bellatorian* warrior for twenty-four hours. I looked over at the clock on my stove. It was still way too early an hour for me to truly process this without any sleep.

"I'm really tired, and this is a lot to get my head around. So I'm going to show you to my guest bedroom." With that I rose from my seat. "Come on, it's this way." I motioned towards the entryway that connected to the hall at the front of the house.

I felt more than heard Dex follow behind me. I pointed to the left. "The room on the left is the living room. If you don't want to sleep, you can go in there. I'll show you the TV and remote in a minute."

Turning to the right, I waved my arm at the doorway.

"This door here is for the bathroom, in case you need to…uhm…relieve yourself." I wasn't sure if he had those functions, and I figured better safe than sorry. "You can also get in through the door in the guest room."

"And this is the guest room." I pointed to the doorway across the hall from the living room and walked into the room. Dex followed me. He turned in a complete circle.

"It looks to be a very comfortable sleeping chamber, *Dunni*."

"Chrissy," I corrected.

He stared at me, confused.

"Sorry. My name is Chrissy Waters. Nice to meet you." I smiled sheepishly and held out my hand.

"Dex, Supreme *Domus Arma* of Bellator." He took my hand and bowed over it, brushing my knuckles with his lips.

I bit my lip and barely suppressed the urge to giggle because it tickled a little. Wow. So that's what that felt like? Kind of neat. I guess chivalry really wasn't dead.

"I'll show you how to use the TV in case you get bored or something." I motioned towards the door and Dex once more followed me out into the living room.

I inwardly shook my head, *again*, at the size of my TV. Dec surprised me with it about a year ago. He said he was out TV shopping for his bedroom and thought I should have a new one too. Why he thought either one of us needed a forty-two inch LG was beyond me. I personally was happy with my old boxy twenty-four inch RCA.

"Okay, so this is a TV." I waved my hand at the big flat screen and picked up the remote from the coffee table.

"This is a remote. You use it to control the TV." I held it out to him.

Dex gingerly took it. I think he thought it might explode or something.

"The green button here on the upper right turns the TV on and off. The blue buttons make the sound louder or softer. And the black buttons next to the blue ones make the channels go bigger or smaller." I pointed out each one and showed him how they worked.

"Get back, *dunni*!" Dex dropped the remote and pulled his sword out in the blink of an eye.

"Whoa! Wait!"

Fortunately, Dex stopped mid-swing and my TV stayed intact. Yeah, my bad. I forgot I'd left the Discovery Channel on. The program that came on was about sharks.

"That can't hurt us. It's just moving pictures in a box. See?" I waved my hand close to the screen.

"*Dunmot.*" I smiled at his awed expression. Thankfully he put his sword away again.

I rescued the remote from the floor and put it back on the coffee table.

"If you get hungry or need a drink, that big room we were in before was called the kitchen. The big white box with the two doors I was standing in front of was called a refrigerator. It has food and drinks in it."

I again motioned for Dex to come with me. I opened the fridge and showed him the things I thought would be easiest for him to deal with and how to open them.

"My room is right across from the bathroom if you need me. I'm going back to sleep." I pointed to my bedroom.

I left Dex opening and closing the refrigerator and freezer doors. I think he was fascinated by the lights inside the compartments. I was tempted to tell him there was a little man in the fridge who controlled the lights. I didn't, afraid he would go looking for him and destroy my fridge. Mentally I winced at my next electric bill. Oh well.

When I woke up, the sun was trying to shine brightly into my room even with the blinds closed. I stumbled out of bed towards my en-suite. I did my thing, washed my hands and face, and squinted at my blurry reflection. Reddish blonde hair currently piled up and clipped with hair clips, brown eyes, and a chubby face. I blew my cheeks out even more and shook my head at myself. Same ole' me. Fortyish, not very tall, pale, and plus sized.

I turned away from the mirror with a sigh and tagged my robe from off the hook on the back of the door. I really wasn't thinking earlier this morning. I mean, if I had been thinking straight, I would have at the very least grabbed my cell phone before I left my bedroom and not just my glasses. At least my shortie PJs (tank and shorts) had decently covered me.

I shoved my arms into the sleeves of my robe and belted it, put my glasses on, and put my phone into the pocket.

The sound from the TV was low, but the rest of the house was quiet enough that I still heard it. I peered around the door and looked into the living room. Dex had his sword resting against the side of the couch and the end table. His boots were crossed at the ankle and resting on my coffee table, and he was flicking through TV channels like a pro.

Satisfied that neither he nor anything in my house was in imminent danger or in need of me, I sort of staggered to the coffee pot. I'm not a morning person. I don't function well without coffee. And I definitely don't do perky. That's grounds for death by coffee mug.

"Damn it, I forgot about the auto shut off," I grumbled. Oh well. I wasn't about to sacrifice a whole pot to the sink drain and anger the coffee gods. Thank the lord for microwaves.

Aahh. Much better.

After about a half dozen sips from my favorite mug, I looked around the kitchen. The detritus on my counter finally registered. Empty plastic water bottles and their caps were scattered along with an empty Fritos bag and what had been a brand new bag of barbeque potato chips. Damn. I guess Dex had found my pantry. A quick inventory of my fridge yielded empty plastic deli bags; I guess he'd also really like the cold cuts and cheese.

The bottles got tossed into the recycle bin in my pantry, and the caps and empty bags went into the trash. I finished cleaning up by wiping down the counter.

Fortified with one cup of Starbucks Christmas Blend under my belt, and a mostly full mug in my hand, it was time to go see what my surprise house guest was up to.

"Good morning, Dex." I winced at how breathless I sounded. In my defense, he was really hot.

"Good morn to ye, *Dunni*." He briefly looked in my direction before gluing his eyes back to the TV.

I guess some things were universal no matter where the male species came from.

"Chrissy. Remember?" I corrected gently.

He grunted. See! Universal.

"The magick in yer world is *amayos*." He flicked his eyes to me and then at the TV.

"Oh? How so?" I braced myself with another sip of coffee.

"This box with moving pictures. It is truly *amayos*. The white box has light, yet everything is cold. And the seat with the big opening and metal controller in the bathing chamber makes sound and the clear liquid disappears and reappears. Just *amayos*."

"No, not so amazing or magical. Just modern plumbing and electricity."

I smiled behind my mug.

"Plumbing?"

"Yes. Water goes through a series of pipes," I explained. The more I thought about it, I guessed one could call it a type of magic.

Ding dong. The sound of the doorbell startled me. My coffee sloshed dangerously close to the rim. I made my way to the front door and checked through my peephole. Shoot! It was Mrs. Darby. She was forever lecturing me about my writing. As in, "You seem like such a nice girl, Chris... I don't understand why you have to write such frivolous smut. Why can't you write *real* books like Jane Austen or the Bronte sisters?" Ugh. I had made the mistake of excitedly showing her the cover art for my first book.

She hit the bell again.

"Quick! Put this on." I hissed at Dex and tossed him Dec's grey zip-up hooded sweatshirt that he'd left hanging on my coat rack. Thank heaven they were the same height and size.

He figured out how to put it on.

"Hide your sword." I hustled over to him and helped him zip up the jacket. He waved his hand at the sword and it disappeared. I blinked. I forgot that he really could do magic.

Mrs. Darby was leaning on the bell now. I opened the door.

"Hello, Mrs. Darby." I hoped my voice and smile didn't look and sound as fake as I suspected they did.

"Harrumph. Merry Christmas, dear." Her smile was more of a grimace than an actual smile.

"Erm.... Yes. Merry Christmas." I clutched my mug to my chest.

"I brought you my angel salad." She held out a plate heavily wrapped in red and green colored plastic wrap.

"Oh, thank you, you shouldn't have. I haven't had time to make anybody anything this year. I've been so busy writing." I forced a laugh.

I opened the door wide enough to accept the plate. Mrs. Darby tried to look around me into my living room. I did my best to block her. Sometimes being plus sized was a good thing.

"It that Dec?"

Nosy old bird.

"Erm…. Yes. He just stopped by to help me get my decorations from the garage." I kept my big smile in place.

"Hello, Dec. Merry Christmas." Mrs. Darby called through the door.

"Merry Christmas," Dex muttered and pointed the remote at the TV again.

"Thank you again, Mrs. Darby. Merry Christmas." I injected forced cheer into my voice, hoping to hurry her along.

"Yes, dear. Merry Christmas." She smiled vaguely at me. "Bye, Dec. Have a merry Christmas."

Dex gave her a chin lift. I guess those are universal too.

I took the Jell-O mold to the kitchen and started to unwrap the million layers of plastic wrap she'd put on it. To be fair, Mrs. Darby's angel salad was good. I'd had it many times at the open house she held every year on the Friday after Thanksgiving. I finally got the last of the red wrap off. Damn, that looked good. Maybe I'd get Dex to try—

"Be very still *D*—Chrissy. That *toxor* is in attack position."

Toxor? Poisonous Bellatorian slime creature. *Oh shit!*

I quickly turned.

"Dex? No!"

Too late. His sword cleaved through the pale green Jell-O, the plate, my counter, and the cabinet below. One half of the Jell-O and the plate bounced off the side of the refrigerator; the half plate shattered on the floor. The Jell-O half flew towards its twin. One piece landed on the stove with a splat and the other splattered against the wall to the left of the sink.

I stared in horror at the broken counter and Jell-O mess. Dex was wearing what could only be called a victorious expression.

"My kitchen!" I burst into tears.

Oh! This was all wrong. I thought if I ever met Dex, it…*he*…would be perfect. In none of my daydreams or wishes did I ever think I would freak out or that he would wreck my house.

Through my tears, I could see that his expression had turned baffled. He looked the way men do when they have no idea why you are crying.

"*D*—Chrissy? The *toxor* is gone. Why ye cry?"

"That wasn't a t-*toxor*. That was f-food." Sniff. Sniff. "Y-you broke my k-ki-kitchen." I bawled harder.

"I am sorry *D*—Chrissy," he said, remorse heavy in his voice.

I grabbed a couple Kleenexes from the box to the right of my sink. I wasn't a pretty crier. I loudly blew my nose.

Dex bowed his head, pointed his sword at the ceiling like he was praying, muttered something I didn't understand under his breath, and pointed the sword at the broken counter. Blue light shot from the tip of the sword. The light hit the counter and expanded, traveling over all of the broken pieces and Jell-O mess. In a few heartbeats my kitchen was as it had been before, including the Jell-O mold and Mrs. Darby's plate.

"Thank you, Dex." I tried to smile.

Dex executed a slight bow, turned on his heel, and left the room.

I have a confession. Christmas is not my favorite holiday. It used to be one of them, but since my divorce three years ago, not so much. Now it was the season of *meh*. Still, I'd been given this magical, dare I say miraculous, gift, and part of me wanted to return it. The other part of me thought I was an ungrateful beyotch for feeling that way. The yin and the yang of my personality. The practical and the dreamer.

As usual, the practical won out. I took a shower and got dressed. Wearing my favorite blue tie-dyed tunic sweatshirt and a pair of my black yoga pants, I stuffed my feet into my slip-on Skechers, adjusted my glasses, and grabbed my cell phone from the vanity counter.

I have another confession. I lied to Mrs. Darby. I don't own any Christmas decorations. I sold, threw out, or gave them all away before I moved to Texas years ago. So I guess I was going to have to go out and buy some.

I didn't feel comfortable leaving Dex alone, also that would be rude, so I would have to take him with me. Other than his eyes, he looked normal enough that no one would bat an eyelash. And really, if anyone said anything about his eyes, I could tell them he was wearing colored contacts.

When I went back into the living room, Dex was once again watching TV. He had taken off the sweatshirt. He glanced briefly at me.

"I, uhm, need to go to the store. You need to come with me." Boy, was this awkward.

Dex turned off the TV, picked up his sword from where it was resting against the end table, and put it on.

"Uhm, maybe you should leave that here." I nodded at the sword.

"A warrior doesn't go without his sword, *dunni.*"

Oh boy. "Okay... Can you conceal it somehow?"

He waved his hand, and the sword disappeared. "I am ready to go."

"Ah, you need to wear the sweatshirt."

Dex frowned. "But it's *caldus.*"

The jacket being too hot for him would be a problem. Even though Lubbock was a college town and had a certain amount of diversity, I was pretty sure an over-six-feet-tall extremely muscular bald man in leather pants and boots with no shirt would attract attention.

Oh! I knew what to do. I had repaired a tank top of Dec's the other day. It had a small hole that ended up being ridiculously easy to fix. The silly man had been about to throw it away. I ran to my laundry closet in the kitchen and grabbed it from the dryer.

"Here, this should fit." I handed him the tank. "Now if you get too hot in the store, you can just take off the jacket."

Dex put on the tank and jacket.

"Lead on, *dunni.*"

The big box store we were in was one of the super ones with a grocery store. The holiday decoration aisles were pretty picked over. Since it was Christmas Eve day, I really wasn't surprised. Still, I managed to find a small tree, garland, ornaments, and a tree skirt. I was even able to grab a few things for dinner tonight before Dex started to get that glazed look most of the men I knew got while shopping. If it wasn't for tools, electronics, automotive products, or weapons, they weren't interested.

It was probably a good idea if we got out of there anyway. I can't tell you how many people, men and women both, stopped and stared or ran into something, or someone, because of Dex. Seems he attracted a lot of attention despite his disguise.

"Do ye always have to go to the bazaar to purchase yer wares?"

"That's not a bazaar. We call that a store. That everything is in one place is for convenience."

"I like the commodities units on *Bellator*. They can make anything ye need."

We loaded all of the bags and box with the tree into the back of my 2009 Saturn Vue. Dex was as fascinated with my SUV as he was with my TV and the refrigerator. He'd asked me tons of questions about it on the drive to the store. We got in the car and headed for home.

"So what else do you like about *Bellator*?" I figured I'd ask. I mean, it's not every day a writer gets to talk to her character and hear what he thinks in the flesh.

"After seeing some of your world, I miss the vividness of my home. This planet is dying. I can see it. Smell it." The wistfulness, sadness in his voice was unmistakable. "I miss Inara."

"What do you like about Inara?" Okay, yes, I was totally going to fish for compliments. After all, Inara was sort of me.

Dex smiled. "I love her. She is my mate."

"Okay." Well, that didn't go as I'd hoped.

"What do you like best about her? Is she pretty? What?"

Yes, I knew I was being stupid to let my insecurities show. I glanced over at Dex. He was giving me a look I couldn't completely read.

"My mate is more *beyda* every *llumine* cycle."

"Do you think she is brave?"

"Aye. Much to her own detriment." Exasperated laughter shot out of Dex. "The *Dunni* drives me to my cups sometimes."

Probably because she is not afraid to stand up to you...

"I am sorry she could not be here. I know she would have liked to meet ye."

I hit the button for the garage door and pulled in. I have to tell you that I was glad I'd stopped. That I was parked. Because what he said next just blew me away.

"I know who she is Dex, I created her character the same as I created yours." I laughed and popped the hatch.

Dex got out of the car. He closed the door hard enough that my SUV rocked violently.

"What the hell?" I glared at him when he came into sight.

He glared back. "Ye speak *blyfima*. My *Dea* created all of *Bellator*, my *auri lex* and *mehi-mo*. Not ye!"

Blasphemy? His goddess created Bellator? I was stunned. Though I probably shouldn't have been. If I had been thinking rationally. I wasn't, so I got mad. I *HATED* being called a liar.

"Come with me." I closed the hatch on my SUV. While I might have been mad, I wasn't so gone that I left my car and the garage open like an invitation to anyone to help themselves. I stalked across the backyard to the house. I'd probably wince later at the dent I'd no doubt left in the wall when I whipped the back door open. At this moment I didn't care. I was on a mission.

Six books I had written. Six. Books. Seven, if you counted the manuscript I completed last night. And this character I had created, now magically made flesh, was going to tell me that I was lying about my own creativity. Oh, hell no.

I grabbed the first of the six binders I kept my final manuscripts in. One of my little quirks was that when I completed a book and finalized the manuscript, I would print it out and put it in a binder. Pages protected, of course, along with my copy of the cover art.

"Here!" I slammed them on my desk one at a time and then leaned over and turned on my laptop. I pulled out my chair for him. "Here. Read these and my notes." I laid my idea book on top of the binders. Pushing past him, I left the room. I couldn't be in there. Not then.

Dex found me scrubbing the bathroom. I cleaned when I was upset. It used to drive my ex-husband crazy. I had no problem turning on the vacuum if he was asleep, or trying too. Bitchy and passive aggressive, I know. It had made me feel better, especially when he was doing his damnedest to make me feel small.

"I don't know how ye know so much about my world. Inara and me. My family. My people. I can only guess that my *dea* wished it so."

Seriously? Disgusting! The look I fried him with should have killed him. I stripped off my rubber gloves.

"You need to leave. Tell your goddess to send you back." I walked out of the bathroom and into my room and closed the door.

"What the hell?"

Dex was standing in front of me.

"I am sorry ye are *vexa. Malu.* I speak true."

I just stared at him. Unbelievable.

"Chrissy, *Bellator* is real. Your knowledge of my home is *amayos.* But, not truly accurate." He sort of smiled, I'd guess to take some of the sting out of his last comment.

I opened my mouth to blast him. He cut me off.

"I have memories of Inara and I being *adali.* We were always meant to be. She is my *auri lex.* My *anma-cumpra.* We did not meet when or the way your stories say," he said seriously.

Say what? I couldn't stop staring at Dex. He had known Inara since they were young. She was his golden light and soul mate, if what he was telling me could be believed. I had been writing about real beings, a real place in another part of the universe. A world that ran parallel to ours in some ways and in others not so much.

Like his being able to read through six books in the half an hour or so I'd been cleaning. I walked on shaky legs over to my bed. It was sit down or fall down. This was too fantastical to be real. I couldn't process it.

"You're seriously telling me that a world with beings with magic powers, trees with leaves the color of lime Jell-O, lavender oceans washing up onto pale gold beaches, and car like vehicles that fly actually exists?"

Dex sat down on my chaise across from me. "Aye Chrissy. I am."

Holy shit.

"How is that even possible?" To say I was stunned would have been a *huge* understatement.

"I don't know. It is *Her* will Chrissy." He shrugged. "She wanted my world to be, and it is. She said I needed to be here with you and I am. She wanted you to tell our stories. So you do."

My stomach rumbled, reminding me that I hadn't eaten all day. How embarrassing. I knew I had to be bright red as hot as my skin felt.

"I'm hungry, and I'm sure you are too."

Dex cautiously nodded.

"Good, let's go eat."

One of the first things I had done after I'd left Dex in my office earlier was to go get the groceries out of the back of my Vue. Dinner wasn't anything terribly fancy. I'm not much of a cook. I made individual pizzas for us. Now before you go getting excited thinking that's impressive, don't. Store bought biscuit dough spread out on a cookie sheet with two teaspoons of tomato paste and a third of a cup or so of cheese was not hard. It doesn't even take long to bake. Just the length of time it says to make the biscuits, give or take an extra minute or two.

Dex thought the pizzas were genius, though. I guess they don't have those on *Bellator*. He ate four of them. Sigh. I envied him his metabolism.

"What is this merry Christmas the *dunni* at the door spoke of?"

Dex had put the tank top and zip sweat jacket back on to help me carry in the tree and decorations I'd bought.

"Christmas is supposed to be a religious event. Celebrating the birth of Jesus Christ, the son of God. For some it is about this. For others it is about fellowship, food, and presents. For big business it is about money," I explained.

"So your Christmas is the celebration of a demi-god?"

I winced and looked around.

"I wouldn't say that too loud around here. Some people could take it the wrong way."

We got the tree and bags with the decorations into the house. Dex put the box with the tree in the living room. I closed and locked the back door.

"Why?" Dex took off the tank and jacket.

To go off topic for a sec, watching him partially strip *never* got old. Inara was so lucky...

"Why what?" I asked.

"Why should I not call your Jesus Christ a demi-god?"

"Uhm...because there are many people who are, erm, *passionate* about their religious beliefs, and believe anyone who doesn't believe as they do is a heathen. Calling him a demi-god would be heathen to their way of thinking. Though technically you are somewhat correct if you go by Greek and Roman mythology. He was the son of a deity and a mortal woman."

I sat on the living room floor and started to open the box for the tree. It had a million pounds of tape on it and thankfully not too many staples.

"What is the purpose of this Christmas tree?" Dex sat on the floor near me and the tree, now out of its box. He took the tree base from me.

"Thank you." I smiled and started pulling the branches down and straightening them out. I could kiss the person who thought up the pre-lit Christmas tree. I hated having to put on the lights. What a pain.

"The Christmas tree is a tradition started in Germany in the fifteenth or sixteenth century, I believe. It had a religious beginning; the decorated trees were done to honor the birth of Jesus. They became popular with everyone sometime in the nineteenth century."

"So after we put yers together and decorate it, do we go to other dwellings to put these strange broken trees together and decorate them?"

I laughed. Dex glared and started to get up.

"Wait. I'm sorry I'm not really laughing at you." I patted his knee.

"The tree is fake, not real, Dex. That's why it comes in a box. If it was real, it would have been cut down from a forest or a farm that grows Christmas trees." I got on my knees to put the middle section in place. "No, we don't have to go to my neighbors' houses to put together and decorate their trees. Everyone who wants a Christmas tree gets and decorates their own. It's not like your, uhm, *Festam Illumini?*"

"Aye. *Festam Illumini.*"

He stood, and we put the top section on. I straightened out the branches, got the bag with the ornaments in it, and we finished decorating the tree. Even though it wasn't very big, I let Dex put the star on top. It wasn't the most beautiful tree I'd ever seen. Still, the red and gold ball ornaments and shiny garland reflecting the lights gave it a cheery feel. So, not bad. Not bad at all.

I showed Dex how to make Christmas cookies next. It was one of my favorite memories of my gran. Gran and I used to make cookies all the time. Sadly, when she died in my teens, my mother and my sisters helped themselves to all her baking equipment and left me nothing. Not even a cookie cutter. Their reasoning for this was that I should be grateful I'd gotten to use it while she was alive, and being as "big" as I was (size 10), having any of those things wouldn't help me.

As I said before, I'm not much of a cook, so even the dough for the cookies was the kind that came in a package or a tube. Just throw on some sprinkles and voila, Christmas cookies.

"What else do you do for this Christmas?" Dex asked.

"Well, people put presents under the Christmas tree, hang Christmas stockings for Santa Claus to fill, leave a plate of cookies and a glass of milk for him in case he gets hungry while filling your stockings."

"What is Santa Claus?" Dex bit into one of the warm cookies I had just put on a plate. "Amayos," he muttered.

"Santa Claus is not a what. He's a magical being who comes every Christmas and goes around the world in twenty-four hours to give everyone a present."

"So he will leave you a present?" Dex took another cookie off the plate.

"No. He is a myth. Not real. Only little children believe in him."

"I thought you said he was magickal?" Dex frowned.

"He supposedly is. Santa Claus is the spirit of Christmas. He's a story that parents tell their children."

"I will ask my dea about him. She will know if he's truth or not. Do ye have presents? To put under yer tree?" He looked at me expectantly.

"No. My family sends me cards with gift memberships for gyms and Weight Watchers or money with notes to cover the grey in my hair," I said brightly. I guess Dex saw through my false cheer.

"*Delica?*"

Hearing Dex call me sweetheart with what suspiciously looked like pity in his eyes…

"It's okay, Dex. They are who they are. I'm used to it. I've been dealing with it all my life. I know it is their version of showing concern." I smiled, resigned.

Dex just looked at me. After being uncomfortably stared at for a few minutes, I cleared my throat.

"What?"

"Chrissy? *Delica*. Ye are *beyda*. Yer gift for telling the tales of my people is *amayos*. I don't *seca* why ye are not told true."

I didn't understand it either. Still it was nice to hear. Even if I didn't really believe him when he said I was beautiful. To my family I am a complete disappointment. My mother and my sisters are all perfect size fours (the fact that I suspect they all suffer from bulimia is irrelevant). I'm not. I'm also not blond enough, or tan. My father disappeared from my life before the ink was dry on my parents' divorce papers. My family's opinion of my body shape (i.e. ME. Because appearance is everything you know) was nothing new. I am just me. Quiet. Bookish. Introverted. Slightly socially awkward. Though I did sign up for a yoga class once... *Naked yoga*! Guess I should have read that description better... Needless to say I didn't stick with it.

I didn't tell Dex any of this.

"Thank you, Dex."

"Ye are *gretas, delica*."

I suspected that he knew I didn't quite believe him, but he was going to be good and not call me on it.

"Here. Close yer eyes."

Dex turned me away from him. We were in my office. My clock had just chimed midnight. Christmas Day. My time with Dex was over. To say that my day with him had been awkward...strange...memorable...would be an understatement. Nothing had gone like I'd thought or dreamed it would.

"Close yer eyes, *delica*," he ordered again.

"Why?"

An impatient growl came from behind me.

"My time is up, *dunni*. I wish to give ye yer gift. Eyes closed anon."

I closed my eyes. Dex put his hands on my neck. My eyes flew open.

"Dex?"

"No *malu delica*."

He promised not to hurt me. I sighed and closed my eyes. Dex put his hands on my neck again. I tensed. I hated having *anyone's* hands on my neck. I heard him mutter in Bellatorian. I couldn't make out all of the words, but my neck got very warm.

"My dea wishes ye to know yer *anma-cumpra* is waiting for ye."

My soul-mate was waiting for me? I don't know why, Dec suddenly filled my thoughts.

"Merry Christmas, *Delica*."

I felt Dex kiss my hair. When I turned around I was alone. Depression almost drove me to my knees. I reached up and touched my neck, still feeling a slight burn. The slightly bumpy texture of a chain and the weight of smooth metal greeted my fingertips. A necklace?

I killed the lights in the office, and ran to the bathroom, where I stared dumbfounded at the mirror. Dex had made me a necklace of delicate silver links and a triquetra-like pendant of silver swirls with a stone in the center that wasn't quite blue and wasn't quite purple. The stone glowed almost as if it was alive.

"Thank you, Dex," I whispered.

I walked around the house turning off lights and making sure everything was locked up. A quick glance at my kitchen reminded me I needed to clean up. Tomorrow. Or later today, rather. On leaden feet I went into my room. I don't know why I grabbed my lavender baby doll nightie instead of my usual tank and sleep shorts. It's not like there was anyone to see it. Hell, my sex life had been non-existent for at least a year. The last time I had sex was——. Nope! Not going to go there. No thinking about that or *him*.

Still, I put the gown on and got into bed. I set my glasses and my phone on my nightstand same as I did every night. Then I turned out the light. And cried myself to sleep.

Samson "Dec" Decker coasted his Fat Boy the last foot or two into the garage. Damn, he was happy to be home. Sure as shit beat another hour of watching his father and younger brother tie one on and then fight with their equally smashed women. Or listen to his old man tell him he acted like he thought his shit didn't stink since he wouldn't drink a *real* fuckin' drink with him. Dec fingered the twenty year sobriety chip in his jeans pocket the same way he had done every day since he'd gotten it six months ago. He still remembered the day he woke up gut tight, eyeballs on fire, head ready to explode, and looked into the bathroom mirror of the dive he'd ended up in to see his father's face staring back at him. He'd made the decision to get sober then and there. His twenty-eighth birthday.

Dec dropped the kickstand, swung off his bike, and unclipped and removed his half helmet. He grabbed the handles of his duffle after he'd unstrapped it and swung it over his shoulder. Helmet dangling from his other hand, he used his elbow to hit the button to close the overhead door.

Standing in the barely sunlit backyard, he debated going to his house. His eyes kept going back towards Chrissy's side of the duplex. Decision made, he headed in her direction. He'd missed his sweetness and delight anyway.

Using his key, he opened her back door. The house was quiet, which was strange since Chris was an early riser. Even more worrisome, her coffee pot was unplugged, and her kitchen was a disaster. Not cool. He closed the door, laid his helmet and shades on the counter, and dropped his duffle in front of the laundry closet.

On his way into her office, he noticed a good sized dent in her wall by the back door, like someone had slammed it open. Her book binders were scattered all over her desk. Her computer was on. So not like her. His gut starting to churn as he headed towards the front of the house. A fast glance in her room showed her bed unmade and no Chrissy.

The tree in the living room brought him up short. His sweetness didn't do Christmas, or so she said. He always got her to go to Santa Land at Mackenzie Park every December to look at the holiday village and the tree. She always left smiling and humming Christmas carols.

Leaving the living room, he went back to her bedroom. Chrissy stumbled out of the master bath wearing a sweet purple and black nightie. Merry fucking Christmas to him. She stopped when she caught sight of him. She leaned forward a little and squinted at him.

"Dex?"

Dex? Who the fuck was that? He started to get pissed that she had called him by another man's name until he remembered that was the name of the character from her books. The one that looked almost exactly like him. Except his facial hair was dark brown, not black, and his eyes were green, not blue. Otherwise they were both bald, had the same build, were the same height, six foot four, and they both had tattoos. He still didn't know how he felt about that one. At least she'd made him a badass with a kick ass sword.

"Merry Christmas, Christmas," he teased.

She grimaced at the use of her given name. "My birthday is in October. I swear, they had to be on drugs," she muttered.

"Nice nightie and necklace. I see your family gave you real presents for a change."

Chrissy's hands flew to her neck. She paled and practically ran for the bathroom. She came out a few minutes later minus the necklace and wearing her robe.

"Don't get your hopes up. The nightie and the necklace didn't come from my family." She put her glasses on and dropped her cell into the robe's pocket. "I thought you were in El Paso, Dec. Why are you here?" She frowned.

"Aren't you happy to see me, sweetness?" Mild disappointment nagged at him.

"I'm always happy to see you. That's not the point."

The happy sparkle in her eyes quickly masked gave truth and lie to her words.

"Then what is?"

"That you should be with your family today and not here. I'm fine on my own. You didn't need to come back. I don't need your pity. I'm not a charity case, Samson."

She stalked out of the room.

Pity? Charity case? What. The. Fuck? He stood frozen for about a minute then followed her out.

"I came home because I wanted to. I rode almost six hours and you dump this shit about pity and being a charity case on me first thing? What the fuck, Christmas?" He watched her put the coffee filter in its basket and scoop the coffee in to it.

"I'm just saying, I know you have better things to do than be here."

Her *with me* was unspoken. She kept her back to him and finished making her coffee.

"This is bullshit Chris. You've been pulling shit like this off and on all year. Enough. We had sex. Fucked. Made love. Whatever you want to call it." He glared at her back.

She slammed the refrigerator door. "That was a mistake. A fluke. We were both drunk." Face pale, her eyes pleaded with him to let it go.

Not happening. He was done. Done giving her time. Done being just her friend. If she couldn't, wouldn't give him more, he was done, period.

Dec quickly closed the short distance between them and hauled her against him. His hand fisted her ponytail and tilted her head back. Her wide eyes pleaded with him not to do this. Pleaded with him not to stop. He dropped his lips on hers and proceeded to kiss the hell out of her. He kissed her for all the months he couldn't kiss her, for all the things she made him feel.

She moaned, clinging to his leather jacket. He broke their kiss and pushed her away from him.

"You kissed me back, sweetness. We're not drunk now. I wasn't then either. I don't drink anymore. I'm a recovering alcoholic. I've been sober for twenty years."

Dec grabbed his gear and slammed out the back door.

Too many bombshells. The first being that Dex was real and my day with him hadn't been a dream or some stress induced hallucination. And more importantly Dec *hadn't been drunk* when we had had sex on New Year's Eve last year. I didn't know what to do with that.

I didn't care that he was a recovering alcoholic. Well, I kind of did, but only because Dec had kept something so huge from me. If anything, I was proud of him for having remained sober and having kicked it. As much as you can kick something like that.

Yer anma-cumpra is waiting for ye.

Dex's words came back to me. Dec was my soul-mate? That couldn't be right. Could it? Why would the universe stick him with a fat little nobody like me?

Chrissy? Delica. Ye are beyda. Yer gift for telling the tales of my people is amayos. I don't seca why ye are not told true.

I was so confused. When in doubt, I always called the one person I knew wouldn't bullshit me or sugarcoat the truth. For me, that was my good friend Rae.

"What's up, hooker? A merry *Chris* muss to ya."

I laughed. "Hey, my Rae of sunshine. Merry Christmas."

"So what's new? How is that hunk of man-candy?"

I couldn't tell Rae about my day with Dex. She'd have me committed, as would most of the other people I knew. No, that one I was going to have to forever keep to myself. Besides, she wasn't asking about him.

"Dec surprised me this morning and came home early from El Paso."

"So that's a good thing. Right?"

All my doubts and insecurities again hit me hard.

"No. Not since it was done out of pity." I sniffed.

"Christmas, use your brain. That man doesn't feel pity for you." A super pissed-off vibe came at me through the phone. "Pity is the last God damn thing Samson Decker feels for you. Jesus, stop giving those jealous bitches and that dumbass head space."

"But Rae—"

"No! But nothing. You naturally have bodacious tatas and a booty. Those toxic bitches had to buy theirs, for fuck sake. And seriously, you're going to take the word of a man whose go to hairstyle is a mullet?"

I didn't know whether to laugh or cry. So I kind of did both.

"Thank you, Rae," I said when I got control of myself again.

"You're welcome. I mean it, babe. Do not give them one more minute of head space. Not. One. Dec loves you."

"Really?" I squeaked, sounding teenage girly hopeful. So much for maturity.

An exasperated sigh hit my ear.

"Yes, Chrissy, really. I saw it with my own eyes when I came to see you over the fourth."

A lifetime of being told I was inferior wasn't easily overcome. Still, if it wasn't for one of Rae's "Come to Jesus" talks, I never would have had the guts to try to self-publish at all. So I knew she was giving me truth.

Have I mentioned how much I adore my feisty redheaded friend? No? Well I do.

I hated having to apologize, mostly because it had been my experience that the people I've had to say sorry to most often didn't accept it graciously (i.e. my family and my ex-husband). Still, I owed Dec an apology. So I shoved my feet into my black suede slippers with the fuzzy leopard trim and hurried out the back door to catch him before he left.

I caught up to him as he was backing his motorcycle out of the garage. He stopped the bike but didn't spare me a glance. Well, that I could tell anyway since he had his sunglasses on along with his helmet and the guard for his nose and mouth. I stopped next to him. One of my arms wrapped around my middle. The other one I used to shield my eyes. The sun glinted off of the heavy silver chain around his neck and briefly touched one of his earrings.

"I need to talk to you. Please." I shouted over the noise of his Harley. Every time I tried to talk to him he revved the engine. Tears of hurt and frustration stung my eyes. I bowed my head, hoping he wouldn't see. I saw Dec move. In desperation, I leaned over to touch his hand.

"Wait. *Please*," I choked out.

He stopped. "Back up, Chris."

His voice was flat. I couldn't get a read on him. I stayed where I was, too afraid if I moved he would leave.

"Chrissy, baby? Back up so I can put the bike back in the garage," he said. That time I heard the exasperation and impatience loud and clear. So I stepped back.

Damn it! Dec had wanted to be hard and give her a bit of what she had given him. He couldn't do it. Her tears wrecked him. He knew she loved him (at least he was pretty sure). He'd caught her looks of adoration more than once when she thought he wasn't looking. Still, her almost constant blowing hot and cold this year felt an awful lot like rejection. Or at least a damn good imitation of it.

He parked his Harley again next to his Chevy Crew Cab truck. Thank God he wouldn't need to be caged in that thing again until Monday. His job as a pipefitter made his truck a must. Otherwise he would ride his HOG everywhere.

Chrissy was still standing in the same place on the driveway. He released the strap on his helmet and took it off, tucking it under his arm. He stalked back to her and grabbed her hand, pulling her through the garage.

"Get the door, sweetness."

She tagged the button to close the overhead door. He knew he was being an asshole by making her practically run in those stupid overpriced slippers of hers; still, he kept a fast pace. They reached his back door, and he opened it.

"Have a seat in the kitchen."

His sweet Chris, just slightly out of breath, shot him an annoyed glance and did as he asked. He put his helmet, shades, and keys on top of the bookcase in his office/workout room, removed his leather chaps, and hung them and his coat up on their wall pegs.

When he entered the kitchen, Chrissy sat on one of the stools for his island, turning a glass of water around in her hands on the granite top. She looked up and quickly down again. He'd swear he saw a flash of fear in her eyes. Damn it, he didn't want her to be afraid of him.

He open the refrigerator and grabbed a Coke. He smiled as he twisted the cap, remembering the first time he'd asked her if she wanted a Coke, then told her he had Mountain Dew and Cherry 7-Up. The look on her face had been priceless.

His poor sweetness; she looked so lost. He took a drink, recapped it, and set the bottle on the counter. Standing next to her, he swiveled her stool to face him.

"Come 'ere, sweetness" He pulled her off the stool and into his arms.

Chrissy wrapped her arms around him tightly and did a face plant in his chest. Her whole body shook.

"Calm down, baby. I can't understand you." Dec pulled the elastic from her hair. He hated those damn things. He threaded his fingers in her hair and tugged her head back to see her face. Watery brown eyes looked back at him.

"I'm sorry. I'm so sorry."

Yep, those tears of hers totally wrecked him. So Dec did the only thing he could. He kissed her.

Damn! The man could kiss me stupid faster than anyone else. Wait... Scratch that. Dec was the *only one* who had ever been able to kiss me stupid. Case in point, somehow I was sitting on his island counter, and I had no idea how I'd gotten here. See! Totally stupid.

I managed to get my hands under the hem of his t-shirt. It was one of his Christmas ones. He had a collection of tees with funny sayings and pictures. Today's shirt had "I can get you on the naughty list" printed on it in red and green letters. Mmhmm, yes he could. I'd so let him.

"Take your shirt off." I pleaded and tugged at the white cotton.

Dec stopped kissing me long enough to pull his shirt over his head one handed. I used those precious seconds to get my arms unstuck from the sleeves of my robe and the straps of my nightie. He had managed to trap my arms when he pushed my robe off my shoulders and untied the tie at the front of my nightie and used the fallen straps to bind me further. I now had a pool of material at my waist, and I didn't care, because I had acres of tanned skin, firm muscle, and ink to reacquaint myself with.

"You have great tits, baby."

Oh...

The hot look in his eyes made my girl parts spasm.

"Offer them to me."

My hands were shaking as I cupped my breasts and lifted them toward Dec. He put his hands over mine and pushed my boobs together before sucking both my nipples into the hot cavern of his mouth. I'd swear there was a direct line between my nipples and my clit because it pulsed with every strong suck.

I managed to get my hands out from under his. Blindly, I fumbled with the button fly of his jeans. I needed to get my hands on him. One of Dec's big hands left my breasts long enough to help me get his jeans and underwear over his cock and down his thighs. I wrapped my hand around the hot velvet of his length, giving it a gentle squeeze. My thumb cruised over the pre-come beaded at the tip.

"Baby." Dec groaned against my breast.

He nibbled and sucked hard at the underside of my breast. I whimpered because holy hell, that felt good.

Ding dong! Dec lifted his head, and we froze staring at one another. The doorbell sounded again. Like someone was leaning on it. That was followed by rapid knocking.

"No." I breathed in horrified disbelief. Cock blocked by the nosy neighbor. No. Just no.

Dec closed his eyes. After a deep breath or two he opened them again. Frustrated rage burned within them.

"Get dressed." He gritted the words out.

Hoo boy, was he pissed.

"I'll get it," I tossed over my shoulder, hurrying towards the front door while struggling to put on my robe and belt it tight. I'd left my nightie in the kitchen. Keeping Dec from murdering Mrs. Darby was more important than being fully dressed.

"Merry Christmas, Mrs. Darby!" I smiled super brightly.

Mrs. Darby looked me over, taking note of my disheveled state. She pursed her lips like she had been sucking on a blue-raspberry Warheads candy.

"Here." She shoved a tin of cookies at the screen door and me. "I made Dec his favorites, chocolate, white chocolate chip with macadamia nuts."

Oh shit! Dec was allergic to nuts.

"Oh, how sweet. You shouldn't have." I smiled big again. "I'll make sure he gets these right away, Mrs. Darby." I lightly shook the festive container for good measure.

She gave me one of her smiles that looked more like a grimace.

"Bless your heart, dear."

I'd been in Texas long enough that I knew that was code for she didn't approve of me. I watched her walk back across the street to her duplex before I closed the door.

"What did she want?" Dec asked me when I came back into the kitchen.

"Mrs. Darby came by to give you some of your favorite cookies. Chocolate, white chocolate chip, with macadamia nuts."

Dec grimaced and shot the container a dirty look.

"Don't worry, I'm going home to throw these away and get dressed. You can take me to the Pancake House for breakfast when I come back." Holding the container far away from him, I kissed his cheek, picked my nightie up from the floor, and headed towards the back door.

"Sweetness, its Christmas. The Pancake House is closed today. Don't you remember Mama Sally telling us that when we were there last weekend?"

"Crud, that's right, I forgot." Damn. Disappointed. I was looking forward to having their pancakes.

"If you want pancakes, I'll make you some." He smiled.

"Thank you. No red velvet," I warned sternly.

"What's wrong with red velvet?" he teased.

I shot him a dirty look and went out the door to the sound of his laughter. Dec was well versed in my extreme dislike of anything red velvet. Yet I'd made him a red velvet cake every year for the last three years for his birthday. At least he never asked for one in the shape of an armadillo.

After a quick shower, I put on a black and white tunic with a deep V-neck that Dec seemed to love—at least he couldn't seem to stop staring at my boobs when I wore it—and a pair of black twill capris. A quick inspection of the polish on my toes showed my favorite OPI red was holding up well. I shoved my feet back into my slippers to travel the few feet from my back door to his.

The kitchen smelled heavenly when I entered. Dec looked over his shoulder at me and nodded his head towards a large steaming mug of coffee. He did that thing where you flip pancakes in the pan without using a spatula.

"Show off," I muttered and took a sip of my coffee.

He snickered. "Pass me my mug, will you, babe."

I walked his coffee over to him and got a kiss for my effort. Yay me.

"Get the plates, baby. These are done."

Dec made me cinnamon pancakes. Awesome. Truth be told, he was always doing nice things like that for me. You'd think after three years I would be used to it. To be completely honest I wasn't. It always surprised and touched me when he did it.

"Thank you, sweetness. I love it. I know just where to put it."

"Over the fireplace?" I teasingly batted my eyelashes. Hopeful.

Dec shot me a sideways look that was part amusement and part exasperation. "I'm not moving Stanley."

Damn. Stanley was the ram's head that Dec had mounted over his fireplace. He got him while on a hunting trip to Tennessee. I personally thought Stanley was creepy. For Christmas I had given Dec a painting of a bull rider. He was a faithful bull riding devotee, at least the watching of it. Thank God I'd never heard him profess a burning desire to ride one.

Dec carefully slid the painting into the space between the arm of the couch and the end table.

"Your turn, sweetness."

Dec handed me a fairly large present. I eagerly tore the paper off. No, I'm not one of those people who carefully unwrap things and save the paper. My gran was that way. I will admit to having done some girly clapping when I saw the name on the top of the box. The box lid got tossed next to me along with the tissue paper. I stopped and stared. So pretty. Black leather and turquoise suede with pink, aqua, and purple stitching. I don't know how he knew I wanted them. Somehow he did. I'd been staring at these boots online for a long time. Every time I could afford them, the site where

I order most of my boots was out of my size. I got a little misty eyed just looking at them.

"Thank you, Dec. I love them. I love you."

Shoot! I hadn't meant to blurt the last part out. I looked over at Dec and froze like a deer caught in headlights. The intensity of his expression scared me a little. With very controlled movements, he removed the box with the boots from my lap and set them on the coffee table. He stood up and pulled me to my feet. Suddenly I found myself over Dec's shoulder. He smacked my ass and headed towards his bedroom.

"'Bout time you said those words to me, Christmas."

Sigh. Such a Dec response.

"Get it, baby. Take what you need."

I kept moving on Dec. I was close. I just couldn't quite get there. I whimpered in frustration. Before I knew what was happening, Dec flipped me to my back. His thumb hit my clit, and he hit a place deep inside me that made me see stars when he put my legs over his shoulders. My orgasm struck with freight train force; I didn't have the breath to scream. Dec slammed into me a few more times then found his own release. He came with a long stuttered groan.

Dec added the last of the ingredients to his large skillet, covered it with the lid, and set it to simmer. Three tablespoons of chili powder shouldn't be too much for his sweetness. After all, it was only one alarm; Chris was kind of a wimp when it came to spicy food.

He looked over his shoulder towards his bedroom doorway; Chrissy, still more asleep than awake, stumbled into view. Call him a Neanderthal; he got a real charge out of knowing he'd put that sated gleam in her eyes.

"My tee looks better on you than it does on me, sweetness." Dec turned to face her.

Chrissy looked down at herself and made a face.

"I highly doubt that, Dec."

Damn. Sometimes her lack of self-confidence almost killed him. Her damn family and fucktard ex sure had a lot to answer for.

"Nothing sexier than a woman in a man's shirt, babe."

"I thought that only applied to the white button up kind?"

She came towards him, stopping about a foot in front of him.

He shrugged.

"Don't care what other people might think; I like my tee on you. You're the prettiest thing I've ever seen."

She rolled her eyes at him and snickered unkindly.

"I'm not wearing make-up and I have sex hair, Dec. I hardly think I look my best."

Chrissy let out a surprised squeak when he pulled her to him.

"Shit, Christmas, learn to take a fuckin' compliment." He punctuated his reprimand with a quick hard kiss.

"More chili, sweetness?"

"Yes, please."

I loved Dec's chili. The one he made today was the quick and easy version. He had one that he made for cook-offs that took longer and was way more complicated.

"Do you want me to pause the movie?" I aimed the remote at his ginormous TV. Seventy-two inches. Such a man thing to buy.

"Sure. I guess." Dec grabbed my empty bowl on his way to the kitchen.

I'd finally gotten him to watch Steel Magnolias with me. He swore he'd never seen it before. We'd been cuddled on the couch for a while now. All in all, not a bad Christmas. In fact, it was the first one I remembered truly enjoying in a very long time.

"Wake up sweetness."

I groaned at Dec's gravelly whisper. I braced myself on his chest and squinted at the clock. Just after five a.m. Waay too frickin' early in my opinion.

"It's your day off. Go back to sleep," I grumbled and lay down again, fully prepared to do that myself.

"I can't. I need to ask you something."

"Now?" I opened one eye and glared at him.

"Yes, now," he returned, laughing.

"Fine." I was so *not* happy. Not only am I not a morning person, I like my sleep. I stumbled out of Dec's bed, pulled the hem of his tee down over my butt, and followed him. He stopped in the bedroom doorway.

"You wanted to show me the doorway?" I snarled.

Dec laughed. "No. I want you to look up." He pointed.

I looked up. "Mistletoe? You got me out of bed to show me dying mistletoe?"

Unbelievable. If looks could kill, Dec would have been a dead man.

"We're standing under it. Give me a kiss, Christmas." He smiled big.

"I'm glad you're enjoying this. I'm not." I decided to humor him, so I stood on my tip toes and gave him a quick peck on the lips.

"There. I've upheld tradition." I turned to go back to bed.

Dec caught my arm. "Kiss me proper, Christmas," he gruffly ordered.

Sigh. I stood on my tip toes again and kissed him proper. At the first slide of his tongue against mine, I was lost. I could stand there all day and kiss him.

Dec squeezed my waist. "Stop a second," he muttered against my lips.

I stopped, blinking in confusion. Dec lowered himself to one knee. Holy Jesus. No way. He took my left hand. Oh. My. God.

"Christmas Waters? I love you. You're my best friend. My lover. Marry me, sweetness. I need you to be my wife."

I could only nod yes. I was too choked up to speak. Dec slipped something on my finger. Through my tears I saw yellow gold. I swiped at the tears and took a better look. The ring was beautiful, yellow gold and diamonds braided together. If I had to guess, I would say it was an antique.

"So does that mean you like it?" he teased me.

Watery laughter rushed past my lips.

"Yes."

So it turned out that the man I had been wishing for and dreaming of all this time was right under my nose all along. Dex and his goddess were right. Samson Decker was my soul mate. And he had been waiting for me.

After I said yes, Dec showed me the plane tickets for Las Vegas for that afternoon. I knew just the dress I wanted to wear.

And that brought us to me, standing in the guest bedroom of Dec's friend's house in Vegas, putting the last of the pins in my hair. Harp music started playing (I don't know where he found a harpist on such short notice.) Smoothing the skirt of my long charcoal grey lace dress, I grabbed the single red rose and Dec's ring.

Dec looked amazing in his black suit and burgundy tie. The backyard was beautiful with the three waterfalls housed in the brick water feature. The assortment of white candles his friend's wife had placed on the ledges of the feature and around it flickered merrily.

The officiant stood off to the side. I walked with sure steps to Dec, knowing with every step I took that wishes and dreams did come true.

"Sweetness." Dec looked at me with notable awe and appreciation.

The officiant cleared his throat. "Shall we get started?"

"You bet," Dec replied.

"We are gathered today…"

Quick 'N Easy Chili

1 lb. ground beef
1/2 c. chopped onion
1 clove garlic or 1 tsp. garlic salt
2 (15 1/2 oz.) cans light red kidney beans
3 (8 oz. each) cans tomato sauce
1/4 tsp. black pepper
1 tsp. chili powder

Brown beef and drain. Add onion and garlic. Cook until tender. Add other ingredients and simmer 30 minutes. Stir occasionally. Serves 5.

The Last Gift

The Possession Series
By Cici Edward

My name is Cici Edward. I love books! Reading them and writing them. As an avid romance reader for many years, I always knew I wanted to write a romance novel of my own. As a kid, I created a list of five life goals. One of those goals was to write a romance novel. I'm happy to say I have been able to cross that off my list (along with visiting Venice, Italy). Once I wrote my first novel, a passion for writing burned inside me and one book was not enough. If you like sweet, steamy paranormal romance, you'll love my haunting ghost stories with heart. When I'm not writing, I love being walked by my Great Pyrenees who never lets me forget to smell the flowers. Learn more about the Possession Series on my website www.ciciedward.com and see where the first book, Possession of the Heart is available.

The tree twinkled with rainbow lights. The scent of cinnamon and pine perfumed the air. Angela Barlow had never felt so content. The air outside was cold and blustery, but a warm fire burned behind the grate of the fireplace, flickering shadow and light across the lion carving in the middle of the mantle.

Angela sat on the floor before the crackling fire with her back resting against the couch. The tree glittered off to the side of the drawing room in front of heavy curtains. Under the tree remained one last present wrapped in blue paper and tied with a silver bow.

"I brought you some mulled cider." Cole entering the room, leaned down, passed the warm mug, and then pressed an even warmer kiss to Angela's lips. She would never get used to those kisses.

She took a sip and set the mug on the end table. This was their first Christmas as a married couple. Her sister Emma was spending the holiday with her fiancé, Drew, and his family, so it was just the two of them. This house, the Penniberg Mansion, had been cleared of all its ghosts, so they were completely cozy and wonderfully alone.

She laced her fingers through the rich thickness of Cole's dark hair and looked into his gray eyes. Their smoky depths reflected the same level of love that she felt for him. She pulled him down for a deeper kiss. He tasted of spices and apples. "Mmm." She hated to pull away, but that final present called to her like a siren's song.

"Is that last gift for me?" Angela bit at her lip, excited to know what the rectangular box, slightly larger than her hand, contained. Could it be jewelry? A necklace to go with her beautiful new bracelet? She'd seen a locket the other day which perfectly matched it. But how would he have known?

"What?" Cole's dark eyebrows lowered, leaving the cutest crinkle above his nose.

"The last gift." Angela pointed to the tree. "Did you save the best for last?"

"I thought we opened all the presents. This isn't from me. Is this a surprise from you?" He bent under the tree. She would never get used to the sexy tightness of his butt.

When he twisted around, he held the box. It looked even smaller in his large hands than it had under the tree.

"You're such a jokester. Thank you for the gift. I didn't think you could spoil me with any more presents." But when she peered at her husband's face he looked confused.

"Honestly, this is not from me."

Angela bit her lip while looking around the drawing room. She and Cole had decorated in traditional green, red and gold for their first Christmas together. She loved this room. It was her favorite place in the mansion and held some of her best memories. She hadn't felt anything strange. "If it's not from you and it definitely didn't come from me..."

"Don't tell me it just appeared out of nowhere." Cole turned pale as he looked around the room too. He licked his lips nervously. "I'm just getting used to this ghost stuff."

"Let me see that box." Angela reached out, but before she even touched the package, she felt the energy emanating from it. It felt like sparks of electricity tingling against her fingertips, making the hairs on her arm stand on end. Oh yeah, the box possessed ghostly energy. She'd had the ability to see and feel ghosts since she'd been a very small child, so she knew that electrical buzz when she felt it.

She bent her fingers and rubbed them over her thumb, building her strength to reach for the box. With trepidation, she touched the outer wrappings of the box with her fingertips. The icy feeling traveled through her hands, along her wrist and up her arm. "It's strong and fresh."

"Am I ever going to get used to this?" Cole sat on the floor beside her, rested his back on the sofa, and ran a hand through his hair. "I can't take another possession. You won't become someone else like last time, will you?"

"No. I took care to protect myself so that would never happen again." She hoped, anyway. Just before their wedding, she'd been possessed by a ghost that haunted her wedding gown. The ghost wanted to take over her life, especially after it saw Cole. "Who could blame Winnie for wanting you? You are the most handsome man I've ever known."

"I never want to lose you." He leaned in and kissed her again.

"You won't." In her business, she knew that to be true. The afterlife existed, and her job was to help the dead move on peacefully to that other realm. She'd help any ghost that needed her.

She turned back to the package. Now that she looked more closely, the blue wrapping paper seemed faded, with edges slightly tattered and yellowed. "Look at the paper, Cole. This is old, years old."

"Let's get this over with. Just open it."

"Okay." Angela slipped a finger under the paper, and the tape released easily, falling away without tearing. The white cardboard box was embossed with a swirling design. Angela lifted the lid. Cole poked a finger into the folded tissue paper, browned with age. Neither of them spoke, as if entranced by the package. He hooked the tissue paper with his finger and folded it back. In the center of the box, sitting on a piece of square cotton, rested a folded letter.

Angela's gaze locked onto Cole's.

"A message from the beyond?" His lips lifted into a half smile.

"Must be." She smiled back.

It seemed to Angela as if they were meant to get this letter together, as a couple. The contentment she'd felt earlier when sipping cider by the fireside enveloped her inside and out. She knew, after all the risks and hardships they'd gone through, that the reward was being with him here and now, always. She loved him so much.

Before she unfolded the brittle paper, Angela looked up at Cole. He held her gaze with his quicksilver eyes. They flashed as he leaned tighter into her. "I love you." His breath tickled her lips moments before he kissed her. When he pulled back, she missed his touch.

"Go ahead and read it," he urged.

Mentally, Angela shook away the cobwebs. With a quick movement, she lifted the first flap and then unfolded the second. She narrowed her gaze at the faded words written in a flowing script of black ink.

"It looks similar to the handwriting in letters I found from my grandfather. Old, as if the person was trained to write by the nuns," Angela said.

A metal pen with a brown tube and a silver tip nestled in the bottom of the slim box. Scratches, marks and scuffs made the pen look old and well used. The name Beatrice was engraved in the metal. That name seemed familiar, though Angela couldn't hook onto the fleeting memory. Who did she know named Beatrice?

"What's it say?" Cole asked.

"Beatrice." Angela held out the pen toward Cole. "Right there on the silver part."

"No, no. I meant the letter."

"Oh." She laughed and turned back to the paper while he took the pen from her fingers.

She scanned the letter and then read it out loud.

To my dearest Michael,

I will miss you dearly. But we'll be together soon, my love.

Until I can be with you, find the ingredients for the cookies you love.

Make them, though they won't be as delicious as those

I will make for my future husband when we are together again.

When you eat those treats think of me and know I will be with you soon.

Love with as large a heart as the cookie I give you. I am also giving you this pen

So you can write me in return.

Yours For Always.

Beatrice

"The name Beatrice rings a bell for me, though I can't put my finger on it." Angela turned the paper over. "Here's the recipe on the reverse of the letter." Who was Beatrice? An image flitted through her brain, but she couldn't grab onto the tail wisp of the thought. Beatrice, Beatrice. The name replayed in her mind like a mantra until she felt calm. Angela's heartbeat ticked gently in her chest like a slow, rhythmic, native drum. She pulled in a long, deep breath and closed her eyes. When she opened them, she peered at the sparkling Christmas tree. The lights twinkled like colored snow until the sparks grew whiter and whiter and merged into one bright light that took the shape of a figure. It was a female form, petite, willowy, with soft edges.

A feeling of confidence and strength filled her. Only one other time had a ghost done that. It was at the Greeley's dinner party when Fran celebrated Cole's prodigal return to Dalewood. She had made such a fool of herself that night.

"Beatrice." The word slipped out like a whisper. Even though she knew Cole stood beside her, his presence felt far, far away. Nothing existed except the wavering apparition before her.

The image solidified and deepened into a woman with pale skin touched by tinges of pink on her high cheekbones. Light brown hair glinted with inner red light. She looked older than the last time Angela had seen her in Fran Greeley's guest bedroom. Today she wore a silken charcoal colored gown which fitted along the top but flowed gauzily around her legs in a mystical wind that Angela could only see and not feel. In her left hand she held two yellow daffodils that seemed almost golden against the gown's dark fabric.

"It's me again, you silly thing. I see my tricks helped." Beatrice's voice sounded like wind chimes. She glanced behind Angela, over her shoulder. "Your eyes are the secrets to all your wishes. Keep batting them, and he's a lost man."

Angela could only assume she was looking at Cole. A sly smile pulled at her lips.

"I'd like to think I had a little bit to do with catching him."

"Tsk, tsk, you were a mess that night. You needed me dearly." Beatrice stilled, peering off into an unseen distance. The arm holding the flowers slackened and drifted from her waist down to her side, though her fist tightened around the green stems, crushing them between her fingers. Her gaze sharpened and locked solidly on Angela's. "But I didn't come tonight to quibble about the past. *I'm* the one who needs *you* now."

That scared Angela. The calm feeling vanished, replaced with something else, a sense of urgency. "Last time, you told me you didn't need my help; you were content to live in limbo."

"Yes, well, things have changed and it's time now."

Angela perked up, back ramrod. "You're ready to move to the light?"

"It's a little more involved than that, sweetie. But yes."

"I'll do whatever it takes."

Light as tinkling chimes, Beatrice's laughter filled the air. "I see you've opened my little present." A gust of wind rushed through Angela and lifted the edge of the letter. It flipped the paper to the recipe side.

"Are you a good baker?" Beatrice reappeared closer to Angela, standing directly in front of her, their faces mere inches apart. A chill ran up Angela's spine as her heat escaped her body. Beatrice's pale skin deepened to a peachier, livelier hue.

"Not really. I'm assuming you need me to bake these cookies?"

"They are special cookies for my sweetheart, so you better not mess around." Beatrice smiled, taking some of the edge off the challenge. "But you need to make them with your true love or else I won't be able to find my true love. No pressure, though." Her gaze flitted over Angela's shoulder again. Angela turned her head to follow Beatrice's gaze. She saw Cole, and the spell she'd been under broke. The electrical charge faded, leaving only a few tingles racing along her skin.

"Are you back?" Cole shifted close and slid his hands along Angela's arms, cupping her elbows, pulling her tightly so her back pressed against his chest. She would never stop enjoying the feel of his strong, protective hands on her. He hadn't always been so... but she'd tamed this beast. She leaned into his embrace, and he kissed her at the base of her ear.

"Yes, though I never really left."

"I don't know if I'll ever get used to it. Physically you're here, but your mind is ten thousand miles away. What happened? Who was here?"

Cole had seen only one ghost, the ghost of his abusive father. He hadn't actually seen the specter. But he'd seen the attack. She didn't remember all of it, but Cole described how she had been lifted off the floor, welts and bruises forming around her neck before she'd passed out and fallen to the ground. He'd been unable to stop his father from abusing him as a child, and he'd been unable to stop his father's ghost as it attacked her then. That interaction had made Cole a believer, a believer in ghosts and a believer in her abilities.

Angela pulled away and lifted the recipe toward him. "The woman who wrote this letter."

He crossed his arms over his chest, his expression dubious. "Why?" He may believe in ghosts, but with all they'd gone through since he'd met Angela, she knew he didn't trust them.

"Beatrice asked us to bake the cookies in this recipe."

"That easy, huh?" He still didn't look convinced.

"She said we had to do it together, otherwise we wouldn't be able to help her."

"What's the catch? There's always some catch."

"All she asked for were some homemade cookies." Angela wrapped her arms around his waist and kissed the dark stubble on his chin. "Plus, I owe her. She helped me."

"What? You're the ghost psychologist. I didn't know they helped you, too."

"This lady was special. She gave me some advice to boost my confidence. She thinks I would never have snagged you if I hadn't taken her advice."

"Oh, really? Then I do owe Beatrice." He leaned down and gave her a deep lingering kiss that sent the strongest electrical vibes down to her toes. When he lifted his head, his eyes seemed smoky. "I guess we need to make some cookies. I owe her big time."

Lacing his fingers through hers, he pulled her toward the kitchen. She really wanted to do something else besides make cookies, but that would have to wait.

When she'd entered this kitchen for the very first time, she'd been terrified. They'd just escaped from one of the many secret passageways in the Penniberg mansion. He'd known the way since the secret hallways had been his refuge as a child. When they'd spilled out into the kitchen, the room had been huge and dark. With Cole in the room, the large kitchen seemed less overwhelming. He'd modernized all the appliances to stainless steel, top-of-the-line equipment. Sunlight spilled through the bank of windows above the sink, covering everything in the room with a cheery yellow hue. Angela spread the letter, recipe side up, on the granite counter top.

"Alright, read off the ingredients and I'll grab them," Cole said.

The paper was worn with faded spots. "It's a little hard to read. Sweetheart Browned Butter Cookies. Okay, the first ingredient is--"

"Let me guess." Cole leaned his hip against the counter on the island across from her. A smile filled his face. "Is it love?"

"No." Angela laughed.

"Are you sure? Let me see that." He leaned closer.

"It's the last ingredient."

"Are you serious? Is that really on there?"

"As a matter of fact, it is." Angela held out the paper for his inspection. "It says 'Bake with love at three hundred fifty degrees.' These are Sweetheart cookies after all."

"Okay. What do we need?"

"First we need one cup of butter, browned butter."

Cole placed the butter in a pan and let it melt over the burner. "How dark does it say?"

"Only slightly browned, more like a golden color. Where did you learn to cook?" She scanned the rest of the ingredients.

"When you grow up like I did, you have to do a lot of things for yourself."

"Once you're done, it says to chill the butter." She was still learning so much about Cole. They had barely been married a few weeks. This was their first holiday together. He was so important to her life that she couldn't imagine herself without him. This thought made her curious about Beatrice. "Beatrice said these cookies were important to finding her true love."

"I'm not seeing how this will help. It's too strange."

"It's strange to me, too. I mean, I've seen ghosts forever, speaking to them since I was twelve. My grandma taught me how to help them. But each ghost was a person with an individual life."

"Life has never been dull since I've met you. Not for one minute." Cole lifted the pan from the stove and placed it on a cooling rack. He dropped the oven mitts onto the counter and looked at Angela. "Will I ever need to worry you'll be possessed again? As much as you were cute in those pin-up outfits, it's disconcerting to think someone else could be in your body again. When I'm with my wife, I want to be with her and no one else."

"Last month was very difficult. I went through it too." She felt shy and a little unsure. All she wanted to do right now was focus on baking cookies and forget this discussion.

He reached a hand over the island and placed his finger under her chin, lifting her lips toward his for a kiss. "No other spirits inside your body but your own, you got that. Your spirit or the spirit of my baby and that's it."

She pulled in a breath. He'd never talked about children before. In fact he'd been afraid of having his own children because of his father. She didn't want to push him too quickly. They had time; they were barely newlyweds. "How about we make some cookies first, and then we'll work on those plans another time?"

"I'm the one who needs to worry about possession. You have possessed me already, Angela, heart, body and soul."

Angela felt like the luckiest woman in the world.

"How are those cookies coming, you lovebirds?" The high-pitched voice caused Angela to jump. "I know you're the only one who can hear me, but I need those cookies soon. I'll be back when it's time."

Angela shifted, searching the room for Beatrice, but she was gone.

"What's going on, babe?" Cole had already pulled the main ingredients from the cupboards-- sugar, flour, vanilla.

"I thought I heard Beatrice. I think we should finish making these cookies. They are very important to her."

"What else is on the list?"

"I'll get the eggs and cherries."

They followed the recipe, rolling the dough around the cherries to create little drops with heart-red centers then dipping them into red sugar sprinkles, the only color they had.

"These are the cutest cookies. The centers will be pink or red. Now I understand why they're called Sweetheart cookies. There is a sweet cherry center at their hearts."

"Let's get them in the oven." Cole slid the cookie sheets in the oven and set the timer. "What are we supposed to do with these treats once they're done?"

"I have no idea. Beatrice?" Angela called into the air. "Beatrice?" she called again, but still nothing. "I don't even feel her."

"Where's that letter? I want to reread it." He scanned the letter and then set it back on the counter. "It's to her love, Michael. He left her before their wedding. I wonder where he was going?"

"He got a job in California," Beatrice's tinny ghost's voice sounded in Angela's ear. She rubbed the curve of her ear where she'd been shocked by a slight fizzle of electricity.

"She just said he went to California," Angela repeated.

"Great, she's back. Ask her what we need to do next. Only a couple minutes left until the cookies are done."

"Though he can't hear me, let him know I can hear him very clearly."

"She says she can hear you, babe."

Angela smiled at the blush that appeared under his tanned cheeks. It was going to take him a long time to get used to having ghosts around. Maybe he never would. It was second nature for her since she'd been living with these strangers shifting in and out of her life for so long.

"Beatrice, we can't wait to taste these cookies. They look very delicious, if I do say so myself," Cole said.

"Oh, no dear, these cookies are for my sweet Michael. You'll have to make a separate batch for yourselves."

"She says we can't have any of these cookies, Cole."

"Not even one taste? What if one gets a little too dark?"

"Not even one cookie from this batch. Each batch is made for a special love." Beatrice's tone was tight, and a chill shimmied up Angela's back.

The bell on the stove rang, causing Angela to start. Why was she so edgy? She'd almost jumped out of her own skin.

"It is time." Beatrice appeared on the opposite end of the room near the stainless steel stove. "Now we must begin."

"We need to begin now," Angela repeated.

"This has become serious business," Cole said as he slid his hand into the heat resistant glove.

"Together. As a couple." Beatrice waved for Angela and Cole to approach.

"Give me one of those gloves, Cole. We have to do this together." He handed her the matching glove, and she slipped her hand into the quilted fabric. A wave of blistering hot air escaped the oven when they lifted out the cookie sheet. The scent of vanilla and cherry with nutty browned butter wafted around them.

"Place each cookie into a box, pile them high." Beatrice leaned over the tray and breathed in a deep sigh, taking in the scent of fresh-baked cookies. Angela's first reaction was to tell Beatrice to be careful not to burn herself, but she stopped before she said a word because as much as Beatrice was lovely, she was already dead and beyond pain.

Just as Angela thought that, Beatrice looked at her with haunted eyes, the blue depths with gray-white around the edges.

"No dear, death does not eliminate the pain. In some ways it turns it into a deep dull ache that takes over your entire being. Trust me, I am not beyond pain." She leaned over the cookies again and took in a second deep breath of the fragrance. "But, alas, that's why I'm here, and that's why I need your help, finally."

"What can I do? Just tell me what you need."

"You're always so eager to please, aren't you?" Beatrice smiled, taking some of the edge off her words. "I guess that's why you do what you do so well."

"Thank you."

"Those on this side call you the White Beacon, you know."

"I didn't know that," Angela said.

"You give off white light as your aura color. It's very comforting and peaceful. That's why they come to you for help-- why I came for help."

Angela had a gift for helping ghosts figure out their issues so they could peacefully move into the light. That was always her number one goal, to help ghosts move on. Her one-track focus had been part of why she'd almost lost Cole and how she had almost died earlier this year. "What do you need me to do? I'll do whatever it takes."

"You see, that's the catch."

Angela pulled in a breath and gritted her teeth. She'd just listen without interrupting. Beatrice would tell her in the way she wanted to tell her.

"This is not an *I* scenario, it's a *we* thing."

"Yes, okay." Angela brightened and gave her a smile. "We, of course. I'm working with you, so we will do this together."

"And I thought he was the hard-headed one." Beatrice shifted her head in Cole's direction.

When this ghostly conversation began, Angela strangely had forgotten he was there. Guilt flooded her. She had a bad habit of blocking everything else out when she focused on the needs of a ghost. Yes, a very bad habit. Heat burned her cheeks as she looked at Cole. He'd continued with the baking process. He'd placed the cookies on a cooling rack in very neat, very organized rows, just like the building contractor he was. God, she loved this man, but how was it so easy for her to block everything else out in her need to assist a spirit? She needed to work on that.

"Trust me," Beatrice spoke in her tinny voice.

Angela twisted quickly to look back at her.

"What we'll need to do will help you work on any of those romantic issues that might have developed. When I said this issue had to be resolved together, I wasn't referring to we, you and me. I was referring to the two of you." Beatrice waggled a finger back and forth between Angela and Cole. "I need two true lovers to help me find my lost true love. Only then can he and I pass on."

"Lost?" Angela croaked. "Lost where?" She'd never heard of a person's soul getting lost. Stolen, captured, imprisoned maybe, but never lost. When she'd been possessed by the pin-up ghost, her soul had been there, never lost or gone, just suppressed.

"If I knew where he was, I wouldn't need you, now would I?" With that last word, Beatrice disappeared.

Angela blinked in the empty space where she'd been.

"Well?" Cole's deep voice broke her spell. "Are you going to let me in on what's been happening?"

"Beatrice came back to tell me a little more information."

"I figured a ghost was around."

"You did?" That thought cheered her. "Are you starting to feel sensations like electricity against your skin?"

He slipped his arms around her waist, pulling her against him. She looked up at him, and he looked down at her and smiled that crooked smile she loved so much. "Nope. I'm starting to learn your body language. I can tell by your movements and your facial expressions when you are interacting. It's kind of cute." He rubbed his thumb along her forehead. "You get this little crinkle right here." He leaned in and kissed the spot where his thumb had just been.

Angela leaned her head against his chest.

"What's wrong, my little angel baby?" He'd started calling her Angel from the start, and she used to hate it so much. Now the endearment made her feel comforted, protected.

"I don't understand much of what she's telling me."

"Why's that? Is she speaking in a different language?"

"No, not that." How interesting that he'd brought up language. She'd never had a language barrier when she helped a ghost, maybe because they communicated on a different level. "I've never been told the things she tells me. For one, she says that we--you and I--need to work on this situation together. She needs help from true lovers."

"True loves? Or lovers?" A laugh rumbled from deep within him. She felt it in his chest more than she heard it. "Because I'm very interested in this 'lovers' idea. All this baking, and now we smell like vanilla. Puts me in the mood." He kissed her neck, and shivers ran down her back.

"You are insatiable."

"I know. We can heat things up while the cookies cool. Let's finish this conversation upstairs." He took her hand, and all thoughts of her ghostly problems abandoned her.

A while later, Angela snuggled deeper into the crook of Cole's side. He combed his fingers through her blond hair, brushing it over and along her shoulder. The fire roared in a fireplace opposite their king-sized bed. Snow fell outside, and the low light gave a soft, blanketed feel to the room.

Penniberg Mansion was built during the roaring twenties by the richest man in town, the owner of the Dalewood Quarries. Cole's father had bought it to show everyone his worth, though appearances were deceiving, and beautiful mansions didn't promise a beautiful home life. Cole had been very damaged by his father's abuse. But Angela had helped him and his father work on a lot of their unresolved issues, and Hank Barlow no longer haunted this mansion or his son. Thinking how thankful she was for that, she snuggled deeper against her husband's side.

"I'm so happy we found each other."

"I thank my lucky stars every single day since I met you." Cole pressed his lips against her neck and nuzzled her. "I love you, my sweet angel girl."

"I love you too, Cole." Ah, contentment. She hoped this would never end. "Thank you for all my wonderful gifts this Christmas." She looked at her arm resting on Cole's tight abdomen. The string of diamonds twinkled. One charm hung off the end and rested on the back of her hand, a heart encrusted in small sparkling pink tourmaline. The bracelet was stunning. She'd never take it off.

"Speaking of gifts, that reminds me of the last present. Tell me more about this thing we need to do together."

"We need to do something together to help her. Are you willing to do that?"

"I wish this Beatrice would ask me herself."

"I'm sure she would if she could, so I'm asking you."

"Of course he'll help." A tinny voice tinkled through the air just before Beatrice's ghostly form appeared. "And I see you've been building up your powers to help me."

"Beatrice," Angela hissed as she pulled the maroon and gray striped covers up over her and Cole's naked bodies. "Knocking is always the polite thing to do."

"I apologize. I've never been able to master the skill of moving things. I can vanish and I have the ability to travel to any place I choose. I've never had the real need to learn how to poltergeist my energy, so…" She put her hands together and bowed in a mea culpa kind of way. "I have no way to knock. Sorry, but not too sorry. Whoo." She waved her hand over her face like a fan. "He's a catch."

"Beatrice," Angela hissed again.

"Should I go and get dressed?" Cole interjected.

"Absolutely not," Angela said.

"Oh yes," Beatrice said at the exact same time. But since Cole could only hear Angela he looked back at her with darkening eyes.

"Okay." He laughed, and one of his straying hands skimmed up her thigh. Angela pressed it with her own to stop him.

Between gritted teeth, she said, "Not a good idea, we have prying eyes. She likes what she sees too much, and I have a problem with that after Winnie decided to take over my body to steal my man. So, if Beatrice thinks she's going to get another glimpse of my husband, she better think a little harder since she needs my help."

Cole laughed. Clearly he knew her little diatribe had been for Beatrice and not for him.

"I'm glad she's here. Can she explain a little more about what she needs us to do?"

Angela looked from Beatrice to Cole. "Beatrice said someone is lost."

"No, dear, not someone. I know where *he* is. It's his soul that has gone missing."

"What do you mean? How can you know where someone is while their spirit is not there? Unless…" Something dawned on Angela. "Is this person alive, or have they passed?"

"He is still alive, though his time is close."

"Then his spirit must still be with him. Maybe it is very weak."

"No." Beatrice smiled sadly. It was such a heartbreaking smile that tears pricked in Angela's eyes. Unbidden, the pain rolled from Beatrice in waves that hit over every nerve ending in Angela's body. She placed her fist over her mouth to stop the sob that threatened to overtake her.

"Baby, are you okay? What is it?" Cole's arm came around Angela's shoulder. He pulled her into a sitting position beside him. "What is going on? Tell me now." His voice was rough. He never could handle her pain, and he hated when she cried.

"Tell him what I told you. Then get dressed, and meet me by your Christmas tree. I'll show you, and then it will make sense."

As quickly as she'd popped in, Beatrice was gone. The overwhelmingly sad feelings faded to a dull ache once Beatrice no longer stood close by. Cole wiped Angela's wet cheek with his thumb.

"This is too much. I won't agree to help."

"We need to help her. I felt her sadness. It was her sadness that made me cry. We must do whatever we can to help her."

"What do we do?"

"I don't know. There are two people needing our help. I know that now. Beatrice as well as her lost love. We need to get dressed. She wants to show us something."

Twenty minutes later, Angela shoved her knit cap low over her ears. She couldn't quite bring herself to unlatch the car door. The tall hospital building with row after row of windows loomed before her. Only the sick or dying were in the hospital, and now she knew that the person she had to help would be dying. She pulled in a shuddering breath. She heard Cole's jacket swoosh then felt his hand cover hers, sweetly, protectively. Just his touch made her feel stronger. She reminded herself that she wasn't doing anything alone this time. They were a *we*. They would be doing this thing *together*.

"We should get inside. There's a little break in the snow," Cole said, breaking the silence.

"Beatrice told us to meet her in room 3733."

"We can do this." Cole's warm hand squeezed hers reassuringly.

She smiled and nodded. There was a confidence in knowing they would be helping together. She had a feeling this journey would take them on an amazing ride.

Angela noticed Beatrice immediately when they entered the hospital room. Beatrice stood at the window with her back to the door. The curtains were open, revealing the snowplowed street below. Only a small amount of light spilled from the fixture above the hospital bed. The room was silent, deadly silent, but for the slow beep of the heart monitor. An antiseptic odor permeated every molecule of air, choking the back of Angela's throat.

In the bed lay the oldest man Angela had ever seen. His eyes were closed and sunken in their sockets. His mouth was stretched open with his skin pulled tight over nothing but bones. He barely had any hair, only a few thin wisps over his head that trailed along his large ears. Other than the slow heart rate on the monitor, only the slight movement of his chest indicated that the man was still alive. Barely, but still alive.

She didn't know what to say or what to do. She couldn't bring herself to speak and break the eerie silence. It was almost like being in a church and a museum combined. Hushed tones were the only kind allowed. Cole took her hand and laced his fingers with hers. She figured he must be feeling the same thing she felt, because he hadn't uttered one word of encouragement since they'd entered the room.

The room's large door swung open, and a whirlwind of a nurse came in.

"I'm so glad you're here. Nancy told me family had arrived." She thrust out her hand to Cole first and then to Angela, a vibrant nurse in a gloomy room of death. Her hands were warm and strong and very reassuring. "I'm nurse Lolly. All this time, I thought he didn't have any family. He was the youngest of six, all of them gone but him."

"And his wife has been gone for a long time, too." Angela found her voice. Beatrice's bereft, slumped shoulders stiffened, though she didn't turn from the window.

"His wife? No. He didn't have a wife." Lolly cupped her hand around the emaciated, gray fingers of the dying man. "Poor Michael, he never did marry, and never had any children either. Too bad since he was such a wonderful man, always making the nurses in the Evergreen Elderly Center laugh. He used to do magic tricks. You know, the silly ones like coins from your ears and the pick the card types. He would have made a wonderful grandpa." She patted the back of his hand. "But he hasn't been with us for quite some time."

When Lolly looked up, her eyes twinkled with moisture. "He's suffered from Alzheimer's. The spirit of this guy has been gone a long time." She leaned in close to Michael's face. He didn't move or even twitch. He probably couldn't hear her anyway, but still, she spoke into his ear. "You've suffered long enough, hon. But now I see why you've held on a little longer. You knew these wonderful people were on the way to see you, I'd bet." She squeezed his hand one last time before straightening and letting go.

"Have a seat, sit next to him, and chat a little. I think it will be good for him. He doesn't have much time. His heart rate is so low and his systems are in failure." She smiled and the tears were gone from her eyes. "I'm glad someone who cares for him will be here when his time comes. I left the window open so his spirit will find his way home. I let the nurses' station know you are in here with him. No one will bother you."

Lolly quietly closed the door as she left the hospital room.

"No family, no wife?" Cole asked. "But the letter with the recipe?"

"Let me ask Beatrice. She's here with us." Angela pointed toward the window. Before she could even ask her question, Beatrice started talking.

"That nurse was so sweet to leave this window shade open. I have been watching and waiting for Michael's return, but he hasn't shown up. He's gone. I watch at this window and wait." She didn't look at them. She spoke as if she needed to voice all her worries out loud, to no one in particular. But Angela was finally a person who could hear.

"Sometimes I travel around, stopping at all his favorite places." Beatrice continued. "He's never at any of them. I search, but never find him. If Michael's body dies before he and his spirit reunite, I fear he will never rest, and his spirit will wander, lost and afraid forever. I have no idea where he could be. I need your true love to help guide back my true love." Beatrice turned, and her pale face was transparent with her fear, her eyes dark with a terror that chilled Angela to her core.

Angela relayed this information to Cole with a voice that felt rusty with the pain. They sat in the uncomfortable chairs and talked and thought and waited.

Beatrice stood at the foot of the bed looking down over Michael. "This is not the man I fell in love with, you know. He was barely a man at twenty. I was just a girl of nineteen. The Second World War had started. We planned to marry, but then he received his transport papers. I was a nurse. I was going to be sent to the same area he was. We planned to marry at the base where he'd be stationed. I ended up leaving first to start work in the hospital, tending the injured soldiers. I caught influenza and never saw him again. As children, we were inseparable. That was the only time we'd ever been separated and look what happened. I have been waiting many years to be with him, and he has waited for me. Now I fear we may never be together again."

"We'll think of something." Angela wanted to encourage Beatrice, but they still didn't have any ideas. This was like no other ghostly scenario she'd ever encountered. She didn't think she could see Michael's ghost because he was not separated from his body. But how would she know if she ever could or couldn't see him, since Michael's spirit was nowhere to be found?

"My mother taught me that cookie recipe. She made them for my father. My grandmother made them for my grandfather before that. It was a family tradition, like a love potion. That was the family legend. I never had any sisters, so there weren't any women who could pass down the recipe to the next generation. Now you know the recipe, Angela. They only work if eaten by true lovers. The legend says that true lovers who eat those cookies will remain in their sweetheart's embrace forever. Michael loved those cookies. Did you bring them with you like I asked?"

"Of course." Angela tapped Cole. "She's asking for the cookies."

Angela's messenger bag rested on a chair close to the window. Cole reached into it and pulled out a tin decorated with red and white candy canes.

Angela took the tin and settled it in her lap. She pulled off the top, releasing a perfume of vanilla and cherries.

Beatrice instantly appeared in front of Angela. "You made a beautiful batch, but that's what I expected since your love is true. I have an idea, and that's part of why I wanted you to bake those cookies."

"Part of the reason?"

"Yes. The other part is, since you were so kind to me at the Greeley's, I thought you should carry on my family's legendary cookie recipe. You can indulge in them with your husband, and when your daughter is born, you can pass on the secret to her." Beatrice's face lightened, and her eyes brightened to a brilliant sky blue. Did she know something Angela didn't know?

"Not yet, but soon. I think we should begin." Beatrice turned around and began pacing.

"Did it get cold in here?" Even Cole felt the chill from her ghostly movements, because he rubbed his arms and then put on his jacket.

"Beatrice is getting ready for us to start. She must be pulling energy from the room, which is why you're feeling cold. Are you ready to help?"

"I hope so," he said and then leaned down for a quick kiss. His lips were warm against her cool skin. It was a lot easier for ghosts to take on her energy since she possessed special abilities.

"Alright, Beatrice," Cole called into the air. "We're ready."

"Tell him that you are going to take a bite of the cookie, and then he will finish the other half. It must be the same cookie, and each of you must eat a part of the sweetheart center. I need both of you to move into the middle realm. Angela, I have the understanding that, if you allow it, I will be able to touch you, and you will be able to see my thoughts and feel my feelings."

"Something like that. It's more of a possession type thing. If you enter my body, it's more along the lines that I become you and you become me, sort of." Angela shook her head. "It's almost impossible to explain."

Beatrice waved her hand dismissively. "The process is meaningless to me. All I care about is that you'll be able to travel through my memories."

"I don't know about this." Repelled by the idea, Angela instinctively stepped away from Beatrice. "It can be dangerous."

"You will not do anything dangerous, is that clear? I almost lost you before, and I can't take that again." Cole gripped her elbow. That crinkle appeared between his eyes. She wanted to smooth away his worry.

"She wants me to do some sort of ghostly walk down memory lane. I'm scared, but I can do it."

"You said *us* before. Both of us. Doing it together, right?" Cole asked. "This is about us being a couple. It's going to be the two of us together or not at all." His eyes flashed, and Angela knew he would have it no other way.

She'd slipped into thinking she was stuck doing this all alone. But she wouldn't be alone. He would be with her. Together. She wanted to cry. Would she ever get used to this idea that they were no longer individuals; they were a couple? To have and to hold, until death do us part. Those were the words they'd spoken. Beatrice and Michael had never had that chance. They'd been waiting for death, and now even that chance might be taken from them. She and Cole were going to help this couple find their happily ever after.

"Yes, we can do this together."

"Thank you." Beatrice's tinkling voice sounded further away. "You need to eat the cookie and that will help both of you become one in spirit, mind and soul. Well, at least that's the family legend. But it's all I've got."

Cole and Angela faced each other holding hands. She told him what they were going to do. Once they transferred into the middle realm, which Angela could only assume meant limbo, the space between heaven and hell, she had no clue what they would do next.

She held a cookie in one hand and gripped Cole's hand with the other one. She took a deep bite into the cookie, making sure to get to the heart center, and then she placed the cookie into his mouth. He smiled and chewed. She chewed, and they both swallowed. Cole's head dipped lower, lower, until their lips touched and they were kissing. The kiss deepened. Her love for him swelled into the recesses of her heart and the depths of her soul until he was all of her and she was all of him. Their smiling lips pressed into each other, and then they were giggling. Their giggles turned into laughs of joy and happiness that wrapped around them like the ribbons on their Christmas presents.

They kept their hands clasped as they pulled away from each other. Angela noticed the sound of the beeping monitors had slipped away, replaced by the gurgling bubbles of a slow flowing stream. Wind rustled through the leaves on towering trees, and the sound of cicadas hung in the heavy humid air.

She felt young, a lot younger than her twenty-eight years. She felt the full passions of a teenager in love. Angela realized she'd been transported into Beatrice's memories.

"It worked." Angela squeezed Cole's hand. "I want to pinch you to be sure you're really here with me, too."

"I'm here too, but where is here?" He looked around at the scenery. "This is beautiful, but I envisioned a more tropical setting for our honeymoon."

"I have to connect with Beatrice to see if I can feel what she feels, know what she knows."

"How do you do that? Connect with her?"

"It's like a tingling sensation that starts on the surface of my skin, almost like the feeling of pulling socks right out of the dryer, popping with static cling."

"You feel that when you're near a ghost?"

"Yes, then I let down my boundaries and let the ghost enter me so I can feel what they feel."

"Wait." Cole tightened his hold on Angela's hand. "I feel like I need to show you something."

"You can feel things here? Oh my God, what can you feel?"

"I get it. I feel it, that fuzzy, electrical buzz. Come this way. Come with me, my love."

Now it was clear to Angela. Beatrice wanted both of them to go into the memories so that Cole could connect with Michael in the hopes of finding his missing soul. It might work. How could it work? But she'd stopped asking how all of this was possible long ago. She didn't know everything about it. All she knew was that these things were possible, unexplainable, and unbelievable, unless they happened to you.

Cole held her hand and pulled her along. She stumbled as she ran behind him, laughing in a childish way that felt like two teens frolicking in the throes of new love.

"I know where I'm going, as if I've been here before. And the closer I get, the stronger the pull. The hairs on my arms are standing on edge." He lifted an arm, but kept up his pace.

They ran through a field of white daisies and the fragrant blooms of lily of the valley. Their feet crushed the grass. They couldn't avoid stomping the flowers as they tore through the meadow.

"This way." He led her toward an outcropping of rock. The sound of rushing water grew louder the closer they came to the rocky ledge. The field diminished into a moss-covered out-cropping where a worn footpath led down through the cracks in the huge stones. "Careful now." His strong hands gripped her hips as he pushed her gently forward, placing her in the lead. "It's at the end of this pathway."

She walked along the path of soft dirt and moss, boulders on either side, until the narrow passage opened up in front of them. Slightly to the right, a waterfall poured from the heights of the rocks they had just descended. The warm misty air from the waterfall's white spray blurred the rocks slicked with green lichen.

"It's breathtaking." She let out a breath. She could barely speak while looking at such beauty. She thought nothing could be more beautiful, until a cloud shifted, and a ray of sunlight spilled into the cavern, hitting the droplets of water suspended in the air. The most vibrant arc of a rainbow soared out from the waterfall. Angela's throat burned at the splendor before them. She felt compelled to thank Beatrice for letting them experience this moment.

"Look." Cole pointed to the ground. Under an ancient willow tree lay a crown of flowers, daisies and lily of the valley intertwined. "They were here." He placed the wreath on Angela's head and scooped her hair forward over her shoulder. "You look like a Goddess." His smile was young and unsure and heartbreakingly sweet, like the smile of someone falling in love for the first time. Then he looked away. "They came here once before, but they aren't here now."

"What do we do? Where do we go next?"

"I'm not sure. I don't know how this works. I'm sorry." He crossed his arms over his chest and turned back toward the waterfall. His foot tapped on a stone. His jaw tightened. She hadn't seen that dangerous tick in his cheek muscle in a long time.

"I was so sure I felt him," Cole continued. "But those feelings are gone, and I have no clue how I connected the first time. I don't know how I was able to do that." His tone was edged with panic. "I was so close to finding him. I could feel his energy on my skin." Usually he was so strong and sure, but here in this situation feeling the emotions of a lost man had an adverse effect on him. His skin took on a gray pallor while his pupils dilated to an almost solid black, his gazed fixed in a faraway stare. It was like he was here and gone at the same time.

"Look at me." She stepped in front of him and grabbed his hand. Sandwiching it between both of hers, she pressed it against her chest so he could feel her heartbeat. His fingers were ice cold and shook against her grip.

"Listen and do what I tell you," she said firmly. But he continued to look blankly out at the water. Fear spilled through her veins. She shook his hand, but he continued to look off into the distance, a lost look on his face.

"We are here to find Michael. We are not here to let your soul lose its way too."

His eyes remained foggy. She was too late. This had been a mistake. They shouldn't have done this. But they had said yes, both of them.

"Cole, you must listen to what I tell you to do." She shook him again, and this time his eyes cleared and focused on her.

"That was so strange. I was here, only I forgot that you were with me, and I forgot where here was. I was circling and circling and not going anywhere, and still I couldn't remember where I was. Then I heard your voice, and it was all clear." His throat muscles tightened as he swallowed.

"Do not let that happen again, do you hear me?" She knew her tone was harsh, but she didn't care. "You cannot get lost here. We are in the middle realm. This is a deathly limbo, like a dream, a memory. Not your memory or mine, but that of the lost and the waiting."

"Don't let go of my hand." His words sounded almost like begging. They practically broke Angela's heart.

"I think that's what happened. I connected with someone lost and then I was lost." His voice was raw, sandpaper gruff.

"I won't let go of you. Okay?" Now she was the one begging and grasping for his fingers, lacing hers between his.

"I won't do that again. Not here." He turned in a semi-circle, hand tightly clamped to hers. "Everything is so strange. It looks real, but it doesn't feel real. Like I could put my hand right through it like a hologram, but my feet are solid on the ground. The wreath in your hair is made of real flowers, the scent so powerful, the white, so stark against your blond hair. Your eyes are as bright as the sun reflecting off gold."

Her hand fluttered to her hair and the flowers she'd forgotten were there. "This place is realer than real. It's filled with Michael and Beatrice's memories. Why did you put this on my head in the first place? Maybe the memories will tell us what to do next."

"Yes. Can we sit though? My legs are wobbly from that experience. So strange." He led her to a fallen log, and she sat beside him. Mist from the waterfall rose before them. The moss on the rocks was painfully green, either from all the water or from the memories.

"So what do you remember?"

"I remember wanting to tell you something by the waterfall. No." He shook his head once. "Not me, it wasn't me. I was Michael, and Michael wanted to tell Beatrice something. What did he want to tell her?" His eyes squinted as he searched his thoughts. Then he smiled, sly, knowing, almost secretive. "Michael wanted to ask her something, but then he got scared. He told her how beautiful she was instead and placed the wreath on her head. She'd woven the flowers together," Cole said. "Come on." He stood quickly. "I know where we're going next."

They set foot back on the path, but as they walked the scenery gradually changed. Angela barely noticed as the temperature shifted from the balmy warmth of late spring into the blazing heat of midsummer.

They were no longer walking along a path in the cool undergrowth of a forest. The trees had morphed into tall grasses, with reeds standing taller than Angela's head. They were at the height of Cole's shoulders, so he could still see above them.

She continued to follow, but his feet moved faster and faster. She could barely keep up. Soon she was running behind his long strides.

She couldn't see the ground, and her foot hooked on something hidden below the grasses. The heat had made her hands slick with sweat. Her tenuous grip on his hand fell loose as she tumbled into the grass. She couldn't see him, but she could hear him as he rustled farther and farther away from her.

Pain tore through her hands and knees, but it was nothing compared to the pain in her heart for fear that she would lose him.

"Cole." Her voice wasn't her own. It sounded like an injured, mewling animal. But still his strides tore through the reeds as he moved away from her.

She rushed to her feet and called him again, but there was no response. The rustling sounds had faded into the quiet sound of winds rushing through the reeds. Oh God, he couldn't be himself anymore. He must be

Michael again. She said a small prayer that he would find his way. Please, keep him from losing himself. She would not let him get lost. She would find him no matter what happened here.

The old adage rang in Angela's mind like the sound of musical words piped through the hollow stems. *The reed that stands tall in the wind will break, while the reed that bends allows the strength of the wind to blow through it.*

She relaxed into the ground and breathed in the scents of heather and lavender on the wind. She smelled the flaxen warm grasses and the musty sweetness of the earth below. She curled her fingers into the crushed grass beneath her palms and listened to the whistling wind. But the whistling was higher pitched. It wasn't the wind at all, but a person whistling an old cheery tune.

A memory of the grandfather she'd barely known flashed in her mind. He held her in his arm when she was a baby. His lips curled into a round O under his white mustache as he created music with his mouth. She hadn't known she'd had any memories of her grandfather because he'd died when she was very young. Her strongest memories were of the grandmother who had raised her, who had taught her to use her gifts and helped her learn how not to be afraid. But now she thought of her grandfather and how he'd held her in his strong arms and whistled to make her happy. She no longer felt panic. She felt sure she could find Cole.

She pushed herself to her feet and followed the tune. The grasses thinned until only reeds stood along the bank of a small lake. But they weren't reeds at all. They were the long sword-like leaves and the brown fuzzy heads of cattails jutting from the edge of the lake. Angela pushed the stems to the side so she could move closer to the lake's glassy surface.

The water was so clear she could see the sandy bottom. Fat silver-skinned fish flashed as their tails flipped against the water's surface. She watched them dart in and out of the underwater foliage, entranced by the beauty. A solitary fish swam to the edge of the water, just below her feet. So alive and so free, in the magical depths of the glistening water, the fish eyed her as she watched it for what seemed like ages. What was the message? Was there even a message at all? Before she could figure it out the fish flipped its fin, twitched its tail, and swam off. She caught a last bit of pink and silver before the fish disappeared into dark waters. Tears burned at the back of her throat, but she had no idea why the image had brought her close to crying. What did it mean? What did it all mean?

A movement rustled to her right. She turned, suddenly afraid an unseen animal was going to jump out at her. A flash of glistening tanned skin made her gasp and jump back. Cole stood before her naked and bent over, drying his backside with a light blue towel. He turned and his deep gray eyes crackled with amusement. His smile made her smile, and she took a step toward him.

"You should have come in for a swim, my love. Even to put your feet in to cool off from the blazing sun. Your cheeks are so rosy." He laughed, a sly knowing smile on his face. His voice was different from Cole's, but she recognized it as well as she knew her own.

She felt shy and glanced away from his nakedness. Then she remembered. All of her skin burned from the memory of his touch and his lovemaking. She remembered his soft caresses and her fear of being caught. And then she realized she was no longer Angela, and he was no longer Cole. These were Beatrice and Michael's memories, not her own. Being here in the middle realm made it a lot easier to slide into someone else's memories, too easy, in fact. She had no doubt that Cole had slipped as easily into Michael.

Fear filled her entire being because she realized that this was the middle realm. They were reliving Beatrice and Michael's memories, but they felt like they were becoming her own memories. Angela and Cole would never find their way back, and they wouldn't be able to help Beatrice and Michael if that happened.

"My love," she called out, not wanting to use any names for fear of startling Cole and forcing him deeper into this world that seemed so magical. She held out her hand, stretching her fingers to him. He grasped them, pulling her tight to his body, wrapping her body against his warm, damp skin. His kiss was deep and powerful. She kissed him back with the same passion.

"I love you, Angela." His head fell into the crook of her neck, and he kissed her soft skin.

Tears wet her cheeks. She held him tighter, afraid to let him go. But he was himself again. They were together. She loved him, and he loved her, but the love she'd felt between Beatrice and Michael had been just as strong.

She wrapped her arms around his head and thrust her fingers into his dark hair that was warm from the sun. "Do you think we can help Michael?"

He brushed her tears off her cheeks with his thumbs. "We are closer, but I think the hardest is yet to come."

"I don't know." Her words hooked in her throat. She swallowed and started again. "I almost lost you twice here. I'm afraid the next time will be forever."

"We've made it this far. We can't turn back." He cupped her face and tilted her chin. She could not look away, and she knew he couldn't either. "Whatever happens, know that I love you, I will always love you. I love you here and beyond for all eternity."

"Eternity is a long time." She tried to laugh through the falling tears and the burning in her throat.

"Know that I mean what I say." He smiled.

"I love you in the same way. I love you through eternity and more."

His kiss pressed into hers, and the rustling of the reeds fell away.

When she opened her eyes again, Cole was squatting on the ground, shoulders hunched, fingers ripping through his hair.

"Cole," Angela cried out. He didn't respond. He didn't move at her call. Then she realized he was Michael again. His shoulders tightened and shook. He threw his head back, his neck muscles taut like wires. Then they rippled and convulsed. A guttural warrior's cry poured from his mouth before he slid to his knees beside a bed.

That's when Angela noticed she wasn't outside anymore. She was in a large room. The only light poured in from the windows on both sides. Many beds--but not really beds, they were more like cots--lined up in rows along the walls. They were filled with people lying under white blankets. A nurse stood at the far end of the long room. She wore an old-time white uniform with a folded cap perched on her head. A clipboard balanced across her arm. They were in an old-time war hospital.

Cole's cries pulled her back to him. She watched him fall over the body of a person in the bed. His body jerked with sobs. Angela pressed her hand against his back, trying to comfort him, not knowing what to do. She had never seen him in such pain. He didn't acknowledge her touch, and she knew he didn't feel it. She was like a ghost in this situation.

She peered over his shoulder, her worst fears coming true. Cole was Michael in the throes of grief as he wept over Beatrice's body.

Even with gaunt skin, she looked just like the pretty-faced girl Angela had seen that first time at Fran Greeley's party. Her heart-shaped lips held a rosy tint. Her dark lashes fell over her cheeks as if she were asleep.

"Pretty as sleeping beauty, right?"

Angela started at the tinny voice.

"I've been waiting for the two of you to get to this point. I couldn't do a thing until he experienced this part."

Angela pressed her hand against Beatrice's arm. She felt solid and whole, because they were all in the place of the spirits.

"I'm so sorry," Angela said, trying to comfort Beatrice. "Your time came too soon."

"It did, didn't it?" Beatrice looked wistfully at her body lying in the bed. Cole, who had once been Michael, lay over her. "But then is there ever any good time?"

"I guess not." They stood back as Cole lifted his head from Beatrice's body. He leaned into her ear and repeated the words that Michael must have said. "I will love you for always. My one and only love."

"Since I'm here, I can help Cole return to you. Now we must find Michael and reunite him with himself."

"I feel weak. How can you be sure you'll bring Cole back to me? It's been so difficult so far. I've almost lost him twice."

This time Beatrice gripped Angela's shoulder. "I'm not sure true love really gets lost. Forgotten for a little while, but not lost. Believe in that. Hope in that."

When Angela turned back to the bed, it was gone. Cole was gone. Beatrice was gone. The hospital was gone. She was alone.

Smoke swirled around her. Light poured from the far end of a tunnel, but it was muted by mist and made the air seem like a spiraling tornado without the sound of rushing wind. The air felt cool against her skin. She looked down, and she was no longer wearing her jeans and t-shirt. They'd been replaced by a gauzy white dress that swirled around her legs, mixing and blending into the smoke.

"Beatrice," she called out, but her voice bounced through the tunnel and echoed back.

"Cole," she shouted louder, more frantically. No response. Her hands reached out, clawing, grasping for anything to hold onto.

"Michael," she screamed so loudly that the words tore painfully from her throat. She was losing it; she was lost. She was in the nothingness, alone with nowhere to go. Fear of the unknown strangled at her throat. Her skin prickled with goose bumps, and she shivered from the wintery solitude. This was death. This was what it felt like. Not the beautiful experience of going into the light she'd been so curious about. She'd experienced rays of rainbow light when Cole's father's ghost had almost killed her. But she'd chosen life then. She'd chosen Cole. Now she was lost and had no way of getting back.

She loved him with all her heart, and now she would lose him. The thought was too much to bear. Her knees buckled. She fell into the mist, but instead of hitting ground, she fell and fell. Her arms and legs flailed, entangling in her skirts until they wrapped around her body like a shroud. She was stuck in an endless fall, never hitting bottom. Time didn't exist except for this eternity. Wind and sky rushed past her without end. There was a calmness in the thought, and she relaxed into the endless falling until her fear slid away. Beatrice's words came back to her.

I'm not sure true love really gets lost. Forgotten for a little while, but not lost. Believe in that. Hope in that.

Forgotten, not lost. Believe in that. Believe in her love. She had found a true love, and she couldn't forget that. She thought of Cole's gray eyes, his tender smile. She remembered the man who had been guarded, a wall of protection so thick around his heart it couldn't be shattered.

As the only one who'd ever pierced through his barriers, she'd saved him, but he'd also saved her. No longer alone, she had him and his love. Together they were a couple, and she could not forget that. She needed him as much as he needed her. And she remembered who she was and where she was. As she closed her eyes and embraced her love for Cole, she stopped falling.

When she opened her eyes she was sitting on a blanket. Cole sat cross-legged across from her. His smile was serene and comforting and filled with the same love she felt for him. She smiled back. The beeping of a heart monitor sounded behind her. She didn't need to look to realize they were back in the hospital room where Michael lay dying.

To Angela's left sat a man with light brown hair parted at the side and combed neatly. "Thank you." His words sounded like rock grinding against rock.

"For what? I don't know what I did to help," Angela said.

"When you called my name, I knew I could follow you. Your energy is white light, better than any flashlight in a dark cave," Michael said.

Beatrice sat cross-legged on the blanket to Angela's right. The four of them made a circle on the blanket.

"Is this a picnic?" Angela asked, feeling strange and uncomfortable. She hadn't done anything to help. She'd been lost herself. She'd been in a state of panic, hoping someone would help her, not the other way around. She hadn't been helping anyone at the time.

"This is a special picnic," Beatrice responded. "A picnic we almost couldn't have. Thank you, Angela, for your self-sacrifice. If you hadn't fallen, Michael would still be lost in the depths. That was how you helped him." Beatrice looked across the blanket at Michael. His cheeks bloomed with color and his pulse seemed to beat strongly under his skin. The monitor's beep matched the rhythm of his pulse. How could Angela sense his heartbeats? She saw a slight tick along his throat, a small vibration at his wrist that rested on his knee. She could even see the small sprinkling of freckles along the bridge of his nose.

Shifting her gaze, she looked at the still body in the bed. He looked very thin, gaunt, a much older version of the spirit of the man sitting to her left.

"You were a beacon of brightness that helped me find my way. I need to apologize. In the end, I lost myself. I kept reliving the old times. The good times mostly, but also the bad." He lifted his hand toward Beatrice, and she took it. "When I was in that place, I relived the worst time of my life. I lost you then, and I kept losing you over and over until I lost myself too. It was a torture I couldn't stop reliving. Ultimately, I lost everything I loved by slipping away into that darkness." With his other hand, he reached for Angela. She laced her fingers into his icy grip. He took only a small, residual amount of her energy. Maybe he didn't need it now. "Angela, you sacrificed your soul. That's how I found you. And you led me back."

In the middle of the circle, lying in the tin, were the cookies Angela and Cole had baked. Angela's stomach rumbled. Her mouth watered at the scent of vanilla and cherries. When her stomach growled again, they all laughed.

"I think it's time to give this girl a cookie." Beatrice reached down and passed the cookie tin to Angela. With a slow, steady movement, she plucked the top cookie from the pyramid, then placed the tin in the middle of the blanket. Her fingers tingled with the importance of something that was about to happen.

"What do we do now?" Cole asked.

Angela glanced at the cookie in her hand. With all its bumps and crevices, its glittering sugar, it looked like any other cookie. "Why is this cookie so important?" Angela asked.

Beatrice smiled a knowing grin that said everything, but told Angela nothing. Beatrice took a cookie, lifted it to her lips. She shifted her eyes to look around the circle at each person in turn. Then she placed it between her teeth.

"When you eat the cookie, make sure to bite through the heart center." Angela repeated the instructions Beatrice had given to her earlier. Was that today? Was that yesterday? Was that a week ago? It all seemed to happen in an eternal instant.

Beatrice bit through the cookie. Chewing, she leaned over the blanket toward Michael. She lifted the cookie to his lips, and he let her place the uneaten half in his mouth. He began chewing, and they smiled at each other. While looking only at each other, they leaned closer and closer until their lips touched, their bodies creating an arch over the tin of cookies. Their kiss deepened like a couple of sixteen-year-olds instead of the ageless, ghostly couple they were. Their fingers tightened in a grip that made them one spirit. As Angela watched, their bodies became less and less solid until Angela could see Cole watching the scene across from her. They had both been watching the ghosts.

It dawned on her suddenly that Cole could see the ghosts. How was that possible while they were in the hospital? And then Angela knew they were not really back in the hospital at all. They were still somewhere in between.

Something caught her attention. She saw a long tunnel with a shining door at the end. Swirling rainbows of iridescent light spiraled through the tunnel. Beatrice and Michael stood deep in the tunnel holding hands. They faced away from the door looking at Angela and Cole, who still sat cross-legged on the blanket.

Beatrice raised her hand while still holding Michael's. "I've waited a long time to be reunited with this man." Michael kissed Beatrice on the cheek. "I thought I'd lost you." She turned to Michael and looked at him like nothing else existed but the two of them. She gripped his other hand, connecting them in a binding circle.

"I was lost, but I never forgot you. I was confused and searching, searching, but always looking for you. I couldn't find you, my love." Michael pulled Beatrice against his chest and wrapped her in his arms, circling her waist. He kissed her, deep and claiming. She kissed him back, and her foot raised in the quintessential old-time image of passion. The two were together as one again.

They pulled away, giggling like schoolchildren, hands clasped in a grip that they would not release again. They ran together toward the light and the door opened. White light poured like ribbons into the room, blinding

Angela, though she couldn't look away. She watched as the couple's silhouette grew smaller and smaller down the tunnel, until they were swallowed by the light.

Before the door to the other side closed, a soft tinkling bell of a voice fluttered back to her.

"Thank you for giving us our happily ever after. We never would have had that without you both. We will be eternally grateful."

From a faraway distance, the slow beeping sound of the heart rate monitor became one shrill, continuous cry.

Tears burned down Angela's cheeks. She had never felt so painfully happy. Cole's solid hand gripped hers, and she remembered that they were in the tunnel as well, but they weren't going to the other side. She and Cole needed to get back to their life, back to the life they had barely begun together. No longer were they individuals. They were one, a couple, not an I or a me, but a we and an us. The tears continued to flow down. She didn't brush them away or try to make them stop. She had accepted Cole with his flaws, and he had accepted her, this strange creature who had dragged him through all these terrifying experiences.

The tinkling voice came again, only it was so soft she could easily have missed it over the roaring in her own ears and heart.

"Do not lose yourselves. You did it once before, but you found your way back to each other. Now take hold of each other's hearts, keep them safe in your soul, and love each other body and mind. Only then will you be able to return home. Remember the way you entered this middle realm, use the same door to go home."

The last rays of light glistened into a glow before the room darkened into nothing but Angela and Cole. Everything was gone. There was no room, no ceiling above them, no floor below them. It was similar to the feeling she'd had just before she'd fallen. Panic filled Angela, and a scream bubbled at the back of her throat. She thrust out her arms, grasping for anything, but her hands only found emptiness. She still held the cookie in one hand. She closed her fingers tight around the cookie, and her other hand, still reaching out, felt the tips of warm, strong fingers.

"Take my hand," Cole called from the darkness. She grasped Cole's hand with her free hand and held tight, never wanting to let him go. She knew she would fall into the abyss of nothingness without him.

"She said to go through the same door. But the door they entered is gone. What do we do?" Cole's voice came to her through the darkness.

"No. We can't go that way." Calmness flowed through her. "I know what she means. Are you ready?"

"I want to be the man you want me to be."

"You already are." She squeezed his hand in hers.

"And you are everything and more to me. I never allowed myself to hope I'd be loved in the way you love me. I will love you for always."

"I will love you for always."

She bit into the cookie, making sure she cut through the center. She knew all this was a legend, but she wanted their souls to become one. She leaned closer to Cole and slipped the cookie into his mouth. They both chewed as they looked into each other's eyes, leaning closer and closer until their lips touched. Maybe it was her imagination, but, as the kiss deepened, she felt their souls touch and entwine. Soft, feathery glitter sprinkled over them, filling the darkness, falling to cover everything in white bright flakes of winter snow. Snowflakes stuck to his dark lashes and fell on his cheeks. She knew they frosted her hair too. She laughed first. Then Cole laughed a deep rumbling growl of a laugh. She blinked and when her eyes opened, Cole stared back, smiling.

They were back in the hospital room, sitting in the uncomfortable plastic chairs next to the hospital bed. The snow was gone except for one melted drop of water that clung to Cole's lashes like a happy, cleansing tear.

The oversized wooden door swung open. Lolly rushed in, moving directly to the bed. She covered Michael's hand and let out a long sigh. "He's gone now. You came just in time. He was happy you came. I know he is at peace now. You see that smile?"

Cole tightened his grip on Angela's hand--the hand he'd never let go of since they'd returned from the middle realm.

After returning to their home, they sat cross-legged in the drawing room of the Penniberg mansion, facing each other in front of the Christmas tree, with the fire crackling cozily behind the grate. The Christmas tree lights twinkled in multi-colored brightness. Snow fell outside the windows, creating a winter wonderland of white frosted trees and a dusted lawn.

Cole sandwiched Angela's hand between both of his and kissed her fingertips. He brought her hand to his chest and pressed it over his heart.

"Do you feel my heart?"

"Yes," she said on a breath.

"I once thought it was broken and damaged beyond repair. You fixed that."

Tears clouded her view.

"This heart beats for you alone. I will never get lost again, because it will always know how to find you."

"I love you, Cole." She took his free hand and brought it to her chest, pressing it over her heart. "When I fell, I felt lost and free-falling to nothingness. That is what Michael must have felt when he was lost and searching for Beatrice. I grasped for anything, but the only thing that helped me were my thoughts of you. I imagined you there. It was like a leap of faith, and I knew you would be there to catch my fall. I will never be lost knowing that our love is true."

"It's not that cookie that binds our souls. We were meant to find each other. Without you, I was broken," Cole said.

"Without you, I was alone," Angela said.

"Our souls are entwined like the roots of the willow tree. We are one spirit, and I'm thankful for you. Beatrice helped us realize that together we are better than who we were when we were apart."

"I saw what happened when they couldn't find each other. I thought I would never find you again."

"What I learned was that we are connected, and we will always find our way back to each other."

"Love you forever." Angela gave him a tremulous smile.

"Love you forever." Cole pulled her against him and kissed her as the snow fell outside, and the lights twinkled on the tree inside. One last gift sat under the Christmas tree, a metal tin of sweetheart cookies with a legend attached that may or may not have helped their souls become one, but definitely helped them understand the strength of their love.

Sweetheart Browned Butter Cookies

1 cup butter

1/2 cup granulated sugar

1/2 cup brown sugar

1 egg

1 tsp vanilla

1 tbsp of Maraschino cherry juice

2 and 1/2 cups all-purpose flour

1 tsp salt

36 Maraschino cherries

Colored decorator sugar

Melt butter over medium-high heat in heavy 2-quart saucepan. Continue cooking, watching closely, until butter foams and just turns a delicate golden color (3 to 5 minutes). Immediately remove from heat; refrigerate 30 minutes.

Heat oven to 350 degrees F. Cream browned butter and both sugars in a large bowl. Combine egg, vanilla and cherry juice into creamed mixture. Beat at medium speed until well mixed. Continue beating, gradually adding flour, until well mixed.

Roll dough around each cherry into 1-inch balls. Roll balls in colored decorator sugar. Place 2 inches apart onto ungreased cookie sheets.

Bake 10 to 12 minutes with love at 350 degrees F or until lightly golden brown. Let stand 1 minute; remove from cookie sheets. Cool completely.

Makes three dozen cookies.

Finally a Family

by Livia Grant

Don't Be
Afraid to
Want it All!
Livia
Grant

Livia Grant lives in Chicago with her husband and two sons... one a teenager, the other a furry rescue dog named Max. She is blessed to have traveled extensively and as much as she loves to visit places around the globe, the Midwest and its changing seasons will always be home. Livia started writing when she felt like she finally had the life experience to write a riveting story that she hopes her readers won't be able to put down. Livia's fans appreciate her deep character driven plots, often rooted in an ensemble cast where the friendships are as important as the romance... well, almost. She writes one hell of an erotic romance. Learn more at www.liviagrant.com.

"I can't thank you enough, Blake. Being home tonight with my girls means so much to me." Debbie leaned in to give her co-worker an awkward hug.

Blake Harrigan moved in to reciprocate, the hug helping to douse the melancholy blanket he'd been shrouded in for the last month. "Hey, I'm happy to help. Working is better than being home alone tonight. Moms should be with their kids on Christmas Eve. You'd better hurry if you're going to make it to the late church service." He released her, and she rushed to grab her belongings and head home through the falling snow.

It felt good to help out the more experienced RN who'd been acting as his unofficial mentor since he started working in the emergency room at Galena Memorial Hospital six months ago. As the newest nurse on staff at the Northwest Illinois hospital, Blake felt it was only fair he work the holiday anyway.

Debbie was almost out the door when she turned, rushing back to hug him again. "Oh my, I just realized this is your first holiday since your mom died. Are you sure you're going to be okay, Blake? Do you have somewhere to go tomorrow when you get off work in the morning? I don't want you going home to that empty house."

His heart contracted with a physical pain that had been his frequent companion since watching his mother pass away from breast cancer in the same hospital less than one month before.

"Thanks for the offer, Debbie, but I'll be fine. I'll need to sleep since I'm on shift tomorrow night again."

"That's not good enough. I'm having my in-laws over for lunch tomorrow. I'd love for you to join us."

This was why Blake loved working in his hometown hospital. He still wasn't used to how friendly everyone was here versus Madison, Wisconsin where he had lived for the last eight years.

He knew she wouldn't leave until he at least considered it. "How about I text you in the morning and let you know?"

"Well, okay, but I'm gonna be waiting for you."

"I'd expect nothing less." Blake smiled, trying to reassure her he would be fine. It wasn't a lie. He'd messed up so many things in his twenty-six years, and yet he'd survived. Being alone on another holiday wouldn't kill him.

After Debbie left, he started to make his rounds of the department. They were short staffed with only two nurses and one doctor on duty, yet three of the four beds in the ER were filled: one with a father who'd cut himself with the knife he was using to assemble his child's Christmas toy; one with a teenage driver who rear-ended a truck while texting; and one holding Mrs. Warski, who was frequently admitted with chest pains. A busy night for Galena.

Blake and Dr. Peterson got the father's knife wound patched up first before fitting the young driver with her neck brace. Only then did Blake return to Mrs. Warski's room. They were waiting on her cardiologist to phone in instructions. Blake didn't say it out loud, but he suspected the kind senior citizen had elected to spend the night in the hospital rather than be alone in her own large house. That suited him fine, as she was decent company.

He pulled back the curtain providing his elderly patient some privacy. "So how are you feeling now, Mrs. Warski?" Blake moved to the monitor to check her vitals.

"I'm doing much better now that you're here to take care of me, Mr. Harrigan. I see they made the new guy work on Christmas Eve."

Blake chuckled. "For the tenth time, call me Blake. And I didn't have to work; I took Debbie's shift so she could be home with her kids."

"You are such a kind young man. I wish I had an eligible granddaughter I could fix you up with. I can't believe you aren't married with your own pack of kids."

His heart contracted with another physical pain, this one stabbing deeper. "I sure have you fooled. I deserve to be alone. I had a chance at that future once, but I screwed it up royally."

"What a bunch of crap!" Her voice warbled with animation.

Blake had been writing on her chart when her shocking exclamation drew his attention. He saw a fire in her eyes. "Excuse me? Did you just say crap?"

"Indeed I did. I'll use shit if you'd prefer." Her face wore a mischievous grin that only the elderly could get away with.

His chuckle filled the cramped area. "You can use whatever word you'd like, although I'm not sure I agree."

"You are a handsome, successful, genuinely nice young man. You don't deserve to be alone, Blake."

He'd been trying to get her to use his first name the last three times she'd come into the ER. The fact she used it in that moment assured him she was sincere.

"I haven't always been so nice."

"I haven't always been a wise old crone, either. We all live and learn. So you made mistakes. Who hasn't? You should be out dating, finding someone special."

Unwanted memories flooded in. "I already found my someone special. The problem is, I lost her. I've tried to date a few people in the last couple years, but none of them can hold a candle to her."

"So where the hell is she?"

"She moved away, and she's with someone else now."

"Well, shit."

"Exactly."

"What could you have done to lose her? You didn't cheat on her, did you?"

Blake sighed, not wanting to dredge up difficult memories. His patient waited for his answer. "It's a long story."

Mrs. Warski's grin confirmed that her primary ailment was loneliness. "Lucky for you, I have all night."

He pulled a chair up to sit beside her bed. "No, I didn't cheat, but I might as well have. What I did hurt her just as much."

"I doubt that. Mr. Warski, rest his soul, strayed once and it almost did us in. If I can forgive him, I'm sure your lady can forgive you for whatever you did."

"I doubt it. I didn't just screw up our relationship, but I also threw away my whole scholarship and career. I was supposed to be a doctor, but goofed around so much in college, I barely got my bachelor's degree. I had to wait for a couple of years until I got my head screwed on straight to go back to nursing school." Blake pushed down his anger at himself for messing up his chance to get into med school.

"It's not too late to go to medical school."

"Yeah, it is. I'm twenty-six."

"Young man, I went back to finish college when my youngest started school. I'd always dreamed of being a schoolteacher. I didn't realize my dream until I was thirty-seven years old with three kids and a husband. If you want to be a doctor, then stop whining and be a doctor. If you want to get your girl back, get on a plane, and go to her and pour your heart out."

"Just like that?" Blake chuckled, assuming she was joking. Her return stare told him she spoke the truth.

"Just like that. Life's short. Be bold. It's that simple."

Blake wanted to think she was only a crazy old lady, but in that moment, he felt a calmness he hadn't felt in a very long time.

Dr. Peterson pulled back the curtain to join them for his examination of his patient, breaking the moment. Mrs. Warski had given him a lot to think about.

Katie downed the last swig of stale coffee from the thermos she'd filled at a rest stop a few hours before. She never should have waited until the last day to drive to her old hometown for Christmas. It had been two years since she'd made the trip from Nashville to northwestern Illinois. She'd forgotten how long the trek took, especially with only one driver.

The wheezing sounds from the back seat of the car drew her concern. Her three-year-old daughter, Brittany, slept fitfully in her car seat. Katie was anxious to get to her dad's house in the next few hours.

Brittany's asthma attacks were not only becoming more frequent, but also more severe. Dealing with them at home where their pediatrician was only a few minutes away was scary enough. Fear gripped Katie at the thought of the most important person in her life needing medical assistance in the middle of the cornfields of Illinois. She'd routed around the Chicago metropolitan area to save time, but she regretted it now as her daughter's breathing became more constricted.

The sound of her cell phone jarred her back into a more alert state of mind. It was her mom's ring tone.

"Hi, Mom. No, I'm not there yet."

"I told you to leave a few hours earlier. It's almost midnight there. Is your father expecting you this late?"

Katie noticed the disdain in her mother's voice as she uttered the word *father*. "Yes, Mom. He knows we're going to arrive in the wee hours of the morning."

"He should have sent you a plane ticket. You shouldn't have to drive all this way on your own."

"I'm not alone. I have Britt with me, and anyway, the car is packed with gifts, remember?"

"I remember you spending more money than you should on gifts for people you rarely see."

Katie sighed. She loved her mom dearly, but hated how bitter she became any time Katie's father, was involved. Their divorce ten years earlier had not been amicable, and as their only daughter, Katie had been pulled back and forth like a tug of war ever since. She was grateful they had at least waited to divorce until she was in high school.

"Enough Dad bashing. It's Christmas Eve."

"Fine." Her mother's tone let Katie know she felt anything but fine about spending her own Christmas without her only daughter and granddaughter in Nashville with her and her new husband.

Katie debated telling her mom how worried she was about the three-year-old sleeping in the back seat, but decided since there was nothing her mom could do to help, it was pointless to worry her.

"Thanks for calling, Mom, but I should focus on driving. I'm only an hour outside of Englewood. Go to bed. I'll talk with you tomorrow."

"Okay, sweetheart. I love you."

"Love you more."

Brittany awoke to a bout of coughing as they passed the sign indicating Englewood was still 43 miles ahead. Katie had hoped they could wait until they arrived at her dad's to give her daughter a breathing treatment, but her symptoms were progressing faster than normal the colder it got.

Her eyes connected with her baby's in the rear view mirror. "Hi, honey. Sorry your cough woke you up."

"Are we almost there, Mommy?" Katie hated the breathy quality of her daughter's voice. She reached into her oversized black bag sitting in the passenger seat, feeling around for the rescue inhaler she never left home without. Of course it was lost in the sea of much less important junk she'd thrown in at the last minute before leaving home.

"We should be at Papa's in less than an hour. Can you hold on, and we'll do a breathing treatment when we get there?"

"Uh-huh." Brittany's left thumb had found its way into her mouth. They'd been working hard at breaking the nasty habit of sucking her thumb, but in that moment, Katie's concern for her daughter's health had a way of putting things into perspective.

Katie stepped on the gas pedal harder, willing her older car to hold it together to get them safely to her dad's. Brittany dozed fitfully for the next twenty miles, and Katie's tension started to recede as she recognized landmarks of where she'd grown up. A whole new kind of apprehension stirred as she passed locations that held painful memories of dreams unrealized.

She hadn't officially lived in Englewood since leaving for college eight years before, yet it still felt like home during her infrequent visits with her dad and his new wife. The irony of how different things had turned out from her well-laid plans never ceased to amaze Katie. Almost nothing in her life had gone according to the dreams she had when she'd left home as a freshman in college. Still, looking in her rear-view mirror, she knew she wouldn't change a thing if it meant not having Brittany in her life.

They had just passed an all-night gas station and diner when Brittany's coughing returned in earnest, and this time, there was no letting up. Katie threw on the interior lights of the sedan, recognizing even in the dim lighting her daughter's pale complexion and the slightest blue tint to her lips. She needed her rescue inhaler.

Katie pulled over to the side of the two-lane highway. She rummaged through her purse until she found the medicine her daughter needed. She rushed out of the driver's seat to open the back door and help her daughter inhale the sweet medicine. The inhaler took the edge off, but Brittany's breathing did not stabilize. There was no way she could give her a full-blown breathing treatment on the side of the road, because the nebulizer needed a charge.

The panic in her daughter's eyes made her decision for her. They needed help.

Katie rushed back behind the wheel, tearing out at the fastest speed her little car could carry them to medical help. She whispered a prayer of thanks it wasn't snowing. Her mind raced to decide where she was heading.

They were still two towns away from Englewood. She didn't remember there being any medical facilities in the town she was entering. She could drive to the fire or police station, but in such a small village, there was no guarantee anyone would be there. And since she wasn't familiar with this area, she made the decision to power through to the next town, Galena. She remembered that the town had a hospital. She couldn't remember if it had an emergency room, but surely there would be medical staff on duty who could help her.

She topped the speed out at eighty, her heart pounding with fear as she listened to her three-year-old daughter struggling for her next breath.

'Please God, watch over us tonight.'

Blake had just sat down in the break room to snack on Christmas cookies and a black coffee when his smartphone alarmed, indicating they'd admitted a new patient to the ER. He jumped up and started rushing back when the priority level of the message indicated it was a priority one emergency. *Life or death.* No one deserved that kind of an emergency on Christmas Eve.

He didn't take the time to stop at the admissions office. He proceeded directly to the examination room where Dr. Peterson was already examining a bundled up little girl. She appeared about three years old. The bluish tint of her lips combined with her gasps for air was alarming.

"Let's get her winter gear off." The men moved into action, working seamlessly. The child's coughing and wheezing confirmed the priority level of this emergency was indeed critical. Dr. Peterson began his initial examination, listening to breath sounds only seconds before calling out instructions.

"The mother told me she'd already tried her rescue inhaler. She has a history of asthma and allergies. It looks like she's encountered one of her triggers in the last few hours."

"Do we have a chart on her?" Blake asked, ready to pull up her medical history on the nearby computer.

"No, first time here. The mother is filling out a history now, but we won't be able to wait. Let's get her on oxygen and prep epinephrine."

"Sure thing." Blake gazed down into the frightened eyes of their young patient. He smiled, trying to comfort her. "Don't you worry about a thing, sweetheart. We're gonna get you all better so you can be home in time to open your presents from Santa in the morning. What's your name?"

"Her name is Brittany." The answer came from behind him, sending Blake into his own panic attack. *That voice.*

He swung around and less than three feet away stood the love of his life, the woman he never thought he'd see again. "Holy shit, Katie."

"Blake?" For the briefest of seconds, surprise replaced terror in her eyes, but the wheezing from the little girl in the bed next to them brought them both back to reality. Blake turned to re-devote his attention to not just any patient, but *Katie's* little girl.

She was a mom.

It took all of his self-discipline and training to keep his mind on the task at hand. Katie had moved to the side where she could watch the medical team work on her daughter, yet not interfere. The only time he risked a peek, he saw her focused solely on her daughter, tears streaming down her face. He longed to reach out, swish her tears away, and hold her, but he knew he couldn't.

Within a few tense minutes, the medicine began to work. While Brittany's breathing hadn't returned to normal yet, she was out of the woods. Dr. Peterson conducted a full exam, ordering up a complete blood workup before leaving to check on their other patients.

When Blake approached the dark haired beauty in the bed with a needle, her brown eyes widened with fear. Katie had stepped forward and was holding her daughter's hand. "It's okay, pumpkin. Let's let Dr. Harrigan take care of you." Her voice quavered with unchecked emotion.

Blake's heart lurched. How he wished he could let her comment stand. "Sorry, but not yet. It's Nurse Harrigan for now."

His patient didn't care. "I hate needles. They hurt." The wheezing was almost gone as she spoke.

"Maybe they hurt when others have used them on you, but I'm a pro at drawing blood. You won't feel more than a small pinch."

"Promise?"

"Promise." He patted her gently.

Blake concentrated on making the draw as painless as possible. When done, he grinned down at a smiling Brittany. "See?" He reached into the pocket of his scrubs and pulled out one of the sugar-free suckers he carried around for young patients.

"I like you." Brittany lit up with joy as she reached for the candy.

His heart contracted with an unexpected kick. "That's fantastic, because I like you, too. Can I ask you a favor?"

The now drowsy little girl nodded the affirmative while sliding her thumb into her mouth, saving the candy for later. "I need to talk with your mom. You wouldn't mind if I asked her to come out to the hall for a few minutes, would you?"

Brittany nodded, but Katie came to life. "We don't have anything to talk about, Blake, and I'm not leaving Britt alone."

They were close enough for him to reach out and touch her forearm lightly. It was innocent, yet the spark, which ignited as they touched for the first time in over four years, filled him with a plethora of unwanted emotions. The most prominent was regret.

"Please, Katie. Just a few minutes?"

When she turned her face to look up at him, a precarious vulnerability shone in her blue eyes. God, he'd missed those expressive eyes that acted like a mirror of her heart. He'd love to know if her trembles were a result of her daughter's severe attack or his proximity. He wished it were the latter.

He saw the doubt in her eyes as he gently stroked her forearm with his thumb, reminding her they were connected, even if in a tenuous way. When she didn't protest his touch, he allowed his hand to slide down to join Katie and her child's entwined fingers, linking the three of them briefly. He saw her surprised longing, but it was so brief he wondered if he'd imagined it when she yanked her hand away as if his touch burned her skin.

"How long until Brittany will be released?" She was pulling away, physically and emotionally.

"She needs to be observed for a couple hours, and it'll take some time to get results back from her blood workup." He never dreamed he'd ever have a chance to talk with Katie again, but now that she was here, he wasn't going to let the opportunity to finally apologize escape. The guilt he'd carried around for almost five years was heavy. Even if she was married with a family, it wasn't too late to at least clear the air between them. "Please step out into the hall—for a minute. I have something I need to say, and it's long overdue."

"You don't need to…"

He cut her off. "Yes, Kathryn, I do. I'm asking for one minute. I think after all we've been through, one minute isn't too much to ask."

"Fine." She sounded anything but fine. She leaned in to kiss the forehead of her now dozing daughter before leaving the room ahead of him. He watched the sway of her hips in her tight jeans, remembering how her round ass had felt in his hands as they'd made love. But that was before he'd thrown his life away. Tonight he'd have to settle for saying he was sorry.

Once in the hall, Blake placed his hand on her right elbow, steering them away from the nursing station and into a private consultation room. His touch was confident, as if he still had a claim on her body.

Katie's heart rate spiked as she realized they would be alone. She moved in, placing her back against the wall, subconsciously putting as much space between them as the cramped room would allow. She hugged her arms around her body nervously, at war with herself and the unexpected feelings seeing her ex-fiancé had dredged up.

His eyes sparked with welcoming warmth as he spoke. "Damn, I've missed you. I've thought of you every single day since you left, but still…. I'd forgotten how beautiful you are, Katie." He wasn't making this any easier.

She reached up to swipe at her face before self-consciously swishing her fingers through her long, messy sandy-blonde hair. Emotions bombarded her and she blurted out the first thing that came to her mind. "I see you're still lying to me. I look like shit."

She'd tried to make her words light, but he visibly flinched as her words cut him. "I deserved that. I'm so very sorry about my lies back then, Kathryn. I don't know if it will make you feel better or not, but for what it's worth, I was lying to myself too."

Katie eyed him suspiciously. "You seem different, Blake."

His bitter laughter filled the small space. "Yeah, well, thank God for that."

She asked the question that was hanging between them. "So, you got help?" Memories from the darkest time of her life invaded. As hard as it was to open up old wounds, she desperately wanted to know why Blake had thrown their relationship away on alcohol.

"It was the one and only good thing that came from you leaving me after you graduated. Losing you was the wake-up call that finally got through to me when nothing else had. I spent a month in an alcoholic stupor before I eventually checked myself into a rehab center. I spent thirty days there the first time, and when I relapsed soon after being discharged, I spent sixty days at a second hospital." His gaze bore into her as she listened to him intently. "I haven't had a drop of alcohol in four years, three months, and twelve days."

She didn't know what to say, but he filled the awkward silence. "I'd fucked up my grades enough that it took me another year to graduate. Even though my MCATs were excellent, I couldn't get accepted into any med schools, so I decided to get my nursing degree. At least I'm working in medicine like I'd planned, and I hope to get into med school at some point in the future."

His words shocked her. All this time she'd pictured Blake in a drunken stupor, as he'd been their entire senior year at the University of Wisconsin. "That's great, Blake. All this time...well, the last time I saw you...I wasn't sure if you were even still alive or not."

"Truthfully, I confess the last few months before you left are a blur."

He really did look sorry, but those dark days weren't easy for Katie to forget. "I'm glad you're better, but unfortunately, I *do* remember every single minute of those horrible last few months."

"I'd give anything to go back and make things better, Katie. My drinking screwed up almost every part of my life. I have to live with my regret every single day." He took a deep breath before continuing. "Losing you is what I regret the most. You have to know how much I loved you. Knowing that I hurt you and threw away our future together guts me. Seeing you here tonight with your daughter...knowing you found someone else and got married. I sure hope he treats you as well as you deserve." His voice trailed off as if he were struggling to control his emotions.

She wasn't prepared to deal with the emotional upheaval of unexpectedly seeing Blake. She'd already been on the edge with Brittany's asthma attack, and now this. Her pulse pounded in her ears, making it hard to concentrate.

"Katie? What is it?" Blake's concern seemed genuine.

She needed space to think. The room closed in on her as she tried to bring the conversation to an abrupt end. "Nothing. Your minute is up. You apologized. I accept your apology. I need to get back to Brittany."

Unfortunately, he stood between her and the door, and the firm set of his jaw told her he had no intention of letting her escape. Blake took a step closer...and another...until they were only inches apart. Katie took a sudden interest in the front of his blue scrubs, refusing to look him in the eye. His finger moved to her chin, tipping her face up to meet his gaze. She felt so damn vulnerable as Blake probed deeper. "Where is Brittany's dad? Why isn't he here with you?"

Panicking, she tried to move away, but he countered by cupping her face in both his palms. He swished at the stray tear streaming down her cheek as she replied, "He left us. We're alone, but we don't need him anyway."

The fury in his eyes alarmed her. "What kind of a moron would leave you and a beautiful little girl like Brittany?"

He had triggered her defenses. "I guess the same kind of idiot who would regularly drink himself into a blackout despite his fiancé's begging him to stop. Lucky me, I keep surrounding myself with guys who love to treat me like shit." She hated feeling so vulnerable. They may have been apart for over four years, but Blake still elicited passion when he was near.

She should have been angry at the glee she saw as he probed, "Wait...so you're single?"

Why did it feel like a trick question? "Yes, Blake, and I've decided I like it that way." The lie fell easily from her lips. She should have left it there, but the next question popped out of its own accord. "How about you?"

"I've dated a couple of women, but not more than a few times before I knew it wasn't going to work out."

"Maybe you were just being too picky."

"Oh, I know I was being too picky. I dumped them when I realized the only person I wanted was you, Kathryn."

Things were moving way too fast. Katie was a planner, an organizer. She needed time to think, yet their bodies were acting as if they were part of a magnetic force, pulling them closer together until Blake closed the last inch between them.

The moment moved in slow motion. The back of her head pressed against the unforgiving wall as his lips lowered, capturing her in a tender kiss full of promise. Blake's left hand strayed to cup her rounded ass through her jeans as his body trapped her against the far wall of the private room. His growing erection sparked a hunger in her she had thought was dead long ago.

Her body hijacked her mind. Resistance seemed futile when her body crumbled into submission, her arms lifting around his neck to run her hands though the thick hair she'd missed. Blake swept his tongue in to tangle with her own as Katie lifted her left leg to wrap it around his thigh, holding him close.

The sexual groan erupting from the man she had never stopped loving had her melting in his arms. The feel of his large hand massaging her clothed breast combined with the feel of his rock-hard cock pressing through his scrubs. In that moment, she wanted nothing more than to have him inside her where he belonged. Her pulse pounded in her ears as their sexual chemistry ignited a fire she'd thought was doused long ago.

The ringing of an alarm on Blake's phone jarred her out of the intimate moment, returning her to an abrupt reality.

"Damn." He stopped their kiss, but remained close, pressing his forehead against hers as they both gasped to regain their breath. He eventually pulled his phone from his pocket to read the message. "We had another patient come in. I need to go back to work, but mark my words...we aren't done here, Katie. We should be ready to release Brittany around the time I get off work. I'd like to spend the day with you tomorrow."

"I can't, Blake." She tried to push him away, hoping to regain control. He wouldn't budge. "This is moving too fast, and anyway, it's Christmas Day. I need to spend time with my dad, and you need to be with your mom."

She knew there was bad news before he spoke. "Mom died about a month ago, after a long battle with breast cancer."

She could see his pain as he broke the news to her.

"Oh, Blake, I'm so sorry to hear that. I know how close you were."

"Yeah, we were. It's why I took the job back here in Galena so I could be near her and help care for her at the end."

A sense of relief washed over her. That was just like something the Blake she had known before alcohol had consumed him would do. "I'm sure it meant a lot to her to have you home."

Another text alerted on his phone. She missed his warmth as he finally put some space between them. "Come on. I'll walk you back to Brittany's room. Promise me, though, you won't leave."

He pinned her with an expectant stare until she whispered what he wanted to hear. "I promise."

This time he wrapped his arm around her waist possessively, pulling her close as they strolled back. She'd dreamed of Blake so much since she'd left him over four years before. It would be so easy to fall back into love with him, but her brain knew she no longer had the luxury of letting her heart rule. She needed to think things through, to make a plan. She wouldn't be able to do that with Blake so near, distracting her with memories of their past.

Ninety minutes later, Blake pulled the curtain back, already suspecting he'd find Brittany's bed empty. Even as she'd promised she wouldn't leave, he'd seen the indecision in Katie's eyes.

Common sense told him he wouldn't be able to erase the pain he'd caused her with a simple apology, yet he was filled with real hope for the first time in a long time. If he were honest with himself, a part of his decision to move back to his hometown of Galena was so he might have a sliver of a chance of running into Katie again one day. She'd grown up only one town away in Englewood. Even in his wildest dreams, Blake hadn't allowed himself to consider winning her back. He'd told himself he would settle for just being able to apologize and clear the air.

But now that he knew she was single and raising a daughter on her own, he dared let a kernel of hope into his heart that he might have a chance to win her back after all. They had been so perfect together before he'd screwed things up. His body tingled with the kind of excitement only Katie had ever been able to ignite.

He was cleaning up Brittany's exam room, prepping it for the next patient, when he picked up her chart from the end of the bed and examined it closely for the first time. Last Name: Conrad. So she hadn't married Brittany's dad. Home Address: an apartment in Nashville. Emergency Contact: Katie's mother, also in Nashville. Health History: severe allergies and juvenile asthma. Poor kid. Date of Birth: December 31st, 2011.

Wait. That had to be a mistake. Brittany couldn't have been born in 2011. That was the year...

A pain feeling akin to a heart attack squeezed his heart as his mind raced to piece together the implications of the adorable little girl who would turn four in one week. That would put her conception date in April of that same year—one month before he and Katie were to graduate. One month before Katie gave him the ultimatum of entering rehab or losing her. She had packed her junky old car with all of her belongings while he watched, still buzzed from the night before. When he failed to seek help, she had driven away from him the day after she graduated, never to be seen again.

Had she been unfaithful to him even before she left him? That one was easy to answer. Impossible.

That left an even scarier conclusion. He examined the evidence as objectively as he could. Kathryn and both of her parents were blondes with blue eyes. Brittany's hair was almost black, and her eyes were a deep chocolate brown. She clearly got her coloring from her father's side of the family.

Blake sought out his reflection in the framed mirror of the examination room. He took in his black hair and brown eyes.

No. Katie wouldn't do that to him. She wouldn't cut him out of his own daughter's life without even knowing she existed.

Even as he thought it, he knew it was the truth. A fury bubbled from deep within. Anger at the lost years. A bitter chuckle erupted when he realized she had gotten the last laugh after all. All these years he had felt a crushing guilt for the lies he had told and the pain he had caused, when she had perpetrated the biggest lie of them all.

His brain tried to reason she had only been trying to protect their daughter from his then growing addiction as he'd buckled under to the pressures of college. But the argument fell flat. She hadn't even tried to contact him with the news. She hadn't even given him a fighting chance at cleaning himself up before deserting him.

"Fuck." The expletive hung in the air, not directed at anyone or anything in particular.

"Such language, Mr. Harrigan." He glanced up to see Mrs. Warski in a wheelchair in the doorway to the examination room. She cracked a smile, but he couldn't reciprocate. "Why don't you tell me what has you so upset?"

"Did you happen to see how long ago the mother and daughter who were in this room left?"

"Yes, I'd say only about ten minutes ago or so. She looked lovely, but if I'm not mistaken, she was crying. I hope there was nothing terribly wrong with the adorable little girl."

Ten minutes. He suspected where she was headed. Could he beat her there or would she hightail it back to Nashville now, suspecting he would put together the truth?

Mrs. Warski's voice cut through his thoughts. "Blake?"

He wasn't sure why the truth spilled out of his mouth in that moment. Maybe it was because his own mom was gone and he was looking for advice from the life-wise elderly patient he'd learned to care for. "I think the little girl is my daughter. Her mother and I dated for four years before breaking up. She left, never telling me I was going to be a father. How could she do that?" He hated how his voice cracked with vulnerable emotion. Anger boiled inside him as he thought of all he'd missed and how unfair it was.

The elderly woman smiled a knowing smile. "So she's the one you lost? You have marvelous taste."

"Didn't you hear what I said? *She lied to me*! She kept the fact I was a father hidden from me." His voice rose with his frustration.

"I heard you," Mrs. Warski calmly replied. "I also heard you say earlier that you'd screwed up and hurt the one woman you had loved. Sounds to me like you two are even. Now what are you going to do about it?"

He worked hard to push down his defensive reflexes at her nonchalant dismissal of Katie's betrayal, but that only made him feel more defeated. "She clearly didn't want me in their lives, so I'm not going to do a damn thing about it."

"That's total crap! Just because she made a huge mistake doesn't mean you need to repeat it. You need to get your ass in your truck and go after her. Remember…life's short. Be bold."

Despite his anger at Katie, he couldn't help but smile at Mrs. Warski. "You really do have a potty mouth, don't you?" When she grinned back, he felt his defenses weakening. "I couldn't even go after her if I wanted to, which I'm not sure I do. I'm not off duty yet."

As if on cue, the day shift nurse sauntered in, carrying a Christmas coffee cake. "Hey, there you are, Blake. I heard you had a busy enough night. I'm here to relieve you."

Mrs. Warski's grin grew. "Looks like you're out of excuses now, young man."

The sun peaked on the horizon as she left the hospital. Katie had to force herself to focus on where she was going. Englewood wasn't very large, but she had already gotten lost twice trying to find her dad and step-mom's new house in the brand new subdivision along the golf course just outside of town. The houses on the winding streets all looked alike. Since her cell phone was dead, she couldn't depend on her GPS to help her locate the right street. She was in desperate need of a hot shower, a good night's sleep, and a stiff drink, and not particularly in that order.

She eventually found Eagle Lane and wound along until she located her dad's address. She pulled into the driveway next to her grandma's car. Of course Nana would already be there to help prepare their traditional

Christmas morning breakfast.

She sat silently behind the wheel after turning off the engine. She still needed time to think about all she'd learned from Blake.

Had her father known Blake was single and back in the area when he'd pressured her to come home for Christmas? Even if he had, there was no way her dad could have caused Brittany's asthma attack. Still, Dad had been very vocal about his disagreement on how Katie had handled her breakup with Blake and subsequent move to Nashville. She knew she couldn't mention seeing Blake until she had a chance to figure out how she felt about it all, and that wouldn't come until later in the day when she might have a few minutes to herself.

"Mommy, why are we sitting in the car?"

Sweet relief that Brittany's asthma attack was completely over filled her with joy. "I needed a minute before we go inside. You ready to go see Papa?"

"Yes! I wanna see if Santa brought my gifts here. You promised he would find me."

"Yes, I did promise that. I'm sure he knew where to deliver all of our presents."

Katie got out, opened the back door to unbuckle her daughter from the car seat, and cradled her on her hip before grabbing her bag of goodies.

Only after closing the car door did she notice Blake standing across the street, his arms crossed across his chest, watching her carefully as he leaned back against his black pick-up truck. She didn't know exactly how, but even from the distance, she felt his accusing eyes boring into her.

She immediately knew he'd figured it out.

They both stood frozen until Brittany called out to him. "Dr. Blake! Dr. Blake!" The smile that broke out on his face gutted her. Even across the street, she could see the love in his eyes as he gazed at his daughter in awe. How was she supposed to resist him if he wasn't going to fight fair?

Katie's heart raced as he moved into motion. Brittany called out to him again as he stalked across the street, taking determined steps towards them. "Yippy! You can have Christmas with us."

"Brittany, don't be silly. He's not staying."

"Yes, I am."

"You're not invited."

"The hell he's not." It was her dad's voice from behind her.

"Papa!" Brittany was wiggling to get down from Katie's arms.

Her father, John, arrived next to Katie, reaching out to grab his granddaughter from her arms before leaning in to place a kiss on his daughter's cheek. She looked up to see him grinning. "Hello there, sweetheart."

"Stop gloating, Dad," she whispered under her breath, hoping to keep Blake from hearing her.

"I'm not gloating. I'm just happy to see my Christmas wish coming true," he whispered back.

Her father offered his hand to Blake. "Welcome back, Blake." The two men shook hands in what appeared to Katie to be a conspiratorial way.

"He's not back, Dad."

"Right. Well, he looks back to me. I can see you two kids have a few things to talk about, so I'm gonna take this adorable granddaughter of mine in the house and get her settled in. Grandma is putting the Christmas casserole into the oven now, and your aunts, uncles and cousins will be arriving soon. You two mosey on in once you get my lovely daughter here straightened out."

"Yes, sir. See you then."

Of course Blake would agree with her father.

The sweet sound of Brittany's giggles as her papa tickled her filled the air, reminding Katie of what was really important.

Blake took a step closer, slowly closing the last distance between them. His eyes were so intense that her heart raced. She couldn't figure out if he wanted to yell at her or kiss her again. She wasn't crazy about either option.

"You left without saying goodbye," he accused evenly.

She took a step backwards, trying to keep some distance between them so she could think. "I figured it would be easier that way."

"Easier for who? Certainly not for me. As you can see, not for Brittany either." He took another step closer. She countered and found her back

182

against her car.

"Fine, easier for me then. You confuse me, Blake." Her voice quavered.

He took another step closer as he pressed her for answers. "Funny. I've never been less confused. I've regretted losing you every day since you left. I've worked my ass off to turn my life around, Katie, so I could be the kind of man you wanted. I've been buried in guilt for how I'd thrown away what we had, and now I find out you've been lying to me all these years." His voice rose with each step forward.

He closed the last few feet between them, grabbing both her biceps in his tight grip. He was a full foot taller than her, and she suddenly felt small as pained anger filled his eyes. "How could you, Katie?" he accused.

She was glad he'd chosen to argue. That she could do. "How could *I*? How could *you*? We were together for four years. We were supposed to get married and spend the rest of our lives together, and then you had to go off the rails and ruin it all. I begged you to stop drinking, Blake. All you did was party. You were throwing away our entire future."

"Why the hell didn't you tell me about Brittany before now? Four years wasted. Don't you think I deserved to know I was going to be a father?" His voice cracked with emotion.

"I tried to tell you. I took the pregnancy test the day before graduation. I wasn't crazy about being pregnant so young, but I was so sure once you knew you were going to be a father you'd clean yourself up. I went straight over to your apartment and used my key to get in. It was almost noon, but you were still in bed. I made you a hot cup of coffee and took it in and was going to have a heart to heart with you about how you needed to stop drinking, but…."

"But what?" He looked confused, as if he was trying to remember that day so long ago.

"But I hadn't made enough coffee's for everyone. I found you curled up in bed with your roommates, Tommy and Jackie. She was naked, and there were empty bottles and cans all around. I stood there for at least thirty minutes, trying to figure out what to do. I cried and prayed, but you were so passed out you didn't even wake up. In the end, I put the coffee on the bed stand and left. The next day I gave you the ultimatum—the drinking or me. You chose drinking. So I left."

She watched him trying to sort out his memories of that day, which had changed their lives forever.

"Christ, I'm so sorry, baby. I'd give anything to go back to that time in my life and hit myself upside the head. I remember waking up and finding the coffee that day. I remember thinking I'd hit rock bottom, but I was wrong. That didn't come until after I discovered you'd really left me."

They stood grounded to their spots. A picture of her, Blake, and Brittany living happily ever after flashed before her, but she pushed it away. Instead, Katie tried to hold on to her righteous anger. She couldn't let Blake close enough to hurt her and Brittany again. She forced herself to remember that last year in college, reminding herself why she'd made the decision she had.

"I wish things had turned out differently, Blake. I really do. But I won't regret leaving you to raise Brittany away from all of that. She didn't deserve to see her father as I saw you that last year. You were broken, and nothing I said or did seemed to matter. I couldn't let her grow up in that kind of environment. I couldn't." She felt her voice crack. She'd kept so much bottled up for so long.

"I've cleaned up my act and I'm ready now, Katie. You can't shut me out of her life any more. I deserve to be in her life."

"You deserve? What makes you think you deserve anything?" Her voice grew louder.

"Listen, I made mistakes, but I've paid for them. I've worked hard to put my addiction behind me."

"That's great, Blake. It really is, but for how long? You've made promises before."

"I don't blame you for doubting me, but this time is different. It's different because I'm sober as I promised. More importantly, I've been sober for years. I got the help I needed. I deserve to be in her life.

The way he declared it made her think Brittany was the only reason he was pushing her. The thought of that left her feeling empty. She took several deep breaths, thinking over her options before answering dejectedly,

"Fine. We'll have to discuss visitation, but it's going to be hard since I live in Nashville now."

"Dammit, Katie! I don't want visitation like some deadbeat dad. I want to be part of her life. I want to be part of *your* life. I fucked it up before, but I'm not going to fuck it up again. We belong together…as a family. I'm not going to just ride off into the sunset, ignoring the fact that I have a daughter with the only woman I've ever loved."

He sounded so sure that Katie dared to let in a glimmer of hope. Could they really be a family?

Blake obviously decided they'd talked enough. It was as if he figured that if he couldn't convince her how he felt with words, he would use his body. He captured her lips in a passionate kiss. He didn't stop until she felt her knees weak beneath her, her body melting against him.

The sound of closing car doors nearby finally pulled them apart. Blake stared into her eyes, a grin on his face as her Uncle Jim called out to them. "Whoa, is that Blake Harrigan? About time you came home, young man."

Her Aunt Jane's voice was next. "Terrific to see you, Blake. I saw the announcement in the paper about your mom. So sorry."

A couple of her younger cousins all passed by on the way into the house, excited to be opening more presents soon. "Hello, Blake! I call dibs on the X-Box. You always used to hog it."

Her Aunt Shari was the last one to comment. She stopped to hug Katie and Blake to her. "So glad to see you two together again. Now, help me carry in this pan of bacon."

When they were finally alone again, Katie sent him an annoyed smirk. "Well, it looks like everyone but me thinks we're back together again."

"Yep. So what's it going to be?"

A peace she hadn't felt in a long time descended on her heart. Still, she couldn't just push aside the horrible memories that fast. She decided on an olive branch. "It's Christmas, Blake. As angry as I was back then, I don't want you to be alone today." When he got a victorious grin on his face, she warned him. "Don't mistake this for something it's not. I'm proposing a truce for the holiday and then we'll talk more about it later."

"Thank you, Katie. You won't regret it."

She hoped she didn't regret it, too. "Let's go inside. I'm starving."

Blake could hardly believe he was sitting in the middle of the open great room filled with people he had once thought of as family. He had to pinch himself at how fast his life had changed for the better. He hoped his mom was looking down from heaven, relieved he wasn't alone.

He was a smart enough man to know he and Katie had a lot to talk about before they were home free. But he also knew they had loved each other very much. They'd created a beautiful, precocious daughter together. Katie hadn't thrown him out on his ass yet.

It was a start.

He glanced up in time to see a freshly showered Katie and Brittany descending the stairs. His heart lurched with love when Katie sought him out in the crowd, smiling shyly. He grinned back before turning his attention to his daughter.

He was a father. He had a daughter. Unfuckingbelievable.

Grandma Conrad broke his concentration when she leaned in to set a yummy smelling casserole on the trivet in front of him. "I'm so glad you're back in the fold, Blake. Our Katie hasn't been the same since you two broke up."

"Hello, Grandma Conrad. In fairness, I haven't been the same either."

"Well, you're here now and that's all that matters."

"I wouldn't miss it for the world. I've missed your Christmas casserole."

"Dr. Blake! Can I sit on your lap?"

You'd never know Brittany had just had a life threatening asthma attack a few hours before. "Of course, but only if your mommy says it's okay." He glanced up at Katie and saw her relief that he hadn't just assumed it would be all right.

"Can I please, mommy? Can I sit on Dr. Blake's lap?"

"Sure, as long as you keep eating. But if you don't eat, then we'll have to get the booster chair."

Katie slid in next to him. The chairs were squished in tight to make room for everyone, which suited Blake fine.

Katie kissed her grandma. "It smells yummy, Grandma. What's in the casserole again?"

"Just eggs, sausage, bread, cheese, and milk. It's easy when you need to serve such a large family in one meal, especially when everyone under the age of twenty only wants to finish eating so they can start opening gifts." She chuckled.

Breakfast was a fun affair, made even better by having a tired Brittany snuggled in his lap sucking her thumb. It still hadn't sunk in that he was a father. He wanted to be angry with Katie for hiding the truth from him, but he couldn't stay mad. He suspected they still had some tense arguments ahead as they sorted through all that had happened, but that could come later. Today was Christmas, and everyone knew miracles could happen on Christmas.

He slid his right hand under the table to grip Katie's thigh, linking them together. The fire in her eyes as she glanced his way assured him she was as affected by their proximity as he was. As much fun as he was having with her family, holding their precious little girl, he couldn't wait to get Katie alone. They had a lot of time to make up for.

An hour later the dishes had been cleared and the tables picked up to make room for the gift exchange. The extended family party measured over twenty-five people in all, so the scene was rowdy. Blake steered Katie and a sleeping Brittany to a love seat near the fireplace where they could collapse, exhausted from being up all night with the stress of the medical emergency.

As the young kids passed out the pile of presents from under the tree, Aunt Shari announced, "I'm so sorry, Blake. If I'd known you were going to be here, I'd have brought you a gift."

Brittany sighed in her sleep, snuggling in closer as she sucked her thumb. Katie smiled shyly at him, looking as if she were thinking of a time when they might be alone as well. Blake grinned, answering Katie's aunt truthfully. "No worries. I already got the best gift I could ever ask for." And he meant it. Surely God had a hand in helping them find their way back to each other even after all of the lies they'd both held secret all of these years.

He didn't care who was watching. Blake pulled Katie in close for a steamy kiss full of promise. The room erupted in hoots and hollers.

Hours later, Katie woke from her nap with her still sleeping daughter snuggled in her arms. The sun had gone down while they'd slept, leaving the room in shadows cast from the dim lamp on the dresser across the room. She took a deep, cleansing breath, relieved to have a few minutes alone to sift through the events of the last twelve hours.

After being up all night, she just couldn't keep her eyes open after the gifts were opened and the family party had wound down. She'd been relieved when her dad suggested his girls go upstairs to lie down for a nap.

She'd tried to say her good-byes to Blake as she'd faded with exhaustion, but her father had once again intervened, offering up their second guest room for Blake to nap, too.

Just knowing her ex-fiancé was one room away had her pulse racing. He'd always had that effect on her. Walking away from him years before had been the hardest thing she'd ever done. Her thoughts drifted, remembering how her dad had been the most vocal of her parents when she'd made the decision to withhold Brittany's existence from Blake. She'd assumed, as a father himself, her dad could better empathize with Blake's position.

Until today, she had never waivered on her decision to raise her daughter as a single mother. Several times over the years her dad had urged her to reach out to Blake, but she'd resisted, certain she couldn't take the heartbreak of seeing the man she loved deteriorate into a drunken bum—or worse. His own father had died of an alcohol related illness while Blake was in high school, and Katie had listened to his stories of the heartache being the child of an alcoholic. All this time, she'd rationalized she was protecting Brittany in a way Blake had wished his own mother had protected him as a child. To realize he'd been sober the entirety of Brittany's life filled her with guilt and regret.

Dad was right. I should have given him a chance.

Would Blake ever forgive her? Even as she thought it, she rebelled against her guilt. She'd given him so many chances that last year together. He'd made dozens of promises he'd never been able to keep. She'd made the right decision at the time. She was certain of it.

So why did the guilt still blanket her like a heavy quilt?

"I know you're awake." Blake's husky voice emerging from the shadowed corner scared the bejesus out of her. Brittany jerked in her sleep as Katie jumped with surprise.

She extricated herself carefully from her daughter's sleepy grasp to lift her head and peer into the dimness of the room. Her breath caught at the sight of Blake reclined in the cushioned chair, his feet on the ottoman looking at her with an intensity that took her breath away. She'd forgotten how handsome he was with his strong jawline, thick black hair, and dark eyes that could devour her. The day's growth of facial hair gave him a scruffy ruggedness that made her long to reach out and touch him.

"What are you doing in here?"

He didn't answer immediately. She saw him open his mouth to speak several times, struggling for his words. "I've missed too damn much. I couldn't be this close and miss watching you two sleeping."

She may not be able to see his eyes, but the anger rang through his words loud and clear. He'd apologized to her at the hospital. She knew it was her turn. Having him across the room, blanketed in darkness, helped.

"I'm sorry, Blake. I mean…I'm not sorry I left. That was the right decision. But…" Her voice trailed off. He let the awkward silence fill the air until she choked out her next words. "But it was wrong of me not to reach out to you after Brittany was born. I should have at least given you a chance to know you were a father."

She didn't expect absolution, but she wasn't prepared for his deep anger. "You think? It's not like you forgot to tell me you'd taken some of my CD's when you left, or planned on keeping the engagement ring that represented our love for each other. No. You fucking left not telling me you had my child growing inside your body." She could make out his chest heaving with emotion before he spat out, "How could you live with yourself, Katie?"

His accusation helped push down her guilt, shoring up the defensive wall she'd worked hard to construct over the years. She detangled herself from Brittany's limbs and pushed herself to her feet, closing in on Blake. He was on his feet in a heartbeat, each moving towards the other, each stopping just short of touching when they met in the middle of the room.

She could see his eyes clearly now and what she found wasn't anger, but fear. It stopped her short, confusing her. They stood in silence, drinking each other in. He looked so vulnerable.

Blake finally broke the standoff, speaking quietly. "We lost so much time, Katie."

"Blake." Her whisper was a plea, for what she wasn't sure. She just knew she couldn't think straight with him so near.

When he brought his right hand up to cup her cheek, her tense body began to relax. She felt him inching closer, closing the gap between them, never taking his eyes from her.

"I hate what you did, Katie, but I understand it. I'm at fault here, too. I should have found you after I got clean. I just thought you'd moved on, and it wasn't fair to interrupt your life. I know now that was a mistake." His anger had dissolved, leaving a melancholy sadness.

Should she tell him? Would it make him feel better or worse?

She felt the tears threatening as her words spilled out. "I used to look for you everywhere I went. It was crazy really, since I was hundreds of miles away from you. But still…in stores…restaurants…in cars in traffic. I had dreams that you tracked us down and demanded to be part of our lives." She let the tears fall freely, unable to stop them as she felt her defensive wall crumbling.

"Oh, baby. Come here." He pulled her into his arms, enveloping her until she felt like she was finally home. Relieved sobs erupted as Katie allowed herself to acknowledge how right it felt to be in this man's embrace again.

Several long minutes passed as they clung to each other, silently working to sew their fragile relationship back together. Katie snuggled against his chest, her ear pressed above his heart, beating strong and true. It brought a calmness she hadn't felt in a very long time.

It was when she felt the strain of his growing erection sandwiched between them that the atmosphere began to change. She felt her body sway against Blake, trying to get even closer while knowing they'd have to lose their clothes in order to make that happen.

Blake whispered against her ear, "God, I've missed you so much, baby."

Katie shuddered in his arms. How easy it would be to let him whisk her off her feet. But they still had so many things to talk about before they could get their happily ever after.

"Blake."

"Kathryn."

She took a deep breath, refusing to look him in the eye as she addressed the elephant in the room. "I've built a life in Nashville. My job is there. Our apartment. My mom babysits Britt."

Blake surprised her by stooping down to whisk her off her feet—literally—scooping her into his arms and returning to the chair in the corner of the room. He plopped down, sitting Katie in his lap, holding her close, their faces only inches apart. He looked so serious.

"Are you listening to me, Katie?"

The intensity in his eyes scared her. Her whimpered "yes" was barely audible.

"I don't care if you and Brittany live on the moon. You just try to get away from me again."

"But…your job…"

She didn't get the sentence finished before he injected, "I'm a nurse. Last time I checked, they need nurses everywhere." His lips formed a small smile as he continued, "Next objection?"

"You own the house in Galena."

"Which is completely paid for and I can rent out. Next?"

"You need to go back to school to be a doctor. It's always been your dream."

That one made him pause for a few seconds. "I do want to become a doctor, Katie, but if it doesn't happen, I'll survive. What I can't fathom, baby, is not being part of your and Brittany's life. You got any other concerns I can help with?"

The electricity between them should have been reassurance enough, but she felt so vulnerable as she allowed hope to spark. Losing Blake had been one of the hardest things she'd ever had to live through. She wasn't sure she could survive losing him again.

There was one final question she needed to ask, but she was afraid she might not like the answer. Blake waited patiently; his roaming hand caressing her lower back through her thin oversized T-shirt. When his other hand began to caress her bare thigh, she was almost distracted enough to forget the question. Almost.

"What exactly...I mean...what do you mean, be part of our lives?"

His sexy grin would have knocked her on her ass if she'd been standing. God, how had she ever walked away from him?

"First thing tomorrow morning when the stores open, we're going to the jewelry store and I'm going to buy you the most amazing engagement ring. The last time we did this, I was a broke college student, and I could hardly afford a small chip of a diamond. The sooner I can walk you down that aisle and make you Mrs. Blake Harrigan, the better I'll feel. Please, baby. Tell me you want that too?"

Katie's heart thumped in her chest. So many nights she had cried herself to sleep wishing things had been different and missing the Blake she had fallen in love with. The fact he was holding her close, asking her to marry him, was a dream come true. They would finally be the family they were meant to be.

She couldn't contain her mischievous smile. "I don't think we should go to the jewelry store."

Blake's face fell with dejected disappointment. She reached out to cup his face in her hands, caressing him lovingly before moving to pull her gold necklace free from under her T-shirt. Blake's eyes followed hers to look down at their engagement ring from many years before. When he glanced up, she saw tears threatening to spill down his cheek.

"You kept it?"

"Of course I did. It's been next to my heart every single day we've been apart. I thought it was all I'd ever have left of the man I loved."

With shaking hands, Blake reached out to unclasp the necklace, freeing the engagement ring with the small chip of a diamond. He took her left hand in his and slipped the ring on her finger. "Finally, back where it belongs."

Blake moved in to capture her lips in a tender kiss, full of promises she knew he was going to be able to keep this time. Katie's heart soared, unsure she could ever be as happy as she was in that moment.

"Mommy, why are you kissing Dr. Blake?" Their daughter's sleepy voice jarred them out of their passionate reunion. Katie caught Blake's eyes as they separated, and saw only love shining there.

Without taking her eyes from her future husband, she called out to her daughter. "Come here, baby girl. Mommy has something important to tell you."

Brittany slid from the bed and toddled over to the couple. Blake's eyes sought out his daughter, and when she approached, he reached out to lift her into his lap with Katie. The girls snuggled into Blake's arms for their first family hug.

It was hard to find the right words. "Remember when you asked me why you didn't have a daddy like all of your friends?"

"Uh-huh." Her sleepy answer slipped out around the thumb in her mouth.

"Well, what if I told you Dr. Blake and Mommy have known each other for a very long time and that he is your daddy?"

Brittany's eyes sparked with excitement. She even removed her thumb to answer, "Really? Dr. Blake can be my daddy?"

Blake answered her. "Nothing would make me happier. How would you like it if I moved down to Nashville to live with you and your mommy?"

Katie was confused by the alarmed look on Brittany's face until her daughter shared her concern. "You aren't going to bring your needles with you, are you?"

Blake pulled them closer as he chuckled. "I promise. No needles. But"—he grinned down at his daughter—"I plan on bringing all of my tickles with me."

The joyful sound of Brittany giggling as Blake tickled her was music to Katie's ears. She couldn't believe they were finally a family, and just in time for Christmas.

Grandma's Christmas Casserole
(AKA Breakfast Casserole)

One pound of ground pork sausage

1/2 teaspoon salt

1/4 teaspoon pepper

6 eggs, beaten

2 cups milk

8 slices white bread, toasted and cut into cubes

8 ounces mild cheddar cheese, shredded

Crumble sausage in skillet and brown over medium heat; drain and set aside

In medium bowl, mix together eggs, milk, salt, pepper

Blend in cubed, toasted bread and shredded cheese - mix well to coat evenly

Pour into greased 9X13 inch baking dish.

Cover and chill in refrigerator for eight hours or overnight.

Preheat oven to 350 degrees F

Cover and bake 45 — 60 minutes.

Uncover and lower heat to 325 degrees F - bake an additional 30 minutes or until set.

Cut and serve.

Christmas Comes Early
by Sherrill Lee

Sherrill Lee is a former teacher, an early childhood specialist and married to her own real life romance hero. Their six terrific kids have provided them with four wonderful grandchildren. Sewing and cooking are among her favorite activities. She is proud to be a member of Windy City RWA, the best writing chapter ever! Her keyboard exclamation point gets far too much use, but she is working on curbing that tendency. Always a voracious reader, she now puts her love of reading into her own stories. Now she is proud to be a contributor to the anthology, A LOVELY MEAL, honoring the late, bestselling author Cathie Linz, who was a dear friend as well as chapter mentor.

Meg pulled on her winter coat and searched the hall closet for her scarf and gloves before picking up the leash. The weatherman predicted an early snow this November, and for once, he was right on target. Her pup, Koko, a rescue dog of unknown origin, had suspiciously large paws and a thick, chocolate-colored furry coat. She shouldn't mind the snow, but this would be the puppy's first time in it. Koko danced around, nearly tripping Meg while she tried to attach the leash.

"Down, Koko, down!" Her eagerness to go out was contagious. "Yes, girl, come on, that's a good dog." Meg maneuvered the big puppy out the door without tripping, which she considered a success. Beyond the sheltered porch the snow was already two inches deep, thick and fluffy, with big flakes softly drifting down. Koko bounded down a few steps before she noticed the snow. When she did, Meg had to smile while she watched the dog touch her paw to the snow and lift it, peering at the paw print left before tasting the white stuff.

A deep, masculine voice startled Meg. "She's a smart dog. Look how carefully she's testing the snow. First she touched it, now she's tasting it."

Acting like she knew she was the topic of conversation, Koko looked first at Meg as if asking for permission, then at the tall man in the camel coat standing on the sidewalk. Her bushy tail began to whip back and forth, clearing the snow from the step. She put her nose in the snow and sneezed.

Both adults laughed at the comical expression on Koko's face. Meg followed her to the front walk where Koko dragged her to the stranger, the pup whimpering with excitement when she reached him. Meg looked up into dark blue eyes ringed with dark lashes and accented by crinkle laugh lines. Deep creases showed in the man's cheeks, dimples really, and a cleft burrowed into his chin. He wore a hat that covered most of his deep brown hair.

He stretched a gloved hand to Meg. "Hello, I'm Dan Braden. I live down the block in the white house."

"The one with blue shutters? I didn't realize anyone had moved in yet. Nancy called in September to tell me it had sold, but I haven't talked to her since she moved." She paused to take a breath, trying to control her runaway chatter. "Oh, my name is Meg. Stanford. Megan Stanford," she stuttered. She hoped she wasn't blushing even though her traitorous redhead's skin felt hot. *Darn.*

He didn't appear to notice. He was watching Koko exploring the snow around Meg's feet, snuffling and sneezing before taking a roll in the fluffy stuff. When she came to her feet again, she shook, flinging snow all over Meg's legs.

"Oh, that was cold!" Meg hadn't yet changed from her work clothes, today a skirt and sweater set. She stomped then lifted one foot to wipe snow off her ankle.

Dan reached out a hand to steady her when she started to wobble. Koko's leash had wrapped around her leg. Meg would've fallen without his support.

She was definitely blushing now! "Thank you. I didn't notice she'd tied me up. Koko, come back here." Meg pulled on the leash and turned around to free herself.

Dan was watching the dog, a smile on his face. "She is a charmer, isn't she?"

Koko came up to him, her tongue hanging out and her whole body wriggling with joy. He reached down to ruffle the fur on her back and scratch under her jaw. He lifted Koko's head and looked her over.

Meg realized she knew who this man was. "You're the Dog Hypnotist, aren't you?"

He turned his head to face her. "Is that what they're calling me?" His smile showed strong white teeth. "I'm a veterinarian with a specialty in dogs. Not sure about the hypnotizing part, but I do have experience with animal behavior."

"My friends, the Jensens, had a problem pooch, and they said you cured him of digging in their yard. Whatever you did was very effective. Now they can really enjoy Buddy. And they've quit calling him Badger," she said with a smile.

Dan stood, brushed the snow off his pant legs, and looked into Meg's eyes. "Thanks for telling me that. I'm glad I could help. The Jensens are a nice family. I enjoyed working with them. And Buddy-not-Badger." His eyes twinkled at this.

"Don't you have a dog?" Meg asked before she could stop herself. A dog specialist without a dog?

"No, not now. The lab I had for a dozen years had to be put down last summer. With the move and all, I decided it would be best to wait before getting another one." He paused. "What made you decide to get Koko?"

"My sister Ellie volunteers at the shelter, and she urged me to adopt Koko. She already has two, so she couldn't handle another one now, but she saw something special in this pup."

"She has good taste in animals. Koko is a winner."

"You can tell this already? In just a few minutes of watching her?"

"I'm one of the vets who serve at the shelter. I considered taking Koko, but your sister had other plans for her. I'm very happy she convinced me to wait for another dog." Dan's dimples deepened as he gazed into her face.

So that's why Ellie kept pushing Koko on her. Ellie kept trying to fix her up with dates even though Meg had asked her to lay off for a while. She was happy being single now, she told Ellie. She had almost convinced herself that was true.

Dan cleared his throat, reminding Meg that their conversation seemed to have broken down. An awkward silence hung between them until Dan said, "Would you mind letting me walk Koko, just a few walks every so often? I do miss my Norton."

"You named your dog Norton? After The Honeymooners?"

"Guilty as charged." He answered with a bittersweet smile.

"Growing up, we once had a dog named Ralph. Also from The Honeymooners." She looked up at Dan and her heart thumped. What was it Ellie said when she promised to quit fixing Meg up? Oh, yes. "I won't need to anymore."

"How about a stroll down to my house? I make a mean cup of hot chocolate."

At this, Koko pulled Meg down the sidewalk. Dan put his hand over Meg's on the leash, his firm grip making a subtle change in the dog's rambunctious gait. His presence seemed to calm her.

When they arrived at his house, he invited them both inside. "Koko is welcome. Don't worry about her." He took Meg's coat and hung it in the hall closet with his own.

She unclipped the leash to let the pup sniff her way around the boxes that lined what had been Meg's friend's living room.

Dan apologized for the cartons. "I've not yet had time to unpack everything, but the kitchen is functional." He led the way into the bright room Meg knew well. Gone were Nancy's colorful curtains and her signature collection of apples—apple cookie jar, apple pot holders hanging from apple magnets on her refrigerator, apples everywhere.

"I see she didn't leave her apples for you."

"No, but she offered." He laughed. "I tactfully said they must mean a lot to her and I'd feel bad about making her leave them behind."

Meg laughed. "Nicely done. I can't see you enjoying them quite as much as Nancy did, and Rob took it all in stride. He said it came with her good cooking." She looked around, wondering if there was a Mrs. Dan.

He must have guessed what she mentally questioned. "My wife passed away a couple of years ago."

Meg's smile vanished. "I lost my husband two years ago. I know what you're going through."

Dan looked at Meg with compassion. "I don't have to explain why I'm alone, you must understand. Any children?" He could read pain in her gray eyes and her fine-boned face with such fair skin showed her emotions clearly. Her earlier blush now gone, she looked pale and lost.

She shook her head. "We'd just started to try. My doctor suggested we both get physicals before we got pregnant. That's when we found Jim's brain cancer. One day I had a healthy husband, the next he was fighting for his life. Not a time to try to have a baby."

Dan took a deep breath. It still hurt to talk about this, so he used the fewest words he could to explain. "My wife was expecting our first child. She was killed in a car accident. They weren't able to save either of them."

Meg's eyes filled with tears. "I'm so very sorry. I can't imagine how difficult it was to lose both of them. Do you have other family?"

Dan busied himself with getting out milk and a pan. "Yes, my folks are retired and live in Florida, and my sister and her family live in Michigan. That's where we grew up and I had my practice." He worked at making the hot drink, keeping his back to Meg. Seeing her sympathy and knowing she understood was too hard. He had to lighten the mood or they'd both be blubbering.

"Marshmallows?" he asked, holding up and shaking the bag while silently thanking his sister's kids who had packed it with the cocoa in a send-off box of goodies.

Meg rallied. "Of course! Can't have hot cocoa without marshmallows."

Dan stirred the mix into the warm milk and got out two of the mugs his nieces had chosen, decorated with their favorite Disney movie characters.

Meg laughed when she saw them. "You into Olaf the snowman and...what's the girl's name? I can't remember."

He lifted up the mug and read, "Elsa? I think that's her. And Anna is the other girl if I remember right. My sister's daughters gave them to me." He handed her the mug and lifted up his own.

"Here's to movies celebrating snow." He clinked his mug against hers.

Meg grinned. "And here's to little girls everywhere." They both sipped.

"This is really good," Meg said, licking the foam off her lips.

Dan watched her tongue tracing her mouth and realized he was aroused, just like that. He stepped behind the table, grabbing a couple of paper napkins while hoping to get himself under control. What a surprise! It'd been a long time since he'd felt any desire at all. And for someone he'd just met. *Wow.*

Meg looked around the room, "You bought a new refrigerator? Anything else?"

"A dishwasher. Nancy said the old one was starting to leak. Nice of her to warn me. I also had the wood floors refinished before moving in."

"I've always loved these floors. My house is still mostly carpeted. Some day..."

"Isn't that the way it goes? We had planned to remodel before the baby came, but I couldn't bring myself to do any of it. The new couple who bought my house got a fixer-upper. And a good deal." He looked away.

Meg cleared her throat and put her mug down. "I hate to drink and run," she said, grinning, "but I do need to get Koko home and fed. I just got home from work and haven't started my dinner yet." She rose, calling to her dog.

Dan walked back around the table and into the living room to get her coat. "It's a pleasure to meet Koko's new owner. I hope to see you both again. Soon," he added, realizing it was true. "Can I walk you home?" He held her coat so she could put her arms in the sleeves, and then he smoothed it over her shoulders.

She turned around, her cheeks pink. "Not necessary, we can manage the one block walk. But yes, I'd like that. To see you, I mean. To walk Koko." She was obviously flustered.

And so cute, thought Dan.

The dog at that moment decided to run off down the hall, leash dangling behind her.

"Koko! Get back here." Meg rushed off after the pup. "Sit, Koko, SIT."

Dan followed, watching Meg trying to catch the playful puppy, who acted as if this is a game, running around the king-sized bed in the bedroom. The dog had a sock in her mouth, shaking it back and forth.

"Koko, no!" Meg sounded frantic. "Let go, now!" She grabbed one end of Dan's sock, trying to pull it away from those puppy teeth. The sock came away with strings still stuck on the dog's teeth. Koko shook her head, growling furiously.

"I think you've killed the demon sock, Koko." Dan came around Meg and knelt to stroke the dog. "There, girl, let's see that you haven't broken any teeth." He expertly held the dog's muzzle in one hand while he opened her mouth. "Ah, lost one tooth, didn't you, girl?"

"I'm so sorry! I never should've let her come inside. I'll buy you a new pair." Meg sounded upset as she picked up the leash from the floor.

Dan stood and placed his hands on her shoulders, which were trembling. "Megan, it's okay, really it is. That's an old sock that I should've put in the rag bag. Koko's acting like the puppy she is, and she's teething."

Meg looked up, confusion apparent. "Teething? She has teeth. Dogs do that?" She shook her head. "I've never had a puppy before."

"You understand you're going to have a big dog here, right?"

Meg groaned. "I was afraid of that. Look at her feet—I mean paws. Huge!"

Dan laughed, "Yes, she'll grow into those feet, as you put it. Just like a teenager, the feet grow first. You're lucky you got a female. Her male counterpart would be larger and heavier."

Meg knelt beside the dog. "You weren't supposed to be this much trouble," she said as she stroked the pup's silky ears. Koko rewarded her with joyous wet doggie kisses. She laughed, trying to avoid that sloppy tongue. "Behave. Now. Let's pretend this never happened, okay? You will walk calmly next to me and we'll go home."

At the magic word "home," the dog pulled her owner to the front door.

"I'm so sorry," she said again. "I guess we need more practice with following orders."

Dan laughed. "I think Koko is doing well for her age. She's pretty young yet, but very trainable. Give her time and she'll behave."

"You think so?" Meg sounded as if she wanted to believe but didn't quite.

"I promise. Look, bring her over and we can start with basics. Do you have any free time this weekend?" He sure hoped so.

"I'm free Saturday afternoon. Are you sure you want to…" She was definitely flustered. And definitely cute.

"I'm sure. I spend the morning at the shelter and will be home by about one. Come on over, and we can start then."

"I can pay you. I know your time is valuable." Her determination to be all business showed.

"We'll think of something," he hedged. He stood at the door and watched as she tried to keep Koko from pulling her down the sidewalk.

He called, "Koko, heel!" and the dog stopped, looked at him, and proceeded to walk sedately.

Meg looked at Koko, then at him. *How?* she mouthed. She turned her attention to her well-behaved animal and continued on home. Dan watched as the pup walked a bit farther, then got frisky again, snapping at the lazy snowflakes floating to the ground.

"Walk! Koko, uh, HEEL!" he heard Meg say, trying to sound firm.

Grinning to himself, he went back inside. This could turn out to be fun. Just what the doctor ordered.

Back in her own home, Megan got Koko settled in the kitchen. She watched the pup eating her kibble noisily while spreading it all over the floor. Why hadn't she gotten the larger plastic mat to put under the dog dishes? But when she closed Koko's food and water dishes in the laundry room, along with her crate, the puppy whined mournfully. Meg couldn't stand the dog's misery for long and she relented.

"You are going to be a good girl, right?" she said sternly as the pup wriggled and licked her hand and arm. Meg relented and knelt to put her arms around the warm body. "Yes, I love you, too."

Tears in her eyes, she turned away from the dog, who was happily gnawing on a chew toy. Koko had quickly made a place in her heart, filled a void that was empty. Not that a dog could replace her Jim, but at least she had a warm body to love. Even if it was furry.

Meg pulled out a frozen dinner and opened it. She really had to start cooking actual food again, but what was the point? Her sister would scold her if she knew what she ate most nights. Jake, her nine-year-old nephew, would worry, too. The meals she used to love to cook for her husband seemed so much work to do for just herself, at least at the end of a work day. Being a librarian might sound easy, but she was tired when she got home. She read the directions on the back of the package. At least this one has vegetables in it and is low in fat and sodium. Healthy, right? She programmed the microwave and pushed START.

When she sat down to eat at the table instead of on the couch with the TV on, Koko came to lean against Meg's legs. She absently stroked the soft fur as she ate, and opened the paperback romance she had just started. It had taken over a year after losing Jim before she could look at one, but she was determined to go back to the genre she loved. Ellie called them her "guilty pleasures". She was as hooked as Meg was on happily-ever-after stories.

At least Ellie is getting to live hers.

Dan collapsed another empty cardboard box in his living room and put it in a growing pile. *Only another couple dozen to go,* he thought. He took the stack out to the garage, ready for the garbage and recycling pick up on Monday. One of the things he liked about this town is its progressive recycling program. The small town exuded atmosphere while providing many big city amenities. He felt comfortable living here, taking over a retiring vet's clinic and seeing firsthand how well the volunteer staff at the animal shelter worked together.

It was Friday evening. He'd worked at the clinic all day and then put in several hours unpacking. What happened to old Dan the Man, party animal? He'd never be caught at home on the weekend doing something as mundane as unpacking. That person from his distant past seemed so very young, much younger than his now thirty-four years. He felt twice that old some days. Except for the day Koko and her new owner came over. Just the memory of Meg's fair skin turning pink stirred him up, and he definitely felt new life. Tomorrow is Saturday, and he anticipated seeing her again. And Koko, of course.

He'd finished the living room, set up his office in the second bedroom, and now needed to unpack boxes marked 'Bedroom'. Dan was tempted to let them go, but the recollection of a certain petite redhead chasing her dog into this room and around the boxes urged him on. *How nice it would be to have company in here,* he mused, feeling a surge of energy. *A surge of something!* He grinned and began whistling as he unpacked.

His mood altered when he pulled out a framed wedding picture of Jenny and himself, one where they looked so young and happy, so much in love.

He started to set it on the dresser where it had been during and after their brief marriage, but decided instead to wrap it back up and put it in a bottom drawer. Jenny would never want him to mope around forever. She'd even mentioned that, in all seriousness, on their honeymoon.

"If something ever happens to me, I want you to go on and live." She'd seemed so earnest when she said this that he couldn't help teasing her.

"You're too perfect. You'll outlive me by a dozen years."

"No, I'm serious," she'd insisted. *"Remember this. I love you now and for always, but if I go before you, don't quit living."*

He'd just wrapped her in his arms and kissed her then, loving her even more. How absurd to think of death when they were young and healthy.

Now this vivid memory taunted him. Did she have a premonition? He didn't think so, but still…

Dan finished emptying the last box while pondering life before and after Jenny. No, she was just being Jenny, always thinking and planning ahead. It was just like her to cover all bases. He went into the kitchen where he got out a short glass and opened a cupboard where he'd stashed his adult beverages. A finger or two of bourbon, and all would be well with his world.

He toasted Jenny one last time, crawled into bed, and slept through the night.

After her Saturday morning children's story hour, Meg drove home from the library at noon, anxious to let her dog out of the crate. Koko had some problems being cooped up for a whole day when she first adopted the puppy two weeks ago, so Meg had since rushed home on her lunch break each day to let her out. Today she'd be able to keep the pup with her all afternoon. Koko had again cried when Meg left for the library this morning, which guilt-tripped her into worrying more about the dog than her work. It had to get better, right? This puppy must be extra sensitive, or had some sort of abandonment issues. She knew of small children who did, so why not her pet? Being a librarian, she brought home an armload of books on dogs.

Meg ate a quick lunch after taking Koko for a long walk. Now it's time for their first session with Dan. Koko seemed to know where they were going since she strained at her leash, trying to pull Meg along faster.

"Koko, walk, uh, heel. Koko, HEEL!"

Meg feared she'd be red-faced and sweaty by the time they got there since she'd bundled up for the thirty degree weather. When they drew near his house, Dan opened his front door and walked out onto the porch. Meg could tell he was watching Koko. She was embarrassed that she didn't have any more control over her dog than before.

He smiled when she arrived at his porch. Koko nearly choked on her collar with the pressure Meg kept on her leash in a vain attempt to show she was in charge. The puppy wiggled and made gleeful noises when Dan reached down to rub her, talking in a calm voice. "Good girl, Koko. Now sit."

Meg was amazed that Koko sat without any further commotion. He was good, she had to give him credit.

"I hope you're going to teach me how to do that," she said, handing Dan the leash. He turned Koko around to walk down to the sidewalk and back, the dog obeying perfectly.

"She knows I'm the alpha. That's all."

"I have to be the alpha dog?" Meg didn't have faith in her ability to pull this off.

"Yes, you do. Don't worry, I'll teach you. Koko wants to please you. You will learn how to show her what you want." He made it sound so easy. He made it look easy too. Koko walked calmly and stopped when Dan gave a hand signal.

Dan had Koko repeat the trip back and forth another two times, then offered the leash to Meg. "You try it. Just use the same hand signals while you speak to her. She'll learn what you want."

Meg felt like she was being judged when Dan watched them while she attempted the same short trip. Koko tried to go to Dan and whined when Meg pulled her back.

"Heel, Koko, heel!" Koko looked back and forth between the two adults, her desire to go to Dan clear in her antics.

"Koko, SIT." Dan's firm order stopped the dog's momentum. "HEEL."

Now Koko walked next to Meg in perfect form. Meg ground her teeth. Would she ever be able to do this without Dan's help? Her temper battled with her chagrin that she couldn't control one young dog.

Dan held out his hand to Koko, dispensing something that the dog gulped down.

"You're giving her treats?" Why didn't she think of this?

"Rewards. This tells her she did it right."

"Give me a couple and maybe I can do it, too." He handed her a few small pieces of dog treats, which she put in her coat pocket. Meg repeated her attempt to get Koko to walk beside her. When she did, Meg gave her a treat. "Good girl." *Finally!*

Meg felt like collapsing from the strain, but Koko was still full of spunk, nosing Meg's pocket where the other treats remained. She saw Dan try to control his grin, not very successfully. She clenched her jaw. She would do this!

Koko more or less behaved the next three times Meg walked her up and down the short walk until she ran out of treats, which the dog couldn't know, could she?

"Will I have to carry treats in my pocket forever?" She had visions of running out of treats and the older, very big dog, pulling her along.

"No, I promise you, you won't. This helps in training her. Can I interest you in more of my famous hot chocolate?" His serious expression lightened.

"Only if you still have marshmallows." She had to grin 'cause he was acting so very nice. He might not spend much time with her when he got his new dog.

"Have you found a rescue you want to adopt? You work at the shelter every week, right?" She hoped she didn't sound nosey, but she suspected she had when he turned away from her without answering. She followed him inside, trying to keep Koko in line.

The pup was hyper-excited again, her tail going from one side to the other in a blur. Meg hoped Dan didn't have any breakables around, as it might be risky with her canine wind machine. She was happy to see Dan wasn't the type to display collectibles on his tables. The living room was now free of boxes, but very Spartan, with nothing decorative in view and no pictures hung. In short, she found nothing to reveal more of his personality.

"Let me hang up your coat," Dan said, as he opened his nearly empty coat closet. When she unzipped her jacket, he took it along with her scarf and gloves. He also hung his coat up and shut the door, much to Koko's disappointment.

"Koko, sit." Meg tried to put authority in her command. The dog didn't obey until Dan turned and looked at her, then she sat. Meg only sighed. Training this dog would take longer than she'd hoped. She bent to stroke the furry back and whispered, "Just remember who buys your meals."

Dan once again fixed their hot drinks, with marshmallows as promised, but served it this time in plain, dark blue earthenware mugs.

Meg took a sip and remarked, "I sort of miss Olaf and Elsa. The hot chocolate just isn't the same." She tried to keep a straight face, but at Dan's challenging gaze she gave up and smirked. "You know you like those cups, too."

"I did call and tell the girls that I've already used my cups for company. They were pleased, telling me they wanted to get me plates to match, but they only came in child size. I assured them that though I'm disappointed, I would make do with just the mugs."

"You must miss them and your sister. I'm sure they miss you."

He looked uncomfortable, but resolute, when he said, "I do miss them, but it's time for me to move on."

She understood and wondered if she should've made a break when Jim died. She still lived in the same house and worked at the same job.

"Would you like to come to dinner? At my house, tonight? If you're not busy, that is." This had been in the back of her mind, the neighborly thing to do for a new…hot guy?

His smile deepened the creases in his cheeks. "I'm not busy, so I'd love to come to dinner. What time?"

Now she had to scramble. "Seven?" She had a thought. "You're not a vegetarian, are you?"

"No, I eat everything. Seven it is."

Dan was dressed and ready at 6:30. He paced until he caught a glimpse of himself in the window, which, with it dark so early in November, made a realistic mirror. *Who is that strange guy?* He missed Norton, who would've come to him and calmed him down. Here he was, being invited for a home-cooked meal with a pretty *and* available redhead, and he was acting like a teen getting ready for his first date.

He grinned. Well, it is a first date, of sorts. So what if he was older and wiser? Who said a guy couldn't get excited about seeing a pretty lady? He had flowers, didn't he? Since he didn't know if she drank wine, or drank at all, he decided flowers were a safe bet. He checked his watch again. Wow, it was almost six-forty. At this rate he'd be sweaty and thirsty before he got down the block. That's the answer, just take a long walk. Cool himself off, so then he wouldn't look so anxious.

He put on his jacket and started off at a brisk pace. But then the beauty of a nearly perfect winter night captured him, and he slowed down to view the light layer of crystalline white, so pretty with the street lights shining on it. The bushes and trees held a sprinkling of snow, just an artist's brush stroke here and there. The quiet was interrupted by a dog's barking and a familiar, "Walk, Koko, um, HEEL!"

He couldn't help but laugh to himself. Should he pretend he never heard her and sneak back to his house? Or should he rescue her? He could only imagine she'd taken the pup out for the evening necessary walk before her dinner guest arrived. He chose the role of savior. He could take the dog from her, let her go back home and get ready for him, and then they'd arrive, the dog exhausted and quiet and the guest hungry. Just as long as he didn't forget to go back for her flowers.

He walked toward the commotion and acted surprised to run into them. "Here, let me take your dog for a walk and we'll come back at seven. Does that work for you?"

Her relief was apparent, and she agreed after weakly offering, "You don't need to do that." So Prince Charming Dan rescued the fair maiden and took the offending dragon off to be tamed.

The parallel analogy of their roles amused him, and the walk with the now charming and obedient Koko made him feel...what? Useful? Needed? Competent? Successful? All of the above? Maybe so, maybe so.

Dan arrived at Meg's house with a tired and happy Koko and the flowers, which he remembered at the last minute, at precisely seven o'clock. *Was he good or what?* His grin felt natural. Watching Meg's flush of pleasure at his arrival with her now-peaceful puppy made him feel even better. It was going to be a great evening.

How did he do it? She'd wrestled with that stupid dog all afternoon, and she was the only one to get tired. She'd made her no-fail dinner, one she perfected when she and Jim were first married. Meatloaf, baked potatoes with all the toppings, and green beans. Very homey. Was it too pedestrian a meal for a professional man? He'd looked so classy in that camel coat the other night. But he wore jeans today. She was doing it again, driving herself crazy worrying about her menu, what she wore, and of course, her unsuccessful attempt to train her dog.

He looked so good, standing on her porch with her rascal on a leash, who was of course being a picture of good manners. She realized she'd stood there for too long and hurried to welcome Dan. Koko walked behind him, calm and quiet. "Who is this dog and where did you leave my Koko?"

He laughed. "She's a good dog, just exuberant. Soon she'll behave for you, too. I promise."

Meg took his coat and scarf and hung them up. She told Koko to sit, which— surprise!—she did in front of Dan. She gave the pup a chew toy in hopes that it would keep her busy for a while.

When Dan produced a lovely bunch of daisies, she melted. "Daisies! Where did you find my favorite flowers? How did you know? Never mind, I'll just put them in water."

She went for the kitchen, but then stopped and turned to ask him, "What would you like to drink? We're having meat loaf and baked potatoes."

At his moan, she squeezed her eyes shut in trepidation, then peeked at him.

"I *love* meat loaf, haven't had it for months." He smiled, really smiled, with his whole face.

She loved the crinkles at the corners of his eyes. He wasn't just saying it to make her feel better, was he?

"You wouldn't have a glass of milk, would you?" he asked, almost hesitantly.

"Is two percent okay? I don't drink skim, and whole milk is just too…you know?" She was chattering again, darn it.

"Two percent is perfect. Thanks."

Meg put the flowers in a small yellow vase that looked lovely with the daisies. It went so nicely on her table with its floral print tablecloth and her grandmother's yellow serving platter filled with meatloaf. She poured them both glasses of milk and set the wine she'd bought aside. She could have it another time.

They sat down to eat while Koko snored softly in the next room and her television played a music channel in the background. Who knew her evening would come together like this?

Dan ate seconds, complimenting her often. "You know how few people can make a truly good meatloaf?"

She shook her head, sipping her milk.

"Not very many, in my experience. My grandmother made one that had canned tomato soup in it. Well, it's not on my list of top ten meat loaves. My mother had her own recipe, better, but not great. Yours, on the other hand, *is* great."

"Mine is a pretty simple recipe. I've tried adding herbs and spices, but it never tasted right." Meg was so relieved he liked it that she gave herself a second slice. She'd been too nervous to take more than a small serving at first, but now she relaxed and enjoyed dinner with this really nice man. "My mother taught me to cook, and she didn't measure except when she baked. Of course, cooking for our family of eight, she gained a lot of experience."

"I only have one sister, and my folks both worked, so dinner was often pretty casual. Sometimes mom cooked, sometimes dad grilled out. My sister Chrissy took to the kitchen in her early teens and did very well. I can feed myself and others when I need to." He looked relaxed at the happy memories.

"We all learned to cook because Mom insisted. She also had each of us cook for the family when we got older, that and we learned to clean and do our own laundry. She said she didn't have time to do it all." Megan grew nostalgic. "I sure miss her. We lost her last year. Afterward, Dad moved to Arizona. I think he couldn't live in our house without her."

"I can relate. It must have been very difficult for him after all those years in that house. I guess that's why I moved here. Jenny was everywhere in our home, and the baby's room...I couldn't go in there." He placed his knife and fork across his empty plate, a pensive look on his face.

Meg jumped up, gathered the dishes, and asked, "Would you like something else to drink? I've got wine and beer, or coffee if you'd prefer." She wished she had a larger selection to offer, even one after dinner drink would be nice. Or made dessert. How could she forget dessert?

"I wouldn't mind a beer, if you'll have one with me."

Meg brought the leftover food into the kitchen. She quickly put it into the refrigerator and brought out two beers, opening them before carrying them back to the table. Just as she handed one bottle to Dan, she realized she should've offered him a glass. When she started to go back to the kitchen, he stopped her.

"I don't need a glass. Please sit with me. It's been a long time since I felt this comfortable with a woman."

"Me, too. I mean, with a man." *Lame!* "I mean, I'm enjoying myself with you. And it's the first evening since I got"—she looked at the sleeping dog and whispered—"my pet two weeks ago that I've gotten to relax and just sit."

He glanced over at Koko and said, "I think she's down for the count."

Meg stood. "Let's go into the living room."

Dan followed her, admiring her petite but shapely figure. For a small woman, she's very nicely proportioned. The same desire he'd had when he was with her before rose to his attention. Hallelujah! A gal who could cook and make a man feel like a man. He smiled for the pure joy of it.

She sat on the couch, placed her beer on a coaster on an end table, and invited him to join her. "Is the music too loud? Or would you like another type of—?"

"No, the music is just right and I've always enjoyed oldies." Dan joined her on the couch and leaned back, his arm braced along the top of the sofa and touching her shoulder when she reclined. He could feel her tension vibrating. He knew she felt this attraction, too.

Meg took a swallow of beer, her movements again showing her nerves. He needed to make her comfortable. Much more comfortable.

Dan reached for her drink and placed it with his on the table. When she looked into his eyes, he saw she knew what he wanted to do. If she'd made any sign that she didn't want him, he would've thanked her and gone home. But she didn't, and he needed to kiss her now. Her eyes were dilated and her breath came quickly. How beautifully her skin shone with the faint flush of color rising from her alabaster neck. He just had to taste her inviting mouth.

When his lips met hers, she made a tiny sound, not quite a moan. It went straight to his groin. He pulled her closer into his arms and she fit perfectly. It was even better when her arms crept around his neck.

They kissed for a few moments, or was it an hour? He had no sense of time. He felt so alive, so aware of everything. Her response, her quickened breath, brought him from simmer to full boil. He couldn't continue or he'd have her on the floor, ripping off her clothes.

Dan pulled back, breathing heavily. "My God, what you do to me."

Meg, her lips swollen and her eyes glazed, said, "What?" and turned scarlet. "I mean… Oh, my."

He pulled her into his arms for a hug. "You are absolutely adorable. I haven't felt this alive in years."

She tensed, and he knew she was embarrassed. When she pulled away and turned her face from him, he figured what he said now would make or break their budding romance.

"Megan, I'm sorry if I offended you."

"No apologies necessary. I'm glad you enjoyed the meal. Thank you so much for giving Koko obedience lessons. I'll work with her." She rose and turned to face him, though she didn't look at him. "I'm sure we both have busy days coming up. Thank you for coming."

Whoa! This was not what he'd expected, not what he wanted. How had he offended her? She was into their kissing as much as he was, he felt sure. He stood and followed her to the door.

Koko woke, came into the foyer, her puppy exuberance radiating. Dan bent to pat her on her head. "You be a good dog, you hear? Mind your manners."

At that, Dan took his jacket and scarf from Meg and went out the door. Before she could close it, he tried one last time. "Megan, I'm sorry if I came on too strong. You are a beautiful woman and I'm very attracted to you." He tried to read her. "Thanks for a great meal and lovely—" At this, she closed the door.

Well, that went well. He slipped on his jacket, zipped it up, and wound the scarf around his neck. The front room window showed her walking away, and then the lights went off.

Damn. What did he do wrong? Should he have stopped sooner? He walked home, feeling decades older than he had on his trip over.

Megan trembled as she turned out the lights. Kissing Dan brought back too many memories of Jim. It was almost like their first date had been, the chemistry between them overwhelming. She hadn't resisted Jim's advances that night because it was just *right*. She *knew*.

But now, with Dan, it couldn't be. It's too soon. She couldn't have that *perfect knowing…again.* Could she?

With Jim, she was so certain, and he was, too. Their courtship took off like the roller coasters he'd loved and had talked her into riding them with him. She'd been frightened at first, but exhilarated when each ride was over. Jim could talk her into anything she was too timid to try by herself. And now that he is gone, she'd reverted to Meek Megan, only even worse. The only thing she'd done on her own since losing Jim was adopt Koko, and

Ellie'd had to talk her into that.

She cringed. What must Dan think of her? First she invites him over for a home cooked meal, responds to his kisses—and boy! did she respond—and then she turns ice cold and sends him packing. He'd had the most baffled expression when she'd told him to go, confused and hurt.

She couldn't ignore him forever since they'd run into each other again. He's a neighbor, after all. And Ellie would see him at the shelter. Meg grimaced. Ellie knew Dan was teaching her how to train the dog. What would Dan tell her after this fiasco?

Meg grabbed her head and moaned. Could she have messed this up any worse?

Oh, Jim, why did you have to die? We had a perfect life.

I can't do this again, she decided. She'd just write Dan an apologetic note and find another puppy obedience school. She didn't need him. Yes, that would work. She'd write a very polite note thanking him for his time. And no more dates!

Megan climbed into her cold bed, wishing she didn't need the electric blanket to warm her. After turning out the light, she curled up on her side and closed her eyes. Dan's face played vividly on the video in her mind. Dan with his eyes closed in pleasure as he ate her meatloaf. Dan smiling as he rubbed Koko's belly. Dan's eyes as they darkened to midnight blue when he came close to kiss her. Then Dan's bewilderment and hurt when she sent him away. This image haunted her until she finally fell asleep, tears drying on her pillow.

Dan got up Sunday morning after a restless night and made a cup of coffee. He'd gone out to pick up his newspaper from the driveway, halfway listening for a familiar bark, but all was silent. His sweats were enough this morning with a warm front coming through. The snow of the past several days was almost gone, the pristine white now a dirty, slushy gray. The pale sky had no color either. Dull. Everything was dull.

He'd scanned the headlines and turned to the sports section, finding his favorite teams had all lost their games. He left the paper on the table next to his half-empty cup and went into his closet, looking for his running shoes. Once he'd changed, he grabbed his keys, opened the garage door, and got into his car.

He drove to the high school and parked by the track where he found a few other cars. He'd hoped to find the place empty, but there were four other people there, two men running around the oval path, one walker, and a skinny boy, bending over and stretching.

"Hi, Dr. Braden," called the boy. "You like to run too?"

Dan recognized him as the owner of a bulldog he'd treated the first week he was in town. The dog had a badly torn ear from a fight with another dog. What was the boy's name? Oh, yes.

"Hi, Brian. How is Winston? His ear healing okay?" The boy had explained his dad was a WWII buff, hence the dog's moniker. Winston Churchill was on the chart. Bullish for bulldogs?

"He's doing great! The scar will hardly be noticeable once his hair grows back in. He sure did hate wearing the cone of shame!" He laughed. "You could tell he was embarrassed."

"I'm glad. As long as he lets the ear heal, he should be fine. You out for basketball?"

Brian nodded and ran in place for a minute, then said, "I'll race you around the track, if you're interested in running, not walking like Mr. Johnson." He indicated the man with the strange, fast gait coming towards them.

"I doubt I could keep up with a jock like you." At this, the young teen looked both pleased and embarrassed.

"I'm not really a jock. I'm in Cross Country and want to keep in condition. Do you, uh, run every day?"

"No. I haven't for a while, what with the move and all. Just thought it would be a good idea this morning. Tell you what, I'll try to make it around the track a few times, but don't let me slow you down." Dan started off at a comfortable pace. The teen soon outran him, his lead growing with each lap. Dan's steady rate left him by himself, the other runners having waved and gone off. Brian showed no sign of slowing down, sprinting along with his earbuds in.

Ah, youth. He knew he'd feel this tomorrow when he woke. No problem. He needed to get back in shape after the move. He'd look for an energetic dog, one he could run with. Norton was a good run partner when he was younger, but the last couple of years he'd slowed down. Dan considered his next pet. Maybe he'd look for a rescue greyhound, if he could find one that wasn't too badly abused. They might be good running partners.

His thoughts were focused on his future dog, and he missed seeing the black cat streaking across his path. *Damn!* He tripped while trying to avoid stepping on the animal, which made him twist his ankle. Down he went, his hands out to break his fall.

"Are you all right, Dr. Braden?" The boy skidded to a stop beside Dan and bent over to inspect Dan's hands. "I can call my dad 'cause he's off duty now. He can take you to the ER. You're going to have to get checked out."

Dan's hands started to sting. The heels of both were shredded with his right palm dripping blood, and his ankle ached. "I think I can make it, my car is just over there." He started to brace himself to stand and realized it wouldn't be as easy as he thought. Of course, this had to happen on the furthest part of the course.

Brian put his hand under Dan's arm to help him try to stand, which caused his slender boy's frame to strain under the weight. Dan's ankle was not going to hold him.

"Dr. Braden, I think you should wait for my dad. He'll be here in a few minutes to pick me up." Brian pulled out his cell and called his dad, explaining about the accident.

Dan settled back on the grassy perimeter of the track, cradling his bleeding hands while extending his injured right ankle. Only the presence of the concerned boy kept him from swearing out loud. Could it get any worse?

Ten minutes later he was in the back of a SUV driven by Chuck, the boy's burly father, who'd easily helped him to the car. "I'll take you to the

Urgent Care Center. You'll get faster service than if you went to the ER. I know; my wife's on duty there this morning. I called and she's getting set up for you."

Dan didn't know what to say to this. It was embarrassing enough to have fallen while running, and if the boy hadn't seen the cat, it would've looked like Dan was just plain clumsy. A veterinarian tripping over a black cat? Good thing Halloween was a few weeks ago.

"Do you have anyone you need to notify?" Chuck asked.

"No." Dan didn't elaborate. Jenny would've been sympathetic and practical. He'd have called her and she'd have come to get him and done what she could to make him more comfortable. Now he'd have to cope on his own.

Carol, Brian's mother, the nurse, cleaned his abraded hands and carefully removed his running shoe, placing his foot gently up on a pillow. Dan felt helpless as his right hand was first stitched up, then bandaged into a mitt-sized bundle, with only the tips of his fingers showing. At least his left hand only required a good cleaning and a smaller bandage. How in the world would he be able to work? Examining animals required two firm hands. He couldn't even drive, he realized.

After the x-ray determined he had no broken bones, just a badly sprained ankle, they fitted Dan with a walking boot and crutches and gave him orders to see an orthopedic doctor the following week. Great. Just what he needed. At least he didn't yet have a dog to walk.

Just like that, Megan popped into his mind. Too bad she had backed off last night. She might have been helpful. Good thing, he decided. He could do without the drama. He stood, balancing on his left foot, grimacing when he forgot and tried to grab onto the crutch with his right hand.

Carol came in just then, his paperwork in her hand. "Here, let me help." She took the right crutch away and showed him how to use just the left crutch to move around. "You'll need to give your stitches at least a week before you try to handle the other crutch. Isn't there anyone, a neighbor or family member, who can help you?"

Once again he thought of Meg, not the Megan who kicked him out, but the one who'd cooked him the meal and whose kisses blew his mind. "No, no one. I'm new in town."

Carol shook her head in sympathy. "Our son Brian can come help you before and after school. Just tell him what you need done."

Dan wanted to argue, but then realized how much he actually did need help. They exchanged phone numbers, and Chuck and Brian settled Dan in the SUV again.

Chuck pulled into Dan's driveway and killed the motor. Brian opened the passenger door, and with his dad, helped Dan up the front steps. Excited barking made Dan turn to look back. Sure enough, Meg and Koko were standing on the sidewalk in front of his house. When her eyes met his, she looked away, only to stare back at his bandaged hands and crutches. She pulled Koko firmly to her side, and for once the pup stilled.

"What happened?" Concern clouded her expression.

Brian jumped in to explain. "There's this black cat! It's like a demon, appearing out of nowhere, and it ran right across Dr. Braden's path. Spooky!" He shuddered. "Then it disappeared."

Dan didn't want to rain on Brian's epic tale, but he had to clarify what really happened. "The cat was chasing something, probably a bird or a squirrel, and I didn't see it until it was too late."

Brian muttered, "No squirrel. I didn't see any bird," as he helped Dan maneuver to the front door. When Dan realized his keys were in his front pants pocket, and his bandaged hand was too big to get it out, he had to have the boy retrieve them, almost wishing it were a feminine hand going into his pocket. Brian deftly removed the keys and fitted one in the front door lock. He held it open while Chuck helped Dan inside.

Megan watched, helpless to act, as Dan entered his house. Poor guy, but not her problem, she tried to convince herself.

"You live nearby?" The boy's dad asked Meg.

At her nod, he continued. "Maybe you could help him out? He's pretty banged up and shouldn't be up and around. He needs to keep his ankle elevated, my wife said. She's the nurse."

Megan nodded. "I can help. Just until he can get around by himself."

This at least would settle her conscience after her behavior last night. She couldn't live with herself if she ignored his obvious need today.

They walked to the open front door where Chuck took Dan's keys from Brian and gave them to Meg. "We need to get his car. You want to take your dog back home, first? Then I can drop you off at the school where Dr. Braden parked, and you can drive it back here for him. Okay, doc?" he asked Dan.

At Dan's muffled reply, Meg turned away to take Koko home.

"I can walk your dog for you while you go with my dad," Brian said, bending over Koko to scratch behind her ears.

They decided that the teen would meet them at Dan's house after walking Koko, while the adults retrieved his car. Chuck asked a few questions of Megan as they rode to the school, like if her puppy came from the shelter and how long she'd known Dan. She answered as briefly as she could, but Chuck had a way of asking that made her volunteer more than she'd planned.

"I was having trouble keeping Koko in line and Dan, uh, Dr. Braden gave me a few pointers. That's all." Her ears were burning, and she hated that her face was probably bright red.

Chuck smiled when he pulled up at the parking lot nearest the track. "I believe that car is Dan's. If you click the key fob, we'll know for sure."

When Meg fumbled with the key, the horn beep-beep-beeped until she grew nervous. She clicked the unlock icon, and this time the lights blinked silently. She breathed a sigh of relief.

"I'll follow you back there so I can pick up my son. I'll give you my cell number and Brian's, too, in case you need us."

Megan got out of the SUV and into Dan's car, a sporty but practical Subaru Forrester that fit a big man and could hold a large dog and supplies. She had to adjust the seat and mirrors since Dan is so much taller, and soon she could see where she was going. Thank goodness he drove an automatic. That's one less hurdle to conquer. She backed out and pulled forward smoothly, giving her confidence that she could handle this car.

She pulled into Dan's driveway and turned off the motor. Chuck parked on the street and got out to talk to Brian, who held Koko's leash. Meg went up to the front door and knocked.

Dan replied, "Come in."

Meg hesitated, if only she hadn't behaved so badly last night. "I'm sorry—""I'm sorry, I shouldn't have—"

They spoke at the same time, then halted abruptly before trying again, Meg more convincingly.

"I need to apologize for last night." She forced herself to look at him. "I was rude to you and it was entirely my fault."

"I'm sorry if I came on too strong." Dan's carefully worded his reply, his expression blank.

"You were..." How could she explain? Too attractive? Too sexy? Too much? Yes, that was obviously the case, but she couldn't use that as an excuse. "I haven't dated in a long time. I'm a bit out of practice."

His smile was reserved, and she couldn't blame him. She'd acted like a mental case.

"Apology accepted. Thanks for retrieving my car. You can put the keys on the table near the door." It was a very polite dismissal.

She knew he must be hurting, and that he probably needed help. "I can bring you some lunch. Would a meatloaf sandwich sound good?"

He grinned then. "That would be wonderful. Thank you." This time he sounded like he meant it.

Megan turned to go, her relief palpable. The tension keeping her rigid faded and she returned his grin. "Ketchup or mustard? I know you liked ketchup on the meatloaf last night, but my favorite way to eat it cold on a sandwich is with mustard."

"What kind of mustard?" he inquired, a hint of suspicion in his voice.

"Good old yellow mustard. Nothing fancy, but then my meatloaf isn't fancy."

"I would be most grateful to you. The only thing better than your meatloaf dinner last night would be a meatloaf sandwich today. With good old yellow mustard."

She left to get her puppy who was outside frolicking with Brian. "Thanks so much for walking Koko. I can see she had a good time."

"Koko is awesome! She's pretty smart, too, for a puppy. She can heel and sit. I think she's a great dog, aren't you, girl?" He gave the dog a belly rub that sent her into ecstasy.

"We're trying to learn our manners." Meg told Brian and his dad. "She can be a bit too excited to behave." Koko barked as if in agreement, and they all laughed.

Chuck and Brian left, and Meg took her dog home. Koko settled down in the kitchen as Meg began pulling food from the fridge. After making the sandwiches, she added a banana and some chips to the meal. *That ought to fill him up.* She debated over bringing enough for them both, and put an extra sandwich in her bag. After all, *he* hadn't done anything wrong, had he?

Dan looked at his foot, propped up in his recliner. Damn, this would make his life miserable, especially with his hand so banged up. The numbness was wearing off and he wished he'd had Chuck stop by the drugstore to get the prescription for pain medication filled. At the time, he thought it wasn't necessary. Now he knew he'd need it, and soon.

The doorbell rang and Dan struggled to get up. His position in his recliner made leverage awkward. No, almost impossible. He forgot about not using his right hand to push himself up, which he regretted immediately and fell back into the chair, his crutch dropping out of reach.

Damn! "Come in!" he yelled, frustration fighting with pain. He sure hoped the door wasn't locked.

The front door opened to Megan, carrying a large basket. Her white winter coat featured a hood that framed her red curls, and she looked so cute and flustered. *Little red with a riding hood?* She took in his position, the crutch on the floor and his no doubt sweaty face, and hurried over to help him.

She placed the basket on the floor next to his chair and picked up the crutch. "Can I help you up? Do you need to go to the..." and she turned a vibrant crimson.

"No, I was trying to answer the door." He clenched his teeth against the pain, but realized that going to the bathroom might be a good idea. He tried to speak more patiently. "If you could help me up, I think I would like to go…" He nodded toward the hall.

Megan looked at his booted foot and bandaged hands, clearly wondering how to help him up. Dan knew he had at least seventy pounds on her and probably eight or nine inches in height, so they'd have to plan this first. "How about you come over on my left side and give me the crutch?"

She did as he asked, but then came the issue of getting him in position to stand. She looked over his chair and came around to pull the lever on the right side, lowering the foot rest.

Why didn't he think of that first? But it was near his bandaged right hand, of course.

This put the chair back in a more vertical position so he could stand up. Together, they got him to his feet, and with his crutch, he stumbled down the hall.

When he returned, having combed his hair and feeling a little more in control, he found she'd put lunch on the table and stood waiting for him. She'd found plates, napkins and glasses. The sandwiches were cut and there were chips and even pickles.

"This looks great!" His stomach rumbled then, causing them both to laugh.

"What can I get you to drink?"

"Milk?"

Her smile indicated she had already guessed that. With the tension broken, he sat down on the chair she'd pulled out. She propped his foot on a couple of throw pillows and placed an ice pack on his ankle. While eating her wonderful meatloaf sandwiches and drinking milk, they talked about Koko, who was at home, probably enjoying a nap after her workout with Brian.

"I want to hire him! He's great with Koko." Meg's grin brought out laugh lines around her green eyes. "She even minded him when he told her to sit and heel. Maybe if she does it often enough with others, she'll obey me too?"

"You can count on it." He ate two big sandwiches to her one and even took advantage of her remaining pickle wedge, pretending to snatch it while she wasn't looking.

Meg cleared their plates and suggested he lie down. "It might help the swelling go down if your foot is higher than the rest of you. Did you get pain meds from the doctor?"

At his head shake, she put out her hand. "Where is the prescription? I can go get it filled for you."

Dan directed her to the hall table where he'd left his wallet. "It's in there, along with my insurance card. There's money in there to pay for it."

She helped him to his bedroom and got him settled on the bed, placing a pillow under his injured foot and refilling the ice pack.

"Can I get anything else for you at the drugstore? Do you need more bandages?"

Dan looked at his hands. "You'd better get me some more gauze and tape, and large band aids. I've got antibiotic ointment."

Megan left him and put on her coat, then picked up her now empty basket.

"You can drive my car if you want. The keys are on the table. And thanks for lunch. That's two meals I owe you," Dan called from the bedroom.

She had to smile. For a guy in pain, he was acting rather nicely. "Thanks, but I'll drive my own car. I'll take your house key, though, so you don't have to answer the door. See you soon."

Dan woke to Megan leaning over him with a glass of water and a vial of pills. She poured out one tablet and gave it to him after helping him sit up.

"Thanks," he said, feeling groggy. "You don't have to stay, I can manage from here."

At her hurt expression, he amended his words. "If you don't mind bringing me something for dinner later, I'd be most grateful." This is the right thing to say, he decided, when he saw her smile. She sure is a pretty little gal, though he should never say it out loud in those terms. Not very PC.

Megan refilled his water glass and placed it along with the prescription bottle on his night stand. "You can take another one in four to six hours. Two pills if you need them, it says." She frowned. "Are you hurting pretty badly?"

Not when you're smiling at me. "Not right now. I'm sure I've had worse." She nodded sympathetically and walked toward the hallway. He spoke loudly enough for her to hear. "Don't forget my keys, so I don't have to let you back in."

"Okay. Call if you need me." The front door opened and closed.

He rested against his pillow and closed his eyes. His ankle now throbbed in time with his pulse. Funny how it didn't hurt when she was here. He hoped the pain pill would kick in soon.

Megan looked through her freezer, hoping she'd find something quick to make for dinner. A Lean Cuisine would not feed a man that size. She moved containers and packages until she found what she was looking for, a package of frozen shrimp. She gathered green and red peppers, celery, and an onion, and started chopping. She hummed while she worked and soon she had neat piles of vegetables. She peeled the thawed shrimp. One can of tomato paste joined her lineup along with paprika. This would be a twist on an old family recipe, one she'd made with chicken many times. Would shrimp work? Why not?

She put some rice on to cook and heated her largest skillet. Soon the veggies were sautéing. When they were just softened, she added the tomato paste and rinsed out the can with chicken broth, a couple of cans worth. She stirred salt and pepper and a generous portion of paprika into the pan. When it had simmered several minutes, she decided to add the now thawed shrimp. By the time the rice was finished, she tested the shrimp. Perfect! She turned off the heat and covered both pans.

A bag of lettuce made a hurried salad, along with diced cucumber and tomatoes. She mixed her special olive oil and rice wine vinegar dressing in a jar and packed it with the salad in her basket. The still warm pans went into a box.

Koko came snooping around, her nose sniffing the wonderful smells in the kitchen.

"You poor baby, I've neglected you, haven't I?" A good head rub and Koko was happy. "Time to go out." The magic words!

She took Koko out for a brief walk. Upon returning, she filled the pup's food and water dishes. "Sorry, girl, you need to stay in tonight. Just for a while. I'll be back pretty soon." She carried her packages out to her car before coming back to lock up. Maybe she shouldn't leave the dog home so long? But she'd have to when she worked a late shift at the library.

When she unlocked Dan's door, she called out, "Dinner delivery." No sense scaring the poor man.

Dan looked better. The tightness around his mouth earlier must have come from pain, and now he wore a sleepy, relaxed expression.

"Wow, those pills sure knocked me out."

"Can't handle the heavy drugs, hmmm?" she teased.

"Nope. Feel a little fuzzy headed, but they did help. I don't think I'll need them much longer, at least I hope not. Can't think clearly on them."

He navigated his crutch more easily this time and was able to get situated without much help. She refilled the ice pack.

"Boy, this is delicious. What do you call it?" He ate hungrily, his skill with his left hand improving.

"I guess I'd call it Shrimp Paprikash. We have an old family recipe made with chicken, Chicken Paprikash, though we used to call it Popikosh when we were little. I just substituted shrimp." She was inordinately pleased with his enjoyment of her cooking.

"I can't imagine the chicken version is better than this." She served him another plateful. "The salad is great, too. Nice light dressing."

When they'd finished the meal, he said, "Want some ice cream for dessert? I've got some in my fridge."

She grinned as she removed their plates and got out his container of chocolate and peanut butter ice cream. "Don't tell me, this is your favorite ice cream? I love this brand, but haven't tried this flavor yet." She dished up a big dish for him and a scoop for herself.

"Hey, you sure you don't want more than that?"

"I'm sure. You need more fuel than I do." She took a bite. "This is yummy!"

"Best flavor ever."

He ate the ice cream with the same gusto that he'd eaten both meals she'd made, and the sandwiches too. It had been fun preparing food for him. She suddenly realized how much she'd missed cooking for someone who appreciated her food.

Dan scooped the last bite from his bowl and licked his spoon. He gave a great sigh of contentment and leaned back in his chair. "Now that is what I call a great meal." He smiled at her. "I can't thank you enough. This morning was a bummer. You've made a bad situation a lot better."

His praise hit just the right note and she relaxed. "You are most welcome. Actually, I've enjoyed getting back to the kitchen. Since I lost Jim, I've not done much in there. No one to cook for."

"*You* are someone, Megan." Dan spoke quietly. "But I do understand. I couldn't enjoy food for the longest time after losing Jenny. I just ate to keep alive. But she'd told me, on our honeymoon, she wanted me to live if she died first. I just brushed her off. How silly to think of death when we were both young, healthy, and very much alive. I didn't remember that until recently."

Megan sat quietly for a few moments and then replied, "You're right. I do try to eat balanced meals, even if they are frozen ones. Not much fast food. But I haven't enjoyed eating very much. These meals I made tasted better than anything I've eaten in a long time."

They sat in silence until Dan started to stand. Meg hurried to help him, removing the ice pack so he could move. "Do you want me to refill this?"

"I think I can do without. I've been icing it off and on all day. Would you like to watch a movie? I think there might be some on TV, or I've got some DVDs."

Meg checked the time. "I'd love to, but I left Koko at home alone. I don't think it's a good idea to leave her so much in one day." She took the plates into the kitchen and loaded his dishwasher.

"I'll run the dishwasher and put the food in the fridge. I can come back in the morning to help you with breakfast." The last was said almost as a question.

He moved into his living room, but this time sat on the couch. "Bring Koko next time. I hate to make you keep coming over just to wait on me."

"I don't mind. Tomorrow is Monday, and I have a late start. I don't have to be at the library until eleven. I work later, though. Koko will need a long walk then." She finished storing the leftovers in his refrigerator and packed up her pans.

Dan watched as she set his kitchen to rights, the dishwasher humming and the table wiped off. She moved efficiently around his house, and he imagined her living here. What would she add to his sterile environment? *Not apples, that's for sure.* And he grinned.

Megan bundled up and put the basket and box by the front door. "Is there anything I can do for you before I leave? I'll be back in the morning."

He shook his head, "Not a thing. Again, I apologize for the other night. Thank you for feeding me so well."

With that, she left while he wished she would stay.

The next week brought challenges. The orthopedic doctor approved of Dan's progress and said he could get rid of the boot in a week if he promised to stay off his ankle as much as possible. The stitches would come out of his hand next Monday, so he'd be able to use it, but driving was still out. The veterinarian whose practice he'd taken over was surprisingly happy about covering for him. And Thursday is Thanksgiving. Both the retired vet and Betty, his office manager, a woman with five kids and four grandkids, invited him for the holiday meal, but he politely declined. There is a certain redhead whose cooking he's enjoying more and more. He could invite her out, couldn't he? She had to be tired of all the cooking she'd done for him this past week.

On Wednesday, Megan arrived with hamburgers and fries and an apology for not cooking.

"What, you ran out of recipes? If you keep feeding me so well, I'll be ten pounds heavier by the time I can walk. Please don't apologize. I'm so grateful to you for all these meals. You must be exhausted, running back and forth between our houses, working and taking care of Koko and me." Hearing the mention of her name, the puppy came running, leash dragging behind her.

"Koko! Sit. Now." Meg put authority in her command, and the dog sat down, waiting at attention. "Good girl. Now leave the poor man alone." She'd picked up the leash and started toward the door when Dan stopped her.

"I'm impressed. You're the alpha now. See how she's watching you, waiting for your next word?"

Megan smiled. "Finally! I don't have time to put up with her running off." She pulled a doggie treat from her pocket and gave it to Koko. "I've also gotten a big supply of T-R-E-A-T-S. Fortunately, she can't spell yet."

Dan guffawed. She looked so darn proud of herself. And Koko adored her. "You have the knack. She's lucky to have you."

Of course, Megan blushed at this.

After they enjoyed their take-out meal, he broached the topic of Thanksgiving dinner. "I'd like to take you out to eat tomorrow, to thank you for all the meals you've made for me."

She stopped stroking Koko. "That's a lovely invitation. I did pick up a turkey breast, though, and have the rest of the meal figured out. It would be easier if you could come over to my house while I fix the food." Meg watched for his response.

"I would never turn down your cooking. But I'm feeling bad about all the work you've had to do while I just sit here." He raised his bandaged hand.

She asked, "Would you have helped me if I was the one who'd gotten hurt?"

"Of course, but…" he blustered.

Her smile provided the answer. "I rest my case."

"I hope you never need my services. I doubt you'd get such great meals if I were cooking." He paused. "Can I give you a thank you kiss?" He held his breath.

"Yes."

She rose and came around the table. She bent to give him a peck, but he had other plans. He wrapped his arms around her and kissed her soundly. She responded slowly at first, then put her arms around his neck and kissed him back. He maneuvered her onto his lap where she fit so very nicely. They continued kissing until Koko barked, at which Dan and Meg said, "Sit." In unison.

They grinned and went back to their most enjoyable task. Koko went to sleep.

Thanksgiving dinner went very well with the turkey breast coming out of the oven juicy and succulent. The dressing was fragrant, and the mashed potatoes had just enough lumps to prove it was homemade. The wine Dan provided was excellent, of course, and the flowers he'd ordered were perfect.

In the next weeks, Dan regained use of his hand and foot and went back to work. Megan continued her job at the library while Koko learned how to sit, heel, and even stay, though the last was painful to watch. She quivered and moaned very softly until Megan gave her the signal to come.

Dan and Megan shared meals at her home and at his. Sometimes they went out, but they were always together.

The week before Christmas found them holding hands as they walked through the mall while carols played softly in the background. Dan pulled her to a stop at the Santa photo booth. It was closing time, but he insisted they needed a picture. He placed Megan on Santa's lap, much to her embarrassment, and got down on one knee. He pulled a small velvet box from his coat pocket, opened it, and held the ring out to her. She had tears in her eyes as she looked into his.

"Megan, would you do me the honor of becoming my wife? I love you so very much."

She, as usual, blushed and burst into tears. But she said, "Yes!" with authority.

She is now the alpha, of course.

It looked like Christmas was coming early this year.

Shrimp Paprikosh

1 red bell pepper
1 green bell pepper
1 onion
2 Tablespoons cooking oil
Salt and Pepper
1 6 oz can tomato paste
1 Tablespoon paprika (NOT smoked paprika or hot paprika)
12 oz. chicken broth
1 lb raw shrimp, peeled and deveined, frozen is fine

Slice and cut into 1" pieces, the peppers and onions, and sauté the veggies in the oil until onions are translucent, seasoning with salt and pepper. Add the tomato paste and rinse the can twice with chicken broth (12 oz broth), adding the paprika and more salt and pepper. Simmer for 10-15 minutes.

Add shrimp, rinsed and patted dry. Simmer until shrimp is done, about 5-10 minutes. If too thick you can thin with more chicken broth. Adjust seasoning.

Serve over cooked rice or noodles, I've also served over fettuccini. Even better the second day!

This is my version of a family recipe, made with chicken. To make Chicken Paprikosh, substituted 2 cups of shredded cooked chicken. You can use a broasted chicken for this, to make it easier.

No Pressure

by Ann Macela

Ann Macela writes award-winning contemporary and contemporary paranormal romance. A native Texan, she now lives in the Chicago area. She started life reading mysteries, then sci-fi and fantasy. When she discovered romances, she saw a way to combine all the aspects of books that she liked into her own stories. Her six-book Magic Series is about a group of people who can cast spells to help them with their everyday jobs. Windswept, a single title contemporary with a historical twist, won the Romantic Times Reviewers' Choice Award for Best Romance, Small Press, 2008. Her latest is the two-book "Wolf Series," now available as both ebooks and in print. Macela has been a public school and university teacher, a writer of academic history, a marketing/PR person, a writer of Word manuals, and a consultant. She holds a Ph.D. in history.

What if . . . you've been dating a fabulous man and, in fact, have fallen in love with him? Not that you've told him so, of course. It's too soon, and you're not sure how he feels about you. But the attraction is definitely there.

What if . . . his wealthy parents are coming to town, and he has the bright idea for you to cook them dinner one night? In your condo, and he'll bring wine and the dessert. It's a chance for you and them to get to know each other, he tells you.

The catch? His mother is a gourmet cook and buddies with the most famous chefs. His father is the head of a law firm in New York and coming to see how his son is handling the Chicago office. Will you be able to make a favorable impression as prospective daughter-in-law material?

You can feel the anxiety building. What can you cook when all you've ever made is good, old, family fare? What if his mother doesn't like what you serve—and doesn't like you, either?

However, you're in love, so you agree. And find out that's just the beginning of pressure.

Chapter One

Date: Saturday, December 1st

"You want me to do what?" Mary Ann Eisermann stared in horror at the man she was in love with.

Not that he knew that last part, of course. Neither of them had used such an important, loaded word—yet. She knew he *liked* her a lot, but that other *L* word? And now this?

Up to this moment, she'd been sure she'd do anything for this man. This request, however, scared the living daylights out of her.

Could he be serious? After dinner in a small local restaurant, he sat on her couch, smiling like all he asked was a simple favor, but she knew better. This could be big, no, huge trouble, with enormous possibilities for disaster.

"I'm just asking you to invite Mother and Dad over for dinner while they're here and before you leave for your family Christmas in Ohio. They're always complaining about restaurant food not being up to standard, and I know they'd appreciate a home-cooked meal." Geoffrey Smithson grinned, ran a hand through his light brown hair, then shrugged. "Besides, it would give them the chance to get to know you, and vice-versa."

Just asking? More like a command performance to Mary Ann. She knew what his mother did "for fun." He'd told her. And what did "get to know you" mean? She could feel the pressure to impress the woman already.

Not questions to be asked right now, she decided, as she gave him a squinty look. "Let me get this straight. You want me to cook for a woman you've told me makes her own gourmet dinners for family and friends, who eats regularly in the best restaurants in the world, and who is cooking buddies with the most famous chefs. And I'm supposed to prepare dinner for her and your father in my small Chicago condo. I am totally *not* in her league."

Geoff frowned slightly, then pulled her into his arms and gave her a small kiss. As usual when being held against his hard body and gazing into those dark brown eyes, Mary Ann wanted to melt. But they needed to discuss what he asked, not pretend it was a simple, easy favor. When she made herself sit up straight to put some space between them, he kept hold of her hands.

"Really, it's no big deal," he said, rubbing her knuckles. "Mother just likes to cook. Neither of my parents is a picky eater. They've traveled the world and are ready to try anything. I'll bring the wine and dessert, so you don't have to worry about that. Simple hors d'oeuvres like veggies and cheese or something from the deli will be fine. They're arriving on Wednesday, the twelfth, in the evening and leaving on the nineteenth. It's only the first of December, so you have plenty of time to plan. I do know how serious you are about planning."

Well, he had that right. As recently appointed manager of planning for a mid-sized company striving to be a large one, she'd better be. At age thirty-two, she'd had to prove herself to her staff. That was work, and she knew how to do it. But this date with his parents had nothing to do with her professional activities, and it had the potential for making or breaking her future with him.

Something didn't fit here, Mary Ann decided, and she slid back so they weren't touching. Only partly joking, she asked, "Whose idea was this get-together? Am I being put on display? Or do your parents check out every woman you date?"

She could almost see the wheels revolving in his lawyer's head as he thought about his answer, which came characteristically quickly. He'd once joked that he was the fastest thinker in Chicago, and she believed him. On handling the unexpected, he gave her a run for her money all the time, and that was part of his appeal.

"It's my idea," he answered. "No display, and they don't check out my dates. You're special to me, Mary Ann, and I know they'll like you and hope you'll like them. You're a really good cook, and we have to eat, so why not do so in a comfortable place? Restaurants are noisy and not private. We can relax here. You know how much I like your condo. It's great and really reflects your personality."

She couldn't help but be flattered by his words. Especially the "special to him" comment. Still . . . having a wealthy set of parents over for dinner? In a definitely not-what-they-were-used-to setting?

Glancing around her living/dining room, she decided she was proud of what she'd done with her space. It had been such a find—affordable, a decent neighborhood, close to public transportation and her company, in good condition—and sold itself to her the minute she walked in. Her promotion and raise, which she'd worked so hard for, had come just at the right moment. Now it was truly hers.

Geoff was correct, her personality was visible all over the place. Her colorful pictures and paintings, the reupholstered sofa and chairs, the garage sale and flea market finds, mementos from trips, they all made the two-bedroom, second-floor unit into her home. Thanks to her parents, who, with all three of the children now on their own, had downsized to a smaller house, she had a dining room table, chairs, and matching buffet, which she loved.

What was she going to do about his request? Despite his protests, she knew this was a check-out-the-woman-our-son-is-dating situation. She'd suffered through those before. None of the parents of the men she dated had rejected her. No, she and their sons simply hadn't matched. She and Geoff did. But was there any way to get out of cooking this dinner?

Concentrate! First, what had caused this visit? Were they coming to Chicago only to check her out? Something didn't make sense. "What happened to your plans to go to New York for the holidays?"

"They're still on. Dad decided to visit my branch of the law firm, show the flag of the home office. He claims to be checking in with a local colleague and another client of his as well. He really wants to see up close how I'm running things after two years as managing partner. He did the same thing last year. Mother's coming along to visit friends and shop. Neither of them wants to miss Christmas with my sister, her husband, and their two kids. When we close the firm for the holidays, I'll leave on the twenty-first. I'll be back before New Years, probably the twenty-eighth."

Mary Ann sighed. Geoff had said his father could be a micro-manager at times. Therefore, this visit wasn't totally about her, but at least half about him. Geoff had to satisfy Dad. His branch of the firm was doing well, so no big problem there.

She, on the other hand, had to satisfy his mother. Even not having met either parent, she expected to have the more difficult job. Wealthy mothers were known to protect sons from what they considered avaricious women, after all. Mrs. Smithson could be one of those. Mary Ann had been on the receiving end of intense and possibly hostile scrutiny like that before, and it was no fun. This time, however, she was in love, and the verdict had become impossibly important.

She could see no way out of the predicament, so she caved. "Are they allergic to anything? Foods, spices, whatever? Any foods they hate?"

"Nope." His lips quirked—what she called his lawyer smile, meaning *Gotcha!* "Dad doesn't like cauliflower, though, and Mother prefers subtle seasoning. I never did understand what 'subtle' means to her. To me, it means I can't taste the stuff at all."

"Okay, I'll do it." Her planning abilities woke up, finally, and she continued, "But it will have to be on Saturday or Sunday evening. I can't get away from the office on a weekday in time to prepare a meal. Let me know what day's best for them. If they like a pre-dinner cocktail or after-dinner cognac, you'll have to provide it. Arrive here at 7 p.m., we'll eat at 8. You'll have to help me get the food on the table—and clean up."

"Mother will be glad to assist, you know."

"She's perfectly welcome to offer, and I'll come up with something for her to do." She looked toward her small kitchen. It was partially hidden by a high counter that separated the cooking area from the dining room. The actual free space in the working part of the kitchen was very close, no, *too close* quarters for two active cooks. Thank goodness. She'd put Mrs. Smithson on one of the bar stools on this side of the counter. So she added, "Or not, as circumstances dictate."

"Agreed as specified. Anything else?" he asked with an oh-so-innocent, wide-eyed look beneath which she could see his satisfaction.

She thought for a moment before throwing all her cares about the dinner out of her head. Worry about that later. It had been a long, busy week for both of them, and they'd managed only two telephone calls. Now she had the man she loved right here.

"Well, now that you mention it . . . It is Saturday night, and neither of us is working tomorrow . . ." She moved closer, leaned in, and gave him a small kiss.

He took the hint and pulled her into his arms. One kiss led to another and another and eventually the bedroom. That was totally fine with Mary Ann.

Chapter Two

The middle of that same night

Geoff woke up and lay there for a minute. What had made his eyes open? Usually he slept straight through, especially when he was lying next to Mary

Ann after they'd had sex. She was a real snuggler, and now on her side, with her butt backed up against his hip, he couldn't resist turning to curl around her. His five-foot-eleven fit so well around her five-foot-four. He loved it.

No, more than that. He loved *her*.

In point of fact and absolute truth, he'd come to the conclusion he wanted her with him always. Making a life together. Married. Living in the same home. Having kids. Kids with brown hair with reddish highlights and green eyes like hers.

Those thoughts stunned him for a moment. No other woman had ever affected him like this one. Never ever had he thought he'd get to this place of wanting *a wife,* much less *kids. Get hold of yourself, Smithson.*

He took a slow deep breath, concentrating on his diaphragm, let it out, repeated twice more, and finally relaxed. How did he get to this situation? He'd enjoyed his bachelorhood. But being named the managing partner of the Chicago branch office of his father's New York firm had been sobering, consuming, and pressure-filled. For the last two years, especially the first one, he'd worked like hell to show that he had the abilities, knowledge, and balls for the job. Some of the older members of the firm had not trusted his then-thirty-five-year-old self, but he'd proved his worth to them—at the cost of his personal life.

Going home to an empty apartment had not been fun, however, and restaurants and especially bars had soon lost their appeal. He enjoyed meeting women but detested having to "pick up" one—he wanted and needed more than sex. He hated even more being seen as the "Pick of the Night," as one tipsy woman had declared. Damn it, he was too old for those games. He wanted companionship and support, serious and frivolous discussions, going places together, true friendship. What his parents had.

Then, eight months ago, at a party given by mutual friends, he had spotted Mary Ann across the room. He'd talked the host, his old college buddy, into introducing him. Something told him to take it easy, not to rush her. So they'd gone on real dates—nice dinners, a movie or two, a play, a baseball game, the latest exhibit at the Field Museum, a concert in Millennium Park, even a picnic. Exchanged quite a few kisses, too, but not much more than that. He had hopes, though, so he made sure to have a couple of condoms in his wallet.

Finally, when he thought he'd explode if they didn't carry this attraction to the next level, he'd brought her home after a date, and she'd asked him in. The next thing he knew, they were kissing, holding on like they were in a wind storm, and then undressing each other. Oh, man, hugging her with no clothes on—he could still remember how that felt. In fact, his body was reminding him of it right now.

Just as he was wondering if Mary Ann might be enticed to wake up, she slid away. Before he could pull her back, she turned to face him, pushed him on his back, and draped herself across his chest, her top leg over his thigh. When she raised her head, there was enough light for him to see her face. She was smiling.

She kissed his shoulder. "I could almost feel you thinking. Can't sleep? Need some help?"

She ran her hand down his side, across his abs, and wrapped it around his shaft, which turned totally hard so fast he gasped. He managed to get the word, "Condom," out of his mouth, but then had to endure her wiggling around to reach over him into the box on the nightstand next to him.

When he raised his hand for it, she straddled his legs and dangled the package out of his reach. "Just relax," she purred. "I'll take care of everything."

If he didn't explode first. She opened the packet and set about rolling the sheath onto him. Very slowly. Geoff took a deep breath and grasped the top of the bed—for dear life. His strangled "Marrrry Annnn" to encourage faster application had no effect on her.

When she had the condom arranged to her liking, she rubbed herself up his now-steel-like cock and slowly took him into her body. Her up-and-down strokes set him off like a firecracker, and she followed him into the explosion.

When the storm subsided and peace returned, his first thought was, *This, just this wonderful, gorgeous, giving woman in my arms and my bed, is all I want and need—forever.*

After he took care of the condom and joined her back in bed, he pulled her into his arms. She lay her head on his shoulder and her arm across his chest. They fell asleep together.

Geoff woke a little later with Mary Ann still holding him tight. As he was her.

The way it's supposed to be. Exhaustion forced him under again—with a smile on his face.

Chapter Three

Monday, December 3rd

What on earth should she cook for his parents?

That night after work, Mary Ann mulled over the coming visit by Geoff's parents. She had searched online for plans for entire dinners, not individual items, and the number was overwhelming. On top of that, so many recipes were exceedingly complicated. She was a pretty good cook and could certainly follow a recipe, but to try to make something "gourmet" like his mother would cook? That way led to doom and destruction . . . and maybe, even worse, ridicule.

At least she had decent place settings of plates, cups, saucers, glasses, and silverware, not to mention various pots, bowls, frying pans, etc. All thanks to her mother, who'd sent her off to the big city with a huge survival kit. Mom had made sure the three of them, she, sister Debbie, and even brother Ron, knew how to cook and set a table. Ron had complained until he found out that women loved a man who knew his way around a kitchen.

She and Geoff had cooked together, various light meals or steaks or pasta. No, those things wouldn't work here. That left only one source of inspiration and information. She reached for the phone.

"Hello, Mom? It's Mary Ann."

"Mary Ann! I was just thinking about you. Is everything all right? Are you still coming for Christmas?"

"Everything is fine. In fact, more than fine, and I'm still coming as scheduled, as long as the snow holds off. How's Ohio and the two of you? Much snow yet?"

"No to the last question. We're doing great, and your father is thinking of building a greenhouse. He misses his gardening in the winter, always has, but never had time to make a place to do it while he was working. I'm encouraging him. As we all expected, retirement hasn't been that easy for him. We're coping together, so don't you worry. How's that young man of yours?"

"Geoff is fine. I need some help." She explained the situation. "With his mother being such a gourmet cook, I'm not about to try anything restaurant-fancy or too complicated, like the Internet is full of. But I'd love to serve something different and at the same time fairly easy *and* tasty."

"Hmmmm." Mom was silent, and Mary Ann could hear her flipping cards in her recipe box. "I agree on the restaurant part. A simple meal cooked well wins every time. Let's talk about it. You're responsible for the main course? What else?"

"Geoff is bringing dessert and wine. We'll need hors d'oeuvres, but he suggested cheese and crackers. I thought I'd get some deli items unless you have a better idea. For the main, I keep coming back to the idea of chicken. Maybe roasted, not fried. Definitely not a heavy meal."

"Roast chicken is good," Mom agreed. "It's hard to ruin a good bird. You might also throw in a half chicken cut into two pieces in case someone wants more or all three want a breast or a drumstick. Aunt Cathie left you that great Dutch oven, and I know it has roasted many a bird."

"That would work." In fact, Mary Ann liked the idea a lot. "For a veggie, I figured some broccoli with almonds. Maybe some rice for a starch? But it feels like I need more."

"I agree. Since Thanksgiving is not that long ago, I wouldn't fix any kind of stuffing, not with bread or cornbread. What else is there?"

Mom's comment set off some ideas in Mary Ann's brain. "But . . . what if . . . fruit or something that could go over the rice? But cooked? Is there anything you know of like that?"

"Apples might work. Let's make something up. Keep talking."

"Oooh, I like the apple idea. What about . . . apples and . . . raisins . . . and nuts of some kind." With those words, Mary Ann could feel her brain kick into gear. "Chop up the apples into bite-sized pieces. Make a lot of it so there'd be seconds. Cooked in a casserole on the top of the stove."

"*And* soaked in dry sherry," Mom added. "That way the apples won't turn, the raisins will get plump, and you've added flavor. I suggest Granny Smith apples. They hold up well in cooking and can counteract the sweetness of the raisins. Be sure to add the chicken drippings to them."

"I like the sherry idea and especially the chicken drippings. Walnuts, too. Maybe a little cinnamon." Mary Ann couldn't help smiling. She and Mom together always came up with something tasty. "This will be light, but filling, I think. Some French bread to sop up the juices, and it should work fine. What about a salad to start? Think that's necessary?"

"I'm not sure about that, what with nibbles before hand."

"I'll ask Geoff if his mother expects one. Oh, I feel much better about this dinner party now. Thanks, Mom, for all the help."

"Just let me know how it turns out. Be sure to write all this down. I want the recipe!"

"Will do. Hi and love to Dad."

After she hung up the phone, Mary Ann quickly finished off her notes. She'd do a little research on-line later to see if anyone had a recipe like what she and Mom had just thought up. All in all, she felt a lot better about this dinner party now.

Chapter Four

Thursday evening, December 13th

After saying goodnight to his parents and dropping them off at their hotel after dinner, Geoff gave a sigh of relief on the way to his condo. He did love them, but they wore him out sometimes.

At least Dad had found nothing wrong at the firm today. Not that Geoff thought he would. The office was doing nicely on all counts, and he'd managed to get the senior attorneys on his side once they recognized that he knew what he was doing. His settling the difficult Trilby case had been the turning point.

Now to see how Mary Ann was. They'd gotten together the previous weekend, but only for Saturday dinner and sex since both were up to their eyeballs in projects requiring weekend work. He'd wait until he got home, however, because she hated him calling while driving. Too many crazy Chicago drivers, she claimed, Bluetooth phone connection or not.

Besides, he really wanted a nightcap. He deserved one. At dinner, his mother had asked questions about Mary Ann and her entire family. Their backgrounds, schooling, professions, to begin with. He had answered carefully because Mother was not a good listener and preferred to jump to her own conclusions. Tonight, some of her observations and conclusions, both on no evidence whatsoever, went farther than her usual innuendos about the women he dated. She had actually strongly implied Mary Ann wasn't good enough for him.

Thank God, Dad had told her to relax and wait until they'd met the woman before jumping to conclusions. But then, he had gone on to talk about how "his only son" needed to think about starting a family. His sister with two children and another on the way was ahead of him in the grandchild race. *Race? What race?*

Geoff could only hope his parents wouldn't interrogate Mary Ann like they did him. Mother had never liked any of his previous girlfriends, but Mary Ann was special. He was sure Mother would love her as he did. Dad would be an absolute pushover, too.

Once home, he stretched out in his recliner with a cognac and hit the speed-dial for Mary Ann.

"Hi," she answered. "How are you holding up under the onslaught of parents?"

"I'm hopeful of surviving. Dad is happy with me as far as the firm goes. Mother has a shopping plan for the grandkids' Christmas presents, and they're both looking forward to meeting you in person on Sunday evening."

"Are you ready for the firm's party for them on Saturday?"

"Yeah, and I wish it included you, but the older attorneys said *spouses only*, and Dad went along with them. Something about a couple of fiascos in the past where some lady guests were not wives, but, and I quote, *totally unsuitable for the dignity of the firm.* I'll let you figure out what that means. So, be happy, you'll miss a really boring evening. How are your preparations coming?"

"Okay, I guess. I'm going grocery shopping tomorrow. Listen to this and tell me if there's anything there your parents hate." She rattled off a list of groceries and stuff.

"No, you're good," he answered. "Just how much food are you making? It sounds like a lot."

"Well, I'm hoping for some leftovers. Warning and truth in advertising, though. I haven't made this complete recipe before, so I hope it comes out all right. My mom made a couple of suggestions, too."

"I really appreciate this, you know."

"We'll get through it together," she answered.

He couldn't help smiling. He really liked the word *together*. "I wish I was there with you."

"Me, too." She said the words in a very breathy, low-pitched tone. "Right now. Snuggled up with *nothing* between us. We'll just have to make up for your absence . . . later."

Oh, damn, he felt her soft voice travel from his ear through his chest and lodge in his cock. Sucking in his breath at the effect, he held back a growl, but just barely. Finally he croaked out, "I'm going to hold you to that, *woman.*"

"You'd better, *man.*" Then she laughed. "Sweet dreams."

He managed a chuckle. "You too."

After they hung up, Geoff took a firm swallow of his drink and looked down at his lap. How was he supposed to sleep with this hard-on? The time-honored method: after a cold shower.

Chapter Five

Sunday, December 16th

The alarm went off, and Mary Ann sat straight up. She grabbed the clock. What, 7 a.m.? It was Sunday. Why had she set the alarm? Then she remembered. She had a refrigerator full of food. Geoff's parents were coming to dinner tonight. She flopped back on her bed.

Thank goodness the law firm entertained the elder Smithsons last night. There was no way she could have put together a meal yesterday. Not after having to spend the morning at work because of mistakes by a vice president. At least the president had realized who caused the problem and thanked her for her extra effort. That particular VP couldn't plan—or execute—his way out of a paper bag.

The afternoon had been spent doing more grocery shopping as well as prepping the chicken. She'd found a shop with very-fresh, never-frozen chicken—no defrosting required, a definite time saver. At home, she rubbed it well with salt and pepper inside and out and put it in the fridge.

There was definitely a lot of work to be done, and she needed to keep to her schedule. So, out of bed and into the bathroom.

By five-thirty that evening, exactly as she had planned, Mary Ann was as ready for her guests as she'd ever be. The table was set and looked pretty nice, in her opinion. The broccoli was ready for steaming, the rice was measured for its pot, the apples, raisins, and walnuts were soaking in sherry in a big bowl, the oven was heating, and it was almost time to put the bird in for slow roasting.

She spooned some of the sherry apple-raisin-walnut mix into the chicken, secured the opening with metal skewers, tied the drumsticks together, folded the wings under, and sprinkled both the whole bird and the extra half (now in two pieces) with rosemary and sage. After oiling the Dutch oven, she transferred the chicken (breast side up) and the other breast and drumstick pieces into it and dotted them with butter. Some sherry went into the bottom of the roaster. Good, with the chicken fat drippings that should coalesce into a nice basting mixture.

Here we go! She slid the large heavy pot into the preheated oven without its cover. Set the temp at 450° and the timer for twenty minutes, then she'd reduce it to 350°. The rest of the apples, etc., went into a stovetop-safe casserole with a little more sherry and butter and cinnamon. A quick stir, but that was it for a while. *Whew!*

A glance at the clock told her she was on schedule. Geoff was one of those people who often arrived early, and she'd warned him against it this time. The last thing she needed was a gourmet cook watching her put this meal together.

Now for a quick shower, in and out. Yea for her short curly hair. No time wasted there. A touch of eyeliner, shadow, mascara, and lipstick and she'd done what she could with her face—especially since she was going to be working over a hot stove.

The timer bell went off, so a trip to the kitchen to turn down the oven. She checked the chicken—it was browning nicely, and it smelled really good. She turned it and the pieces over for even cooking and set the timer again. As she spooned a little of the sherry/butter/drippings combo from the bottom of the pan over the bird, she thought of her mother, who always swore by basting.

Back to the bedroom. As for her simple V-necked dress, the green went with her eyes, and the skirt allowed freedom of movement. Low heeled kitten pumps wouldn't leave her with sore feet or make her wobbly with the heavy pots. Gold earrings and the matching necklace her parents had given her when she graduated the last time would have to do for jewelry. If his mother didn't like her outfit, too bad.

When the timer went off, she wrapped herself in an apron and turned the chicken over again. The browning was coming along nicely, she thought as she basted some more. Smelled good, too.

Once more around the table and the living room, just to make sure all was in place. Yes, the pre-dinner munchies were already on the coffee table. She'd actually run out of things to do.

She told herself sternly, *"Don't fidget!"* But even out loud, the words had little effect, and she walked from the front door to the bedroom and back—twice. She made herself stand still. Even when she defended her dissertation, she hadn't been this nervous. Was that what love did to her?

The sound of a car stopping drew her to the window. Looked like it was show time! How she managed to wait for the doorbell to ring so she could let them inside the building, she had no idea, but within seconds, she was greeting her guests from her open door as they got off the elevator.

Geoff gave her a wink and ushered in his parents. "Mother and Dad, I'd like to introduce Mary Ann Eisermann. Mary Ann, Alexandra and Herbert Smithson."

"Welcome to my home," she said with a smile.

His father was what she had expected, an older version of the son—or should that be vice versa? No matter. Both men wore what Mary Ann thought of as "high-priced attorney" suits and their overcoats were dark, impeccable, probably cashmere.

His mother was immaculately dressed and absolutely gorgeous. A blond coiffure, a dark blue sheath, perfect dark red fingernails, and fashionably thin. Her jewelry consisted of earrings and a circle of gold pin—both shining with diamonds and emeralds—along with the obligatory gold engagement and wedding bands, the former with what had to be a two-caret diamond. Alexandra had beautiful skin, too, the type her own mother would give her favorite sewing machine for, Mary Ann estimated. Over it all, the obligatory fur coat—sable, from the look of it.

Mary Ann shook hands with his parents—father's handshake hardy, mother's limp. Geoff and his father then left to get the wine and dessert out of the car.

Leaving the two women alone. *Thanks so much, Geoff,* Mary Ann thought, but said, "Let me help with your coat."

"You have a lovely home," his mother said, looking around after Mary Ann put the fur coat in the closet. "So convenient and comfortable."

"Thank you, Mrs. Smithson. It's small, but fits me well."

"Please call me Alexandra," the older woman replied with a smile. "Is there anything I can do to help?"

And wasn't that a loaded question, Mary Ann thought, but she answered, "Not right now, thanks. Excuse me, I just need to see how the chicken is doing. Please make yourself comfortable."

While she basted the chicken, his mother checked the condo out, but said nothing. Mary Ann couldn't tell if Alexandra approved or not. Didn't matter, Geoff did, and that's what counted.

The men came in, Mary Ann found a place on her little kitchen table for the cherry pie dessert Geoff had brought, and Mr. Smithson told her to call him Herbert and give him a corkscrew to open the wine.

"Thanks for having us," his father said. "It sure smells good in here. I'm looking forward to home cooking. I really am tired of restaurant food."

"Geoffrey tells me we're having chicken with apples and raisins," Alexandra said. "I don't believe I've had that combination before."

Mary Ann smiled as if unconcerned. "It's an old family recipe of my mother's."

Geoff poured the wine, and everybody sat down and nibbled on the deli treats. Herbert started the interrogation. "I understand you're originally from Ohio."

The expected quizzing followed about her parents, siblings, her own education, her fast rise in her profession, and living in Chicago. In a totally polite, even subtle manner, Alexandra took Mary Ann's life apart and put it back together again.

At least that was the impression Mary Ann let her assume. This wasn't her first ride on the parents' merry-go-round. She answered calmly and was just a little bit gratified to see his mother blink a couple of times at her very sketchy report of her accomplishments. Telling her whole story just made people think she was a braggart, and she'd learned it was better to be underestimated at times. Without much detail, she also mentioned a couple of achievements by her parents, brother, and sister, just to be clear that she didn't come from lowly, stupid peasants, but from lowly successful peasants with brains.

Geoff, bless him, knew what she was doing and gave her a wink before moving the conversation into more neutral topics. Mary Ann checked on the chicken, stirred the apples, and started the rice. Finally, it was time to take the chicken out of the Dutch oven and finish the other dishes.

Alexandra stood by the counter to watch as Mary Ann moved the chicken to the serving platter, scooped out the apple mixture and added it to the simmering casserole along with some of the drippings from the bottom of the pot. "Oh, that looks and smells delicious."

"Yes, it does, doesn't it?" Mary Ann answered, rather pleased with herself. Nothing ventured, nothing gained, she decided, so she picked up a spoonful of the apples concoction and offered it to his mother. "Does this need anything?"

Alexandra tasted the offering and pronounced it "very good indeed."

Mary Ann could have done a happy dance, but controlled herself.

Behind his mother's back, Geoff grinned and gave her a thumbs up. Then he organized his parents into helping put the dishes on the table, plus cutting the French bread, and opening another bottle of wine.

Conversation for the rest of the meal was general, if a little pointed over politics and a little contentious over Chicago vs. New York sports teams. Alexandra was mostly quiet, but Mary Ann noticed she was watching both her and Geoff closely as she almost cleaned her plate. The recipe she and mom had invented was evidently a success.

After the dessert and coffee, Geoff helped clear the table while Mary Ann put the remaining food away and filled the dishwasher. Herbert and Alexandra sat on the high stools and sipped the cognac Geoff had brought, and the conversation shifted to a discussion of the difference between living in New York and Chicago. After one more cup of coffee, Herbert announced it was time to leave if they were to be worth anything at work the next day. Mary Ann was a little surprised to realize it was 10:30 already.

The Smithsons put on their coats, and both parents thanked her for the "wonderful" meal and the fine company. Geoff handed his keys to his father and said he'd be out to the car in a few minutes. Herbert clapped him on the back, smirked, and said, "Take your time, son."

The door had hardly shut behind them before Geoff had her in his arms. "Damn, but you were absolutely wonderful tonight. And the food was great.

I hope Mother didn't get to you too badly. I apologize for the interrogation."

"No need. It was no more or less than I expected." She smiled up at him as the tension in her back and shoulders dissolved. "But I need this hug right now."

"Me, too, and one thing more . . ." He kissed her long and deep. They were both slow to let go when they separated. "Damn, I wish I didn't have to leave."

"Take your parents to the hotel. I have a horrible week coming up, and yours probably will be as bad, but let's talk after they're gone home."

"I'll try to come by or at least call on Wednesday. I hope we can get together Thursday night. We have to exchange presents, you know. I'm still leaving for New York on Friday."

"Oh, I do understand," she groaned. "I've gotten inundated with so much work, I'm just living a day at a time. I do have your present, so Thursday night is ours, together, no matter what. If the roads are clear, I'm driving to Ohio on Friday. Now, your parents are waiting." *And leave before I can't let you go.*

After one more kiss, he left. She closed the door behind him and leaned against it. She missed him already.

On the way to the kitchen to make sure it was tidy, she thought about the Smithsons' visit. That was the most exhausting *interview* she'd ever had. Because it definitely was an interview for the position of daughter-in-law. Worse than her dissertation defense when one of the profs didn't agree with her conclusions until she pulled out her laptop and showed him the numbers, worse than her first boss's condescension, and even worse than the mother of her first date.

Well, like all those previous aggravations, she'd survived in good shape and ready for the next battle. Because there would be one. She knew she hadn't "won" anything where his mother was concerned. But, oh, how she wished she had a bug in that car to hear the conversation going on right now.

Chapter Six

Sunday night in the car on the way to the hotel after the dinner at Mary Ann's

"Are you planning to *marry* that *woman*, Geoffrey?"

His mother's voice came out of the back seat in the low, somewhat menacing tone that had signaled her strong displeasure as long as he could remember. She was usually complaining about one of his girlfriends, how uncultured they were. But she had *never* said the word "marry" like that, no matter how long they'd been dating. *Marry* like it would be, at the least, a horrible mistake and, at the worst, the downfall of the entire family. Then there was her emphasis on *woman* like she wanted to use another term— gold digger, or prostitute, or whore.

He flicked a glance at his father sitting next to him in the front. Dad was looking straight ahead and frowning. No help there.

"Why do you ask?" Had he spent too long saying good night to Mary Ann? Had Mother seen something in his or her demeanor she didn't like? He needed information before answering that question of hers. Her innocent-seeming inquiries were often full of traps. He'd fall back on typical lawyer tactics: ask questions, not give answers.

"Because I'm thinking about your *future*," his mother responded, almost biting off the last word. "It's a huge responsibility to run this branch of our firm. It will be even larger when you succeed your father. You need a helpmate who understands the demands on an attorney, who can support you without reservation, who can be a stellar hostess, who can fit in with your colleagues and their wives, who makes you the center of her universe."

"Give the man a break, Alexandra," his father put in. "There's nothing wrong with Mary Ann. Her accomplishments and the woman herself are quite impressive, aren't they? I had a good time tonight. The food was tasty and the conversation interesting once you stopped interrogating her. They're only at the dating stage. Who knows if the relationship will go any farther. Right, son?"

Geoff was ready with a comment until that last question. He knew how far he wanted the relationship to go. Exactly how far. *All the way.* But he'd be damned if he gave either parent a voice in the ultimate decision. That was for him and Mary Ann to make.

"Why do you think Mary Ann doesn't fit your criteria? What did she do or say that caused you to think so?" He kept his tone neutral, curious. Dad would catch the nuance, but Mother wouldn't. She hadn't been hearing anything but her own opinions for far too long.

"It's her background, most of all. The daughter of a school teacher and an ironworker? What could she possibly have in common with you and your colleagues? Does she understand the pressures on you to run the branch of a large law firm? Can she entertain in the manner that will give clients confidence in you and the firm? Yes, it was a pleasant *little meal,* her academic credentials are good, and she seems to be up to planning for a small firm, but will she be able to help you and deal with the kind of people you will have as partners and clients? What if she continues to work full time? Will she be there when you need her?"

Well, the outright sneer in her voice did it. Sparked Geoff's need to make a few salient points about Mary Ann. In no uncertain terms. His mother never understood subtlety.

Geoff pulled over into an open parking place and put the gear shift in park. Releasing his seat belt, he turned to face his mother. Keeping his tone as neutral as possible wasn't easy. "Where is all this anger and denigration coming from, Mother? Didn't you pay any attention to what Mary Ann was telling you during your interrogation? The brother is a PhD engineer with a slew of patents, the sister is a high-ranking computer geek with Google, and Mary Ann has a double Masters *and* a PhD in planning, accounting, and I don't know all. God only knows what the IQ is for anyone in that family, but it's probably in the 140s or 150s.

"We didn't talk much about her parents," he continued, "but her dad has patents on machinery for working iron, and her mother has all sorts of recognition for stellar secondary-school teaching. The question you should be asking is, why would anybody so smart want to associate with a plain lawyer like me?"

Might as well go for broke. "Look, Mother, it's the twenty-first century. If we do marry, and neither of us has said a word about that, I'd expect Mary Ann to continue to work. By the time she's your age, I expect she'll be president of a large company, not 'my little helpmate' out of the 1950s. She's been to my offices and impressed the hell out of every single person she met. The world has changed. Deal with it."

Mother opened and shut her mouth a couple of times, but before she managed to say anything, Dad jumped in, twisting around to see his wife. "Don't say I didn't warn you, honey, when you brought this up last night. You're jumping to conclusions and going into protective mode for a full-grown man who makes his own decisions. Now, to keep the peace in this family, let's just drop the subject, okay?"

"Fine with me," Geoff muttered and faced front to buckle himself in.

"Alexandra?" Dad asked.

In the rearview mirror, Geoff could see her jerk her head a couple of times. He'd consider that a yes. Taking a deep breath, he buckled himself in and watched for traffic before pulling the car back onto the road.

He knew she had his best interests at heart, but Mother could be a real pain in the ass at times. When she got on one of her angry tirades, she didn't listen to anyone. His sister said the medicine she was on helped to restore calm. He hoped she had brought some to Chicago. He'd stay out of her way in New York. Let Dad handle the situation. At least Laura's kids would take her mind off him and Mary Ann.

He'd keep the word "marriage" out of the conversation, too. He wasn't ready to say that one out loud around Mother until Mary Ann had given him the right to—although he'd told Dad of his goal and then swore him to secrecy. Did he think she'd say no? Not really. Damn, how could he get out of going to New York? Find a way to go with her to Ohio? Not by any means he could imagine. At least, he'd see her before they both left town. Should he ask her then to marry him?

Chapter Seven

Tuesday, December 18th, 7 p.m.

Mary Ann let herself into her condo and looked at her watch. Seven in the evening already? Or maybe the question should be "Only seven?" The last two days had flown by, totally filled with the company's plans for the next three years as well as the present year-end evaluations. She was on top of all the situations, but it was good she'd be coming back from Ohio on the twenty-seventh. She needed to do some hard, clear thinking—some of it work, but definitely not all.

As she went through the mail, she found one of those perfume sample envelopes with a heavy scent that reminded her of Alexandra's. Even after thinking through that dinner party, Mary Ann still didn't know what to make of Geoff's mother. She had been cordial until somewhere toward the end of the meal when she'd been following the conversation of the three of them, but not participating. Then she grew even quieter and seemed to scrutinize Geoff and Herbert carefully before turning her attention solely to her hostess. Alexandra had looked at her with a totally blank expression that somehow carried a whiff of menace.

What had they been talking about when that happened? Oh, yes, Herbert had asked how she would go about planning for a law office. She warned him that she was thinking off the top of her head, before she gave him four examples.

After a lively discussion, Herbert had said, "You know, I'm going to try a couple of those ideas. Son, don't let this one get away." Geoff had answered, "Don't worry, Dad, I won't." Alexandra had stared at her son for at least thirty seconds. Then they got up to clear the table, and she started taking part in the conversation again.

Weird. But maybe the older woman was just tired from all the shopping she'd been doing. Mary Ann certainly would be.

Enough of this. First, get into something comfortable like her old sweats, then finish off the remains of the Sunday meal. She'd have to make the chicken and apples again for her family. Mental note: send the recipe to Mom.

She'd accomplished her first goal and was standing in front of the fridge singing The Beatles' *All You Need Is Love* when the doorbell rang. *Oh, please let it be Geoff surprising me!* She ran to the window but saw only a cab down below. *Not Geoff. But who?* She went to the door panel and pressed the talk button. "Yes?"

"May I speak to you for a moment?" *Alexandra. What could she want?*

"Of course," she answered, hit the release for the door below, and stood in her own doorway as Geoff's mother came out of the elevator.

"I need to talk to you," her unexpected guest stated. She didn't sound very happy about it.

"Please come in." Mary Ann stepped back, and Alexandra sailed past her and stopped in the middle of the living room. She looked a little frazzled, like she'd been running her fingers through her hair. Her lipstick was also smudged, and her makeup wasn't perfect.

"Is everything all right?" Mary Ann asked.

"No, it is not," Alexandra answered angrily as though she'd been asked a stupid question. "It's clear that you're a gold digger with your eyes on my son as a possible husband, and I'm here to tell you that will never happen."

Mary Ann was dumbfounded for a second or two, but then asked the first question that popped into her head. "Why on earth do you think I'm after him or his money? How have you arrived at that conclusion?"

"Just look around here," Alexandra answered with a sweep of her arm that included the entire condo. She began to pace around the room as contempt dripped from her lips. "Reupholstered sofa, reclaimed dining set, dishware and silverware that you must have found at a discount store, and that dress on Sunday? Bargain basement surely." She waved at Mary Ann's current clothing. "And now, a ragamuffin."

Mary Ann definitely regretted letting this mad woman into her home, but she kept her mouth shut. No shouting match for her. Instead, she took a minute to gather her thoughts and picked up her purse as a distraction. Carefully she moved behind her kitchen counter where she surreptitiously took her phone out and set it to video and record. Then she propped it up, semi-hidden between a book and an ivy plant. If Alexandra attacked her physically, she wanted proof.

Her visitor paid no attention to her, but continued to pace and rant about how poorly decorated the condo was and how awful Mary Ann's clothes. How she had probably bought her university degrees off the Internet. Everything was a sure sign her son's inamorata was not worthy of him. She picked up Mary Ann's favorite vase, and for a minute, looked like she was going to throw it against the wall.

Reason definitely wouldn't work with this woman, but Mary Ann had to stand up for herself and Geoff—and her vase. "I really don't care what you think of my home or my clothes. I do care about Geoff. I don't know where our relationship is going to end up, but I do know that I love him."

The distracting statements seemed to work because Alexandra put down the vase with a thump. Then she stood in the middle of the room, her hands on her hips, and laughed rather shrilly. "Love him? Hah! I've driven off bigger threats to him and his career than you."

"Does he know you're here?" *Surely not.*

"Of course not, you simpleton. I've been chasing avaricious women away from him for years. All of them professed to love him, but every single one fled when the going got rough. When I took a hand in saving him. At least I could keep an eye on him when he was in New York. Look what moving here got him. *You.*" Her last word dripped with hate.

Mary Ann tried to decide what to do that might calm down Geoff's mother. Would explaining more or maybe asking where all the rage was coming from help? No, clearly not. The woman was so erratic, so venomous for no reason, she had to be on something, some kind of drugs or too much liquor, to be this irrational—or have another more serious mental problem altogether.

Best to maneuver Alexandra out of here before she decided the only way to get rid of the threat to her son was to attack physically. Mary Ann kept her voice as matter-of-fact as she could. "I'll take what you've told me under advisement. Shouldn't you be getting back to your husband and son?"

Alexandra came over to the high counter and leaned over it, but appeared not to notice the phone. Her tone vitriolic, her look furious, she spat out, "I'll go, but stay away from Geoffrey, or you'll be sorry."

With that, she turned, wrapped her coat closely around her, stumbled on her way to the door, flung it open, stalked out, and slammed the door behind her.

Mary Ann ran over to the window. Alexandra got into a cab waiting down below, and it drove off. That's right, she'd noticed it when she let the woman in. Well, at least she didn't have to worry about his mother freezing or trying to walk somewhere looking for transportation.

What to do about the situation? Call Geoff? To warn him about his mother? But he and his father were at some sort of lawyer gathering, weren't they? With important clients? He always set his phone on no-vibration and no-ring or turned it off entirely when in one of those meetings.

She called anyway and left a message asking Geoff to call but didn't explain why. They needed to discuss this mess in person and together. She'd try again tomorrow.

And tonight, what could she do? Call the cops? No, that was ridiculous. Alexandra hadn't attacked her physically. She had transportation, and the cabbie could call for help if necessary. Surely Herbert had some idea of his wife's overprotective and erratic behavior. Did Geoff? Mary Ann thought the woman needed help that only the family and a good doctor—or two—could give.

Herbert and Alexandra would be on the plane for New York by the afternoon. She and Geoff would be together tomorrow night. Mary Ann sighed in relief and went to eat leftovers. And have a glass of wine. She'd earned it.

Chapter Eight

Wednesday morning, December 19th, 7 a.m.

Geoff arrived at his parents' hotel in a hired limo to pick up his father to go to the office. Good, he was waiting in front. Geoff had no desire to see his mother after her diatribe last night. Besides, they had work to do. There were always last minute office details to be taken care of that only he and his father could handle. They usually made a lot of good decisions in limos— excellent privacy and no worry about driving.

Dad got into the car quickly and pulled out a folder as he mumbled something about his mother being on one of her rants and "at it again."

"What's the subject this time?" Geoff asked.

"You and Mary Ann. You know how she is about your girlfriends. Nobody is good enough for you, and everyone is after your money."

Geoff sighed. "Unfortunately, I know all too well. She was never so unkind to any of my girlfriends before. I thought we settled that issue long ago. I was surprised when it came back on Sunday."

"So was I. She never has given up on her opinions easily, but she's getting more erratic in her anger and expressions about several matters. I haven't said anything about it to you because she's seeing a doctor who is able to settle her down. I'll make sure we see him together when we get back. Now, what's up first this morning? If Carnell and Bixson act like the idiots they are, I'm going to cut them short, and you're going to take us to the airport where I can have some peace and quiet."

Geoff pulled out his own folder and they got to work.

At eleven, Dad pulled the plug on "C & B," and it was back to the hotel to pick up Mother.

When they walked into the suite, however, they could hear her shouting in the bedroom, the place was a mess with clothes strewn everywhere, and the smell of bourbon hung in the air.

"Oh, my God!" Herbert rushed for the other room. "Alexandra!"

Geoff followed and stopped in the doorway. His mother was crying in his father's arms, but he couldn't understand what she was saying. He told his father, "I'll call the desk for a doctor and an ambulance and cancel our plane reservations. I'll be in to help you with her as soon as I can."

"Call the police, too." His father held up bottles of pills with no prescription labels. "I think we have a larger problem."

Deep shit now, Geoff thought as he dialed. But what was wrong with

Mother? Before their visit, he'd had such hopes all was well with her. She'd always disliked any woman he dated, never saw them as good enough for him—or was it good enough for *her*? He had been certain she'd approve of Mary Ann—how could anyone in their right mind dislike her? Then came the tirade in the car after they left her condo. And now this breakdown.

What did Dad mean about Mother being "at it again?" Obviously, more was going on that he didn't know. Something had gone wrong in the last two years. Wrong in Mother's mind. Dad knew what. Geoff would start with him for an explanation.

Chapter Nine

Wednesday, December 19th, 7 p.m.

Geoff was never so happy to see someone as he was when Mary Ann opened her condo door to him that night. It had been a long, exhausting, frightening day full of revelations and decisions. He needed her so much, he'd just come over without calling first.

After he dropped his briefcase and she closed the door, she literally fell into his arms and they both held on for a while. She clearly needed to be held as much as he did—although it was probably for very different reasons. Body to body, a fierce hug, a couple of kisses, a long inhale of her scent, and he knew he'd come home.

Eventually she stepped back, and he took off his overcoat, tie, and suit coat, slung them over a chair, and collapsed on the sofa with her by his side.

"You okay?" she asked, turning sideways so she faced him.

"I am now. How are you?" He raised her hands, kissed each, and kept them on his chest.

"I'm fine now, too. Did your parents make the plane all right?"

He winced. "No, we've had some problems. I need to tell you about my mother. I'd like to do it now to get it over with."

"Okay." She frowned. "What happened? Is she all right?"

"You don't sound surprised at the topic."

"I'm not. Did you listen to your voice mail last night or today? I left messages."

She sounded sad. What did she know that he didn't? He took a deep breath as his stomach began to hurt. "No. I never got to it. What happened?"

She took his hands in hers. Her voice was calm, but he could hear anguish around the edges. "Your mother visited me yesterday after I got home from work. She was very angry and spiteful and nasty and warned me to stay away from you. She said she's been chasing gold diggers like me away for years.

"Geoff, she really acted weird, like she was on drugs or sick. She didn't threaten to kill me, if that's any consolation. I did make a video secretly on my phone if you want to see it. When she left, it was on her own. I never touched her. I watched to see if she had a car or if I'd have to help her find a taxi, but she had one waiting. I hoped she had the sense to return to the hotel."

"So that's what set her off. That and those damn pills." He ran a hand over his face and sighed. "Here's the story from my end. Dad and I went back to the hotel together around eleven this morning to pick her up and go to the airport. When we walked into their suite, Mother was crying, sitting in a heap on the floor in the bedroom, along with three bottles of pills and an empty bottle of bourbon. The room was a wreck. She saw us and started throwing up. We called the hotel doctor, arranged for an ambulance, and the physician the firm uses here met us at the hospital."

He took a deep breath and continued. "Here's what we pieced together with my sister's help. In their house, Laura went through the medicine cabinets and Mother's closet. She found lots of pill bottles. Long story short, in New York, Mother's been seeing a quack of some kind who's been selling her pills that are supposed to keep her slim, give her energy, and somehow rejuvenate her skin. Dad thought they were some kind of vitamins.

"She never told Laura or me, and she never acted out like she did with you. She has, however, been nervous, losing weight, and very touchy when someone disagrees with her. A couple of her long-time friends asked Dad if he had noticed the changes, but he just thought it was because of the diet. Of course, he's now blaming himself for not investigating."

"I have the feeling that Alexandra is a very good actress when Herbert's around," Mary Ann said.

"When anyone's around," he said, nodding in agreement. "Anyway, Mother had two kinds of pills on her today—the old ones and a new bottle with no label. Three hours ago, she was finally coherent enough to tell us what happened. It turns out the New York quack referred Mother to his buddy here who runs the same scam, only with much worse drugs. She picked up the new ones from him while 'shopping' on Monday. She didn't start taking them until Tuesday. We've called in the police and the Feds. They recognized the pills as ones causing havoc among the junkies."

"Where is she now? Still in the hospital?"

"Yeah. Dad's there. We're going to take Mother home to our family doctor and specialists as soon as she's able to travel. The doctors think that could be as early as Friday if she's stable. They're also saying that, since she's only had a couple of doses of the really evil pill, she has a good chance for a full recovery. We'll get her off the quack's prescriptions also."

"Oh, I am so sorry to hear all this. I knew something was wrong, but she seemed mostly in control of herself. I didn't think to try to keep her here or go back with her to the hotel where help was available."

"None of this is your fault, Mary Ann. Mother has been working herself up over any woman I go out with since I was a teenager. That's one of the reasons I jumped on the chance to move here."

Mary Ann gave him another hug. When she leaned back to see his face, his expression was not one she's expected. He looked almost . . . defeated. "What is it, Geoff? I know you and your family will see that your mother gets clean, gets help, and back to her old self."

Although, now that she thought of it, that might not be the best outcome if Alexandra kept up her nasty ways. But she kept her own counsel on that.

He sighed and took her hands in his. "What I am, I guess, is exhausted. Dad's beating himself up for not realizing what was going on with her. I haven't been with Mother except on holidays and she always seemed fine. Her 'normal' for a long while has been picky and irritable and bossy and demanding as hell. But then Laura and her husband saw her often and never recognized what was happening either. That's not the true cause of my exhaustion, though."

"Of course you're exhausted. Look what you've been through the last week," she stated firmly. The pressure would have killed a lesser man. Where, however, was he going with this line of thought? "What's wrong? *Really* wrong?"

He took a deep breath like he was going to deliver bad news, so she braced herself.

"I so wanted this visit by my parents to be wonderful for all four of us. I wanted you to meet them and realize at heart they're good parents, good people. For me, I wanted to show off for Dad about how well the firm is doing. He's pleased, so that's good.

"I wanted to show Mother that I am a man who is capable of making my own decisions about my life. That I'm an adult, and she should let me be one the same way she lets Laura and her husband be adults. All my life, she's been trying to make me do what *she* wants, to organize my life, to decide who my friends are. Who I date."

"Geoff, I know that both of them have your best interests at heart. I suspect they just display that in different ways. Alexandra wants you to be careful about your choice of a girlfriend or a wife. Unfortunately, she never realized or accepted that you've grown up. Those horrible pills must have helped warp her thinking and her actions. It's clear that your father thinks very highly of you and trusts you totally, or he wouldn't have appointed you to run the office here. He's so proud of you, it sticks out all over him." She gave his hands a squeeze and got one in return, so maybe he was hearing what she was telling him.

"Thank you. I needed to hear that, and it gives me hope we'll work it out with Mother. There's more, though," he said softly. "I wanted them to get to know you and realize how good you are for me, how well we get along, and how much . . ."

"How much . . .? What, Geoff?"

"Mary Ann, I love you."

"You love me?" The words came out like a squeak. The very words she wanted so much to hear. The last words she'd expected right now from him. What did he think was wrong about that? At his pronouncement, she wanted to scream with joy, but he continued before she could.

His smile was a little crooked. "I've loved you since our second date, I think. But I didn't want to come on too strong or do anything to scare you off, so I tried to play it cool. Finally, I just said to myself, 'Do more than kiss her, you fool,' and I'm sure you remember what happened then. At least I hope you do."

Mary Ann wanted to grab him and kiss him and show him how much she loved him, but Geoff still looked miserable, so some more bad news must be coming. She braced herself. This up-and-down, back-and-forth, good-news-bad-news was going to drive her crazy. "Yes, I remember. What's next?"

"Dad came up for a quick visit in early September, and I told him about you, that basically I had found the love of my life, and if I had my way, he'd have a daughter-in-law by spring. I asked him to say *absolutely nothing* about you to Mother. When he told me that he and Mother were coming here in December, I knew I really wanted them to meet you. Stupid me, I expected Mother to realize how great you are. I was planning on proposing when we got back from the holidays and work had settled down for both of us."

She was beginning to get more than a little frustrated. After the holidays? If Geoff didn't get on with it and propose to her *right now*, she'd do it to him! What in the world was the bad news?

He cleared his throat and looked into her eyes. "You've seen and experienced how Mother treats people, how she's determined that her daughter-in-law will be just like her, what she considers 'high class' and a society type, what she expects her to do for the law firm—be the total hostess. Well, I've been afraid that she would drive you off.

"Then Dad said that after her nasty questions and statements in the car, he decided to try to get through to her. Convince her to leave the two of us alone. When they returned to the hotel after your dinner party, he told her I was going to marry you, and he made her promise to do nothing but be polite and relaxed and welcoming. She said yes, but then she pulled that stunt coming to your home last night. This morning she bragged about it to him. He blew up and said she was going to see a psychiatrist when they got home if he had to carry her there. Then he left to go with me to the office."

"And she fell apart and OD'ed," Mary Ann said slowly.

"We don't know what will happen next. Even with the best treatment in the world, there's no guarantee that she will change her mindset towards anyone I marry. You need to think about this, and I'll abide by your decision. I love you, but if my family is too much for you to have to deal with, all you need to do is say the word 'no.' I'll understand totally."

Oh, my God! Men!!! Mary Ann barely managed not to scream, not to laugh, and not to hit the man in front of her. Did he think she was a wimp who couldn't handle his mother? Someone who buckled under pressure? It was time to set the record straight here.

She cleared her throat and said rather primly, "First, you haven't met my extended family, especially my obnoxious Uncle Gerhart. Second, I love you, too. Third, how can I say that word or any other when you haven't *asked* me to marry you?"

He dropped her hands into her lap and stared at her.

Come on! Geoff! Get with the program! She kept utterly still. He needed to work this out on his own or they'd never be together.

He squinted at her like he was trying to decipher her question. Honestly, she'd used plain English. She could tell when the lawyer's brain in him started working because his face cleared and his lips quirked. *Hah! Gotcha, you attorney, you!*

"Oh." Geoff sat up straight, picked up her hands again, looked her in the eyes, said in a strong voice, "Mary Ann Eisermann, will you do me the honor of becoming my wife, to have and to hold until death do us part?"

Fireworks were going off inside her, but she managed to speak as he had. "Yes, Geoffrey Smithson, I will. Will you do me the honor of becoming my husband, to have and to hold until death do us part?"

A big grin broke out on his face. "Yes, I will."

She knew they'd argue later over whether he had hauled her into his arms or she had hurled herself into his. The kisses went on forever. Finally they just held on to each other.

After a few minutes of that, Geoff sat back, stood up, and held out his hand to her. "Shall we anticipate our vows?"

"Oh, you're such a lawyer. Don't you know I have it all planned? Of course, we shall."

Epilogue

One year later, Mary Ann looked around the dining room of her parents' home in Ohio. Set with the Eisermann great-grandmother's Paul Müller china, the Tremonte great-grandmother's Joan of Arc International sterling silver, and festive red candles in crystal holders, the table looked grand and welcoming. All ready for Christmas dinner.

The best part? She didn't have to cook!

No way was she even setting foot into the kitchen. Not with her mother and Geoff's mother busy with the meal to come. She was staying out of the way, as were Geoff, her sister and brother, his sister, husband, and three kids, and both Dad and Herbert. Nobody was going to get in the middle between two cooks like Katie Eisermann and Alexandra Smithson.

Not that there were any arguments. Quite the contrary, the two women seemed to be getting along splendidly. Like they'd cooked together for years. Thank goodness.

All in all, Mary Ann mused, it had been an exciting, harrowing, complicated year. The big hurtle had been Alexandra's addiction and her subsequent hospital and halfway house stay. Her therapy had revealed that *her* mother had instilled in her what she tried to force into her own daughter and then Mary Ann. Linda had found her husband early and gotten out of the house. That left Alexandra focused on Geoff. She seemed to be doing fine now, clean and sober and determined never to repeat the experience.

Mary Ann and Geoff had welcomed her to their wedding in June, and

Alexandra had been a changed woman—gracious, pleasant, even funny, exchanging tales of their children with the Eisermanns. Everybody had a good time.

Her mother came into the dining room, looked at the table, and nodded. "Go get everyone," she ordered. "We need help putting it all on the table."

Two hours later, Mary Ann pushed her dessert plate away. Geoff, sitting next to her, did the same, then gave her an eyebrow wiggle. "Ready for this?"

She grinned at him and nodded.

Geoff rose and pulled her up with him. "We have an announcement."

All four parents said together, "You're going to have a baby!"

Mary Ann and Geoff started laughing. They had each claimed the other's parents would be clueless about the pregnancy.

"The big question is," Herbert intoned in a solemn tone, "which ones of us are you going to name the baby after?"

Oh, dear. They hadn't thought that far ahead. They didn't even know if it was a boy or girl. Whose name to pick? Mary Ann couldn't help herself, she started laughing so hard she had to hang on to Geoff to stay vertical. When she could speak again, she pulled his head down to whisper in his ear, "I thought you told me this time there would be *no pressure.*"

Chicken Macela

This recipe is a blend of several chicken-roasting recipes and techniques as well as what I learned from my mother and dreamed up when I needed something different for guests. So, have fun! Be creative! Anything goes here.

The dressing or stuffing or whatever you want to call the apple-raisins-walnut-sherry no-bread mix is my own, as far as I know. A long while ago, I needed to come up with a meal for company that wasn't heavy or difficult. I couldn't find a recipe that worked for me. So I channeled Julia Child and came up with this one.

Warning: The measurements and ingredients themselves aren't set in stone. More of practically anything in the mix will work. Of course, there's the factor of how many people you're feeding and their tastes.

About measurements like pounds of apples. I have no idea. I just pick up a bunch that look good. If I don't use all of them, well, an apple a day . . .

In the story, Mary Ann serves broccoli as a "real" vegetable. Again, your choice to have one and what it is.

Pans & Utensils
A good roasting pot or pan. I prefer my old heavy aluminum Dutch oven with lid. I particularly like a pot with a top in case the chicken is getting too brown.

I don't use a rack, but that's up to you.

A big enough casserole for the apples, etc., that will be used on top of the stove. Again, a lid is helpful. I use CorningWare.

A pot to cook the rice in and a bowl to serve it in. Totally your choice.

Nice sharp knives and some big spoons.

Ingredients

1 good chicken, defrosted if necessary, a day or two before the meal.

If you want to add some chicken quarters, that's fine also, but make sure your pan will hold them and the whole bird.

The neck, gizzard, and any other parts can be used in other dishes or discarded. I like to put the liver in the bottom of the pan for anyone who wants to eat it. (me)

Rice. I prefer Uncle Ben's. The kind you have to cook. I really don't like instant rice.

If you prefer something else, even not a rice, but noodles, that's fine.

Apples. I suggest Granny Smith. They don't go mushy.

Raisins, a good sized box. I haven't tried dried cranberries, but they're a possibility.

Walnut pieces, chopped. 1 bag. Pecans also a possibility.

Vegetables, as in green beans or broccoli or asparagus or . . . Your choice or not with the meal.

Salad. Ditto the above.

Bread. A good French bread or sourdough goes really well, and you need something to sop up the juices.

Dry Sherry. I use a cheap basic one. Plan on using the whole bottle.

Butter. I like the real stuff, but unsalted.

Preparation

A day or two before the dinner, make sure the chicken has thawed completely. Wash it off, including the insides. The neck, gizzard, and any other parts can be used in other dishes or discarded.

Rub some salt and pepper over and inside the bird.

Cover and refrigerate.

The day of the meal, take the chicken out of the fridge an hour or two before cooking.

Preheat the oven to 400 to 450 degrees. The setting will depend on your stove's temp idiosyncrasy. Cookbooks and recipes vary.

Peel and chop the apples into bite-sized pieces, put them in a bowl and add sherry to cover.

Add the raisins to the bowl. Ditto the walnut pieces. Put in the fridge. Stir from time to time.

Note, this can be done earlier because the sherry will keep the apples from turning.

While the oven is heating, stuff the whole chicken full with some of the apple mix and secure the flaps with metal skewers or needle and thread. You don't want apples all over. Tie the drumsticks together and tuck the wings under the breast.

Now, there is the question of to flip or not flip the bird. Some recipes call for first putting the breast side up, then twenty minutes later or so, flip so the breast side is down, repeat twenty minutes later. Do what works for you.

While all this flipping is going on, remember to flip the breast and leg quarters you also put in the pan.

Roast, flipping or not, for about an hour to an hour and a half. It all depends on your oven. Baste with the pan juices from time to time. Also scoop up some of the juices/drippings and put them in the casserole with the apples, etc. (See below.) You may want to also add a little more sherry in with the bird.

Timing is important, and you know how crucial it is to get everything to the table done and hot, so work out your schedule. This usually smells so good that there's not much problem getting people to the table.

While the bird is cooking, put the remaining apples, et al, into the casserole and add some of the drippings from the roaster. Maybe some more sherry. Cook on a bubbling low heat for about fifteen minutes before you take the chicken out of the oven.

Test at the leg joints with a knife and/or a thermometer for doneness. The meat should not be red.

Don't forget a lid on the pot if the top of the bird gets too brown.

When you take the bird out of the oven, put it on a platter or cutting board and let it rest for a while. Take out the apples you stuffed into the bird and put them in the casserole with the rest of the mix. Stir that pretty good.

While the above is all going on, you're in a timing merry-go-round. Fixing whatever other vegetable is going with the meal, cooking the rice as the label says, remembering to put the bread in the oven to warm, cleaning up after yourself, and maybe having some of that sherry yourself.

Carve the chicken and put the pieces into a serving casserole. I like CorningWare with tops because it keeps thing warmer.

One other thing. I don't "carve" the chicken as is usually done with a turkey. A chicken, to me, just isn't made for taking slices off the breast. So, each person gets the quarter of his or her choice. Or you can split the thigh and leg. And you can cut off the wing and save it for another time. Do whatever works for you.

Then it's time to put it all on the table.

Wine? Whatever you like. Red or white.

Play with the recipe. Use whatever your parents taught you about cooking chicken. This one works for me, my hubby, and guests. If you try it, please let me know how you liked it.

The Thanksgiving Caper
by Cindy Maday

Cindy Maday's writing career began when a story formed in her mind while reading the Da Vinci Code. When her girlfriend said she wanted to read the book, she wrote the book, although the book is hidden under the bed where it will remain. She writes humorous contemporary romances. She's a yearly participant in Nanowrimo (National Novel Writing Month) where she begins the holiday season writing a new Christmas Novel. When she's not writing, taking writing classes, she works full time as an Accounts Payable Manager, and babysits for her beautiful grandchildren, and country line dances with her friends.

"In two days, I will be cooking Thanksgiving dinner. I promise no one will suffer from food poisoning. Besides, the last time I cooked, Iris was the only one affected, and the actual diagnosis was an allergic reaction. There's no reason to worry, since Iris has eaten this dinner before."

Standing by her mother's chair in her parents' family room with her hands on her hips, Annie Hutchinson dared her brother Jack, her sister Iris, and her brother's friend Parker Anderson to say another word.

Parker moaned. Although she gave him the evil eye, her chest tightened. The kind of tightening brought on by wanting— by wanting someone so much it hurt. Her fingers itched to run her hand through the tousled spikes of his dark blond hair and gaze into those deep set hazel eyes. To think she'd once wanted to have this man's babies. After the way he dumped her how could she still want him?

Yet, she did.

Her jaw clenched as she glared at him. "What are you doing here?"

He was the last person she wanted to see. Of course, he was Jack's best friend since they were ten. He was practically a member of her family. When she was a kid, he tugged on her braid every time he walked past her. She'd get so mad she'd punch him. To think of the merciless teasing she endured from both Parker and Jack. Parker was a popular jock not given to sentiment. Yet, there was the one time after she broke up with her first boyfriend in high school when Parker revealed his tenderness by wrapping his arms around her while she cried. That's when she realized he was the man she wanted to marry. Her girlhood crush turned into love. Not that he paid her much attention after he went off to college. Well, at least not until her brother Jason's wedding.

"If you're cooking, maybe I will leave. I came to visit your mother to check on how she's doing since her hip replacement," he said, adding a sexy smile as he glanced at her mother while Annie rolled her eyes.

"La de da. Aren't you the sweet one?" Surprised at her snarky remark, she realized she was jealous of her own mother. She'd been hoping he'd stopped by to claim his love for her. Her mind filtered back to her brother's wedding again, where she had spent the night on the dance floor wrapped in Parker's arms. A few heart rending kisses at a wedding obviously weren't enough to make a man drop down on his knees—yes, she liked the idea — to declare his love.

"Well, I'm thrilled Parker came over," said Annie's mother, Mary. She waved Parker over to the sofa where she sat wrapped in the afghan Annie made her for Mother's Day. "Come sit by me. Tell me what you've been up to. I saw your article in the Times on that rotten scoundrel who shot his wife. Good thing they didn't have children. Jack, get Parker a beer."

"Thanks. That was my big break. Now I'm working on real news stories instead of local events. Though, I still help my dad doing construction work on the weekends."

Annie figured this was a good time to escape. "Well, I've got lots to do, so I'll leave you to visit."

"Wait, Annie," said Iris while cuddling her new son, Will, named after their father. "Tell you what. You make the turkey and dressing. The rest of the family will bring the vegetable dishes."

Annie ran over to her sister and hugged her, dropping a kiss on Will. "This is going to be the best Thanksgiving ever. Don't worry about a thing." She grinned at her mother. "Take a load off, Mom. Enjoy yourself. Is the recipe box still in the pantry? I'll write the dressing recipe down and head to the store."

"Use Williams-Sonoma's brine," said Mary in a voice of barely concealed pain.

"Mom, do you need your pain medicine?" Worried, Annie looked over at her mom.

"Just took a pill and should be fine in about ten to fifteen minutes."

"All right then. See you all in two days." Before she left, she turned to her mother. "I'll be back later after I pick some stuff up from my place."

"Good. Your Dad can use some down time."

"No kidding." With a wave, she disappeared in a flash.

Annie has more energy than the ComEd electrical plant for all of Chicago, Parker noted silently. He longed to pull that rubber thing from the bottom of the braid hanging half way down her back and unravel all that glorious hair. The image of brushing her hair nightly while seducing her with his lips made him yearn for her; he almost groaned aloud.

Ignoring his baser nature, he turned to Mrs. Hutchinson. "What possesses Annie?

"Still got a thing for Annie, Parker?" Jack nudged him before handing him a bottle of beer.

"I see a disaster coming. She'll be humiliated again. How can we stop this?"

"When one of my children offers to do something out of their heart, you won't find me saying no." Mary Hutchinson gave them a look that brooked no argument.

Jack swore. Iris shook her head, and Parker bit his lip.

With her foot tapping, Annie checked the time on the Christmas clock on the counter while waiting in line at Williams-Sonoma. Again. The hand of the clock moved, but she did not. Of all days for her client to call with an assignment to edit an article for their website. Of course, everyone in the mall had decided to go to Williams-Sonoma. Good thing she did all her baking last weekend. At least she got the turkey, although it was smaller than she would like. Hopefully, there was enough to feed everyone. Running to not one, or two, but five stores for nuts for the dressing put her behind schedule. She couldn't find cashews, but bought almonds instead. Nuts are nuts, their all the same. Shaking her head, she prayed she didn't mess this up.

After she finally made it through the checkout line, she was putting her change away, when someone tapped her on the shoulder.

"Oh my God. Erin." She grabbed her old friend in a hug. "When did you get to town?"

"Today. My sister, Cheryl, had a beautiful baby girl yesterday. Seven pounds three ounces."

"Congratulations! What did they name her?"

"Abigail. I'm calling her Abbie."

Annie laughed. "Abbie's nice. So how are the newlyweds doing? Gosh, I wish you still lived here."

A woman pushed Annie out of line, so they moved to a space where they could talk. "We're doing great. Oh, you need to get married. Marriage is blissful, heavenly, simply wonderful."

Glad for her friend, Annie fought the silly emotion of envy. "Good for you, Erin. Any chance of you moving back here?"

"No, I wish. I miss my family and friends. Steve's job is in Raleigh. Also, I landed a great job at the nearby hospital. Raleigh's a nice place to live. Why don't you come for a visit?"

Annie glanced towards the exit.

"Some day. I better get going. I've got work to do yet. Mom had hip surgery, and I'm helping out," said Annie.

"Dating anyone?" asked Erin, shifting away to avoid a running child who almost knocked over the display of cookie cutters.

"No one serious."

"Hey, what happened between you and Parker?"

"Not interested in his friend's sister."

"Well, change his mind. You two are hot together. Steam was rising from the two of you on the dance floor at your brother's wedding."

"Hot, huh." *If only.*

"Well, I better get going. Let's get together while you're here." She handed Erin her business card, getting antsy about the time, made a move to leave.

"Sounds great. Maybe Jan can join us."

"Of course she can. We're going over to the Fox Hole tomorrow night.

Do you want to meet us there?" asked Annie, hoping this wasn't a mistake. In the past, when the three of them got together the night before Thanksgiving, they had stayed out until four in the morning.

"Steve mentioned going out with your brother so, yeah, I'd like to join you. Let's go for dinner so we can catch up."

Annie nodded. "How about a later dinner though? I'm cooking Thanksgiving dinner, so I have a lot to prepare the day before. I'm not sure when I'll get done. Karaoke night is on Wednesday, so tune up your voice."

Erin looked worried. "You're cooking dinner?"

Annie rolled her eyes. "Not you too. It will be fine. What can go wrong? I've got my Mom's family recipes."

Erin didn't look convinced even as she said, "You'll do great. Listen, I'll be home at my Mom's on Thanksgiving. My siblings are going to their in-laws for dinner. Mom's cooking us dinner, so I'm available if you need to talk to me after your dinner."

"There won't be a need, but thanks. Better head out, or I won't get everything done. See you tomorrow. I'll call to let you know the time."

As she hurried toward the exit, she nearly ran over Parker. He grabbed her before she fell. "What are you doing here?" she asked, her body reacting to his touch with a ticklish sensation.

"You keep asking me that question," he said, as his gaze roamed over her, making her melt in a few private places.

"I always come here. I add to my kitchen whenever I get time to shop."

Annie didn't quite believe him, but she didn't have time to argue. "I better skedaddle."

"No time to grab a coke or something."

She wished. *Wait. Parker Anderson is asking me to go for a coke?* She checked her watch. Her deadline for the editing job was looming. Damn. He was looking at her as if he wanted to…kiss her. *Crap. I can't go through this again, or can I?* A few kisses from Parker would last her imagination for maybe a week. *What kind of girl are you? You can't. You are not going there again.*

"I'm sorry. Maybe another time. I have an edit to finish among other things." She made a move to leave, but he bent closer, landing a quick kiss on her lips. Stunned, she stared at him and then decided to leave, before she changed her mind. Why was she making this into a big deal? He's kissed her like this before and it never meant anything before? Except to her.

"Another time, then." He headed into the store, leaving her staring after him.

Parker swore to himself as he entered the store. What a dupe he was? Kissing her like that. She's going to hate him for sure. Yet, he couldn't be too sad as she tasted wonderful. Or maybe it was that gloss. He wanted to do more. Hell, he wanted to toss her over his shoulder and head back home with her. Forever. He'd get no sleep tonight.

Annie examined the menu for the umpteenth time. Iris was bringing both sweet potatoes and mashed potatoes. Beth, her sister-in-law, was bringing the carrot and the broccoli casseroles, two dishes that made Annie's mouth water in anticipation. Jack—wine, beer, and rolls. Red cabbage and a cranberry mold from her grandmother.

Parker was bringing himself. After all, he was a guest. *Bull! Since when?* He practically lived at their house growing up. To think she used to follow him around like a puppy dog. Talk about stupid. Except the truth was, the man still took her breath away. She didn't dare think about the kiss yesterday, so she turned her attention back to dinner.

Luckily, the heavy turkey didn't break when she dropped it on the bread board. *Yuck!* Grimacing, she stuck her hand inside the turkey and pulled out the bag of giblets. Keeping the giblets in the bag so she didn't touch them, she sliced the top of the bag and dropped them in a big pan of water. Next, she dropped a cleaned onion into the pot. The night before, she'd slit the plastic wrap on four loaves of bread to dry them out a bit, the way her mother did for years. While the giblets and onion cooked, she cut the crust of the bread off, broke the bread into pieces, tossing it in a large roasting pan.

"Hey Annie. How's the chef doing?"

She jumped, putting her hand on her heart.

"You scared me. I'm great, Parker. What are you doing here?" The man looked scrumptious, but when didn't he?

"I'm visiting your mom. Jack called to say he's on his way over. This is the best drinking night of the year. Are you going out later?"

"Jan, Erin and I are going out, but I'm not staying out long."

"Right, you don't want anything to go wrong tomorrow."

Her eyes narrowed accusingly, "Are you insinuating..."

Putting his hand up to ward off her anger, he chuckled. "I wouldn't dare. Are you dating anyone?"

The subject change threw her for a moment. "Nobody serious. You?"

"No. Been thinking about your brother's wedding."

Jason's wedding—the place of her humiliation, or at least the day after. She bit her lip as her brain fumbled with memories that led her gaze to his lips. Wanting him filled her heart and soul; fear filled her brain. She moved toward the refrigerator just as he stepped around the center island. Stopping inches from each other, their eyes met, like steel to a magnet. Seeing Parker Anderson looking confused gave her confidence a boost, almost as good as her vision of him on his knees.

"I'm going to make a fool out of myself and tell you I can't get that wedding out of my head. Correction, I can't get your kisses out of my head."

"Get in line," she said as if she couldn't care less, even though her heart was pounding hard and fast, as if she were—*don't think about what's hard and fast*—running a marathon. Damn, now the man was messing with her metaphors.

His eyebrow arched in a sexy way. She wished she had a camera to take a picture. Of course, the last thing she needed was another picture of Parker in her house.

"Other men tell you they can't get your kisses out of their minds?"

Now who sounds accusing, thought Annie. Liking the hint of the little green monster in his eyes, she shrugged. "You know what they say; I don't kiss and tell."

Anger flashed in his eyes, and then cooled just as quickly. What was she doing? Setting herself up to be hurt again?

Hiding his face, he looked down at a book on the counter. "I can't believe you read this stuff. Since you're a professional editor, I figured you for more literary fiction, not romances."

She glanced at the book cover of Cathie Anderson's, alias Ellen Parker's, newest novel, *Falling in Love is Not Picnic*. It showed a gorgeous woman leaning against a sexy man's chest, a picnic basket at their feet as they looked out over a mountain top. She was enjoying it so much, she hated to finish it.

"That's your mother's book. She wrote it! Don't you read her books?" she asked, surprised that anyone wouldn't want to read Ellen Parker's books.

"No. All that garbage about the women's idea of the alpha hero. Men wouldn't have such a hard time if women were more realistic about relationships. Instead they want someone from a book or a movie."

Using the moment, she backed away some, grieving the distance. Safe was better.

"I disagree. Look at my father."

His eyebrow rose, making her stomach turn into fluttering butterflies of excitement.

"Your father?"

His skepticism made her chuckle. "My father. The man who stood by my mother's side when she had surgery, carrying her up the steps to bed, sitting by her bedside because she is the most important person in his life and he loves her.

"All right, I guess," he said, his head tilted in acknowledgement. "So this makes him your hero?"

She grinned, her gaze turning dreamy, wishing for a hero of her own. With a sigh, she said, "Yeah, it does. What woman doesn't dream of having someone to care enough about her to do something heroic?"

"Mmm. What would you do with this hero? Would you declare your love to him?"

"The idea of a man performing a heroic deed to show he cares about me or loves me sounds exciting. Declare my love for him?" She shook her head.

"No. I'd need to be a little better acquainted with the man before declaring my love."

"How much better? Like us? We've known each other all our lives. Like that?"

Taken back at the seriousness on Parker's face, she studied him. Normally, he'd be cracking jokes, making her laugh or angry depending on the joke. *Who is this man and what has he done with Parker Anderson? Looks the same. Talks the same. Yet, the words don't fit.* "Not quite. We've never dated. Kissed but not dated."

He looked down at his mother's book and frowned. His chest drew tight revealing taut muscles as he took a deep breath, and then his head lifted and he said, "Annie, you deserve a hero."

What was he up to? The man claimed he didn't believe in heroes, so why tell her she deserved one? His eyes seemed sincere. *He didn't get the hint about us not dating as he didn't ask me out, so I guess nothing has changed. So what's he up to?*

Parker's gaze grew in intensity. He moved closer, lifting his hands to her face.

"Annie Hutchinson, I want to be your hero."

Stunned with pleasure, her gaze went to his lips, wanting a kiss so bad. She wanted to believe he was serious. Yet hadn't she believed they had a date scheduled for the day after the wedding? But instead he blew her off. Could she trust him now? Her mind screamed, *No, no, no,* her body screamed, *Yes, yes, yes.*

"I thought you didn't want anything to do with your best friend's sister," she said in a flippant voice.

"Yeah, I thought so too."

Parker lowered his lips to hers. Tingles ran wild, overflowing into erotic currents of desire. Great possibilities expanded in her heart. As the kiss deepened, she threw her arms around him. Their bodies touched, leaving her quivering with need. When he ended the kiss, he stared at her with confidence.

"Is that how your hero kisses?"

"Mmm. Maybe, but we'd better try again. To make sure," she murmured in a husky voice.

Instead he caressed her cheek. "Nope. I think I'll let the anticipation build. Have to make up for my stupidity in not calling you after the wedding."

Without another word, he walked out of the room. She chuckled when she heard her brother ask Parker why he was in the kitchen, but didn't catch his reply. Thinking about the kiss and the chance he was serious blew her mind. Shaking her head, she lifted the turkey into the bag to marinate overnight in the fridge, and then finished the dressing before leaving to meet Erin and Jan.

The Fox Hole was decorated with garlands and lights over the bar. Annie spotted her friends at a table in front of the stage. She waved to several people she knew, realizing the normal crowd was out tonight. Lacey, the waitress asked if she wanted her usual drink, and she nodded.

"Hey, you beat me here. I'm starved," said Annie, hugging both friends.

"We were getting worried about you. We're starved too," said Jan, grabbing some nuts from the dish on the table.

"Is Steve out with Jack and Parker?" asked Annie, sitting down.

"Yeah, along with a few other guys he used to hang out with," said Erin.

Annie turned to Jan. "So how's everything with you? Where's Ben tonight? "

"Out with his friends. Everything is great. I'm having dinner with Ben's family tomorrow. I don't want to hurt you but I think this is getting serious."

Standing, Annie wrapped her arms around her friend. "Nothing would make me happier than to see you with Ben. You two are perfect for each other. I told you this before. Let's see, you've been going out eight months now. Maybe you'll be getting a ring for Christmas."

"Did he say something to you?" asked Jan, her eyes narrowing.

Annie frowned as she sat back down. "No. It's just a feeling I have. I watched him when we double dated that last time. He's flipped over you. You're flipped over him. It's a match. Aren't you glad I introduced you?"

Jan looked down, nodding. The waitress brought Annie's beer and took their dinner order. The DJ began to play music, indicating karaoke would start soon. They caught up with each other's lives during dinner. Erin's explained their life in Raleigh, inviting them both to come for a visit.

Jan looked pointedly at Annie. "All right, Annie. You've been fidgeting all night. What happened?"

"Nothing," she said, her voice pitched higher than normal.

"Is is something to do with that Dan character you introduced us to last week?" asked Jan.

"Dan. No. I've decided not to see him again."

They stared at her without a word, waiting for Annie to break.

"I'm not sure if I want to talk about it yet. I'm confused."

"That's what girlfriends are for," said Jan.

Annie bit her bottom lip. "Oh, all right. You both know how Parker stood me up the day after the wedding?"

They both nodded.

"Well, today he came in the kitchen claiming he wanted to be my hero. That he can't get my kisses out of his mind. This is just the type of joke my brother and he would play on me. I can't tell if he's serious or not."

"Tell us exactly what happened," said Erin while Jan moved closer to hear the story.

After explaining everything, Erin grinned. "I was right on. He's as in love with you as you are with him."

Jan lifted her drink to toast. "I agree, girlfriend."

"No. I'm telling you it's not that. If he was in love with me, why wouldn't he just ask me out? Why all this hero stuff? No, he's up to something," said Annie, tapping her fingers on the table to the music.

"Annie, just roll with it for once in your life. Let the guy make amends for being an asshole in the first place," said Erin.

Tom Williamson sang the first song, "When The Sun Goes Down", by Kenny Chesney.

"I love the way Tom sings that song. What are we singing tonight?"

"Going To The Chapel," "suggested Erin.

Annie left to go to the washroom. When she came back Jan winked at Erin, completely oblivious to Annie whose mind was still on Parker. The three of them headed to the stage. But to Annie's surprise, her two friends abandoned her, and she was facing a crowd waiting for her to begin. She turned to the DJ, and he winked. The screen lit up, but it was not the song they normally sang. Annie's eyes narrowed and she said, "The song should be "Friends n Low Places."All right, you two. This is for you."

The crowd laughed. Annie knew most of the audience, went to school with a lot of the people here. Heck, half the high school choir was here tonight.

When she sang "The Wind Beneath My Wings" in her beautiful mezzo-soprano voice, the crowd was mesmerized. Her eyes' narrowed at her friends when she sang the line, "Did You Ever Know That You're My Hero?" After she finished, she received a standing ovation. Her friends joined her on stage, where they rocked the house with Little Big Town's, "Little White Church."

They left early, as they had a big day the next day. Annie wondered if she should just roll with this— whatever— with Parker. She was afraid of getting her hopes up to have them dashed once again.

On the morning of Thanksgiving, the sun shone through the windows, making her mother's kitchen bright, even more so due to its new, pale yellow wallpaper covered with colorful fruits and flowers. One day Annie hoped to have her own big country kitchen like her mother's. Sooner than later if all went well, she thought, remembering the house the realtor recently showed her.

Memories of her brothers and sister fighting over their favorite cereals in the morning at the kitchen table made her heart lighter. Annie grabbed a cup off the buffet and poured some coffee, noting it was nearing eight o'clock. Glad she hadn't missed the Macy's Thanksgiving Parade pre-show, she flipped on the television to channel five. Her ritual was to pick out the Broadway shows she wanted to see—if she ever got to New York. *Hey, a girl can dream.* She sipped her coffee, her body awakening with the caffeine jolt to her system. Good, she hadn't missed the *Rockettes*. One day, she'd go to Radio City for the show. New York or Bust. She refused to see them in Chicago.

Pulling the turkey out of the bag, she noticed it looked no different than last night. Something was wrong. Pressing her fingers to her lips to keep from screaming, she shook with frustration. The package of brine was nowhere to be found. The store would be closed. *Oh my God. I don't remember taking the bag from the store. The new thermometer is still at the store. Damn!*

Banging her hand on the top of her head, she ran upstairs to get her laptop to look up ingredients for Williams-Sonoma's brine.

"Oh man. Which recipe do I choose?" She scanned at least five different recipes on the website. She finally found a recipe that wouldn't require another trip to the store, and set to work. After pouring the brine over the turkey, stuffing an apple inside the bird, she put the turkey in the oven and heaved a sigh of relief.

"Whew. Talk about scary. Who forgets to put their turkey in brine? Me!"

Thinking back, she realized she'd first gotten distracted when she ran into Erin at the store. Later, Parker distracted her with the hero stuff. *Was he sincere? Or did he say all those things as a joke? No, he wouldn't. Would he?* Sick of thinking the same thing over and over again, she set to finish her work.

After making the rice pudding, she did the dishes and set the dining room table. A pecan pie sat on the buffet along with various types of cookies and her mother's favorite banana cake. A pumpkin pie waited in the fridge. Baking was Annie's thing. Getting everything on the table for a dinner at the same time was another story. She was relieved everyone else had volunteered to make the side dishes. Why she baked like a pro but couldn't cook would forever be her life's mystery. Iris did both admirably. Even Jack cooked well.

Back in the den, Annie fell asleep in her favorite spot on the couch. When her alarm went off, she hurried back to the kitchen to finish her duties before heading up to change. After basting the turkey and dressing with the juices from the pan, she set the dishes of dressing in the oven. Pushing her nose up, she took a whiff of her mother's secret seasoning filling the air. Her mother always told her you could never go wrong with Season All, and she didn't want anything to go wrong today. She hoped this small adjustment to the brine recipe worked.

Her father, Bill, came into the kitchen and stopped short. "Annie!"

"Good morning, Dad. How's Mom?"

"Fine. All dressed and watching the Macy's Parade. Why don't you join her?" Her father walked to the kitchen door and waved.

"Who are you waving to—a bird?" She chuckled at her own joke.

She watched her father who seemed preoccupied with something outside.

"Is everything all right, Dad?"

He nodded.

"I'll check on mom, before I go finish my hair."

"Later, sweetie."

As soon as she left, Annie's father ran to the door. "Hurry, Parker, before she comes back. I can't believe I agreed to this. But your bird is perfection."

"Good thing you found you're wife's duplicate pan and checked on the ceramic dishes used for the dressing so we match. One turkey and two dishes of dressing as requested." Bill opened the oven door while Parker set down his dishes.

"What is that smell?" Parker wiggled his nose, his lips pushed out in a-yuck-that's-gross face. "Season All, and at least a whole jar."

"Good grief. Does Mary put Season All on her turkey? Thought she used brine."

"She does use brine. No Season All is involved. "said Parker.

"What are those brown things in her dressing?" asked Bill.

Bending down closer, Parker pulled the dressing out. "Almonds?"

Bill bit his lips but couldn't hold his chuckle in. "Almonds in cashew dressing. My daughter sure is creative."

Chuckling, Parker swapped out his turkey and two dishes of cashew dressing for Annie's whatever.

"Someone's coming."

"Shit." Parker grabbed Annie's turkey in his covered hands, one dish of dressing resting on top, the other wrapped in a towel under the roasting pan.

"Hurry." Bill pushed him out the door. Stumbling as the door slammed shut behind him, Parker quickly turned away from the window, tossing Annie's turkey dinner in the stones on the side of the house.

Inside the house, Bill turned with a smile when Annie returned to the kitchen.

"What's so fascinating in the yard?"

Heated curlers bobbed all over Annie's head as she spoke. Bill smiled. His baby girl was as pretty as a flower in spring. His Annie. She could do almost anything, except cook.

"Bob from next door stopped by. Always complaining about something."

"Oh, that explains the voices. Are you going to play your annual football game?"

"Yes, but I need a cup of coffee first. What time is dinner?"

"One."

"Great," he gasped as she opened the oven door. Taking the baster, she sucked up some juice from the turkey, putting some on the dressing as well as on the turkey.

"Dad?" She glanced up at him.

"What, honey?"

"Can a turkey grow in the oven?

"What do you mean?" He walked over glancing at the scrumptious bird. "Looks great, Annie."

She peeked up at him with a grin. "It does, doesn't it?" She walked over to the coffee pot.

Jack came walking in with donuts. Her father snatched one as Annie handed him a cup of coffee. "Hey, Dad. Ready." Jack sniffed the air and opened the oven door. "Wow. Good job, kid."

Beaming with pride, as Jack rarely gave compliments, she said, "Thank you. My first turkey is going to be delicious."

Parker walked into the kitchen, looking all gorgeous with his lower face roughened with new outgrowth, a tight t-shirt revealing taut muscles underneath, and fitted jeans emphasizing his great butt. "Come on. The Wozinicks and Smiths are already down at the park."

"Crap. Didn't we say eleven thirty?" asked Bill before taking a gulp of his coffee to wash down the donut.

Annie rolled her eyes. "You've got ten minutes. Maybe they need more practice than you guys."

Her father rinsed his cup, setting it in the sink. He grabbed his baseball cap out of his pocket. "Let's go kick ass."

Parker eyed Annie's rollers with a grin. Self-consciously, she put her hands over her head. "By the way, my parents came home early. Your mom said to invite them to dinner."

Her mouth dropped. "Ellen Parker is coming for dinner."

"No. Cathie Anderson is coming to dinner, along with Ed Anderson."

"Oh. My. God."

Parker laughed as Jack pulled him out of the house.

Limping on her walker into the kitchen, her mom looked worried. "We need more plates set. Parker's parents are coming to dinner. Dan stopped by when you were upstairs getting ready, so I also invited him for dinner."

"Dan? Dan who?"

"Dan, the guy you brought over that night we ordered pizza. The man stopped by wanting to take you to dinner."

Annie sat down and put her head in her hands. The weight of her curlers fell forward around her face. "Oh, Mom. We only went on a few dates. I decided to tell him I didn't want to go out with him anymore. With Parker and his parents here, oh, what a mess."

"Dan said he was from out of town. No one should be alone on Thanksgiving. So I invited him here. We have more than enough food. I probably should have checked with you first, sorry. We've no time to worry now. Extra leaves need to be put in the table. You'll have to reset for fourteen people."

She looked at her mother. "What are you doing up?"

"I came to check on the dinner. I'm nervous."

"You don't trust me."

"I do, Annie. But Cathie Anderson is coming. I don't want to hurt your feelings, but this is too important." She winced as she opened the oven door to look at the turkey. Her mother's wince shook Annie to her soul until she saw her smile.

"Annie, I'm so proud of you. Everything looks perfect. Even better than mine."

Still hurt, Annie's lips lifted slightly. "I'll set the table with those beautiful Thanksgiving dishes. Why we don't use them every year…"

In the dining room, Annie pulled the plates off the table. "There's some silk flowers downstairs. I have more in the car. Mom, go sit down. I'll fix everything. Good thing I baked a lot of different desserts."

Mary smiled at her daughter who headed downstairs, while she headed to the dining room to help clear the table. She wondered why Annie and Parker haven't hooked up yet. Everyone could see those two are in love. Everyone except Annie and Parker. Maybe, this Thanksgiving will give them the nudge they need. She smiled at the thought.

Annie headed down the stairs in crepe pleated brown palazzo pants, dotted with fall colors. A rib-knit brown sweater accentuated her hour glass figure. Soft brown hair fell in loose curls around her face, down past her shoulders. Parker stood at the door looking up at her. The way he stared at her made her feel feminine and happy.

"Who won the football game?" she asked, stepping into the foyer.

"We did in the last quarter," said Parker, moving closer. "You look beautiful, Annie.""

She smiled up at him, deciding to not get too excited until she saw how this played out.

"Where are your parents?" she asked, with a glance toward the door.

"They're on the way. We took separate cars. I haven't lived with my parents since I left for college."

"Right."

Iris came in with a diaper bag hanging over one shoulder, a car seat with a sleeping baby in the other, while her husband, Ben, entered carrying a crock pot. "Happy Thanksgiving. We come bearing mashed potatoes."

"Babe, plug the crock pot in the kitchen," said Iris while removing the baby from the car seat.

"Bring my grandson over here by Grandma," yelled her mother, who rested in the lazy boy chair. Iris went to the den with the baby where the cooing sounds of both her parents made Annie laugh.

The door opened again as Annie's brother, Jason and his wife, Beth came in carrying three dishes. "Let's bring these in the kitchen," said Beth as Annie ran to help. "Happy Thanksgiving, Annie. Love your outfit."

Parker banged his forehead with his hand. "I made some cauliflower in cheese sauce. Darn, I left the dish in the car." As he headed back out, Beth nodded to Annie to follow.

Parker met her in the driveway with his dish in his hands. "Annie, did I mention how great you look?"

A grin a yard wide spread across her face. "You might have, but a girl can't have enough compliments. Thank you. You didn't need to bring anything."

"This is one of my favorite dishes, so I decided to share." He brushed against her, but with his hands full, he couldn't hold hers. She resisted an offer to carry the dish, freeing him to wrap those arms around her waist.

"When did you find time, having been out late last night and up to play football this morning?"

"Cooking is my thing. My dad taught me when I was ten. Mom can't cook at all, but we humor her. Maybe I'll invite you to dinner one night for my special Veal Paprika."

Stunned, her eyes widened. "You're serious, aren't you? The stuff you said yesterday."

"If my hands weren't filled, I'd show you how serious I am."

"What about Jack?" They glanced at each other. Parker stopped and turned to face her.

"Hell, Annie. I've thought of nothing but you since the wedding. I wanted to call, but I worried if we started dating and our relationship went sour, we'd be uncomfortable if Jack invited me to family gatherings. Then I thought, the hell with it. You're worth it."

"I am," she said in a dream like state, before realizing she sounded like a pansy. She added more confidently, "I am."

He smiled. "How's the dinner coming along?"

"Perfect. Better get inside, because I need to take the turkey out of the oven to cool before carving. Then I can start the gravy."

Parker grimaced. *Oh boy, we forgot about the gravy.*

Everyone gathered in the kitchen. Setting his dish down, Parker headed to the oven with Annie. He grabbed a couple of towels to pull the bird out and set it on the carving board.

"Hello, anyone home?" Annie's grandmother walked in with another crock pot.

"Gram, you made red cabbage. Mmm. My favorite," said Annie, walking over to help her.

"Yes, I did," said Grandma Mae. "Funny how you hated this as a child but love red cabbage now."

Nodding, she said, "Thanks, Gram." She took the crock pot and plugged the cord into a nearby socket before turning to give her grandmother a kiss. "Where's Grandpa?"

"Right here." Grandpa Andy came in carrying the cranberry mold. Her grandmother took the mold to put it in the fridge while her grandpa walked around kissing and flirting with the ladies.

Jack arrived with several bottles of champagne and wine, along with two bags of rolls. "Annie, should I pour the champagne yet?"

"Yes, thanks."

Her grandmother went to the stove and began making gravy, to Annie's relief, so she laid out the rolls on the cookie sheet.

The doorbell rang, and the excitement in her mother's voice reached the kitchen as she greeted her guests. Parker looked at Annie, "Guess my parents are here."

They all headed out to the den where Cathie Anderson stood cooing over Annie's two-month-old nephew. Parker gave his mother a kiss and shook his father's hand before he introduced everyone. Although, Jack and Jason knew his parents, the rest of the family never met his mom and dad.

"Annie," said Cathie, "so you're the chef who made the perfect turkey and dressing. I'm so impressed. Ed does all the cooking because I can't cook a thing."

"You bake like a dream, Mom."

"Thanks, dear."

"Dad, did you still need help on the Collins's house? I can give you a hand next week. I'm not traveling next week," said Parker standing next to his dad who watched his mother cuddle the baby.

"I thought you had that article to write?" said Ed turning toward his son.

"Done. Piece of cake. Boss told me to take a break," said Parker.

"Then your help would be welcome. We're almost done putting up the wall board and we could use all the help we can get. I had to pull two of my guys for some emergency jobs."

Standing nearby, Jason said, "I can help, Mr. Anderson. I've got some time off over the weekend. We could use the extra funds. I can work this weekend starting tomorrow."

"Great. The couple is desperate to get out of her mother's house, and they would like to be in their new home for Christmas. I'm determined to make it happen for them."

"Ed, dear, are you talking shop on a holiday?" Cathie, having relinquished the baby, slid over near her husband.

"No more than, you babe. I saw you sign that book for Mary."

Cathie snapped her fingers. "Darn. You caught me, hon."

The table glowed with her mother's gold-rimmed Thanksgiving dishes. Bands of green leaves adorned the edges of the plates, while the centers featured bright red apples, blueberries, squash, and autumn leaves flowing from a cornucopia. Annie had made a matching centerpiece for the center of the table with the dried fruits and flowers in the basement. Crystal glasses glistening with sparkling champagne stood next to crystal water glasses. Gold silverware added a festive touch to the china and crystal.

Annie moved the centerpiece off the table to make room for the side dishes as they were brought out the kitchen. Soon afterward, her father carried a big plate of turkey into the dining room. Her Grandmother followed with the rolls, and everyone sat down to eat. Parker took a seat next to Annie and slid his hand into hers after the prayers were said. The doorbell rang just as everyone finished passing the food.

"Annie, Dan's probably at the door," said her Mom.

Parker glared at her. "Dan? Dan Walker."

Annie was surprised Parker knew Dan, because Dan was on temporary assignment. He didn't live in the area.

With a scowl, he asked, "What's he doing here? Why would you answer the door for him?"

The man looked ready to blow his cork. Not understanding the problem, she stared at him while the doorbell rang again.

"You didn't answer my question," he said in a demanding tone of voice

"You're embarrassing me, Parker. We'll discuss this later." Ending the subject, Annie went to find a smiling Dan at the door.

"Happy Thanksgiving. Sorry I'm late, but everyone in my family decided to call me." He walked in, following her to the dining room table.

"I bet," said Parker, earning him an inquisitive gaze from Iris.

Dan greeted everyone at the table, gushing over Parker's mother before noticing Parker. He sat down on the other side of Annie, glancing over at Parker with a raised eyebrow.

"So, Anderson, what brings you here?" he asked as he filled his plate.

All gazes shifted, along with a few raised eyebrows, to Parker.

"I was invited."

Parker stated this as if Dan was not, Annie noted. *Could this get any worse?* she wondered. *And in front of Cathie and Ed Anderson?*

Looking unperturbed, Dan said, "Mrs. Hutchinson, thank you so much for inviting me."

Annie's mother shrugged as Parker glared at her. Annie nudged him, hoping to stop his tirade. When he turned to look at her, she smiled, while her eyes warned him. "How do you two know each other?"

"We went to college together. Actually we roomed together for a year," said Dan after swallowing some dressing. "Mmm, this is delicious."

"Correction, we both went to the same college."

Dan laughed. "You're not still sore at me for copying your paper, are you?"

"You almost got me expelled," said Parker, annoyance in his voice.

"But you weren't. Besides, I should be mad at you."

Parker stared at him without comment. Jack intervened, "Oh man. I remember you. You're the dude who stole Parker's dates."

"Those days are over since I found Annie," said Dan as he stared adoringly at Annie. She felt sick. The man had to be kidding.

All gazes shot to Annie, who dropped her fork on the ground in shock. She and Parker bent to pick up the fork at the same time, bumping heads so hard they moaned. Parker's face filled with concern, "You all right?"

She nodded. "You?"

"Nothing an ice pack couldn't cure. Damn, talk about a hard head."

"And yours is so soft?" she whispered. This was kind of romantic, being under the table with Parker in the midst of table full of guests. Too bad they couldn't stay here.

"Not at the moment," he said with a wink. She glared at him. He glared back. "So you're not dating anyone, huh," he whispered as he grabbed her fork.

"No one serious. I don't count Dan as someone I'm dating."

The smile that claimed his face made her stomach jump for joy. "Get rid of the creep. He's bad news, just ask Jack."

"I can't. My mother invited him."

"Let's get together tonight to discuss this. If we don't get up soon, our families might decide to join us."

She giggled as they both lifted their heads at the same time, bumping them once again, only this time Annie rubbed the top of her forehead.

"You two are going to knock each other out with your hard heads," said her father.

"Dad, please," said Annie, totally embarrassed.

She glanced at Mrs. Anderson, who smiled at her. "This meal is marvelous. I love this dressing. Maybe I can get the recipe so Ed can make this dressing for our Christmas dinner."

Annie's mother smiled. "I'll type out the recipe myself. My Aunt Ruthie gave me this recipe when I took over Thanksgiving dinner some twenty-five years ago."

Iris jumped into the conversation, "Annie, this is as good as Mom's. You did great."

"Thanks, Iris." She smiled. She'd outdone herself. The almonds tasted like cashews, proving her point—nuts are nuts, no matter what kind you use.

Compliments flowed around the table as they ate, drank, joked, and talked.

With dinner over, the women cleared the table while the men settled in the den to watch football before coffee and dessert were served.

In the kitchen, Iris rinsed the dishes, while the rest of the women packed the food away in containers. Annie's grandmother gave her a hug. Beth patted her on the back. Cathie filled the sink with soapy water, against Mary's wishes. The women settled in, singing Christmas carols while they worked. Her father brought in a chaise lounge for her mother.

Their singing came to an abrupt end as they heard chirps and squeals from the yard.

"Guess the animals don't like our voices," said Annie.

"What do you mean? We're booked at every nearby forest for our a cappella sound," said Cathie. Laughs filled the kitchen until a bark and a deep growl came from the yard.

"We're not singing now. Mom doesn't have a dog," said Iris, heading to the door, followed by the other women.

They stood on the patio looking toward the animal sounds. Birds and squirrels chattered in the trees while two dogs feasted on a turkey carcass and piles of dressing in the stones. Annie cried out as she saw almonds scattered among the rocks. She turned to her sister, humiliated to the core. "Did you do this?"

"Do what?" asked Iris, moving to the edge of the patio.

Parker and her dad showed up, and the looks on their faces said everything. Her grandmother stared at her father. "Bill, was this one of your ideas?"

All the women turned and stared at the men.

Iris shook her head. "I'm guessing your Thanksgiving dinner is on the rocks."

Parker and her father looked sheepish.

Cathie Anderson glared at her son. "Parker Anderson."

"Mom!"

His mother tapped her foot, waiting for her son's explanation.

Annie stared at him, more confused. "Parker?"

"Damn, should have figured this wouldn't work," said her father.

"What wouldn't work?" asked Cathie and Annie in harmony.

Parker waved the rest of the women into the house until only Annie, her father, and his mother remained. "Remember when we discussed heroes yesterday? Well, I wanted to save you from being humiliated again like the last time you cooked dinner. So your dad got me your mother's recipes. I made a duplicate dinner, dishes and all, except when we made the swap you came into the kitchen. When your dad pushed me out the door, I dropped everything in the stones. There was no way I could pick it all up, so I ran to the front of the house as if I'd just arrived. Annie, I'm so sorry. I wanted you to believe in yourself."

"But you didn't believe in me. You assumed I'd make a mess out of the dinner."

All heads turned to watch the animals enjoying their dinner. Annie glared at Parker. "Do you humiliate people for fun? I almost believed you were interested in me."

"Annie, I am. I care about you." His voice floated behind her as she walked back into the house slamming the door. Annie's father followed her, leaving mother and son alone on the patio.

Parker's mother made a sad face. "I'll talk to her. Maybe I can use this in a book."

Parker shook his head. "Not on your life."

"Is this the girl you've been mooning over since Jack's brother's wedding?"

He nodded. "Now I lost her. She thinks I'm playing her. Mom, she's the one. The one I want to marry."

Parker's heart was breaking at the idea that he lost Annie before they even had a chance. He loved her so much. Even when she was an annoying kid, he always had a soft spot for Annie, but never realized it. Not until her brother's wedding.

"Well, you better get in the house and start eating crow. Going down on your knees and begging for forgiveness might help."

He rolled his eyes. "Part of this situation is your fault. If she didn't love the heroes in your books so much she wouldn't be looking for one of her own. I could've asked her out the way normal people ask someone out."

Cathie laughed. "This is the perfect book. I'm going in for dessert. By the way, who made the desserts?"

"Annie."

"Good, because I'd be worried if you baked anything."

"Thanks a lot, Mom."

Parker walked into the house to find Dan Walker looking rather smug. He'd wrapped his arm securely around Annie, consoling her. One punch to his jaw would be all it took to wipe the look off Dan's face. When the woman he loved looked up at him, then back at Dan, while moving closer to Dan, Parker's heart sunk. Frustrated, Parker ran his hand through his hair. But then he noticed her watching him and it gave him hope. Somehow he would make this up to her. He just had to get her to talk to him again.

"Who makes cashew dressing with almonds?" asked Jason, teasing his sister.

"Only Annie could make a new recipe out of an old recipe. The animals liked her cooking. Man, that turkey reeked of something familiar." Jack looked at his sister. "Don't tell us you used Season All on the turkey and dressing?"

"That's it! You two are off my Christmas list," exclaimed Annie. Both brothers laughed, knowing it was an empty threat. Parker knew no matter how mad Annie was at her brothers she would still give them a gift for Christmas. Once, when she wasn't speaking to Iris at Christmas, she still gave her a gift.

"What about the three dishes of rice pudding you ate, Jack? Jason, what about the two pieces of Annie's banana cake you wolfed down?" Parker's eyebrow rose, waiting for them to comment.

The two brothers stared at Parker with grins on their faces. Jack asked, "When did you become the gourmet chef? Hey, do you cater? Been thinking of throwing a New Year's bash."

Parker swore, earning him a look from his mother.

"No really, Parker. When did you learn how to cook?" asked Jack, "I've known you most of your life. You never cooked."

Cathie smiled, "His father taught him. Ed was going out of town on a job and worried we would starve, so he taught Parker everything he knows. What were you, ten, Parker?"

Parker rolled his eyes, "So I can cook. Big deal."

"Annie, my dear, you may not cook well, but you bake like a dream," said Ed Anderson, while eating a piece of pecan pie.

Cathie Anderson smiled. "Annie, you're the perfect person for Parker. He can do the cooking. You can do the baking."

A beeping sound came from Dan's pants pocket. When he extracted his cell phone, Annie noted Barb Wilson's name on the screen. Close enough to read the message, she bit her lip. 'Babe, I'm naked and all wet for you. Come over quick.'

She couldn't believe it. *Barb and Dan? When did he meet Barb? Geez, this guy gets around, but then again so does Barb.* Good thing she never went to bed with him. The guy turned her off.

She glared at Dan, leaving him no doubt that she'd read the text. Taking him by the arm, she grabbed his coat from the front hall closet and hauled him to the door.

"Annie, let me explain!" He tried to pull back.

"You want to get going while she's wet for you," said Annie, as her eyebrows rose.

"But you're the one I want."

"Too bad, because you're not the one I want. We've been out three times and you made my mother feel sorry for you so she invited you to dinner."

"No, I didn't. I want a relationship with you, Annie."

"Dan, I planned on telling you I didn't want to continue seeing you. This isn't working for me."

"Annie… All right. But I really did like you."

Right! She watched him run to his car while pulling out his phone. Most likely he was calling Barb to continue their sex talk.

Annie was glad her father had put an end to the jokes; it helped her survive the rest of the evening. She decided to escape when her grandparents left. Every time she thought about what had happened, she became sick to her stomach. Worse, Cathie Anderson mentioned that she wanted to use this scenario in a book. All she needed was her catastrophic Thanksgiving dinner immortalized in a book. She needed distance from everybody, especially Parker. He tried to follow her, but she put her hand up to stop him.

After entering her small two bedroom apartment, she flipped the light on, threw off her clothes, and put on her warmest flannel pajamas. Then she grabbed the bag of Garrett's Chicago Mix popcorn her neighbor had given her when she came home. Not in the mood for the movie on Hallmark, she plugged in one of her favorite DVD's, *Borrowed Hearts*, settling down to enjoy the popcorn and movie.

Instead, she cried. Tears ran down her face when she thought of believing everyone was enjoying her wonderful dinner, when the truth was her dinner had literally gone to the dogs. Tears for the hope of fulfilling her dream of a marriage to Parker. She hadn't even realized she saw the dream as a reality for the past few days. Now she'd never get married because she couldn't fathom loving anyone but Parker.

Parker may have saved her from humiliation at the dinner table, but what made her mad is how he tricked her by lying. As if lying was ever right. It's a double whammy. She may want to blame Parker for humiliating her, but to tell the truth, she was more disappointed in herself.

The next morning, Annie lay on the couch curled under her afghan. She stretched her arms up over her head ending in a yawn. Sleepily, she curled back under the covers as the smell of freshly brewed coffee wafted her way. Usually she loved coffee maker timers. But today she warred with the idea of going back to sleep or sipping herself awake with caffeine.

A pounding on the door brought her to her feet, startling her fully awake. Wrapping the blanket around her, she rushed to the door. No one ever came to her apartment.

She peeked through her peep hole; there stood Parker Anderson. "Annie, please let me in."

Rolling her eyes, she did as requested. "What do you want now?"

"You. I never meant to humiliate or hurt you."

She moved to the side to let him in, not because she wanted him there, but because he was letting in the cold air, and she was freezing. He leaned down and picked up a poinsettia plant he must have set down before pounding on her door.

"This is for you. I want to make this up to you. I'll go down on my knees and beg your forgiveness."

"That would help," said Annie.

His eyes narrowed. "Did you talk to my mom?"

"She wants to write a book using yesterday's scenario."

"Figures. I meant about going down on my knees." Annie couldn't help but giggle as he continued, "Can you forgive me if I promise never to cook for you again?"

"No."

"No?" His sorrowful hazel eyes seemed blue, looking like he barely slept a wink. Even at his worst, the man still looked great. He moved towards her, and her whole body simmered with anticipation. Parker stopped abruptly, looking unsure of his welcome.

"If you hadn't made a replica dinner, our guests would have had to eat what I'd cooked…" She shuddered. "I forgave you last night for making the dinner, but not for lying. Did you ever think of offering to help me with the food?" Putting her hands up, she said "I know, I know. You're going to say how determined I was to cook the dinner myself."

He nodded. "You might have taken my head off if I'd suggested we cook dinner together."

"Maybe. Probably," she said with a bit more certainty.

"But then, you shouldn't trust me when it comes to making rice pudding, banana cake, or any kind of cookies. My cookies come out burnt. Biting into one is like biting into a rock. Once I forgot the eggs in a cake. My frosting comes out harder than a baseball bat."

She giggled. "Maybe you can bake for the next holiday, and I'll trade my desserts for yours."

He pulled her into his arms and kissed her forehead. "By the way, Mom wants to invite you to join her friends for a cookie baking day. She's got three ovens. They make breads and cookies for baskets for the poor."

"Ellen Parker—I mean your mom—wants me to help bake for gift baskets? When, Parker? Of course, I'd love to."

He frowned. "Am I always going to take a back seat to my mother?"

Incredulous as she found his words, she saw the truth in his eyes. He was sincere. He wanted her. Wanted her as much as she wanted him. "You'll only ever ride in my front seat, Parker Anderson."

"Yeah?" He grinned.

"Yeah." Her lips found his as the blanket slipped down. *Why didn't I wear my sexy negligee last night? Oh, who cares?* She wrapped her arms around Parker's neck, pulling him closer.

"Get dressed, babe. Let's go Christmas shopping." He pulled out a long list of names, topped with hers. "Tomorrow, if you're not busy, we can decorate my apartment for Christmas. Afterward, we can go to the town tree lighting ceremony then come back to my place. I mean, if you're not busy. Annie, I'm sorry. I didn't mean to assume…"

"Sounds perfect."

Before she turned toward her room to go change, Parker said, "Annie, I think I'm in love with you."

Her mouth dropped. "You're quick."

"Quick? This began when you were seven years old. I remember you wore pony tails on each side of your head. I used to love to watch those things flop around."

She frowned. "How romantic? Hey, you acted like you didn't like me."

"I would have been tortured by the guys."

She walked back over to him, putting her arms around his neck. "Parker, I promise to torture you for the rest of your life." Her lips met his, he pulled her closer, as she got lost when he deepened the kiss.

"This kind of torture I can get into," he said in a deep, husky voice.

She chuckled and backed away. "I'll be ready in a bit."

"I'm ready now," he said, making her laugh.

"Mom, I can't believe you're letting Annie cook Thanksgiving dinner again. Wasn't last year's disaster enough?" Iris stopped her one-year-old son from grabbing the candy dish on her mother's table.

"Parker assures me Annie will be a success this year. Plus, he's keeping an eye on her. You have to admit his dinner was delicious last year."

Married, five months, Parker and Annie were hosting their first holiday dinner. Thanks to his father, Ed, with Parker, Jason plus a whole crew from Ed's construction business, the old house they bought was transformed into their dream house.

Everyone shared a before dinner drink while staring up at the seven-foot frosted tree filled with sparkly ornaments that spun in the revolving tree stand. Annie explained how they found ornaments throughout the year.

One real tree stood in the front hall to fill the house with the scent of Christmas. Trees adorned every room. Even the window of her third floor office boasted a special tree filled with ornaments Parker bought her from all their travels over the past year.

As a journalist, Parker sometimes traveled, taking Annie with him. As her work was done on the computer, she rarely had to visit one of her clients. Often they went to different writers' conventions for her work. The rest of the time they spent at home filling the house with warmth, home cooked smells, and treasures Annie and Parker couldn't resist.

The table was set with Lenox Christmas dishes. The chandelier sparkled with a wire wreath of red ornaments and thick plaid, gold-rimmed ribbon. Cathie Anderson, alias Ellen Parker, gave signed copies of her latest book, *The Thanksgiving Caper,* to all their guests. The only guest from last year's Thanksgiving who was not present was Dan Walker. No loss.

When they all sat down for dinner, Parker rose, lifting his glass to his wife, Annie.

"To the most amazing cook in the world."

When guests eyed the dishes, there were a few gulps, a few wandering eyes, and of course, her immature brother Jack stuck his finger down his throat. Hunger won out, though, and they filled their plates. Annie's father, the first brave soul to taste the dressing, gave a look of delightful surprise.

"Delicious. Annie, are you sure you cooked today?"

She nodded. "Parker made the desserts."

His mother groaned, glancing at the cakes and cookies. "Tell me he didn't make the rice pudding. Please tell me Parker didn't make the pudding."

Annie grinned. "He did, and I can guarantee the pudding is going to be delicious."

Her mother stared at her. "How did this change happen?"

"We took cooking and baking lessons together. We're always trying new recipes as well as old ones. We decided if something should happen to him, we didn't want our children to starve. Parker didn't want them to miss out on any of my baked goods if something happened to me."

Iris shook her head. "I'm so impressed with both of you."

"Me too," said Jack. "So when are you due, Annie?"

"In June. How did you know?"

"You're boobs are getting bigger." Their mother slapped him on the head.

In the future, Parker and Annie hosted all the holidays except New Year's and Labor Day. With their built-in pool and colorful garden, they became famous for the loving meals and delicious desserts served at the Anderson home.

Aunt Ruthie's Cashew Dressing
(From The Thanksgiving Caper)

4 loaves of bread

The night before, slit the plastic on the top to let the bread dry out some.

Giblets from the turkey

Piece of onion

In a large saucepan, slowly boil the giblets and the onion until the giblets are tender.

When done, take the onion and giblets out of the water. Throw the onion out.

Save the water.

Grind the giblets and two fresh onions together.

Melt 1 stick of butter or margarine (we use butter)

Break up the bread in to small pieces without the crust and toss in a big roasting pan. Add the ground giblets and onion. Dampen the bread with the giblet water and melted butter. Add water if needed.

Optional: Can add a small amount of chopped parsley and celery. (If you don't have this in the house, don't worry. We don't use either and our dressing is fantastic without it.)

Cut up cashews and add last.

Season with sage, salt, and pepper. (Use your judgment on the seasonings.)

Grease or spray Pam on oven proof glass bowls or Pyrex dish.

This can be made the night before. Pull out the dressing dish from the fridge in the morning to take the chill off the dish before putting it in the oven.

Bake for an hour or until done. Top should brown.

We cook the dressing in the oven with the turkey. As your turkey is cooking, take some of the juice from the turkey and drizzle on your dressing.

Note: Over the years we used to stuff our turkey with the dressing but heard this was bad. Now we put an apple in the turkey and our turkey comes out so tender it melts in your mouth. We also use Williams-Sonoma Brine.

I want to take this opportunity to wish you a Happy Thanksgiving. Thank you for supporting the Windy City RWA chapter with donations for this worthwhile cause in honor of an outstanding author and our friend, Cathie Linz.

Thanksgiving Orphans

By Rachael Passan

Rachael Passan works as head of the fiction collection in a large suburban library and has won multiple awards for her work in Readers' Advisory. A long-time television/movie aficionado, she's been published in non-fiction and has been a contributing author to two editions of the Museum of Broadcast Communication's Encyclopedia of Television (1997 and 2004). She is currently working on a paranormal mystery series featuring the ghost of a 1940s Hollywood leading man.

"Somebody dial 9-1-1!"

Not exactly the words you want to hear at your very first Thanksgiving party. It's important to leave an impression, not poison someone.

But I'm getting ahead of myself.

I love to cook, especially baked goods, but I also love to eat what I make. So, in order not to gain weight from all my baking endeavors, I love to share my labors with friends, especially with potential friends.

I got a new job this year. I work in the library of a big-name entertainment company in Southern California—I'd tell you the name of the company, but I signed all kinds of non-disclosure documents when I was hired, so I'm keeping my mouth shut. I just moved here from the great State of Texas, and I've been taking a lot of ribbing about my drawl, my Texas-isms (all thanks to my grandpappy), and my red cowboy boots. How to win friends and influence people? With all due respect to Dale Carnegie who wrote a book by that name, I discovered many years ago that the way to just about anybody's heart is through food. And, if you're working with a bunch of women, I highly recommend baking anything with chocolate. Works pretty near every time.

As an ice-breaker on my first day of work, I brought baskets of homemade muffins. Since I didn't know the likes and dislikes of everybody, I made a mix of blueberry, chocolate, and banana-nut. And I kept them all separate in case there was anyone who might have a food allergy or two. My cousin J.T.—short for James Tyler—has a peanut allergy. I never saw him have a reaction, but I hear it can be pretty serious. And lots of people are lactose-intolerant, so I made my muffins with a soy substitute. Personally, I wouldn't drink that stuff straight, but used in a recipe, it's hard to tell the difference.

You'd swear these women hadn't seen food in a week, that's how fast those muffins disappeared; by lunchtime, there weren't enough crumbs to feed a gopher. Nobody bothered to ask what was in them, so I assumed food allergies wouldn't be a problem in my new job.

That first week involved a lot of introductions—various department heads, artists, and some of the library "regulars" who heavily used the resources or just liked to hang out and not be stuck in their little cubicles. My job was to assist people with research, although most people liked to do that for themselves and used me as more of a signpost on where to find things. When my supervisor, Joyce, wasn't around—and that wasn't very often since she keeps an eagle eye on us most of the time—I might be called on to give a tour to other new hires when their orientation groups came around.

As much as I try to commit names to faces, after a while, they all started looking alike. Until a couple of months later, when *he* walked in.

I'm not one to believe in love at first sight, more like love after a whole lotta sights and getting to know the person. But at that exact moment, I knew what all those romance novels were talking about.

And here I had just been silently cursing out Joyce. We had three people out with the flu, including Joyce who never took a day off for fear we couldn't survive without her guidance. I didn't mind picking up the slack, but Joyce had called to tell me to work the front desk because our regular receptionist, Divya, was also out sick. I reminded myself to make Divya a huge pot of vegetable soup. Normally, I'd make a hearty chicken stock, but she's vegetarian.

I knew right away this guy was from the "Gold Coast"—that was the nickname the company gave a line of offices of various vice presidents. And you could tell them right off. Every last one of them wore a starched white shirt with some kind of conservative striped tie; they could add a bit of color to the tie if they wanted, although most didn't vary beyond the blues and greys, but they were always striped. The VPs' only concession to "business casual" was that they didn't wear suit jackets. Shirt sleeves were never rolled up, and I'm sure every one of them kept a spare shirt in case they got a wrinkle after an intense business meeting.

If this guy ever had a wrinkle or a perspiration stain, I guarantee you'd never notice it. Once you looked into those blue eyes fringed with the thickest, darkest lashes I pay good money on mascara for, you might not even notice if he were naked. Okay, maybe you *would* notice him naked, but it would take a minute or two. That man had a killer smile, too, and it looked like he was just about to introduce himself, but Harold from Human Resources jumped in first.

"Hey, Shel, where's Div today?"

One of Harold's more annoying habits, of which he has many, is shortening your name like he's your good buddy, completely disregarding that many of us don't like our names shortened. Me—Shelby—for one. Divya for another. And pretty much everyone else here.

"Divya's out with the flu so I'm filling in. How can we help you today?"

"Joyce around? Hunter here is our new VP of Creative. I was hoping she could give him a quick tour." That meant Hunter was, technically, our boss since the library was under his particular jurisdiction.

"Oh, darn, Harold, Joyce is out sick today, too." I even vowed to bring *her* some chicken soup, although maybe a canned version. "But, I'd be happy to give y'all the nickel tour."

"Maybe we better wait until she gets back. Hunter's a VP after all." Meaning that a lowly librarian like myself couldn't handle such an important task.

"I wouldn't want to be a bother." If velvet had a voice, it would sound like Hunter. The guy was getting better and better every second. He was almost too perfect. He had to be gay.

"Never a bother," I said. "I love to show off everything we can do."

Harold was about to say something to make me hate him more, but his phone rang—a tinny rendition of "We Are the Champions."

"Excuse me. I gotta take this. This is Hal, talk to me," and his voice faded as he stepped a few feet away so we couldn't be privy to this "important" conversation.

"We haven't been properly introduced. I'm Shelby Foote, no relation to the writer."

"Same family?"

"Not even a distant relation."

"Too bad. I loved his books. Hunter Thoreau. No relation to the writer either, not even distantly. Nice to meet you."

Hunter smiled. He must spend a small fortune on his dentist or on whitening products.

I was about to say something witty, but then Harold returned, essentially saving me from trying to think of something witty.

"So sorry, Hunt. Pete needs me back in the office. Since Joyce isn't here, I'll walk you back to your office. I'm sure she can set up a tour for you when she's back."

"Why don't you go ahead without me?" Hunter suggested. "I'm pretty sure I can find my way back, and I don't think you should keep Peter waiting." He placed a slight emphasis on Mr. Sheldrake's full first name, although I doubt Harold noticed.

"Thanks, Hunt."

"Hunter."

Harold didn't hear that because he was already halfway out the double glass doors.

"Now," Hunter said as he perched a hip on the desk and turned his blues eyes on mine, "how about that nickel tour?"

Wish I could say our little tour ended with him asking me out to dinner, but sadly, no. I did receive a nice email later that afternoon from him, copied to Joyce, thanking me for giving such insight into our operations. Official, but nice. I didn't hear from him again for three weeks. In another email.

To: Shelby Foote
From: Hunter Thoreau
Subject: Movie trivia

We're having an argument I hope you can settle on the Academy Awards. I thought *Gone with the Wind* was the first color film nominated for Best Picture. Is that correct?
Thanks, Hunter.

Easy peasy. I'm all for movie trivia and I get questions like this all the time from friends, but Hunter Thoreau is a VP and my not-so-immediate supervisor. We have a rule in the library that we're not supposed to do personal research, but when you work in any kind of corporate setting, a good rule to follow is never say "no" to a director or above. I was going to answer this question as seriously as any other.

And Joyce, control freak that she is, has very specific rules in the library. Any question must be answered using a prescribed answer form—in writing or via email—and she needs to be copied on all replies. As much as I would like to be more friendly, or even a bit flirty in my reply, I have to do things Joyce's way.

To: Hunter Thoreau
From: Shelby Foote
Subject: RE: Movie Trivia

Dear Mr. Thoreau,
In reply to your question, a definitive answer depends on the wording of the original question. *Gone with the Wind* (1939) is the first color picture to <u>win</u> an Academy Award for Best Picture in the awards ceremony held on February 29, 1940. *The Wizard of Oz*, also nominated for Best Picture that same year, is partially in color.

However, if the original question asked what was the first full color picture to be <u>nominated</u> for an Academy Award, then the answer would be *The Adventures of Robin Hood* (1938), although the Best Picture award that year went to *You Can't Take it with You*, a black-and-white film.

Partially because Joyce was keeping tabs on me, and partially because, as a librarian, I just love to give people as much detail as I can find, I provided the sources where I found this information. I also included the fact that *The Broadway Melody* (1929), which was the second film to win Best Picture and the first sound and musical film to win, included one Technicolor sequence, but probably could not be considered a "color" film.

His reply was succinct:

> Thank you very much for your prompt reply. I appreciate that detailed and informative answer.

I hoped he realized I was cc'ing my boss and not being all hat and no cattle.

Over the next few months, I'd get other emails from him, usually asking some question, and I would answer like a good little employee would to a vice president. Never got much of reply other than a "thanks," so I figured he didn't have any interest in me apart from my being a walking encyclopedia.

Then one day, instead of an email, he came into the library. The first time of many after that.

He was still asking what I would consider trivia questions, but he was coming in person. I'd show him the resources that would answer his questions, or he would sit across from my desk while I searched computer databases.

Joyce was all over him like fleas on a bloodhound, asking what she could do to help him, but he'd always say something like "Thank you, but this is a follow-up to something Shelby was helping me with."

Joyce never admitted I was doing a good job, not to my face anyway. But when Mr. Thoreau—I always made sure to be very formal in her presence lest she complain I was being too friendly—complimented my work, she could do nothing but agree with him and say she was glad he was pleased.

One time I found a Coke—or more specifically, a can of Diet Doctor

Pepper since, in Texas, we call all sodas Coke—on my desk with a note saying "Thanks for helping me win a bet," so I can truly say he bought me a drink. But still no invitation to dinner or lunch.

Now if you want the 4-1-1 on anyone in the company, all you have to do is contact Javier, one of our phone operators. I swear that man is former CIA. I don't know how or where he gets his information, but he knows, or can get, the low-down on everything about everybody.

I asked Javier for lunch—off-site, of course—and asked him what he knew about the new VP of Creative. Javier didn't hesitate for one second and rattled off everything he knew about Hunter, everything committed to memory. Like me, Hunter was a transplant, from Chicago. He was 37 years old, born on March 2, which made him a Pisces, although I don't pay attention to that kind of thing. His last job was at a graphics firm in the Valley. He wasn't married and not gay, a relief to me and more than a bit of a disappointment to Javier. He loved Italian food, especially from this one restaurant on Pico Boulevard. His parents and two sisters' families still lived in the Midwest, and he had no plans to fly home for Thanksgiving.

"Now how can you possibly know that?"

"Bernice"—one of the executive assistants on the Gold Coast—"handles all the travel arrangements for the VPs, and she didn't book anything for him. Besides, even though it's a holiday weekend, he's the newbie, so they put him in charge in case anything happens. He's staying put, Chica."

"A lot of us are. No big deal." I was more than a bit homesick and really wanted to go home myself, but I also didn't want to spend *beaucoups bucks* to fly home for a short weekend.

That's when I got the idea.

I would throw a Thanksgiving dinner for all us "orphans," people who didn't have family in the area. I didn't want to do a traditional Thanksgiving dinner because that would just remind everyone of family. No, I'd throw one big non-traditional blowout.

Divya, as I said before, is a vegetarian and I wasn't planning on a traditional bird. But now I had a perfect excuse to go through all of my cookbooks and all those downloaded recipes I've been collecting.

My baking had made me a number of friends at work so, once the word got out, a lot of people sort of invited themselves. By the beginning of November, I could expect about twenty people to come to supper. Everyone was really nice and wanted to contribute something to the dinner, but I was hell-bent on doing it all myself. I did, however, accept the idea of people bringing extra tables and chairs. I wouldn't turn down a bottle or two of wine, either.

The guest list included people of different nationalities and cultural backgrounds, so I planned for a little bit of everything. For appetizers: baked brie and crackers, dips, crudités, and stuffed mushrooms. Also, seeing as how I hail from Texas and grew up on Tex-Mex, guacamole, salsa, and chips were an absolute must. For the entrées, I planned on dishes from Mexico (enchiladas), India (a masala), and a variation on barbeque meatballs that had a bit of Asian influence.

Okay, I had this blind hope that Hunter might hear about the party and want to come along and, in case that happened, I also planned on having something Italian. I was going to make lasagna, but settled on a turkey tetrazzini which might be Italian enough for his tastes and could also appease anyone who might miss a regular turkey. Best of all, most of the dishes could be made well in advance, so I wouldn't kill myself between Wednesday night and Thursday afternoon.

The week before Thanksgiving, Hunter walked into the library again and found me in our little kitchen area in the back of the department. Joyce had just reamed me out for some minor infraction, and I was in desperate need of anything chocolate. My heart skipped a beat when I saw him, but it was lodged in my throat right alongside one of my death-by-chocolate brownies that I'd stuffed whole into my mouth.

I grabbed a piece of paper towel to cover my mouth; the brownie was too big to swallow and too good to spit out.

"Those look very good. Mind if I have one?"

I still couldn't talk around the mouthful of brownie, but I nodded and mumbled something I hoped sounded like, "Please, go ahead."

Unlike me, he took a far more delicate bite, and then emitted a small moan of ecstasy-slash-approval—high praise indeed.

"Did you make these? They're terrific." And he popped the rest of the brownie into his mouth while I nodded my thanks.

We stood there in an awkward silence, chewing away. I finally swallowed my brownie and could get back to business, but waited for him to finish.

"You're quite a cook," he said, licking the frosting off his fingers. "What do you know about cooking a turkey?"

Obviously, he never heard of 1-800-Butterball. "Stick it in the oven and wait for the skin to turn brown and crispy."

"I'm a little disappointed in you, Ms. Foote. Your research prior to this point has always been far more detailed than that."

"A more detailed answer depends on a number of factors."

"Such as?"

"How many people are you cooking for? I mean, how big is the bird?"

He extended his hands out in front of him, about eight inches apart. "It's about this big."

"That won't feed a lot of people." Not unless they were all emaciated supermodels.

"Well, since it's just me, it's probably more than enough. Funny thing, I'm not much of a fan of turkey, but I thought I'd give it a try."

He was a VP and I was pretty much at the bottom of the corporate totem pole. I should have referred him to Joyce who would bend over backwards and do somersaults to appease a vice president who could have a great deal of say over our operations. But standing there in our little break room/kitchen looking very *un*–vice presidential picking chocolate crumbs off his pink and gray polka dotted tie, he was so cute that, before I knew it, I invited him to my "orphan" party.

When he answered, "I'd love to," I was as pleased as a puppy with two tails.

Thanksgiving Day suddenly took on a whole new meaning. It wasn't just a get-together with friends. Now I desperately wanted to impress Hunter.

Even though I planned to make certain dishes ahead of time, nothing went according to plan.

I put on a dozen eggs to boil to make a Cajun-style deviled egg, but got distracted ironing my fancy tablecloth and only remembered the eggs when I heard them explode all over the kitchen ceiling.

For the crudités, I decided to save money and not buy the pre-cut versions at the grocery store. But I just sharpened all of my knives and ended up cutting off a few tips of my fingers.

My first pie crust burned because I didn't hear the timer go off and let it cook an extra twenty minutes.

I made about a dozen trips back and forth to the grocery store to replenish, rebuy, or regroup.

On Thanksgiving morning, I was crazy as popcorn on a hot skillet trying to make sure that anything that needed to be heated was put into the oven or on the stove at just the right time so that everything would come out hot at the same time.

I'd barely showered and dressed before the guests started arriving at four o'clock—even though the original invitation was for four-thirty—each bringing a bottle of wine as a hostess gift. Lucky for me, I liked this cheap brand from the local market because I now had about five bottles of red and seven of the white. While they attacked the appetizers, I went to finish my make-up.

At 4:31, Hunter arrived. I was busy in the kitchen, but Javier gave me the head's up. Hunter brought a red wine that I could only afford if I bought a winning lottery ticket. I tucked it behind the paper towels in the pantry so this would *not* be a bottle I opened tonight.

People were so busy eating, there wasn't much conversation, and I was running back and forth making sure all the appetizers were replenished. Hunter came into the kitchen as I was refilling the guacamole bowl.

"Quite a spread. Everything looks delicious. That," he said, indicating the green mess I was stirring, "seems to be particularly popular. That's guacamole, isn't it?"

"You've never had guacamole? You must have had a deprived

childhood."

"My family isn't one to venture out beyond basic meat and potatoes. I've never really tried Mexican food.

"Then you do not know what you're missing." I took a chip and dipped it generously in the guac. I stopped short of feeding it to him; that'd be a might too personal. But he ate it with gusto and even went back for more.

Everything was going well, and I was going to develop callouses from patting myself on the back if the night continued on like this. The guests were eating and chawing and having a good ol' time. A gentle tapping of plastic ware on glass cut through the background noise.

It was Hunter.

"If I can have everyone's attention for a moment," he said quietly and stood, clearing his throat. "Not in any kind of official capacity, I just wanted to express my gratitude to Shelby for this…. uh, this…. sorry."

As if it were possible for him to be any cuter, his cheeks flushed with embarrassment. He loosened his tie and undid his collar button.

"Sorry, something's caught in my….." He emitted a weak cough and looked like he might pass out.

When he tried to speak again, his words slurred like his tongue was too big for his mouth.

And then he keeled over.

"Somebody dial 9-1-1!"

That's where you came in.

We didn't have a doctor in the house, but nearly as good. Javier's significant other, Ben, had some medical school training and took charge until the paramedics got there, which was a good thing because nobody knew what to do.

"Help him up," someone shouted.

Turns out that's not something you're supposed to do. I'm not quite sure why because I never really heard what Ben said about that; I was too busy watching my life flash before me.

The paramedics arrived and pulled out all kinds of gadgets. I heard them mutter phrases like "rapid heartbeat" and "BP is low," none of which sounded good. Eventually, they bundled Hunter up on a gurney and high-tailed him out of there, but right as he was passing me, Hunter grabbed my hand and squeezed it weakly. I couldn't see his face because a big oxygen mask covered most of it. Just why he grabbed me, I wasn't sure. It was gentle and probably not code for "I'll see you in court." After all, would you shake someone's hand you were later going to charge with attempted murder? Maybe it was "Thanks for dinner, but you're fired."

I couldn't just stand there. Javier and Ben assured me they would take care of everyone, so I followed the ambulance to the hospital.

When I got there, they wouldn't let me in to see him at first because I wasn't family. (Hell, at this point, I wasn't even a friend.) But Hunter's tongue had swelled so much and they put in a breathing tube so he couldn't talk at all. But they had lots of questions they thought I could help with.

They led me into a curtained cubicle. Hunter was all trussed up with tubes and IVs and oxygen, but his hand raised slightly. I wasn't sure if that was "welcome" or a weak "get the hell out of here." I sat in a chair against the wall by the foot of the bed.

"We think he's having an allergic reaction to something," the guy in the white coat said. "We've given him a shot of **epinephrine**, but it will take a few minutes to take effect. Mr. Thoreau says he doesn't have any known allergies, isn't that correct?"

Hunter gave a shaky nod.

"Do you know what he ate tonight?"

He might as well have asked me to recite the periodic table backwards and in Chinese. I couldn't even remember what *I* ate tonight. "I'm not sure…."

The doctor had a pen at the ready and rooted around in his pockets for something to write on. When he couldn't find something to write on, he sent a nurse out for some paper. Hunter waved his hand to get my attention and then brought his hand up to his mouth in a C-shape.

"Drink?" I asked and he nodded.

We went through a list of what I served to drink at the party. Wine? No. Water? I knew the minute I said it, it wouldn't be the water, but that was the second thing that came to mind. No. Iced tea? Yes!

"What else?"

Hunter brought his hands together and formed a circle.

"Brie?" Yes. "There was baked brie with crackers. What else?"

Hunter mimed making a snowball.

"Meatballs?" Yes. "I made barbeque meatballs," I said to the doctor person.

"Was there anything he could have eaten that no one else had? Maybe something he'd never eaten before?"

The nurse came back with a legal pad but, by that time, we were all involved in this game of charades.

Hunter slapped the bed to get my attention and mimed scooping with one hand.

"The mushrooms?" No.

"The veggie dip?" No.

He frantically pointed to the blonde nurse next to him fiddling with his IV.

I'd fixed a plate of blondies as one of the desserts, but we were still in the middle of dinner when all this happened. Frustrated at my lack of understanding, he tugged at the nurse's scrubs.

Still not getting it.

Then he pointed to my red cowboy boots.

"My boots? You ate something that looked leathery?"

He pointed to the boots again and sort of spread his hand out, palm towards me and made a circular motion.

"Red," the doctor said. "He's indicating the color." Hunter nodded.

There were a lot of reddish dishes. He said "no" to the meatballs, which were kind of reddish. "The marsala?"

Hunter shook his head and grabbed for the nurse's scrubs again.

"Green," the doctor guessed. "He just pointed to your boots to indicate color. Not something red, but green."

"The guacamole."

Hunter collapsed back on the pillows, his energy spent.

"It could either be the spices or the peppers in the dish. He might even be allergic to avocados, although that's an uncommon allergy," the doctor said, "but we're going to take good care of you, Mr. Thoreau."

Now that they knew the probable cause of Hunter's reaction, I gave them a list of ingredients in the dish. After that, they didn't need me anymore and the nurse ushered me back to the waiting room. Hunter sure as hell didn't want me around, so I left the hospital.

By the time I got back home, everyone had left—poisoning a dinner guest can really put a damper on things. Javier and Ben, bless their hearts, stuck around to help clean up and put away the leftovers. They offered to stay, but I just wanted to be alone. I opened a bottle of the cheap wine; I didn't enjoy it at all. I probably should have opened Hunter's wine, but I figured he'd ask for it back.

On Friday afternoon—the company had given us that extra day off—Javier called to check up on me. Don't know how he knew it, but he told me Hunter only stayed overnight and was released that morning.

Going to work on Monday morning was like walking to the guillotine. You knew your head was going to be chopped off, you just didn't know when the axe was going to drop. I couldn't work up any kind of appetite after the debacle Thursday night, so I brought in all the dessert leftovers and left them in our break room. I planned to leave the plastic containers there too, figuring I might as well start getting rid of stuff before I had to pack up and go back to Dallas.

Joyce must have known something happened on Thanksgiving. Not that she was being nice or anything like that, but she wasn't her usual picky self either.

Divya grilled me on my trip to the hospital, but it was a busy day and she got the story in bits and pieces between projects and when no one was within earshot.

Every time my computer pinged with a new email, I cringed. I knew I wouldn't hear from Hunter—well, maybe some cease-and-desist letter kind of thing from his lawyers—but I surely expected to be called into HR. Or would they come to me and fire me in front of everybody?

Nothing. All day, nothing.

Nothing happened on Tuesday either.

I didn't let my guard down all week, but still no calls, no emails, *nada.*

The following Monday, I got to work about an hour early to finish a project, but the message light on my phone was already blinking. I took a deep, resigned breath and dialed into my voice mail. It was Harold and he wanted to see me ASAP.

"Shel, c'mon in and have a seat."

Harold had a really nice office high up in the corporate building with a wall of windows overlooking the '10' Freeway. Not the best view, but I was still a bit jealous. The library was in one of the outlying buildings with only a couple of skylight slits to let in some natural light.

I sat down in a lumpy, worn leather chair while Harold shuffled paperwork, looking for the right folder. It took him a couple of tries, but he finally found it.

"Here we go." He leaned back and read through a bunch of papers in the folder, his lips moving as he read.

The suspense was killing me and I finally blurted out, "Can we please just get on with it?"

Instead of being shocked by my outburst, he just smiled and asked, "A little anxious, are we?"

"I love my job. I don't *want* to be fired, but if you're going to do it, do it!"

"Shelby," he said, his brows knitting together, "you're not being fired."

"I'm not?"

"No. Why should we?"

Well, if he didn't know, I wasn't going to be the one to tell him.

"No, in fact, we're moving you to a different division. Consider it a promotion, but without additional compensation," he was quick to add, although at that point, I didn't care.

"We've been very impressed with your skills as a researcher. Our Research and Development division has always been asking for their own dedicated staff, so effective immediately, you'll be working for R&D. I've notified Facilities Management. They'll be moving your office this afternoon, so you better get back and start packing. Congratulations."

R&D! The company owned lots of different buildings all over. That particular group occupied a multi-storied building in the next city over. I'd surely miss all my friends here, but I most definitely didn't get fired! Whereas the library fell under Creative and Hunter, R&D belonged to Strategic Planning, meaning I'd be indirectly reporting to a different vice president.

Hunter had still gotten rid of me, but it was nice of him not to fire me. For that, I would be eternally grateful.

Back at the library, everyone was grinning like cats in a cream factory. News travels fast in a corporate environment, but this was like the Indianapolis Speedway of gossip. My co-workers weren't grinning about my new job, though. The object of their amusement sat on my desk—the biggest bouquet of flowers I've ever seen outside of a funeral. Everyone, including me, was dying to know who sent them, but there was no card.

I packed up my desk and, carrying the last box, eventually headed out to the parking lot where I found Hunter standing next to my car.

"Here, let me help you with that," he said, taking the box from me. We stood there for a bit until I couldn't hold my tongue any longer.

"I really appreciate you getting me this new job instead of firing me."

"Fire you?"

"Because of the dinner."

"Shelby, you didn't know I was allergic to avocados. *I* didn't know I was allergic to avocados. It was an accident. That's why I sent the flowers."

"*You* sent the flowers? There was no card."

He said he had written a nice card thanking me for the dinner and saying that he didn't hold any grudge against me because what he ate that night he really liked.

"But you *are* one of the reasons I'm being transferred to R&D."

"Well," he said, blushing, "yes, I have to admit I had a hand in it."

"Because you wanted to get rid of me."

"Because, (a) I knew it would be a great opportunity for you and (b) they can really use a person of your talents." After a few seconds, he added, "and (c) because I'd like to ask you out."

"You didn't have to give me a different job just to ask me out."

"Actually, I do. Corporate frowns on executives who 'fraternize' with subordinates. But now you report to Jim Goldthwait."

Well, that was as unexpected as a fifth ace in a poker deck. But it sure gave me a little more 'git' in my git-along. "Since you're no longer officially my boss, how 'bout we go to dinner tonight to celebrate my new job? It doesn't have to be a date-date, but I would sure love to go out with you. Where would you like to eat?"

"Any place but Mexican."

Asparagus Guacamole

- 1½ pound(s) uncooked asparagus, trimmed
- 1 tablespoon reduced-calorie mayonnaise
- 1 tablespoon fresh lime juice
- ¼ cup cilantro, coarsely chopped
- 3 medium uncooked scallions, thinly sliced
- ½ medium jalapeño pepper, minced
- 1 medium-sized garlic clove, minced
- 1/8 tablespoon Worcestershire sauce
- 1/8 teaspoon hot pepper sauce
- 1/8 teaspoon table salt, or to taste
- 1/8 teaspoon black pepper, or to taste

Instructions

1. Bring large pot of water to boil. Add asparagus and cook until tender, about 10 minutes. Drain.

2. Place asparagus into food processor and purée until smooth. Stir in remaining ingredients and serve.

Echoes of Time

A novelette from the Timeless Series
By Savannah Reynard

Savannah Reynard wanted to have a star on the Hollywood Walk of Fame and win an Oscar for best actress until she stumbled upon an abnormal psychology class and fell in love with the human psyche. She now combines her creative side with her experience working in the mental health field to write about characters who rise from their lowest points and achieve their undiscovered potential in her fantasy and paranormal romances. In these worlds, she makes sure everyone gets their happily ever afters. Savannah's own storybook ending consists of living in the Chicagoland area with her two favorite men in the world, her husband and son, along with two quirky cats and one very lovable black lab.

Every so often, the echoes of time dance with the present. On the breath of a butterfly, with the whisper of the wind, time crosses for many reasons, the most meaningful, true love.

Madison sat fuming in the passenger seat while the blizzard beat down on their tiny Kia. "Shit, Tom, why did you get off the highway?"

Her almost ex-husband sighed, "The GPS said to exit, so I exited. What the hell was I supposed to do?"

"Well, it's worse down here." She stared out the window at the blanket of white. No streetlights, no moonlight, only the dark coal-gray of the night sky mixed with the blinding white snow. It was hard to tell where the road ended and the trees began, and where the trees ended and the houses began. At least she thought they were houses. The whole state of Illinois had become a frozen tundra.

"I'm well aware of that. I'm the one who's driving."

"Pull over. Just pull over, for God's sake. We're going to get killed. I don't know why I let you talk me into this stupid idea in the first place."

"I don't know why you came either, if you were going to bitch at me the whole way."

"It was your grand plan we rent some house and drive up here together. How could you even think for one minute I wouldn't bitch at you the whole way?"

Tom pulled off to the side of the road. "Now what?"

"I don't know. I guess we sit here and wait it out."

"Right...and get buried alive."

"Got a better idea?"

"Not really." Tom rested his arms on top of the steering wheel and peered out into the blowing snow.

Madison leaned up against the passenger door, crossed her arms over her chest, flicked her brown curls in front of her face for good measure, and refused to look in his direction. She didn't know whom she was more pissed at, Tom for suggesting this last hurrah or herself for agreeing to go.

The wind whirred outside as piles of snow fell. Madison looked out the window. "I hope the kids are okay," she said, unable to hide the concern in her voice.

His face softened. "They are. They've been at my parents' since finals ended, and you told them to stay put if the weather got bad. They're being stuffed with all kinds of goodies by my mother."

"You're right." Madison rubbed her hands together nervously. The twins, James and Jenna, were in their first year at the University of Illinois, and she hadn't seen them since her visit to Champaign in October. She had been looking forward to spending the holidays with them. Her heart hitched. "But now, because of the snow, we won't get to see them for Christmas."

"I know." Tom sounded genuinely disappointed too, but that wasn't surprising. He was a great dad—a shitty husband, but a great dad.

Madison wiped the fog off the window with the sleeve of her puffy teal coat and stared at the blanket of white outside. "God, I've never seen snow like this in my life." She felt better knowing the kids weren't driving in the stuff, even if it meant she was going to have to spend Christmas alone with her soon-to-be ex.

"Yeah, it's freaky the way it just seemed to dump all of a sudden. I wish I knew where we were." He stared blankly at his phone.

"What does the GPS say?"

"It's broken."

"What?" Madison snatched the phone out of Tom's hand and stared at it. She swiped at the screen feverishly but nothing, just a black screen. "Christ, you don't have a signal."

"I know. I haven't been able to get anything on the damn thing since the last exit."

Madison dug in her purse and pulled out her own phone. With furrowed brows, she tapped the glass a few times, turned it off and then back on, and nothing. Panic rose from deep within her gut. "Mine's not working either." She stared at Tom as her heart raced and her stomach knotted. "We're stranded." She searched Tom's face. "People don't survive in cars for long."

"Nonsense. We've got gas, so we've got heat. It'll be fine." He peered out her side of the car and glanced around. "Maybe the house is around here somewhere. I noticed we were almost there before the GPS cut out. It looks like we could be in a residential neighborhood. A sparse one maybe." Tom buttoned up his coat, settled his hat on his head, and then reached for the door.

"What are you doing? You can't go out there. You'll freeze."

"Don't tell me you'll actually care if I do."

"Don't be a jerk. I'm serious."

"I can barely see, but it looks like there's a glow coming from over there. Maybe it's the house we're looking for?"

"Yeah, or one with killers. You're on your own, buddy. No way I'm going to some strange house in the middle of nowhere." She didn't even know what city they were in. She thought there might be houses around, but visibility was nil.

"Suit yourself. I'll leave the keys so you can keep warm." Tom opened the door and a gust of wind blew in, sending a shiver down her spine and a slap of snow to her face. She wiped the remnants off her cheek, but her irritation remained.

She watched Tom walk away until he was covered in white. They hadn't lived together in almost six months, and she was sure he had arranged this little family holiday weekend to get her to sign the divorce papers. But she couldn't let him die in the snow alone. After all, he was the father of her children. They had been married for almost twenty years, most of which she had thought were good until last June. Her heart squeezed, and all the ache came back again.

"Goddamnit." Madison buttoned her coat up to her chin, wrapped a scarf around her neck twice, and opened the door. When she stepped out of the car, the wind whipped at her face, sending snowflakes—or rather, ice flakes—into her eyes, and nose, and every other orifice that wasn't covered. Despite the sting of the weather, she hoisted her legs out of the snowdrifts and trudged after Tom.

Squinting, she managed to see the glow too. What the hell were they getting into? But the alternative was freezing to death in the car. That was the last thing she wanted to do, die in a Kia. So much ice and snow blew in her face that she couldn't make out the exterior of the house until she came upon the stairs, or at least she assumed they were stairs, more like graded levels of snow. She could barely see Tom's footprints on the steps; they were already being covered up by newly fallen snow. When she reached the top of the porch, she found the door open and Tom standing in the foyer.

"What are you doing?" she yelled at him in her loudest whisper. "You can't just barge in."

"It's okay; no one lives here. It's the one, the house I rented for the weekend." He smiled smugly. "I did take the right exit. The key was left in the lock box, just like the owner said it would be."

"No way." She couldn't believe it. They had made it. If she believed in miracles, then this would definitely be one. The second one might be if she managed not to kill her husband by the end of the weekend. She shot a weary glance in his direction. Well, one out of two miracles wasn't bad.

Madison looked outside at the small, Kia-shaped mountain of snow they had just left and shivered at the thought of being buried alive inside it. She started to unwrap her snow-laden scarf, causing chunks of ice to fall to the floor. "We need to get the bags and start a fire. It's freezing in here."

Tom smiled and instantly she felt warmer. He always did have great teeth and a charming smile. Tingles buzzed in her belly, and then she remembered why they were there. She stomped the snow off her boots, shook off the nostalgia, and took a deep breath.

"I'll grab the stuff from the car, whatever I can carry in one trip," said Tom, pulling up his gloves.

Madison closed the door behind him and stripped off her wet coat and boots. Better him than her. Plus, he was due for a little penance. Her heart and gut twisted into a ball. Tom had really let her down. After all those years, he had truly disappointed her. More than disappointed her, he'd broken her damn heart. She figured this was a last goodbye for her and the kids, a last holiday before they actually called it quits for good, and a good way to corner her and get her to sign the divorce papers. It was a strange way to do things, but the kids had been into it, and secretly, if she were being honest with herself, she wanted one last time too. Now she was stuck here with her soon-to-be ex-husband—in a snowstorm, without any kids to buffer the tension. Son-of-a-bitch.

Madison flicked the nearest light switch to illuminate the chandelier hanging from the ceiling above. She stared at the twinkling lights for a moment, finding them slightly familiar, but shrugged the feeling off. The house was an old Victorian, dusty yet somehow still refined. Her mouth dropped open as she scanned the foyer. Breathtaking. Red carpet lined the stairs bordered by dark wood and intricately carved banisters. A bench sat to the left of the stairs, flanked by a wall-sized mirror framed in ornate gold. The place hadn't had any TLC in a long time, but was amazing nonetheless. This is what she had always wanted, an old Victorian, but Tom had wanted a modern new building, said it would outlast them. It sure the hell did.

She skimmed her hand along the dark wood of the staircase and closed her eyes. A prickle of energy danced under her fingertips, and then zipped through her arm to the rest of her body. She opened her eyes with a flicker of recognition and gasped. Her heart pounded as she stumbled in a circle. *Oh my God.* She knew this place. She knew the stairs and the tapestries and the wood. She had been coming to this house for years.

She had been coming to this house for years—in her dreams.

A blast of frigid air grabbed her attention. Tom had returned carrying two suitcases and all the grocery bags, his form hardly recognizable under all the snow covering him. He shook the layer of white off his head before dropping his armfuls on the bench along the wall.

"Nice job," was all she could manage, still reeling from the familiarity of the house.

"Thanks." He tossed aside his black wool coat and hat. "Let's see if we can heat this place up." He walked around looking for a thermostat. "Hmmm. Thank God it's been updated somewhat, but it'll take a while to warm the whole house with these radiators." He walked into the next room and Madison followed. "Ah, one of the fireplaces. Now to find the wood."

Madison stared at the brown leather trunk adjacent to the fireplace. Her senses stirred as a flutter of a memory flashed in her mind. The wood should be in there, to keep it out of sight. "What about the chest next to it?" she asked tentatively.

"Good idea."

Madison crossed her arms over her chest and rubbed the sides of her sleeves. "I wonder how long this place hasn't been lived in."

Tom walked over to the large trunk and tinkered with the latch. "Looks like awhile. The dust is a few inches thick." He opened it and peered inside. "Hey, look! Firewood. It's like you knew."

Madison smiled. She had her moments.

Tom began putting logs in the fireplace. "If the stove doesn't work, we can cook here. It'll be like camping." He always had a way of pointing out the fun or the positive in almost anything. Almost. He dug into one of his bags. "I know I bought a new lighter and a candle."

"A candle? Why a candle?"

"What? It's festive."

"Yes, festive." And kind of romantic, if she didn't know better. Madison grabbed the bag of groceries she'd brought and made her way to the kitchen. She unpacked the perishables and found the refrigerator in working condition. Might as well start getting dinner ready. Besides, she was starving, and cooking gave her something to do. She wished the kids were there. She had made James' Christmas Eve favorite. Now it was just the two of them and a whole lot of awkwardness, not to mention a whole lot of lasagna. She closed her eyes and sighed. She just wanted this to be over. Instead, she was going to have to make nice with the man who abandoned her for following her dream.

"Hey, I got it." Tom yelled from the other room. "Come on in and warm up."

The fire crackled while Tom grinned at his handiwork. He'd also strategically placed more "festive" candles around the living room. The fire roared for a few minutes, but then smoke began to back up into the room. Madison covered her mouth, unable to stop herself from coughing. "What's going on?"

"I don't know." Tom peered up the chimney. "The smoke's coming back in for some reason."

She sighed. "Did you check the flue?"

Tom jabbed a poker into the chimney. "Of course I did. I think something's lodged in here." He gave whatever it was a few more jabs. "I can feel it."

"Stop! What if there's something dead in there?"

He waggled his eyebrows. "Then we'll have more for dinner."

"Eww. You're gross." Madison wanted to laugh, but she kept it inside. A part of her didn't want to give him the satisfaction that being together might be anything other than awful for her.

Tom gave one more good jab and dislodged a big, black lump that landed in the fire. The lump didn't jump out, so it must have been dead, or never alive in the first place. Madison watched as Tom stuck his poker into the flames and knocked the mass out onto the floor. The thing was starting to smolder but hadn't caught fire yet.

"Be careful, and don't damage the floor."

"You mean don't make us have to pay more money for damage. You couldn't care less about me."

"That's not fair. Of course I care if you get burned." Maybe singed a little bit might be okay though. She walked closer to the fireplace. As she neared it, she realized the black lump was actually dark velvet material wrapped around something small and kind of square-shaped.

Tom knelt down and began to unwrap the layers cautiously. "I wonder what it is."

"What if it's a head or something demonic?"

"What if it's cash?"

He removed the last layer, and there sat an old, leather-bound book and a small wooden box. Tom grabbed the box, while Madison reached for the book. When she opened it, she saw blue ink and wispy penmanship. Someone's journal. A thrill crawled up her spine. Someone at some point had written in this book. How old could it be? Madison thumbed through the yellowed pages before settling on a specific one. Drawn to the ivory chaise dotted with tiny red flowers, she sat down and started to read. She bit her bottom lip as she devoured the words.

My sweet Georgie.

No fire could burn as bright as my desire.

You have set my soul aflame.

It was as if she were peeking into someone else's mind. A kindred spirit. A fellow writer. She drew the book to her chest and sucked in a breath. What a gift.

Madison had only set out on her own writing career a year and a half ago, and the whole journey made her heart sing. She'd always dreamed of being an author, so after the kids finished high school and went off to college, she decided to follow her dream. That's when Tom mucked it all up.

The mucker himself got up from the floor and walked over to her. "Look, Mads, cufflinks." He dropped them into the palm of her hand.

They were gorgeous—gold, ruby, sapphire, diamond. She rubbed one between her thumb and forefinger, the ridges of the stones scratching her skin. The image of the cufflink clinging to the edge of a sleeve as two hands clasped each other flickered in her mind and caused an ache in her heart. The vision dissipated just as quickly as it came. The sight of Tom leaning over her brought her back to the present. Wait a minute…Mads? Who's he calling Mads? That name was reserved for the young, sweet man she had married, not the one who gave up on her. "They're magnificent," she said, keeping her other thoughts to herself.

"What did you find?"

"Nothing. A book is all."

"A book? Let me see." He went to grab for it, but she snatched it away and hid it behind her back.

Just then, the timer in the other room beeped, signaling the oven was preheated. "Oven's ready," she sang, walking towards the kitchen and tucking the journal under her arm. She didn't know why she was protecting it. All she knew was she wanted to be alone with the words and how they made her feel for a little while longer.

Madison put the lasagna in the oven and sat at the kitchen table. The overhead leaded-glass lamp created a soft glow, a perfect background for reading an old book full of honeyed words and beautiful memories. She opened up her newest treasure and turned to another page. On it, she found another poem to Georgie.

The sun, the moon, the stars cower in your sight.
Love as true ne'er burned as bright.
Without you, there is only night.
Dearest Georgie, you are my light.

She traced the last line of cursive with her index finger then brought the journal to her chest, giving it a hug. Tears welled in the corners of her eyes. True love, how beautiful. How she craved it for her own.

The timer ticked away as Madison read on. She could hear Tom bustling about in the other rooms, presumably unpacking, but she was lost in this woman's words, lost in another time, lost in someone else's love. Tom came into the kitchen, opening and closing the wooden box. Madison looked up, her face flushed hot as if she had just been caught doing something wrong.

"Wow, what's got you so intent?"

"Nothing, it's just a journal." She put the book behind her back again, shielding it from Tom.

"Okay, if you don't want to share, you don't have to."

A smile curved her lips. She was being silly, but she couldn't help herself. Even so, he wasn't going to get a peek just yet. It was hers and hers alone. "Dinner's almost ready. Grab some paper plates out of the grocery bag, will you?"

"On it." Tom casually walked over to the cupboard and pulled out two pieces of china. Then he opened a drawer, pulled out some silverware, and brought the settings to the table.

Madison paused as she removed the lasagna from the oven. She eyed him suspiciously. "Have you been here before?" she asked.

"Me? No. Why?"

"You got dishes right from the cabinet, like you knew where they were kept. And the silverware too."

Tom glanced over at the cabinets, then the drawer and furrowed his brows. "I did, didn't I?" He set the plates down. "No, I swear. I–I just grabbed them."

Madison felt a surge of anger tear at her insides. "Did you bring her here too?"

"What? No. No way. I swear, Mads."

She stuffed back the tears that threatened to flow. The "her" was a coworker he'd talked about a little too much. About how she was a devoted wife and mother. How she needed nothing for herself. A regular martyr that one. But Madison, she was the selfish one who wanted to do something more with her life, to become something more. Her heart disappeared into the black hole of pain that had been the past six months. "And don't call me Mads."

Tom reached out and stroked her forearm. His touch felt warm and firm as he gently rubbed her skin. "We had coffee is all. Nothing happened, and I sure didn't bring her here."

Madison peered down at his hand as if it were burning her, and he pulled it away. But the feel of his skin on hers didn't burn, goddamnit. It felt nice. Sweet even. But she didn't want him to know that.

"Fine." She had no real proof anyway, just a worry, or an obsession with the fact that the "her" was buxom and blond and he'd talked about her, a lot. Well, not a lot really, maybe he had brought her up once or twice. Somehow, when Tom left, "the her" became Madison's own personal villain, however undeserved.

She would have pushed his familiarity with the house more, but it was familiar to her too. She knew the walls, the rugs, the stairs. She had dreamt about them since she was little. She had always figured the Victorian home in her dreams was her made-up safe house. Her happy place. She had had no idea the location actually existed until now.

After Tom served the lasagna, he pulled his phone from his pocket and gave it a few taps. "Still blank. I'll have to take it in to the Apple store when we get back."

"If ever." She rested her chin on her palm and looked out at the night sky and the ever-growing mountain of snow. She wondered if the white beast could swallow up the whole house, and if they'd be frozen, unearthed when the world thawed.

Tom hopped up and went over to one of the other bags. "Might as well bust these out." He held up two bottles of wine. One bottle of red and one bottle of white. She smiled to herself. When they bought wine, they always bought two bottles, one red and one white, reminiscent of one of their favorite songs. He went into the pantry and came out with two goblets.

Again? "You got directions from the owner, didn't you? Come on, don't lie."

He looked at the glasses in his hands. "Er...no. Honest, Mads—I mean Madison." He brought the crystal over to the table, wiped them down with a dishtowel, and then uncorked the wine. He held the white over hers, waiting for permission.

"By all means." She gestured towards her glass.

Tom smiled and looked down with those lush eyelashes of his. Long and black, the perfect frame for his big brown eyes. Traitorous big brown eyes, that is. Madison stabbed her lasagna, jammed a piece into her mouth, and washed it down with a big gulp of Pinot Grigio.

The two of them ate in silence for a while. She finished her first glass of wine, and he quickly filled it again. They made small talk about the kids and their Christmas gifts, what each of the in-laws was up to. Nothing of consequence. By her third glass, her insides felt pretty good. Her belly was full with some damn good lasagna, her head was buzzy, and even her heart, which had been so heavy for so many months, seemed lighter, softer, less achy.

"It was delicious as always. Thank you," said Tom, quite sincerely.

Actually, so sincerely it took Madison by surprise. "You're welcome."

"You always were a superb cook. Always."

She grabbed her plate and his and took them to the sink. "Thanks, you're getting all complimentary on me. Must be the wine." She laughed and set the dishes in the sink. It was more like an uncomfortable change-the-subject kind of laugh than a real one. What was he trying to do anyway? The candles, the wine, this house? It was as if he were planning to schmooze her. Schmooze her into signing something which benefitted him more than her, or was the whole weekend something completely different?

"Maybe," he said. "But maybe it's something I should've said more." He sat with his elbows on the table, staring into space.

She turned towards him and swallowed. "Thank you."

"I'll do the dishes. You go sit by the fire and read your secret book." He looked at her, mischief in his eyes.

"Really? A girl can't argue with that." Madison walked—no, practically ran—over to the table and picked up her goblet. "Fill her up....please."

"You bet." He stood next to her and filled her glass, not spilling a drop.

They both paused, transfixed by the other. She got a whiff of his soap, his scent, him. Her stomach knotted, and a flush of heat and heartache swelled in her chest. She turned on her heels and sped into the living room. She had to get away from that feeling. She thought it was gone. She thought she had set it free. She did everything the self-help websites said to, everything except actually talking to him, that is. She wrote him letters about how she felt and then burned them. She went to a therapist. She tried to heal, tried to forget. She tried, but all of her efforts unraveled with each smile he gave her, with each sweet word, with each sentimental gesture.

In her heart, she knew the whole mess wasn't only his fault. She was the one who had actually filed for the divorce the day after he suggested they get some space. And by space, he meant he was renting a fancy, new, high-rise apartment minus her. There was no talking, no counseling, no attempts at making peace, just cold, hard, agonizing silence.

She was so angry and so hurt that she had asked for everything, a boatload of spousal support, full payment of the kids' college tuition by him alone, the house, both cars, the dog, and even his beloved cat, Ringo. She would have asked for his blood, if it were legal. All her venom and pain were enveloped in the first draft of those divorce papers. She wasn't surprised when he hired a lawyer and drafted his own version, a version she had refused to even look at until this week. She didn't know why she hadn't looked at them. Perhaps she was waiting for him to take them back, to say something, maybe even to move back home. Maybe he was waiting for her to do the same. It's not like she hadn't thought about it, or hadn't started to pick up the phone and dial even, but she never went through with making the call. Stubbornness, pride, and the overwhelming feeling that if he was the one who left, he should ultimately be the one to crawl back home, ate at her.

When it came down to it, they had loved so passionately for so many years. It wasn't surprising that when they fought, the pain of their battle was just as intense. She could remember at least two other times when they had been on the brink of divorce, but this time was their worst, and the one that had lasted the longest.

Madison sighed as she sat down on the chaise lounge in front of the fireplace. She pressed the book to her forehead as if it were her savior. She wanted to forget her own life, her own loss, with that book. She sipped her wine and opened to the beginning. It read:

This book belongs to: Margaret Pennywise Martin

As she read, the writings revealed that Margaret, or Peg as she called herself, married a man named George at the height of Prohibition. The journal was a mixture of a diary, and love letters, and an ode to George, who she lovingly referred to as Georgie.

Yesterday Georgie forgot to tell me he loved me. Today, he said it every hour just to make up for it.

Madison consumed every scripted word, every rhyme, every bit of Peg's daily life. The more she read, the more she could see Peg and George in this house. Their presence filled every corner.

Last night, Georgie and I made love all night long, in almost every room in the house. We started in the kitchen and didn't stop until we heard the birds chirping from our third floor bedroom.

She closed her eyes, letting the soft seduction of the wine seep over her. In her head, she could hear the jazz music and the crooner singing of love or love gone bad.

"Hey, you asleep?" Tom stood in front of her holding his glass of wine and another unopened bottle.

Madison sat up and cleared her throat. "No, not at all."

He sat next to her on the chaise, half on half off. "More?"

"Ah, what the heck." She glanced out the window at the world covered in white. "I'm not driving anywhere tonight."

They both laughed, easy laughs, laughs like old times. She looked at his warm brown eyes. Once, she would have done anything for those eyes. Once. Those eyes dropped to the book in her hands. "Feel like sharing yet?"

She looked at her precious secret pages. She felt so vulnerable, so raw at revealing what lay on them. That was ridiculous. It was as if they were her own words. As if she had penned them herself. She shook off the tightness that balled in her chest. "Okay, you've been good."

"Sweet." He sat on the floor next to the chaise and laid the box with the cufflinks in his lap. He sipped his wine, looking up at her as he waited. Madison started with the first poem. She couldn't reveal Peg's thoughts just yet, but she could read her beautiful poems.

The soothing words of love pirouetted off her tongue. The emotion poured off the pages, invoking thoughts of days gone by, of deep bonds, and of love of the truest kind. Madison's heart opened as she read each syllable. Tom listened intently while he rested an arm on her leg. The fire glowed, time stood still, and a comforting stillness settled in the room. Each object in the room, the whole room itself, even the crackling flames that licked the chimney walls, waited for each breath of her words.

Lips press.

Tongues explore.

Hot breath brings me back to life.

Wake me.

Wake me.
From this dreamless sleep of life.
I was nothing.
I am something.
I am loved by you.

Madison looked down at Tom.

"They must have lived here." He opened the box, removed the cufflinks, and rolled them between his fingers. "These must be George's." He eyed them closely. "Keep going."

Madison read a few more poems. The fire was warm, the wine was sweet, and Tom was as charming as he was the day they had first met.

"She's a good writer," he said. "Not as good as you, though."

Tom's last sentence snapped Madison out of her wine and love-poem induced trance. "What?"

"Remember how, back in college, you used to write poems. All kinds too; political ones, philosophical ones, and some pretty hot ones." Madison shot daggers at him. His gaze dropped to the floor. "You used to read them to me in the dorm. Don't you remember?"

Irritation crawled down her spine. "Yes, *I* remember." It had been hard enough to write a novel, alone and in secret, while the kids were in their last year of high school. Then, when they went away to college and she got the guts to reveal her work to Tom, he laughed. He laughed in that self-preserving, don't-know-what-to-say kind of way that she'd seen him do when he felt taken by surprise. But whatever the reason, the sting of that laugh left an invisible scar. He laughed at her dream when she thought he would have been proud of her, when he should have said he loved her and wanted her to be happy. When she needed him to say that he knew she had it in her all along. What came next was the last thing she would have expected—an unreadable blank face and the words, "I need some space. I think I need to be alone for a while, maybe get my own apartment." Not exactly the response she had pictured.

Tom stared at the floor and cleared his throat. "I had forgotten." He twisted the wedding band on his finger. "How could I have forgotten?" He stared up at her with sadness in his eyes. He wore a look that tore at her insides, a look that melted her heart.

"And you remembered, now?" Madison sat up straighter. Now when she was ready to let go? Now after she had spent the last six months hurting? She stared at him, daring him to speak.

"No, not now. I remembered a couple of months ago, but it seemed too late to take everything back." He shook his head, presumably in disbelief at his own stupidity. "How could I have forgotten that?" The hand resting on her thigh began to caress it. "You've always loved to write, and I loved listening to your writing. You said all the things I wanted to say, and so perfectly."

She snapped the book closed, anger soaring through her veins. She spat out, "You sure as hell did forget." She started to get up, but Tom kept his hand firmly in place to stop her.

"I'm sorry, Mads. I was stupid."

"Yeah, you were." She leaned back in the chaise and looked out the window. She hadn't prepared for this: the sweetness, the apologies, the kind words. She had prepared to fight for her territory, for money, to get what she could and get out. She didn't want to admit it, but she liked the unexpected way Tom was acting better. She chastised herself for being so weak, for being sucked in, for still being in love with him.

Tom leaned over her and rested his head on his elbow. "Please don't stop. Read something else. Please?"

Madison took a deep breath in. She didn't want to stop either. She liked how this felt, goddamnit. She liked reading to him. She had forgotten how much time they spent doing this in college. She wanted to stay in that moment for just a little while longer. Was that stupid of her? Was she making a mistake? "Okay, I'll keep on."

New Year's Eve. Georgie put on the Ritz for the party, spared no expense.

We danced until we were dizzy. Drank until we were jazzed (Georgie has the best hooch ever). Ate until we stuffed ourselves silly.

Georgie got a tip from a Bull down at the precinct that we were going to have uninvited guests. While we were in the cellar, we didn't even hear them bust down the door.

Madison stopped reading. "There's a cellar."

Tom's eyes sparkled. "Let's look for it."

But she didn't have to look. She already knew its location, in the back, under the third floorboard, the loose one with the scratch on it. She didn't know how she knew, she just did. She giggled as a surge of excitement lit her up. She closed the book and they walked into the kitchen towards the back porch together. Without looking or thinking, they simultaneously knelt down and reached for the same board. Their hands touched. Madison felt the warmth of that old feeling and a familiar tingle between her thighs. Tom looked at her and she looked back at him. Their eyes fixed on one another's.

"How did you know?" they said in unison.

Then they both laughed.

"Oh my gosh." Like before, they said it together.

Madison grabbed her stomach, rolled onto her back, and started to really laugh. She couldn't help herself and she couldn't stop. Tom leaned over her, laughing too.

"I–I can't believe this." She managed to say through bouts of giggles.

"I know," he said. "I guess I should ask if you've been here before."

Yes. No. Not really. She didn't know how to explain the situation and worse, she didn't trust him with her answer. "No, just a guess, I guess." She rolled onto her belly. "Go ahead, you try."

She watched as he removed the board and found the release for the trap door. It was old and rusty, and he had to work hard to loosen it. But after a little twisting and some muscle on his part, she heard the lock release.

"Got it." Tom pulled the door open, and a waft of stale wine and dust drifted out.

Madison practically trembled with eagerness to get in. She dangled her feet over the edge while Tom lowered himself halfway into the cellar. "I'll go down first. Can you grab two candles?"

Madison rushed into the living room without speaking a word and brought two candles and a lighter back with her. Her heart beat fast; she couldn't wait to see what was below the house. At least they had a distraction, something besides the awkwardness of the weekend. She handed Tom a candle while keeping one for herself. Tom eased into the hole in the floor. She followed, first inserting her legs into the opening. She had expected to find a ladder on the wall, but as she lowered herself down, her feet hit a level surface. She pulled the candle in with her, lit the wick, and immediately noticed she stood on a staircase, but not just any staircase, a gorgeous cherry one with wrought iron railings. She held her breath. This was no run-of-the-mill wine cellar. She tentatively walked down the steps, holding her candle close.

"Look, there's a bar over there," said Tom.

Sure enough, flanked by leather stools, a bar stretched along one entire wall. The cellar must have been at least the length of the house, if not bigger. Velvet couches sat in one corner, and at the far end of the room, she saw a square space with oak hardwood flooring. She gasped. A dance floor. Madison smiled inside and closed her eyes. She envisioned Peg in her flapper gown with George in a tuxedo. "Tom, this isn't a wine cellar. I think it's a speakeasy."

Tom snapped his head from side-to-side. "You're right." His face lit up as he walked behind the bar. "And there's liquor still here."

Madison made her way over to one of the velvet couches in the candlelit darkness. She noted they were covered in almost a hundred years' worth of dust, which seemed to wash out their color while casting a grayish film over everything. Was it possible the owners didn't know this even existed? "Do you think anyone's been down here since Peg and George?" She had to laugh at herself and at how she referred to them as if they were old friends. But they almost were. She couldn't explain it, couldn't put it into words, but she knew them, maybe even as well as she knew herself.

Tom moved back and forth behind the bar, poking at things. "It doesn't look like it. But could that be possible? No one?" He pulled out an old bottle of wine. "Want to try it?" He waggled his eyebrows up and down.

"Are you sure it's safe?"

"Hon, it's vintage."

Madison crinkled her brows at him and shot him a dirty look for slipping the hon into his response.

"Sorry, Mads...I mean, Madison."

He was acting so strangely, and by strangely she meant normal, like old times. Acting like the past six months had never happened, like he hadn't left her. It bugged her a lot, and it bugged her even more because she liked it. She watched him trying to uncork the wine, his sandy hair in his eyes like always, his lips dark pink with a killer smile. Her heart tightened. Why did you have to be such an asshole? She should have asked him, but instead she said, "I'm game if you are."

"Alright, but these glasses are filthy. Let me go and wash them upstairs. I'll be right back." He padded up the stairs, glasses in hand.

"Grab more candles," she yelled up after him.

The cellar was darker than dark and damp too. Madison walked the length of it to the dance floor. She'd been drawn to the area as soon as she set foot in the room. Mirrors spanned the walls around it, giving it a larger feel. They were old and cloudy, but she imagined how they might have sparkled in the light with the beading of the dresses and clinking glasses. She set her candle down on a nearby table and stood in the center of the floor with her eyes closed. She heard the slow rhythm of an old jazz song in her head and swayed to the music. The scent of a light perfume enveloped her.

Oh Georgie. Come dance with me.

She heard a far off voice reply. *Not now, babe. I gotta do inventory. We owe our share to the boss soon.*

Come on, Georgie, one little dance for your sweets.

Why do I get the feeling this ain't gonna be no short dance.

Madison felt the warm touch of a hand in hers. She clasped her fingers around it, eyes still closed. She felt the heat of a body close to hers and smelled wine and spice. Her head seemed fuzzy and light.

"Why do I get the feeling you're not dancing alone?" asked Tom, breaking her trance.

Her eyes shot open and fixed on Tom. "What?" She lost her breath for a moment. "What do you mean?" She blinked her eyes to regain focus then shook her head to clear it. She...she wasn't alone. She looked in mirrors and then back at Tom. She had heard the music. She had heard the voices. She had smelled the perfume that was not her own. What could she say to him? How could she explain what was going on?

"You looked like you were dancing with someone, so I thought I'd fill in the space." He nodded to his hand holding hers. Their fingers entwined, their bodies close.

She tried to brush the situation off so he wouldn't ask any more questions. "That's silly."

Tom had placed the candles from upstairs all around them. There were two glasses and a dusty bottle on the elaborately hand-carved table at the end of the dance floor. And there he was, swaying to the non-existent music with her.

"Ready for some old wine?"

She let go of his hand, needing to be out of his arms, yet wanting to stay there forever. She spun away from him, laughing nervously. "You mean vintage?"

"Exactly." Tom followed closely behind her.

Just to the side of the dance floor sat a pink couch. Maybe it had been red at some point, but time and a coating of dust had dulled the color. Madison brushed the back of it, and Tom batted the pillow. Dust spewed into the air creating a haze all around them. Coughing, she sat down, trying to settle herself. She needed to distance herself from the hallucination, or the ghosts, or the memory. Because that's what it felt like, a memory, like it was all around her yet in her mind's eye. And she was still reeling from being so close to Tom. Damn that man. She had felt it all again when he held her in his arms, the tingles, the heartbeats, their rhythmic breaths. Jackass. It was all his fault they were divorcing. Or was it really? They had both made rash decisions. They had both been stubborn, and now they were both paying the price in silent separation.

Tom poured the rich, dark wine into the long forgotten glasses. He spun the liquid in the crystal, gave it a whiff, and then held it up to her nose. "What do you think?"

She inhaled. "Fruity, with hints of oak," said Madison, almost surprised this one-hundred-year-old wine could smell so, so good.

They lifted the glasses to their mouths as they watched each other, both of them pausing with the edge at their lips. They laughed in unison, light, easy, genuine laughs.

"Okay, on the count of three," said Madison. "One, two, three, drink." She squeezed her eyes shut and opened her mouth the tiniest bit to let the red liquid flow in. She tasted the berries, still sweet, then the woody earth taste of oak, then a slight bitter hint of something else. She smiled with her whole face. "It's pretty good." She giggled and took another sip. "This is kind of fun."

Tom's face turned serious. "I'm so glad. I wanted this to be fun for you."

She looked away. She wanted to avoid a conversation when they were enjoying the moment, enjoying each other. A conversation meant seriousness, heartbreak, pain. She didn't want pain to ruin her secret speakeasy, but there was going to be no way she could avoid "the talk," so she let it out. "Stop, just stop."

"Stop what?"

"Stop being so nice, so complimentary, so like you were before. So like, you love me. Just stop it." Madison set down her glass and stared him straight in the eyes. "Why go through all this? Why not just give me the papers and have me sign? I'll do it, you know. I never said I wouldn't."

Tom looked down. "I don't want you to."

"To what?"

"To sign."

Madison sat up straighter. "What?"

Tom grabbed her hand in his, teardrops brimming behind his dark lashes. "I'm sorry," he said, his voice barely a whisper. "I was stupid and selfish, and I wouldn't blame you if you never wanted to see me again, but I don't want a divorce."

Madison's head reeled. Fury at his stupidity swirled in her chest. Tears fought their way to the forefront of her eyes, bringing to memory all the times she'd cried, all the times she couldn't sleep. Her stomach lurched, and she could feel the bitter taste of the wine that had come up. "Fuck you,

Tom."

He let go of her and sunk his head in his hands. "I know, I know, I know. You hate me."

But she didn't. She didn't hate him. She loved him. Still loved him. Loved everything about him, his eyes, his smile, his way. She didn't know the right way to feel. She didn't know what to say to all this. How could they go back? How could they pick up where they left off after so much silence between them? "I don't hate you."

He looked up, his eyes red and bleary. "You don't?"

Madison gulped down the last of her wine. "No, I don't. I want to punch you in the face. I want to shame you for centuries." She stared at him, raw and vulnerable. She stared at him and remembered how many times she had wished he'd said that he didn't want a divorce. She stared and felt that enduring quiver in her belly. "I want to yell at you until my voice is hoarse and then...and then...I want to kiss your lips until the pain of the past six months goes away." Tears streamed down her cheeks, and she swiped them away with the palm of her hand.

Those words were all he needed to wrap his arms around her, tangle his hands in her hair, and press two vintage wine-soaked lips onto hers. His kiss was hot and wet, and she felt it to her toes. Madison was just as eager, opening herself up, exploring him, letting her tongue lead the way. Goosebumps pebbled her skin, and she flushed hot everywhere. *I've missed you. Oh how I've missed you.*

Their hands explored all the familiar places on each other. His fingers found all the right places to make her want more. His tongue traveled to all of her hot spots. She should say something. She should stop, but she didn't want to. She liked the way he felt. She liked the things he did. She loved the way he made her feel again; it had been so long since she'd felt the rush of desire burn through her.

Feel now, talk later.

Tom found his way to her bra clasp and unhooked it. He cupped both breasts in his hands under her sweater. Somehow, this felt so naughty in their secret room. So naughty and so damn good. He pulled her on top of him, and she straddled his lap. Her legs hung over his strong muscular thighs, hidden beneath his faded blue jeans, her favorite faded blue jeans of his. He slid off her sweater and bra, taking one breast into his mouth, sucking on the nipple, then the other, slowly, methodically, with purpose. Madison trembled under his touch. Each contact of his mouth on her bare skin sent her higher. Should she let him in? Was this right? To hell with right.

She grasped his hair between her hands and kissed him, pressing hard against him. He paused only to pull off his white thermal, revealing his shaped pecs and lean abs. She had always loved those abs. Madison trailed a tongue along his neck and over the curve of his smooth shoulder. She scraped her teeth along the spot, which had always been ticklish for him. He giggled like he always had and squirmed in her grasp, but it didn't detract his attention from her breasts. Tom licked and nipped across her chest as she arched her back so he could taste more of her. Closing her eyes, she soaked all the sensations in.

This is my favorite kind of dancing, sweets.

Mine too. We have to hurry before our guests come.

It don't matter. We don't gotta open the doors til we're good'n ready.

Madison sat up and pulled away from Tom. "Did you hear that?"

He looked up at her, his eyelids hooded. "Hear what?"

"The people talking?"

"Down here? No."

But there had been, twice. Like she was there with them. Almost as if she were one of them. No. She shook her head in answer to her own thought. No way, that was ridiculous. But it felt so real. She had no explanation for what had just happened, and she felt a little, actually a lot, crazy. Something wasn't right. This wasn't right. She slid off Tom and reached for her sweater at the other end of the sofa.

"Don't, don't cover up."

"What, I should walk around shirtless now?"

"Could be a whole new thing?"

A laugh escaped her lips even though she didn't want it to. "Stop," she said as she pulled her sweater on. She needed to clear her head and reel things back in, not only because she was hearing things but also because she hadn't planned on their reuniting. "We have to talk about some things."

Tom leaned his head back against the wall. "I figured. I knew we couldn't just jump in the sack and make it all better." He looked up at her. "Or can we?"

She lightly slapped him on the chest. "No. We can't." She stood up and picked up her glass. "Let's go upstairs. We'll run out of candles soon anyway."

"That's okay by me."

They made their way upstairs and closed the trap door.

"More wine?" asked Tom.

Madison needed to sort through her feelings. She needed to decide what she wanted. She needed to see if she had forgiveness left in her heart. She knew she did, but she wanted to sleep on it just the same. But most of all, she needed to figure out the strange feelings and voices that started ever since she set foot in this house. "No, I think I'm going to bed now."

"No talking?"

"Not tonight. I've got some thinking to do."

Tom's usual grin turned upside down. He looked sad and disappointed and even a little pitiful. She grabbed her purse and looked for her suitcase. She found it in the master bedroom upstairs. She saw Tom's in another bedroom. Relief that he hadn't assumed they'd be sleeping in the same bed for the weekend washed over her. She locked the door behind her, and that's when she noticed her exquisite and pleasantly dust-free surroundings. Had Tom been in there earlier sprucing up the room, or did the owner make sure the bedrooms were clean at least?

Drawn to the plush red comforter of the bed, she crawled onto it and lay on her back staring up at the gold and red draperies cascading from the canopy above. She reached out to touch the lush fabric and tiny currents passed through her body. A filmstrip of images flickered through her mind, heated bodies, tears, laughing, the crash of a vase, humming, whispers, and the most palpable, the unmistakable rush of love. The snap of hot wood caught her attention. Directly across from her sat an elegant ivory fireplace complete with a toasty fire, compliments of her Tom. Madison melted into the bed as her heart was reduced to a molten glob. She could have her family back in one piece. She pulled her phone from her purse but still no signal. She attempted a text to her kids but nothing. From the bed, she could see outside through a small part of the heavily draped window. What should have been darkness, the black of night, appeared more like gray with blinding white specks, as the snow continued to fall.

Madison found herself standing in the middle of the kitchen downstairs. The room was decorated for Christmas, and she held some sort of fancy drink. She took a sip, minty, strong, with a hint of sweetness from the candy cane garnish. She felt arms wrap around her from behind. *Georgie.* She snuggled back into him. Her heart was warm and full. *I love you, Georgie.*

A pounding sound thundered from the other room, and she turned towards the front entrance.

"Get in the cellar. Get in the cellar," yelled George.

"Who is it, baby?"

"I dunno, could be the cops."

Madison threw the remnants of her drink in the sink and ran the water to rinse out the glass.

"Hurry, sweets, there ain't much time."

Her heart pounded as she scrambled for the trap door in the floor, but she was too slow. The front door burst open and in came four men dressed in black, each toting a gun. Madison bolted to George. He placed his body between her and the men. "Freddy. Freddy. What's going on?" he said, fear in his voice.

"Sorry, George, boss's orders. Let's take a little ride."

"He double-crossed me, you gotta know that."

"Freddy, Johnny, Stanny-boy, what's happening?" asked Madison.

"George here didn't pay the boss, so now I got orders. Sorry, Peg." Fred looked away, unable to face her.

She stared at George through tear-filled eyes. "No, Georgie, I won't let them take you." She fisted his shirt in her hands, clinging desperately to him. "They can't take you," she screamed.

George cradled her chin in his fingers. "I'll see you again, sweets. Don't worry."

But she did worry. There were tears in his eyes, and she knew if he left, he would never come back. Madison looked from face to face, pleading through blurry eyes. She glanced around the room, her heart racing, but everything else seemed to be in slow motion.

She noticed the butcher knife on the cutting board near the sink where she'd been chopping shallots to put in their Christmas dinner. Before she could think, before she could tell herself that she wouldn't win, she pulled out of George's arms and lunged for the knife. Stabbing forward she charged at Fred, screaming. Madison felt a strong hand grasp her shoulder; the force of it pulled back on her. Ra tat tat. Piercing pain, hot and sharp, exploded through several parts of her body. Fred had fired shots at them. She grabbed her stomach and collapsed, noticing that she had fallen on something soft. She turned her head and found George crumpled underneath her. Blood gushed from his temple. She tried to speak, but the darkness was growing all around her. She heard voices, yelling, curses. She lay there unable to move. She lay there, dying. She felt the warm hand of her Georgie slowly wrap around her waist. She willed her hand to move over to it and placed her numbing fingers over his. *Oh, Georgie. I love you. I will see you again.*

Before the darkness consumed her, she saw a face, grief-stricken and wrought with tears, hovering above her. She recognized the face of her brother Stan. He knelt down and whispered to her. "I'll take care of your stuff for yah. I promise. I'm so sorry Peg, so sorry." She couldn't focus, couldn't keep her eyes on him. Her eyelids were so heavy, and she felt so sleepy. She tried to speak again, but her words were stuck inside. Deep inside of her, Madison recognized the face too. No, it wasn't just Stan. It wasn't just Peg's brother. The face belonged to her son, James.

Madison opened her eyes to find a haze of snow blowing past her window in the morning light. She lay there, cemented by the most vivid dream she had ever had in her life. The whole thing had felt real, the drink, the guns, the pain, the blood. She saw the world as herself, but all the men had kept calling her Peg. Peg, the woman whose diary she and Tom had been reading, the woman who had lived in this house. Georgie, if she didn't know better, resembled her Tom. She remembered the feel of his arm sliding around her waist and the smell of blood filling her nose. Panic surged through her hard and fast. Tom. Somehow, after her dream, there seemed to be more at stake. The yearning for Tom and the home they shared consumed her, leaving her breathless.

She shook her head and tried to put the rest together. Her dreams of this house when she was young, the fact that Tom knew his way around as if he lived here, and her horrific dream last night. Was there something to it all? Could she find proof? What kind of proof she didn't know, but she had to start looking. As she slipped on a pair of socks, she could still taste the mint and candy cane on her tongue. The drink, the speakeasy—that was it. She hurried down the stairs in her red flannel pajamas and got a whiff of something wonderful. Breakfast. Tom stood by the stove already dressed in a snug black Henley, scrambling eggs and making pancakes.

"Good morning! Breakfast is almost ready."

"Thanks, I'll eat later." She couldn't think of anything else but the bar downstairs. She headed straight for the trap door and yanked the handle with all her might.

"Where are you going?"

"Downstairs to find something." She leapt into the opening and then poked her head right back out. "Can you bring me a candle?"

Tom walked over to her, handed her a candle, and lit it. "Is everything okay?"

"I–I don't know." She didn't have any answers for him.

She stepped carefully into their secret underground lounge and crept down the steps, her mind unable to focus on anything else. It had to be here, it had to be here. What had to be here? She knew she had left it there the last time she had it. Had what? Inside, she felt this insatiable urge to search. Her gut knotted and pulled, leading her to the bar. She put her hand underneath the counter top and began to feel around. It was there, she knew something was there, somewhere. She just didn't know what that something was. She moved along the bar, sliding her hands underneath from front to back. When she reached the center, she felt something she knew didn't belong. Yes. An extra flap protruded underneath the bar with something wedged in there. Her fingers brushed the surface and with a tingle she knew instantly what lay hidden. With a firm grip, she yanked the bound papers out. Tom's—er—Georgie's drink book. He had invented all of his own drinks and had written the recipes down in a small notebook.

A prickle of energy buzzed through her as she turned the notebook over in her hands. She read each recipe, page by page. Her head burst when she stopped at a specific one. It was in there, her favorite drink, the drink she had been holding in her dream, the drink she had been drinking when she died. She covered her mouth with her hand and leaned against the counter behind her, drawing in a breath. Her stomach balled, and she could no longer see as the tears gushed. She brought the notebook to her forehead and squeezed her eyes shut. She had lived here and died here and so had Tom. Shivers crawled up and down her arms, snaking their way down her back. It was all real. It had to be.

Madison's legs felt weak and wobbly beneath her. She managed to make her way to the stairs with the candle and the recipe book. Her thoughts raced as she sat down across from Tom at the breakfast table. She stared at the waffles and eggs that had cooled in front of her.

"Merry Christmas," said Tom over his empty breakfast plate. His face was sullen, and he could barely look her in the eyes.

Madison clenched the book with both hands. She couldn't put her thoughts to words and just stared at him. What could she say? How could she explain? It sounded ludicrous. It was ludicrous.

"Is this what you want?" Tom nudged a stack of papers towards her.

Madison glanced at them. They were the divorce papers. "Is that what you think this is about?"

"What else could it be? Why did you let me say all those things if you had already decided?"

"I hadn't decided. I was just surprised is all. I thought you had decided six months ago when you decided to move into your own apartment. I thought you had decided when you never called to apologize. So don't try to pin anything on me about deciding just because you have decided you made the wrong decision now." She stabbed her eggs with her fork and shoved some into her mouth. The nerve of him. Sometimes she just wanted to punch him in that stupid face of his. That stupid face, that same stupid, bloodied face that lay beneath her as she bled to death. *Oh Tom, we've been both been so stupid. We've wasted so much time.* Her bottom lip quivered as her dream came to mind, the smell of the liquor, the sound of guns, the feel of the blood oozing out of her abdomen. She had so much to say to this man, but yet again, her words were stuck inside.

"I'm sorry. I just don't know what you're thinking or feeling and it's making me nuts. I deserve everything you say, everything. And if you do choose to forgive me, I know I don't deserve that most of all."

"Here, I found you something." She passed the recipe book across the table to Tom. Her heart hammered. She wanted him desperately to know exactly what it was. "Recognize it?"

He picked it up and turned it over. "No, should I?'

She stared into his eyes for a glimmer of recognition, something familiar, but nothing.

"I guess not." She lowered her gaze and played with the cold eggs. She thought about her dream. It must have been Christmas Day. Her chest tightened as she glanced around the room. Almost a hundred years ago, she had died here in this house, on this very day, and so had Tom. She knew it, but he had no clue. She pushed back the tears. She had no idea why she wanted to cry. It was silly. Or was it, to cry about your own death or what you thought could be your own death? She shook her head and got up from the table. The realization of a past life and connection to this house and to Tom tangled her thoughts and weighed her down. It seemed impossible, yet she knew it to be true. She needed to work through everything in her mind before talking to Tom. "I—I think I need to be alone for a while."

"I understand," said Tom as he turned away from her.

"No, I don't think you do. Not yet anyway."

Madison walked around the house in search of herself. She brushed her fingers along the staircase. She closed her eyes and felt the vibrations of the old house. She went from room to room as her dreams and her memories and the present converged. She lingered in the powder room where she had dressed in the mornings and made love to Georgie braced against the pedestal sink. The sound of beads dropping and rolling across the floor filled her mind.

Georgie, that was my favorite necklace. Her words came out amidst hard breaths.

I'll buy you a thousand of those, sweets. He bent over her, kissing the back of her neck.

Madison's core buzzed at the memory. She moved to the parlor where she had entertained nice and not-so-nice people. The patter of rain sounded in her head, and the smell of cigarette smoke tangled with the humid air that hung around her. The heat was stifling. She had hoped the rain would bring a cool breeze and, with it, Georgie home safely. She felt the impression of a pen in her hand.

I hate when he leaves to do business with those men. I don't trust them, any of them.

The cellar beckoned to her. Rummaging around in nooks and dark places, she found the knob for the gas that lit the lights down in the speakeasy. In the soft glow of lamplight, the lounge looked more spectacular than she could have ever imagined. When she closed her eyes, the walls told her their secrets; they were filled with life and laughter. She felt at home down there most of all and yearned for Tom's presence. Without him, there was a dull ache inside her heart along with the feeling of being incomplete. No matter what Tom had done, no matter how broken their relationship had become, she knew she needed to mend it. He was ready, apparently had been ready before they even came here, and if Madison was honest with herself, she was ready too. Before she could move on though, she had to tell him about her discovery. Maybe he would understand or maybe, just maybe, he would accuse her of being crazy and let her down once again.

Curled up on a corner couch, she wished they never had to leave this house. She wished they could start anew there, or maybe anew wasn't the right word. Perhaps continue where they'd left off in their old Victorian. Opening the book, she read the rest of Peg's memories and poems. The writings didn't go all the way to the end. Peg's early death had left many pages blank, so many memories left unwritten. Her heart tugged and then her stomach grumbled. The time had come for her to leave her haven and go upstairs. Time to stop avoiding Tom. Time to tell him he was her Georgie.

She got dressed and then started to prepare dinner as planned, getting the lemon, garlic, and brown sugar out for the rack of lamb. On automatic pilot, she took out the knife and began to finely chop the cashews. Tom came in, his movements tentative.

"Hey," he said.

"Hey back."

"You're cooking dinner?"

"Of course, why wouldn't I."

He leaned on the wall. "I don't know. I just thought—"

"I guess you thought wrong. I have some things on my mind I have to talk to you about. I just don't know quite how to do it."

"You're in love with someone else."

"What? No. Where did you get that idea?"

"I don't know. You seem…different, is all."

Madison chuckled. "Well, yes, but I can guarantee you, I'm not in love with anyone else."

Tom let out a sigh. "That's good to know."

She was in love with someone else, but he was still Tom, just in another life, at another time. Those words sounded so ridiculous when she put it that way. Another life. Another time. She would have researched things if she could, looked it up on her phone if she only had a signal, but they were stranded there. Stranded with just each other and the echoes of time.

"How about making me a drink from that book?" She smiled at him. "A festive one. Can you guess my favorite?" What was she doing? Why did she just say that? Would he make her the same drink from her dream? Did she even want him to make her the same drink? Had she lost her mind?

He eyed her wearily. "Alright. I bet most of the ingredients are downstairs." She bet they were too. He carefully studied each page and she watched as his eyes brightened. He turned his back towards her and fumbled in the fridge. Hiding his loot under his shirt, he gave her a mischievous grin. "You can't see until I'm done."

She smiled. "I promise not to peek."

An old radio sat in the corner of the kitchen. She turned the knob and heard static mixed with choppy bits of music. She fiddled with the tuner until she could get a clear audio. Huh, jazz. Swanky. She liked it. She swayed to the music as she continued prepping. Tom came up from the cellar with two drinks in hand. In an instant, she knew he had chosen correctly. He had made it with a candy cane and everything.

"I found the candy in one of the grocery bags, mint too."

She had bought the candy canes to top off the presents for the twins, and mint jelly had always been a Christmas tradition in her family. "Thanks," was all she could manage. She looked at him, the past and present swirling around them. The heaviness of the truth weighed on her.

On the verge of blurting everything out, Madison opened her mouth to speak when Tom asked, "Where's that music coming from?" He looked puzzled.

"The radio, where else?"

"Really?" He walked over to it and stared. "Hrmph."

"What?"

"The owner said it was just for show."

"I guess he doesn't know what he's talking about, because there's definitely music coming from it."

"Does it get any other stations?"

"No, that was all I could find."

Tom turned to her with that grin of his. "It's kind of cool, isn't it?"

"Yeah, yeah it is." Madison started chopping her mint and thyme. She sipped on her candy cane drink as she moved to the smooth music. "Start cutting the potatoes, will you?"

"Sure." Tom flushed, looking as if he were honored she had asked him to help. He stood close to her as they worked together to prepare their Christmas dinner. They finished one drink and then another. Madison was again feeling brave, maybe ready to tell him what she had discovered.

"What does one ho plus two ho make?" asked Tom.

"I have no idea."

"A jolly Santa."

A whole-hearted laugh came out of Madison's mouth. She could feel Tom's presence as he moved behind her, standing close enough she could feel the heat of his breath on her ear. Warmth enveloped her.

"Mads?" He slid his arms around her waist from behind.

Georgie. She snuggled back into him. Her heart sighed with contentment. *I love you, Georgie.* Madison's body froze as her mind became a mix of pleasure and pain, but she didn't quite know why. "Yes?" she asked, her breath catching. A strange feeling of unease battled with the comforting sensation of his body next to hers.

A loud bang sounded and a blast of cold air swept through the kitchen. A sudden wave of terror gripped Madison. Her heart leapt to her throat and she couldn't get a word out. Tom grabbed her by the hand as both of them sprinted into the foyer. There they found the front door blown open and snow gushing in. They ran over and pushed the door closed.

"Now that was a gust of wind," said Tom.

Madison stood immobile next to him, her feet cemented to the floor by fear. Her heart pounded as the memories of her dream, of that horrific Christmas Day, filled her. Men, guns, blood. The chill surrounding her wasn't just because of the snow and wind. She rubbed her icy arms. All she could manage was, "Yeah, gust of wind."

"Are you okay?" Tom moved in front of her, his body close and lingering. He smelled of soap and something else. She closed her eyes and inhaled. He smelled of late nights and bottle feedings. He smelled of anniversary dinners and BBQ's. He smelled of sweaty passion on summer days, cuddles and coffee on cold winter nights. When she put it all together, the feel of him, the scent of him, he smelled like Tom, he smelled like home.

Madison looked up at him, slowly thawing. "Why did you do it? Why did you leave me?"

He swallowed and, clasping her hand in his, led her into the kitchen. He resumed his place by the potatoes and took in a deep breath. "I was afraid of losing you." He laughed a sad kind of laugh and shook his head.

"You left because you were afraid of losing me? You do know that sounds asinine, don't you?"

"I know. My therapist helped me figure things out."

"You have a therapist?"

"Yeah, the kids suggested it." He shook his head again and began to quarter a potato. "I was afraid I wouldn't be enough for you anymore. I was afraid you wouldn't have room or need to love me anymore." He stopped slicing and hung his head. "Because of my own issues, I made the biggest mistake of my life." He looked up at her. "I don't think I can ever say how sorry I am."

Tears of bliss and relief threatened to escape. He had seen a therapist for her, for them.

"Wow," was all she could say and then the ability to speak disappeared. She looked at him as he laid out all his flaws. It was uncanny, his voice, his eyes, so like Georgie. She could imagine Tom with his hair slicked back wearing a tuxedo with a silk handkerchief adorning his pocket, and those cufflinks, those beautiful cufflinks, shimmering in the glow of the candlelight. She wanted to kiss him and hold him and never let go again. There were no words to express her emotions, so she just smiled and continued to chop her herbs.

Wordlessly, they continued to cook and connect. The kitchen had plenty of room, but they seemed to take up a sliver of the same space together. They laughed and brushed up against each other when they could. With the lamb and potatoes in the oven, Tom switched to making his famous chocolate lava cakes for dessert. Madison could smell the delicious aroma of cocoa and butter and cinnamon. She eyed the bowl with hungry eyes.

"Would you like a preview?" asked Tom, holding up a spoonful of chocolate.

"You even need to ask?" He stepped closer and lifted the spoon to her lips. She opened her mouth and a burst of warm, chocolaty goodness coated her tongue. "Hmmmmmm. It's better than I remembered."

Tom licked his lips as he watched her enjoy her spoonful. "Sure is."

She stuck her finger in the bowl and stole another taste. Sucking on it, a tickle of recognition whirled in her head.

Chocolate and Georgie, my two favorite vices.

They spent the next few hours cooking and eating and being together. The snow still blew, the phones were still dead, but the rekindled flame between them made Madison feel more alive than ever. After finishing her favorite dessert, they retired to the living room. Tom put some more logs on the fire. Madison sat down on the deep red rug in front of it, still nursing a rather potent candy cane drink. Tom sat down next to her. "So, how's the book coming?"

"I finished it today. I loved every one of her poems."

He chuckled. "Not that book, yours?"

She became a blob of goo. She didn't think he'd ever ask how her writing was going. That's all she had wanted—Tom, her family, and her passion for the written word. "Oh, it's good. I finally finished my last revision, had a few requests to see it. We'll see how it goes."

"That's great." He cupped her cheek, brushing his thumb along her skin. "I knew you had it in you all along."

"Thanks...thanks for asking." She could barely contain her enthusiasm. She had so much more to share with him. She wanted to tell him her stories, wanted to read her new words to him like she had read Peg's, wanted to hug him for simply being the supportive man she knew him to be.

"So, can I help you with any kind of research?" He waggled his eyebrows up and down. Madison slapped him on the chest. He caught her hand and kept it, pressing it into the warmth of his body. "I still love you, Mads."

The pieces of her once broken heart slid back into place. She nodded, snaked her arm around his neck, and brought her lips to his. She pressed them against his and felt the whole house sigh. Tom wrapped his arms around her waist and they knelt, knee to knee, pelvis to pelvis, chest to chest, lip to lip. Madison nibbled his bottom lip, and she could feel his physical response, his hardness rubbing against her. Desire dampened the need between her legs. She couldn't put him off any longer. She wanted him back in her life, in her bed, until death in this life and the next.

Tom kissed her harder and she welcomed him, sucking his tongue, devouring him. Their sweet touches grew hungry, fierce even. Desire turned to need. Need turned to cannot-live-without. Cannot-live-without turned to touching the farthest depths of each other. He tangled his hands in her hair. She fisted his shirt in her hands. She wanted more. She needed to feel him, all of him. She needed to relieve the ache only he could satisfy. That only the love of all her lives could quench.

Madison looked into Tom's eyes. She had forgotten how wonderful it was to touch him. She had forgotten what it meant to her when he looked at her the way he was right now. She unbuttoned her blouse, revealing her white lace bra, unfastening the front clasp. Tom responded in an approving, breathless moan. Worshipping them as he always had, he cupped her breasts and traced his tongue along her neck down to her nipple. She ran her fingers through his hair as his tongue worked its magic with her senses. Her hands moved over his shoulders, down his back, all the way to the firm, roundness of his butt, recalling every curve, every contour, every precious inch.

"I need you. Don't tease me, please."

"I need you too," she whispered breathlessly, grabbing his backside and pressing him into her.

Tom removed his shirt, exposing his broad chest. With the tip of her finger, Madison traced the outline of his pec, over the tattoo of their children's names, over the old scar from his attempt at fixing the roof, all the things that made him Tom. Slowly, she brushed her fingers along the trail of hair down his abs leading below.

With a purposeful stare, she unbuttoned his pants and slid them off his hips. "I promise, I'm not teasing." And she definitely wasn't.

He breathed in a slow, deep inhale as he watched her undress him. Anticipation and pleasure darkened his eyes. It didn't take him long before he stripped off her jeans and panties, finding his way to her soft curls, wet, ready. Instantly, his fingers found her sweet spot. No fumbling, no need to urge him in the right direction. He knew exactly where it was and exactly what she liked. Memories flooded her mind of Tom and George and endless nights of hot, sweaty love. He had always been great with his hands, his mouth, his everything. A flush of need overcame her and she couldn't stand to wait anymore. It had always been like this. How had they let almost six months go by? How had they gone without touching for so long?

Lying down, she pulled Tom on top of her. He nestled between her legs as she wrapped them around him. He kissed her deep, exploring, grinding his erection against her. Yes. More. She guided him between her legs, into her warm folds, and he slid into her. They fit together perfectly and both let out a moan of pleasure, of relief. Nothing else existed but the two of them in this moment. Two bodies pressed together, two souls entwined, two people, madly in love. A gush of emotion embodied in tears trickled down her cheeks. She grabbed him tighter, pulling him closer, closer still, burying her face in his shoulder. Tom slid in and out slowly, working his hips. She arched into him, feeling his rhythm, aching for him to keep going. Just when she began to climb, began to lose sense of this world, he paused and fixed on her, his chocolate brown eyes consuming her. "I need you to say it, Mads."

She closed her eyes. "Yes, I need you too." She tilted her pelvis into him, pushing on his butt to keep going. Don't stop. Don't stop now.

"No, not just that." He lowered his head and nuzzled her. "You never said it, that you loved me."

She looked at him and let out a light giggle. "Do you think I'd be doing this with you if I didn't?" She felt a warm sensation run through her as she hugged him closer to her body with her legs. He was actually worried she didn't love him. He was worried she was just doing this for the sex. Of course, he would. He was still her loving Tom, who wanted to be loved too.

"A woman has needs too, doesn't she?"

"Yes, but there are toys for such things. We don't need to be getting involved with almost ex's for a good O."

He kissed her lips lightly, teasingly. "Say it."

"I love you too, I swear. I never really stopped." And she hadn't. No matter what she wanted to tell herself. No matter what she wanted to believe. She had never stopped loving him and never would. Not this life or the next.

That was what Tom had been waiting for. He pushed deep inside, and she let out a half-moan, half-laugh. Their hips ground into each other, their mouths pressed together, their hands clung to sweaty skin, as they effortlessly found their rhythm. It was as if they had never stopped. Never stopped touching, or talking, or making love. Madison closed her eyes and felt their connection hum through her veins. The fire, the house, the music in the background, all a piece of their union. Tom touched her in ways only he could. He used his hands, his tongue, the whole length of him until she couldn't take it anymore, until she couldn't hold back and succumbed to the wave of mindless pleasure. Tom's rush of heat followed seconds later. Filled with relief, and love, and contentment, they lay in a tangle of arms, and legs, and naked skin. They stayed there wordless, motionless for a long while. Madison closed her eyes and inhaled. She was thankful for the most precious of Christmas gifts ever.

In a haze of afterglow and sweat, Madison looked at the old Grandfather clock in the corner; it displayed ten minutes after midnight. Officially the day after Christmas. She glanced out the window. *Oh my God.* She leaned high up on her elbow and craned her neck to see. Finally, the snow had stopped. She let out a sigh and settled back down next to Tom. A soothing calm enveloped her and wrapped them in warmth. The house was quiet and all was well. Better than it had been in a long time. A strange kind of peace presided. Christmas was over, they were in a house they had lived in almost hundred years ago, where they had died almost a hundred years ago, and this time, they had lived through it. Not only lived through it, but also reconnected with each other and with themselves on an almost inconceivable level.

Madison rolled over onto her belly and watched her husband sleep, or seem to sleep.

He opened one eye to peer up at her. "Yes," he said as if he knew she had something on her mind.

She summoned up the guts to speak. "I have something to share with you."

"Anything." He propped himself up, his hand cradling his head, giving her his undivided attention.

Madison braced herself on both elbows. "I don't know where to start. But, those cufflinks, that recipe book..." She stalled on the words.

"Go ahead."

"They were yours."

He looked confused, like she knew he would. "This is going to sound off, but I've been to this house before. Many times actually." She could see the questions in his eyes, but he listened. "In my dreams. I have been dreaming about this house since I was a kid. And I think the reason I've been dreaming about this house is because I used to live here, with you." She waited for a response but got only silence. "I know you think I'm crazy, but it's true. You know where everything is in this house. Both of us knew about the trap door when no one has been down there since we lived here before. And that book, Peg's journal, that's my writing, my words. I know it."

Tom caressed her arm soothingly. "You're sure about this?"

"As sure as one can be without proof, I guess." She searched his eyes for anything to tell her if he believed her, but she couldn't get a read on him. Even so, she decided to spill all the details. "And there's more."

"What more could there be?"

"I dreamt about our death last night. Here, on Christmas night, we were both shot to death."

Tom closed his eyes and shook his head back and forth. *Oh God, he thought she was nuts. Oh God, she should have kept it her little secret.* She felt like her heart might burst under the pressure of the uncertainty of it all. "I know, you think I'm crazy."

Tom stood up. "I'll be right back."

"Where are you going?"

"I have to get something." He started up the stairs stark naked, taking them two at a time.

Madison pulled his shirt over her, covering the front of her body, feeling too open, too vulnerable in her nakedness. Why had she said anything? But then again, if she couldn't speak her mind, her heart, then they might as well not be together.

Tom came down holding a photo album of some sort with a bunch of random papers tucked underneath.

"I have a confession to make." He sat down gingerly next to her.

Madison's breath seized and she didn't say a word. She just sat there waiting for what he might dump on her.

Tom presented her with a stack of papers and bit his lip. "Merry Christmas, Mads." He handed them to her. His eyes sparkled and he seemed like he might burst from the excitement within.

Madison skimmed over them. She held a deed. A deed to the house. Her heart stuttered over the idea. "You bought this house?"

He nodded. "Uh huh."

"How...when...wh...what?'

Tom ran a hand through his sandy waves. "I–I can't explain it. I was looking at the paper one day and saw it, the house for sale. It just popped up at me. Something came over me and I called about it. It was crazy, we were supposed to be divorcing and all, but I had to find out about it." He gripped the album tightly and rubbed the edges nervously. "It was a great deal. I just kept thinking you've always wanted a Victorian, so why not?" He shook his head again as if he couldn't believe it himself. "Then I bought it, just like that. I know, it was an insane thing to do, but I had to have it. I figured if you didn't want to get back together, you could have this house. And, if by chance we did get back together, we could move here, or you could use it as a getaway to write." He stared at her, his brown eyes teary. "I have been so selfish, so ungrateful." His hand brushed lightly back and forth over the album. "I've been so stupid. You were happy just to see us happy, and when you actually asked for something of your own, I flaked, big time. Anyway, I figured it might be a nice peace offering."

"How did you—"

"Cashed in some things. I'll tell you the details later."

Madison clutched the deed to this beautiful house in her hands. Goosebumps traveled up her arms and she trembled. "That's one hell of a peace offering." She loved this house, and now it was hers. Again.

"It was worth it to see that look on your face. And after what you just told me, it's all making a little more sense." He handed her the photo album. As she took it into her lap, she noticed it wasn't just a photo album but more like a scrapbook.

Madison thumbed through the old fabric-covered book. It appeared to be a history of the house. Someone, or a few someones, had been saving information about it down through the years. Her brows crinkled in confusion. "Where did you get this?"

"I found it, today, when you were downstairs sulking, or what I thought was sulking."

"It was in this house?"

"Yes, upstairs. There were other things too, some clothes and jewelry. This house is full of secrets. I found a sliding panel behind one of the closets. I wouldn't have noticed it if it weren't for the ghost tour we took a few years back. You know, that house with all the secret rooms." He glanced around. "It's as if it's all been preserved for us."

"It's unbelievable." But was it? Peg's brother's words echoed from her dream. "I'll take care of your stuff for yah. I promise." And he did. He really did.

"That's not all. Wait until you see this." Tom flipped the scrapbook all the way to the front. He pointed to a grainy black and white photo. "It's George and Peg."

Madison's eyes opened wide as she pulled the album closer to see. She just stared at the old black and white image. Her finger traced the paper lightly. "I–it's us." She looked up at Tom. Tears slid down his cheeks as he silently nodded.

It was them, but not. They were dressed in eveningwear. Tom wore a tuxedo complete with hanky and cufflinks, his hair slicked back, and Madison was in a form-fitting, floor-length, silk gown. Wavy blond hair framed her face. Her heart ached, ached for a time she really couldn't remember, but knew she loved. Ached for a love that was gone but not really. Ached to be closer to her love than ever before. Her eyes met Tom's. She sobbed and pushed the album off her lap and knelt to hug him. Tom returned the tears and snug embrace. He knew too. He knew they had found each other again. He knew they were always meant to be together, whether it was in this life, the next, or even a previous one. Their arms wrapped around each other tighter. She felt as though she couldn't let go. As though he might slip through her fingers and disappear.

Tom leaned back and lifted Madison's chin to look at him. "So, am I forgiven?"

She nodded. "I think I know of something we can add to the fire. Can I have the divorce papers?"

Tom closed his eyes and let out a sigh of obvious relief. He pulled more documents from underneath the pile and handed them to Madison. "I thought you'd never ask."

She threw the last remnants of their almost divorce into the fire, sat back in Tom's arms, and watched their moment of separation burn to pieces. Their blip in the connection of eternity dissolved into nothingness. She looked around at her dream home, in more ways than one. The rich mahogany, all the embellishments, and her insides lit up. This was all hers. Boy, when Tom apologized, he did it in a big way. She sighed and glanced around as she imagined herself with her laptop on the chaise behind her, clicking away at her newest novel.

She thought of the cellar, her secret speakeasy, and how she adored it. One day, when she was ready, they might share their find with the world. For now, though, it belonged to her and Tom, Peg and Georgie. Her heart lifted, thinking about all of the stories she could dream up and write from this very room. Yes, there would be more stories, lots of them, and there would be Tom to share them with. She grabbed Peg's—or rather her—old journal and opened it to the last words she had written ages ago. She picked up a pen and began to write.

Tom and I kissed today. When he kisses me, I feel as though no one in the world, no one in the history of kisses, has ever kissed with as much love as we do.

South Side Christmas

Slip on your silk and pearls or Fedora and enjoy this 1920's classic named for the old stomping grounds of Al Capone.

2 ounces gin, vodka or white rum
1 ounce fresh lemon juice
2 tsp of sugar
Five or six fresh mint leaves

Mix ingredients in a cocktail shaker. Shake just enough to bruise the mint leaves. Pour mixture into a highball glass filled with ice. Top with soda, if desired. Add a splash of Grenadine for a festive addition of color, or even the macabre. Garnish with a candy cane and a sprig of mint.

- You may exchange the lemon juice for lime.
- Serve short option: shake the ingredients with ice and strain into a cocktail glass.

Now, sit back, put on your favorite early jazz or ragtime music, and enjoy!

Furry Fiancé
By Shelley Tracy

Tracy Harte is a Mother, Grandmother, Retired Teacher and Published Poet. She is happiest when she is spoiling her grandkids or writing. Currently, she is working on a paranormal story.

8 years ago

"Just a little farther up the hill, Jason." Jill encouraged her brother as they walked in the familiar Black Hills of South Dakota.

"Sure, easy for you to say. Tell me again why I got talked into this hike?" Jason shook his head and continued to trudge up the unmarked camping trail.

"Great tasting berries sprang up where the last airplane dropped its load during the forest fire. I don't know what's in the mix to suppress fire, but it results in wild berries for the pies. You're here to help me pick them because I promised to make the berry pie now and your favorite apple pie for Thanksgiving. You love the smells of baking in the house. May means pie. We need to get this hike in before the tourists arrive Memorial Weekend. "Jill once again pushed her brother.

Ignoring the hit to his stomach, he asked, "Where do you get these facts about fires and berries? You're like a walking encyclopedia. If I wasn't your older brother, I'd run the other way."

"Like you're normal spending every weekend at the pet clinic."

"Hey!" He turned abruptly. "I'm going to be a vet."

"Yeah, you stick with that. We both know that animals are easier to deal with than people."

As she walked, Jill absently reached up and redid her sleek chestnut hair, which had fallen out of its scrunchie. She cocked her head, "What's that sound? Is that a dog?" The puppy was all alone and quietly whimpering into its soft, silvery fur. It seemed caught in the brambles at the side of the path.

She couldn't resist helping animals any more than she could stop breathing. Cautiously stepping forward so that she didn't scare him, Jill knelt down and extended her fingers while crooning gently. If he didn't nip at her, maybe she could see what was wrong.

Unbelievably, the little thing was caught in a trap. What was a big cat trap doing in Custer State Park?

Hearing the bushes rustle, she sighed in relief at seeing her brother. "He's caught in a trap, Jason." Trying not to cry, she blinked wet eyes at him. "We have to help him."

Jason's eyes widened with alarm, but he continued to approach. Speaking softly, he drew near the pup. "Poor little thing. You do know that you're a wolf so there must be a pack nobody knew was here. They won't take kindly to meddling."

Jill stroked behind the wolf's ears while murmuring, "Don't worry, little one, we won't let a little thing like that bother us. Granny says the Lupas family is wolf clan. All this time I thought we were part Native American. Your mommy and daddy will know we mean no harm."

Jason just snorted as he transferred his backpack to the ground for easy access to his first aid kit. He waved Jill toward the cub's muzzle. Used to this form of silent communication, she complied. At the growl coming from behind them, Jason and Jill froze in mid crouch. "Um, Jason." Jill jerked her chin towards the creature and was immediately captured by pale green eyes flecked with amber. At the wolf's swift intake of breath, she started to shake. It only added to her confusion when she felt a matching heartbeat. Her fear grew when she realized they were alone in a deserted part of the parkland. Neither she nor her brother had told anyone where they were headed. Now they were far off the beaten track surrounded by miles of pine trees.

Gregory stood frozen as he beheld his mate. Who knew that helping other shapeshifters search for their missing youngster would lead to him finding his soulmate? What was he supposed to do with a pintsize gangly child? He took in her chestnut hair tied in a careless braid half way down her back and green piercing eyes locked on him? He was far too young for them to bond.

While these thoughts ran thru his head, his wolf side growled 'mine'. Controlling his wolf half, he spoke to her mind to. "No, my Gem. I mean you no harm."

Conversationally, she asked her brother, "Do you remember Granny telling us we're descended from the Wolf Clan?"

"Now? You want to talk about this now?"

"It's relevant. I think she meant werewolf. I also think the big guy over there doesn't want us to risk getting bitten by the little one."

"You got all that from a growl." Any normal person would laugh, but all their relatives could hear or sense thoughts to some degree. "Maybe," he conceded, reaching toward her. The wolf growled.

"Knock it off," she snapped. "That's my brother."

A blink of those incredible eyes, and the wolf bowed. 'Good', Gregory thought. 'I can leave her to grow strong with her family.'

The siblings held their ground as he paced slowly forward and placed his jaws around the pup's scruff.

Only then did Jason pull open the trap while Jill yanked the pup's paw free. Then Jason grabbed a purple coneflower to crush the stem with a bit of water from his canteen to form a paste. Knowing the Echinacea stem numbed Jason rubbed around the abraded area. Then, he waited a count of ten for it to work its magic. Finally, he meticulously cleaned the cut, applied salve, and put on a dressing.

While they worked together, Jill reached over to run her hands down the big wolf's back. It felt so natural, like coming home.

Just then, two more wolves appeared in the trees. These were timber wolves, unlike her russet colored wolf. The pup yipped, wriggled free, turned to lick their hands, and then scampered to the pair.

Jill's wolf turned. They both heard him in their heads. 'His parents are grateful. You are so young, my mate. I will see you soon. Grow strong.'

In the quiet that followed, brother and sister gathered their berries. There was a lot of information to consider. Breaking the silence before heading home, Jill asked. "Should we say something?"

Jason snorted, "Who would believe us? No, I'll give this trap to our cousin Samuel. As law enforcement, he'll be able to do something. Other than that, nope."

"I'm going to tell Granny. Maybe she'll explain the mate thing."

Present Day

As Jill pulled the pan out of the rinse water she said, "Isn't Thanksgiving great."

Her cousin Rachael muttered, "Doing K.P. is not my idea of great."

"No." Jill giggled. "But I love getting together in Granny's kitchen. I love everything from rolling out pie dough and Granny's tea roll dough to doing dishes with the girls. And the aromas. Don't you wait for this time of year?"

"I do," said Mom. "All the family gets together. We get out all the secret recipes and then need lots of exercise to lose the extra calories."

"Speaking of exercise, who's riding in whose car for the annual assault on Rapid City for Black Friday?" asked Rachael.

Jill turned and said, "I'm going on-line this year."

Her mom looked at her with her mouth open and eyes wide. "You're kidding. Miss, this is the strategy for the early birds guys."

"Not this year. The deals are better on-line, and I won't have to get up at dawn."

"Each to her own," said Granny. "I think I'm going to pass this year too."

With that pronouncement, everyone assumed that Jill had chosen to stay for Granny. She didn't contradict their beliefs.

First thing in the morning, Jill pulled out the crock pot for Veggie Lasagna. She took two zucchini and peeled them. Then she cut them vertically and put them at the bottom of the pot. Next, she put in spaghetti sauce. Finally, she added cottage cheese, egg, and one package of Italian cheese mixed together. She sprinkled Parmesan cheese over the top and set the temperature at low.

Feeling less guilty now that she'd started their dinner, Jill grabbed her backpack and hopped on her Scooter. Then she parked the bike in the shrubs and hurried up the old abandoned fire road which was so overgrown in grass and brush that it was forgotten. Muttering to herself, she headed to the dormant berry patch. "Why do I think Gregory will be here? It's been eight long years. It's not even May. If it weren't for the earrings made from Black Hills Gems arriving each year, I'd think he'd forgotten me."

The holidays were a guessing game for the whole family on what earrings would arrive. The whole wolf thing was taken in stride. The first gift of garnet earrings had come with a card addressed to his mate Jill from Gregory. There was no place to return them, and Granny, the Matriarch, pronounced it acceptable.

Her legs propelled her forward as she thought of Gregory and his gifts. She knew she needed to come here. He had captured a piece of her since their first encounter.

When she reached the area, she turned to the spot where he had appeared so long ago. She grabbed her chest in shock as a man with pale green eyes flecked with amber moved closer, Her lips trembled, and her knees grew weak at the six foot plus vision in front of her.

Without hesitation, he pulled her into his arms. "At last."

She shoved him back. "That's it, you jerk. Eight years. If you hadn't signed the cards 'Gregory', I wouldn't have even known your name. No letter, phone call, e-mail, Skype, nothing." She poked him to punctuate each point.

"I sent you a gift, Mate, every year."

"Yeah. Big whoop. If Granny hadn't explained the mate thing you'd have been history."

He snorted. "The mate thing"—he finger quoted the words—made that impossible. You are my other half."

"The conveniently misplaced other half."

"Never. You needed to grow. I couldn't cheat you out of maturing. I saw what that was like."

"What do you mean?" she said as she tugged his shirt to guide him to a fallen log.

Gregory began the story. "On a trip to Canada in '67, a couple and their barely sixteen-year-old daughter went to Montreal to see the Expo. They ate at the Swiss Chalet where they experienced their first fondue. While there, the waiter, a shapeshifter, claimed their daughter. Since they were kin to an old shapeshifter clan there were no questions asked.

"The young waiter took her hand, placed a kiss on it, and as was the custom, they were formally bonded at the full moon. She was already pregnant when he left to fulfill his military service. When he returned, he bestowed the claiming bite that turned her. If it wasn't for that tour of duty, she might have lost the child because he didn't have the patience to wait."

When she Jill held up her hand, he filled in, "Werewolves turn at the full moon. Some have complications. That's why our numbers are small."

"I want children. No mating bites." The words came unbidden from her. "What am I getting myself in to? This is crazy."

"I will control myself, but the point is, that young girl let the male dictate her choices. That's not the equal mating I want. You needed to be allowed to grow."

This time she placed her hand on his cheek. "How do you know every decision was the male's?"

"They were my parents, my Gem."

"Okay." She pulled his chin towards her. "Granny says that mates are our other half. It was that way for her parents. Maybe they were on the same page."

"No, whenever they argued, I was sent to spend the night with my fraternal grandparents. The next day there was no disagreement."

She giggled, then held her sides as she laughed until tears leaked. "Oh, honey." She tried to stop the guffaws at his offended look. "That was make-up sex." As the grown man turned red, she lost it again.

Growling, he snatched her close and placed a kiss to stop the conversation, then soon forgot his annoyance as her lips softened, and passion crept up on them both. He licked, sampled, and devoured her mouth.

"Wow. So that's why I waited." She put a trembling hand to her swollen lips.

"We should talk to your parents. I can't stay long." He pulled her to her feet.

She dug in. "You are not leaving me again."

"True mates are a monogamous pair. They're rarely far apart for any length of time. Once we bond, distance would be a problem. We'll be going home together."

"Home where? I have a job that I like. You remember wanting me to grow. Also, don't think one kiss makes it a done deal."

"We can learn all about each other when we get home."

"Again with the home bit. Where is this elusive place?"

"It's in Washington State. That's why I..." His voice trailed off.

She opened her mouth and closed it. "You didn't. How did know I would answer that ad?"

"I asked my friend Ben to make the ad appealing to you. I knew you could do it. You had all the skills that drew you to apply for the position. German, Greek, and Japanese are unusual languages for one person. It was the lack of experience that was the main stumbling block."

She raised a traffic stop hand. "Whoa, Dude. We need to talk. How do you know all this?"

He interrupted with a hard kiss to her lips. "My gem. We are mates. The other half of each other. There can be no greater bond. I am forever yours. There is no stronger loyalty. I would sacrifice myself before you were hurt. I kept a discreet watch."

." Greg. Before we bond, don't you think we should date? Let's exchange favorite foods, colors, movies and music. How about a walk in the woods?"

"Don't be nervous. I would never hurt you."

"Right," she muttered. "You just want to give me a little love bite that will turn me furry when the moon is full."

He laughed. "Oh, sweetheart. I promise you a wonderful long life filled with adventure. Besides, you've always wanted to run free in the woods."

"Not yet, bub." She circled her hand. "Go back to the, I wanted you to grow so I manipulated a position where I live."

"What would be the point in getting a job you'd have to quit? This one is near the house. You proved yourself."

Just then her phone chirped. She automatically pulled it out and checked. It was an amber alert. Blond, blue eyed, seven year old missing and seen with a possible suspect in Custer Park. Gregory leaned in to read. Then he stood and calmly shrugged out of his shirt. "I'll have better luck hunting in my wolf form. Have that sheriff cousin of yours meet me so I don't get shot."

As he kicked off his shoes and shed the sweats, the shock of seeing him commando had her speechless. Finally, he dropped to all fours as his mouth elongated and his skin sprouted fur, paws appeared and a tail flicked.

He leaned forward and licked her cheek, sniffed around, then bounded away with a few yips. In the distance she heard the same vocalization.

She shook herself and texted Samuel. 'My friend of 8 yrs. ago wants to meet by rocks, he changed to track.' She wrapped his clothes in the jacket and headed down the track to stuff them in the pack.

Oddly enough, Samuel answered. 'K'

While waiting, she texted her brother. 'Greg back. Helping amber alert.'

'Do you need me?'

'I'm good.'

'Got study group later.'

After an agonizing time, Sam texted. 'Got trail. He's headed for the exit by trailer park that volunteers use. Smart. It's empty this time of year. Greg says his friends are herding a buffalo to block road to slow him down at lay out by old track.'

'Bringing bike-we can cut across-wait'

Again he surprised her. 'Waiting for faster ride'

She hopped on and cut across all the back ways she'd learned over the years. When she reached Sam, she hopped off the bike and got back behind her cousin. He was even better at the back trails.

When they hit the trailer park, she realized her cousin had been busy arranging a blockade while she drove to him. Jill bailed at the sight of her wolf. She led Greg to the back entrance. "Here's your clothes, change fast."

"When we see the car, we act. As law enforcement he has to have probable cause to search. That's what the impromtu blockade is. We'll be there with an exit sheet of questions. I'll lean in to pop the trunk. You get her out."

When to car holding the suspect that the wolves had spotted pulled up, Jill and Greg acted together. She distracted him and popped the trunk. Thank goodness it was an older model. Greg grabbed the child from the trunk the minute she pulled the latch."

The guy was stuck, and the little girl was rescued. She clung to Gregory until a car pulled up and her parents jumped out. Then she scampered down and met them half way.

Sam stopped long enough to talk to Jill and Greg after he stuck the suspect in the sheriff's vehicle that had pulled up after the bust. Greg stood behind Jill with his arms wrapped tightly around her waist and his chin resting on her head. "Sam, meet Greg. Greg, my cousin Sam."

"That was good work. Thank your friends. You'll be coming to dinner, right? By the way, who's house are we doing tonight?"

Jill laughed. "Your sister Sharon."

"No." He moaned

"Don't worry. It's mostly leftovers from Thanksgiving."

Turning to her Furry Fiancé, she said, "You earned some brownie points today, so you'll meet the family. This is Thanksgiving break, and everyone will be there. Lots of food."

"Does that mean I can taste that berry pie?"

"Wrong season. All the other pies were devoured Thanksgiving Day, but I saved half of my Tea Roll dough for today. You'll love it."

Tea Roll

Dough:

1 8oz. pkg. cream cheese

1/2 lb. (2 sticks) butter (can substitute margarine)

2 1/4 cups flour

Blend well in to a ball and chill at least 3 hours

Filling:

Preserves or jam

Cut dough in fourths.

Roll individually on well-floured surface.

Spread preserves or jam

Sprinkle Cinnamon-sugar

Sprinkle with chopped walnuts (Can substitute sunflowers if there is a nut allergy)

Roll length wise

Bake at 400 degrees for 25 minutes until light brown

Sprinkle lightly with sifted powdered sugar when slightly cooled.

Measuring Excellence

by Lynne Wall

Dedication

For John, my kind of Hero

Enjoy!

l. Lynne Wall

Lynne Wall has worked in a public library for over 10 years and that is where she fell in love with Romance books. The only things she enjoys as much as reading are eating, shopping, and binge watching TV shows. Visit her online at www.lynnewall.com

It's happening again. I can feel them staring at me, waiting, wondering what the problem is. I'm awake, I'm breathing, my eyes are blinking, my mouth is opening and closing, but no sound is coming out. I must look like a guppy. Just answer the question. The words are floating around in my head, if only I could just grab them and shove them out my mouth.

"Okay, John, I think we have enough information. We'll make a decision today and contact you by close of business tomorrow." The two interviewers got up and walked to the door; they made small talk with John Berry on the way to the elevator.

John entered the elevator, knowing in his heart he'd ruined his chance for the promotion. *Sure, they'll call me tomorrow, at my desk, in the office where I'll be sitting, in the same spot, doing the same thing, the same way, and feeling like a failure.*

John walked to the Round Table, a coffee shop a few blocks from where he worked at the East Branch of the public library in Aurora, Illinois. Angie Bonner, John's co-worker and confidante, entered the shop a few minutes later. She spotted John, and his face told her everything.

"Oh no, it didn't go well, did it." Angie said.

Even John's eyebrows seemed to droop in defeat as he answered, "I was late; I couldn't find a spot in the employee, lot so I parked on the bridge. Of course I didn't have change for the meter, so I detoured through the sub shop and bought a bag of chips to get change. When I finally got there, I looked like I had been running from the police. Worst of all, I couldn't find the right words—or any words— to explain why I was the man for the job. This is a cycle I need to stop. I know I'm better than this."

"John, I've told you, my cousin's group would be perfect for you. He's a life coach. He can help you make a plan for where you want to go."

John looked down at his coffee cup, "I know, Angie, I know."

"I would have to get help to be more confused than I am right now." Sara Brooks pushed the website brochures to the side of her desk and put her head in her hands. *I am so overwhelmed, and I don't like the feeling.* Sara was the administrative assistant to the pastor of the True Light Community Church. She had wasted the morning looking at vendor resources for the new church website and understood none of them. Sara pulled open her desk drawer and took out a small mirror and comb. She tended to her hair, and then stood and smoothed out the wrinkles in her silver pencil skirt. She folded the sleeves of her white blouse up to her elbows. The thought of one of the staff coming into her office and finding her looking frazzled was not acceptable.

Before she could finish the thought, Daniel walked in. "Sara, you look beautiful as always, but I can feel the tension in here. What's the problem? And do not tell me you have everything under control."

Daniel Bonner also served on staff at the True Light, as the head of the Care Ministry. Daniel was a psychologist and certified Life Coach. He had a way of asking questions that made you respond even when you didn't want to.

Sara sighed as she answered, "It's the church website. We need to have it professionally designed and administered. I've read through the brochures from the recommended companies, but I honestly don't understand what I'm reading."

Puzzled, Daniel asked, "Isn't Will Miller handling the technical end of the technology upgrade?" Sara looked away and began straightening her desk. "Sara," Daniel persisted, "tell me you're not trying to do this alone."

"Well, you know, Will and Nita just had triplets. Caring for them has become more than Nita can handle by herself. Will is working from home now as an independent contractor in order to help with the babies. He volunteers as much time as he can to the church, but it's not enough to get the website up before Thanksgiving," Sara explained.

"Sara, I've told you before, needing help does not equal incompetence, and it doesn't mean you aren't doing your best," Daniel said earnestly.

"I feel an assignment coming," she said.

He smiled widely. "Absolutely right. Make a list of what needs to be done, and I'll find you some help."

Later that evening, John sat in front of his computer in his small apartment. He lived on the east side of Aurora, across the street from the library branch where he worked. Following Angie's advice, he had decided to give her cousin's group a try. He pulled up the True Light Community Church website and groaned. One look at the blinging, blinking font and giant clipart cross gave him an immediate flashback to the '90s Geocities web pages, and not in a good way.

I hope their group therapy is more advanced than their technology, he said to himself before muttering aloud, "I'll make the call to Cousin Daniel tomorrow."

Earlier, John had downloaded a video lecture that he wanted to watch. The presentation was about teaching teens to write computer code. He thought it would make a great library program.

He went into the kitchen and grabbed a bag of chips from the grocery bag on the kitchen floor. Still in the bag were some boxed items and canned goods that should have been put in the cabinets. *I'll do it later,* he thought, knowing it would never happen.

Heading to the living room, he pushed aside a pile of clean laundry that needed to be folded; another chore that wouldn't get done. He plopped down on the couch, grabbed the remote, and started watching the video.

After a long day at work, Sara made a small salad and placed it on the breakfast bar in her kitchen. She put all the salad fixings back in the refrigerator, wiped down the counters, and retrieved a spiral pad from her tote by the front door.

She lived in a condo in the downtown area of Aurora on the west side of the city. Her condo was small but very neat, and she strived to keep it that way. She prided herself on being able to receive impromptu visitors at any time because her home was always presentable.

Sara sat down to eat and began to write the list Daniel had assigned her. The last thing Sara wanted was to tell her boss, Pastor Thompson, that the upgrade plans were not on schedule. As the pastor's administrative assistant, it was her job to handle the office functions. The pastor relied on her keen eye for detail, organization, timeliness, and her ability to provide direction. She wanted people to look up to her the way she looked up to Pastor Thompson. She didn't just want it: it was what she needed.

At work the next day, John took a break to call Daniel, the church's life coach, about the men's group. "I'm not sure this is for me. I haven't been to church in years. I don't believe in it anymore, and I'm not sure I ever did. I don't want God and scriptures shoved down my throat. I had that growing up."

"No shoving allowed," replied Daniel. "God's principles work regardless of whether or not you believe in Him. You read them in self-help books, and you hear them in your daily life."

"Really", said John.

"Yes. For instance, the saying 'what goes around, comes around' reflects the biblical principle of sowing and reaping. Let's just start with this. Angie is your friend, you trust her, she pointed you toward this group, and you made the call. Come to the group meeting tomorrow night, and we'll talk more after that."

John arrived at the church the next evening just in time for the session. He walked past the huge auditorium, the offices, and the gym/café area. He spotted the room where the group meeting would be held. Daniel waved him in, and they each took a seat in the circle.

The group consisted of John, group leader Daniel, and three other men. Each man was asked to introduce himself and talk briefly about why he was there. One guy was plagued with anger and violent thoughts after a bitter divorce, while another man was trying to re-establish himself with his family and find employment after serving jail time for a white collar crime. One poor fellow named Calvin was so depressed that John feared he wouldn't make it to the end of the session. John found himself looking around to make sure there were no open windows the guy could plunge out of. When it was John's turn to share, not only did he have to face down his trepidation of speaking in front of strangers but he also worried that his problem didn't measure up. A guy being stressed at work because of social anxiety wasn't even on the radar with this group.

After the introductions, Daniel explained how the group would run. "I expect you to participate in the group discussions. I'll give you individual assignments to complete before your scheduled one- on- one sessions with me. "I am committed to coaching each of you until you reach your goals but, you must commit to the process. That brings us to tonight's discussion topic: *What's important to you?*" Daniel ended the session with giving an assignment to be completed before the next meeting.

As the group was dismissed, John noticed that Daniel pulled Calvin aside. They spoke in hushed tones, but when they bowed their heads, John recognized they were praying. *"Seriously, that's all you got? The guy needs a shrink and some meds, not prayer."*

The next day during his lunch hour, John looked over the assignment. Sure that Angie would ask how the meeting went, he wanted to be able to tell her he gave it a serious try.

Question 1: What is important in your life?

John considered his answer. *Being independent and free to indulge in my interest in computer technology*, he wrote. *The liberty to follow my thoughts and ideas wherever they lead without being subject to ridicule.*

Question 2: What or who do you give your time to?

Becoming proficient in computer software and applications is what I give my time to. Helping Angie with the teens at the library, and helping co-workers with their technology problems I'd say answers the who portion of the question

Question 3: Where are you, what are you doing, and who are you with when you feel good, feel like you are in the right place?

In front of a computer is where I feel smarter, more confident, understood, John wrote boldly. *Helping someone learn is the doing part,* he added. As for who he felt right with, that he would leave that blank for now. Apart from his work environment, there was no one in his life, no woman, that made him feel that way,

As he finished his answers, Angie walked into the room.

"I've been trying to get free all day so I could find out how your group went," Angie exclaimed.

"I'm shocked. I didn't think it would take you this long to catch up with me," John replied.

"Okay funny guy, spill." After John described the meeting and the assignment, Angie asked, "Well, are you going to stay with the group?"

"Not sure. I have a follow-up session with Daniel tomorrow, and then I'll decide.

The following day, John went to Daniel's office at the church to review the first session and the homework assignment.

"After reading your bio and listening to you share with the group, I think you have the knowledge and skills to be successful. With some coaching, you can narrow your goals, learn how to use your strengths, and most of all learn how to shut off that voice that's telling you there's something wrong with what you want," Daniel said seriously. "So what do you say, do you want to give it a go?"

Daniel had a way of making people feel at ease. The way he phrased his words inspired confidence to the listener. He imparted a *can do* attitude. That may have been a result of learning to be a Life Coach or because it came naturally to him, John didn't know yet. Nevertheless, he would give it a try. "Alright coach, let's go," John replied.

John arrived at work the following morning with his list completed. He ran into Angie in the employee break room. She put down the cup of coffee, she was about to drink and asked to see his list.

"You can only look at it if you promise not to tell anyone else or pick it apart," John demanded as he held paper over Angie's head, just out of her reach.

"You know, John, you behave like a juvenile sometimes," Angie huffed.

"And you can be so nosey and critical sometimes. No promise. No list."

"All right, all right, I promise."

He handed the list to her and she began to read. From her facial expressions he could tell how desperately she wanted to comment. He ended her misery. "Tell me what you think about the list, without the nit-picking."

Take more care of physical appearance. "I can help you with that," Angie said excitedly. "Your bod is in great shape. You just need some staging."

""Staging? You mean like a theater set for a play?" John asked.

"No, like a room on one of those makeover shows," Angie replied. "You're structurally sound, but you need some curb appeal."

"That sounds like I need new shingles and a coat of paint."

"What you need are more professional clothes, a serious beard trim, and a haircut."

Angie continued reading. *Initiate a conversation with a patron or colleague every day.* "I don't get it. You talk to people all day long at the library."

"According to Daniel, people talk *at* me, and I try to deflect them. He says I have to initiate the exchange, take charge, and move the conversation the way I want it to go."

Curious, Angie asked, "Why does he want you to do that?"

"He thinks part of my issue with clamming up when asked a question is that I'm anticipating what they want to hear and all the while internalizing that I'll give the wrong answer, not enough of an answer, et cetera. He thinks that if I initiate conversation, then I can talk about what I want, knowing I have the right responses ready. It will take me out of my head and into the actual exchange."

Angie read the last item on the list. *Have my work area reflect that of a professional as much as possible.* "This I've got to see," Angie shouted. "Your desk is a disaster. You have piles of papers, letters, books, cards from last Christmas…. How are you going to organize? You'd have to hire need a cleaning—"

John interrupted, "You promised, but now you're being picky. Daniel scheduled me for some one-on-one sessions. There's also a church project that he wants me to consider. He said it would be a practical application of my plan. Oh, I almost forgot. I'm going to church this Sunday."

After Sunday service at True Light, John sat at a table in the café area with Daniel, who asked, "How would you like to help with the church's technology upgrade?"

"In what way?" John asked.

"As you probably know, our church building is only about a year old. We have all the exterior projects completed and most of the interior areas ready. We've taken our time and done each one without going into debt. Either the funds were donated, or we put together fundraisers to finance each aspect. We want our last big project, the technology upgrade, completed by Thanksgiving week, the one year anniversary of our new building."

Very interested now, John inquired, "Do you have a plan in place?"

"Yes, we do. Mainly, installing a wireless network throughout the building, and installing a computer lab for technology education for our youth and adults who do not have access to computer equipment at home. We also want to hire a full-time IT manager."

"Let me guess, you need money in the budget," John speculated.

"Correct," said Daniel. "We had an IT guy, Will Chambers, from the congregation that had been spearheading the process. But because of family obligations, he's not able to put in as much time as we need. He was handling the equipment purchasing and searching for a permanent staff person."

"Is Will the person I'll be helping?" asked John.

"No, you'll be working with Sara, the pastor's administrative assistant. She's a master of organization, so she'll handle scheduling the classes and lab volunteers. Which leads us to the problem I think you can help with. Your expertise would be an asset in designing the classes and training the volunteers."

Without hesitation, John said, "I can do that!"

"You'll also work with Sara on the fund raiser that will be a big part of paying for the equipment and new web design. I believe you'll benefit by having the opportunity to use your technology expertise in an environment where no one has any history with you. You'll be free to stretch yourself creatively and gain supervisory experience. It will be clear to you when the bad habits creep in. You'll be able to recognize how they hinder you from success and you'll be less likely to tolerate them."

"All that from this one project?"

"That, and we'll continue our group sessions and private follow-ups. You and Sara would be good for each other. She has somewhat of a control issue, so it will be good for her to be in a team dynamic."

"I'm curious now. This woman sounds dangerous."

A big smile appeared on Daniel's face. "Well, her personal motto is 'Excellence in Everything', and her favorite Bible verse is 1 Corinthians 14:40 'But be sure that everything is done properly and in order.'"

"Wow, just what I need, a scripture loaded control freak. Where do I sign up?"

Daniel walked John down the hall to Sara's office. His phone rang and he excused himself to take the call. Turning back to John, Daniel said, "Sorry, I have to handle a situation. Sara's across the hall in the Pastor's office. Go on in, she shouldn't be long. I'd told her we'd stop by. I wanted to introduce you, but I've got to run, so see you at group." As Daniel disappeared around the corner, John took in the full effect of Sara's office. It was immaculate, cold, like an operating room. Was she an admin or a surgeon? He wondered. He had the odd feeling that he should sterilize his hands before he entered.

At that moment, he heard a lovely voice coming through the partially closed door of the pastor's office. It was Sara's voice and the sound of it brushed over him like a warm breeze. In that same moment he knew, from somewhere deep inside, that he was not prepared to meet Sara Brooks. John took another glance at Sara's sterile office space then looked down at his outfit. He had a flashback, and again, not a good one. He was reminded of his appearance at the failed interview. He needed to give her the best first impression possible. Despite how he felt inside, he wanted to appear confident and professional. He would help with that and he knew just the person to ask.

He grabbed a pen and note paper off of her desk he jotted a note to Sara. He wrote down his phone number and asked her to call him to set–up a time to meet.

Sara took a quick glance at her watch, she was so involved in listening to the anecdote Pastor Thompson was telling her that she almost forgot about her meeting with Daniel. She quickly excused herself and went to her office. She found a note from John Berry, the computer expert that Daniel had recruited to help with the technology upgrade. Again she looked at her watch, if she hurried she could take a walk with Brother Winters while the sun was still out. She would call John later.

Sara hurried to her car in the church parking lot. She heard leaves crunching under her feet with every step. She thought about Brother Winters, a long-time member of True Light. As he had gotten older, his health had deteriorated. He lived alone and enjoyed getting visits from Sara. It was fall, and the weather was getting colder. She wanted him to enjoy being outside as much as possible before the season changed. Her thoughts quickly skipped to her to-do list. "No, I'm not going to worry about that list. I'm going to enjoy the walk." she said out loud, but in her mind, she knew she would worry.

The next day when John checked his voicemail, there had been a message from Sara. Even hearing her voice over the phone affected him. She informed him of the when and where of the first committee meeting. They would be meeting with Will Chambers and Sharon West, the person who would be in charge of marketing. He was sitting with Angie at the coffee shop. He looked up from his phone screen and exclaimed, "I need clothes! I need that woman to think I'm cool, calm and collected, the ultimate professional.

"What woman?" Angie asked?

"Sara Brooks, she works at True Light Church."

"Of course, I know Sara, she's good friends with Daniel. I don't think she'll be that easily fooled. She sees you one day and you're a mess, then the next day you're the perfect cover shot for a business magazine." "Actually, we haven't met yet, but I want to be prepared."

"You want to do all this for someone you haven't met?"

I heard her voice and there was just something about it, I know she's going to look as lovely as her voice sounded.

Wait a minute John. I thought you were trying to get your professional life on track, now it sounds as if you're trying to impress a lady.

Why can't I do both? Why can't I have a great career and a relationship?

Angie liked the sound of that. "I absolutely believe you can have both. "Let's go shopping!

Walking toward Sara's office later that week, John contemplated how to approach her. *I won't lead in with how bad the website is because she already knows it's a problem. I'll be her solution. I know what to do to fix the website. I have my suggestions for the computer classes and volunteer training. I'll concentrate on saying the words.*

John took one last look at himself before entering Sara's office. He had paid more attention to his clothes in the last week than he had in his entire adult life. Angie had chosen the entire outfit except for his shoes. Standing there in his stiff collared shirt and creased dress pants, he felt as though he was in costume. Maybe that was a good thing, because it would help him stay in character.

As he approached the office, he saw her through the glass panel on the side of the door—the most beautiful face, long brown hair, and that smile—he fell into full guppy mode. He felt thankful he hadn't entered the room yet. He was speechless, and she would have thought him to be a complete idiot, not even being able to say hello. John collected himself and took a deep breath. He summoned up every ounce of courage he possessed and went in.

Inside her office, Sara looked at the clock on the wall. The rest of the committee had arrived with the exception of the new person, John. She sighed, hopefully he's not one of those unprofessional types...her thoughts and her breath ceased. The man walking into her office was tall, well dressed and gorgeous. He had brown eyes that held her gaze and looked into her soul. He had a beard, and she didn't particularly like beards, but his was close- trimmed and neat. He held out his hand.

"You must be Sara," he said.

"And you must be John."

John wanted to hold her hand forever, but he let it go and answered her. "Yes I am. I hope I didn't keep you waiting."

"No, you're right on time."

Sara did her best not to stare at John the entire meeting, but every time she looked at him their eyes met. Well, she was leading the meeting, so of course his eyes were on her. He was paying attention. He was a librarian. She had never met a male librarian before. She expected him to be...well...bookish or nerdy. John was neither. He was very well dressed except for his shoes. His physique definitely exceeded her expectations. John was over six feet tall, with muscular arms and...

"Sara, Sara, are you listening?" Will started to laugh. "At least I'm not the only one with concentration problems, but mine come from living with infant triplets."

Sara wanted to run out of the room and stick her head in the nearest potted plant. Of all times to be doing seventy miles per hour down the carnal highway, right in the middle of a meeting she was supposed to be leading. *Quick! Pull it together girl. You're in control.*

"I apologize, Will. I was picturing something in my mind and wandered off for a moment. Please repeat what you were saying."

"I wasn't speaking. Sharon was," said Will.

Unbelievable! "Again, my apologies, Sharon. What were you saying?"

When Sharon waved her off, Sara started speaking again, "Will, you're taking the lead with the hardware and drafting a job description for the IT position. John and I will meet to review the classes and volunteer requirements. Sharon will handle the marketing for our fundraiser, which leads me to our next item. For our fundraiser, I wanted it to be something that would appeal not only to our members but to the community as a whole; something that would be relevant."

"I'm getting excited," said Sharon. "What do you have in mind?"

"A church cookbook."

"A cookbook? Now I'm bored. That is so 1980's."

Sara continued, "Cooking shows are popular today, and so is healthy eating."

Will frowned. "Healthy eating, popular? Only to veggie eating types like you, Sara. At my house, we're meat and potatoes people."

Everyone laughed. John listened to the exchange and thought, if Sara saw his assortment of processed food at home, she wouldn't approve.

Starting again, Sara elaborated. "I looked at the old, plastic, spiral-bound cookbook the church produced years ago. By today's standards, many of those recipes are not very healthy, which could limit their appeal."

"Wait a minute, Sara. The old folks are not going to be happy with you messin' with their cooking."

"Especially since we still eat everything they bring in here," added Will.

"I completely agree," Sara continued. "We want to honor our beloved members' contributions, so leaving them out is not an option. Just because our generation has access to more knowledge about nutrition doesn't mean we never want to eat Grandma's cornbread dressing again at Thanksgiving."

Everyone, including John, said "amen" to that.

Sara brightened up, "My thought was to do a cookbook that featured a traditional recipe on one page and a newer version of the same recipe on the opposite page. We would add an appendix of ingredient substitutions for people who need to lower their fat intake or have food allergies."

"That's a great idea!" John blurted out, a little too loudly.

"I'm glad you think so because this is where we need your help again. In addition to a print version, I want it to be an e-book that's available for purchase on our website."

John groaned. "The church website? Not possible under its current condition. It will require new software and a complete redesign."

"Absolutely," said Sara. "Can you get it done by October, in time for our harvest festival?"

"Absolutely," John said echoing Sara's own remark a little too quickly. The work itself would not be a big problem. Pretending to be a cool, calm, A-type personality while working beside Sara would not be as easy.

"I have the perfect name for it," Sharon chimed in. "The Side-by-Side Generations Cookbook."

When the meeting ended, John sprinted to his car, propelled by energy and excitement. He had been right about Sara. She was all business on the outside, just like that sterile office of hers, but when she spoke, when she said his name, took his hand, looked into his eyes she was warm and appealing. Holding onto the steering wheel, John looked upward. He made a declaration and a request. "I will dress and speak like a confident, successful, professional. I will achieve my goals. I want a promotion at the library and, God, if you're really up there and listening, I want Sara."

It had been almost a week since the meeting. John had not spoken to Sara again until today, although he'd emailed her a proposal for the teen/young adult volunteer group that he named the Computer Geek Team.

"I'm so impressed by your proposal for the Geek Team. What made you think of it?" Sara asked John.

Not wanting to meet in her ultra clean office, and knowing his wreck of an apartment was a no go, he'd suggested they meet at the coffee shop.

"I wanted to mentor them, like Mr. Keyes did for me."

"Who is Mr. Keyes?" Sara asked.

"He was our county bookmobile librarian in Wonder County, Kansas. He helped me develop my interests and taught me about librarianship. When I returned to Kansas after college, I assisted him on the bookmobile. When he retired, I was hired into his position. I spent a lot of time updating the technology services with the assistance of state library technology grants."

"How did you wind up in Aurora?"

"I got bored with the job and living in the same town all my life. One day I met a woman named Lena who had moved to the county to be closer to her daughter and grandchildren. She'd been a library circulation manager for several years, but couldn't find any library openings in the area. That was the catalyst for me. I decided to make a change. She wanted to go back to work, so I suggested that she volunteer on the bookmobile for a few months to see if she would want my job. I started applying for every open library position I could find outside of Kansas. Lena became the new bookmobile librarian for Wonder County and I accepted an Adult Services Librarian position in Aurora."

Sara hesitated and then asked quietly, "Do you mind telling me why you're in the men's group? Honestly, you don't seem to need it."

Don't panic, you knew this would come up, which begs the question why didn't I prepare an answer. I don't want her to change her impression of me but I can't lie... uhm, "I have a resentment against church and religion. I'm not sure I can believe in God" he blurted out. Sara looked shocked. *Maybe I should have lied,* John thought.

"I had no idea, John. What happened to make you feel that way?"

"I grew up in a small town where everyone went to the same church. The church leadership was not very good. They had limited acceptance of anything or anyone that was different. I was a reader; I liked to learn about science, inventions, space. I wasn't into sports like most of the other boys. I was too different and wasn't accepted."

Sara looked at John sympathetically, "that must have made you feel awful." A feeling she was all too familiar with as she grew up.

"Religion was the most important thing to my parents; I had religion forced on me; the only thing that mattered was what the pastor or church leaders cared about. My parents couldn't understand my fascination with computers and science fiction. With them everything was God, the Lord this, the Lord that.... The things I read about in books, the subjects I liked, were nonsense to them."

Leaning in toward John, Sara asked, "Was it your fascination that lead you to be a librarian?"

"In a way, but mostly it was my relationship with Mr. Keyes. He saw my enthusiasm for reading and made sure I had access to books that interested me. He was the only one I could talk to about what I liked. He even spoke with my folks about letting me go away to college. I think the only reason my parents let me go to college was because they thought I would take over the bookmobile when I graduated and stay in Kansas forever.

I got my BA in Iowa and my MLIS from University of Illinois. After Mr. Keyes was gone, I stopped sharing my ideas with anyone, because they just didn't get me. Instead, I kept to myself. I was tired of being laughed at, rebuffed or misunderstood."

Sara understood the pain of being rejected all too well. After taking a sip of her tea, she probed, "The negative reactions of people caused you to turn away from faith?

"Why would I want to be a Christian if it means I can't do what I love, what I'm good at? Although, participating in the group at True Light is allowing me to see religion and church folk in a better light."

"How do you feel about the services?" asked Sara. "I noticed that you've been attending regularly."

John perked up. She *noticed* him. God bless True Light Church!

"Daniel convinced me to forget about what happened in the past. He told me not to judge all the faith community by one group of people. He brought up a good point, that my view of church from a child's perspective was limited. As an adult I can analyze faith with a wider perspective."

"Does it seem different to you?"

"Yes," John responded happily. "Instead of making me feel angry and defeated, I feel at peace. I find myself reading the Bible to find out if what Pastor Thomas is preaching is actually in there."

"I'm glad to hear that. Ever since I was a child, church was the only place I felt peace."

"What about you, Sara. Did you have any negative experiences growing up?"

Not going there tonight.... "It's getting late," replied Sara. "I need to get home. John, I'm very glad Daniel sent you to me...I mean to the committee. We need what you're good at. What God made you to do."

The next committee meeting was held at Sharon's house. She insisted on cooking dinner for everyone. After Sara recapped the previous meeting, Sharon took over and outlined the marketing campaign.

"We'll do a program with one of our seniors as the presenter. Maddie Booker is well-known for her pies; everyone likes them. She'll teach a class on making apple pie. We've also scheduled an outing for the teens and tweens to go apple picking at a local farm, followed by a hayride and marshmallow roast. The apples they pick will be used for the pie making class.

He was totally in, John thought as he listened. He knew how to pick apples. There were apple trees on the farm where he grew up. Upon hearing that Sara was on the list of mandatory chaperones, he had no trouble finding the words to volunteer as bus driver for the trip. It was an opportunity to spend the entire day with Sara, oh yeah!

Sara felt herself smile knowing that John would be with her at the orchard. Thinking about spending the day with John, delighted her more than it should have. It certainly made it easier to tolerate being cooped up with a bunch of teens on a long bus ride. They tended to be disorderly, impatient, and even worse, messy, not her ideal situation

Sharon continued. "We'll tape portions of the pie-making class and upload them to the web. There will be an information crawl at the bottom of the screen inviting the viewers to the Harvest Festival. We'll give out samples of the apple pie to entice visitors to buy something from our bake sale booth.

Sara looked at John and Will. "The website needs to be ready."

"In keeping with our multi-generational theme, we're doing a grandparents trip to the pumpkin farm. Our seniors will be paired up with our primary grade children to pick pumpkins. The filling from those pumpkins will be used for a desert. We'll tape the Jones cousins demonstrating how to use the filling to make a traditional versus vegan pumpkin trifle dessert," Sharon explained.

"Yuck", said Will. "I'll pass on the trifle."

"The final video segment," Sharon concluded, "will be with the father and son team, Kevin and Brandt Chambers. The have agreed to tape a segment at their restaurant. They'll demonstrate Kevin's barbeque short ribs recipe versus his son Brandt's recipe for barbequed salmon. Both will use their special family barbeque sauce. The sauce will be available for purchase at the Harvest Festival. All the recipes used in the clips were included in the cookbook."

Sara interjected again, "the website has to be ready so we can start running these clips."

John made eye contact with Sara and spoke calmly. "Sara, we know what needs to be done."

"But are you on schedule?" Sara said, sounding agitated.

"You gave me the responsibility of the web design. I know what to do, so relax. I've got a picture of the cookbook cover and a description ready to go up on bookselling sites so we can take pre-orders. We want to reach more than the people who visit the church website. Having the book available through online bookstores will attract lots of buyers."

Sara let it drop, but she wouldn't be at ease until she saw the final product.

The weekend came and Sara was probably more excited than teens about being at the apple orchard. Her favorite dessert was apple pie. When she was a little girl, her mother would buy her the small ones that came in a box for fifty cents at the corner market. They were mostly sweet tasting goo, but she didn't care. One year at school, her teacher taught a unit on apples. As a special treat, the teacher brought in homemade apple pie squares. When Sara bit into hers, she knew she would never eat those boxed pies again. She got a cookbook from the library, found a recipe for apple pie, and begged her mother to buy the ingredients. Her pie didn't taste as good as the teacher's, but it was way better than the box pies.

Sara remembered learning to cook more dishes, and reading library books on home organization so she could get family's messy apartment in order. She thought about on how long it had been since she had eaten pie. It was years ago, when she found how devastating sugary desserts were for diabetics, as she watched her mother struggling with the disease.

They had been at the orchard for a few hours when Sara saw some exceptional looking apples far up and way out on a branch. *I bet I can reach them.* She asked a couple of teens to bring a ladder over to the tree. As she climbed the ladder, it started to shake, so the kids offered to steady it while she climbed. She got to the top and stretched out her arms toward some beautiful apples at the end of the branch. As she reached, her thoughts drifted back to the excitement of making her first apple pie. In the distance she heard someone shout, "Watch out Sara".

John was across the way, putting heavy bushel baskets of apples in the church bus. He turned to pick up another basket and saw Sara. *Oh my lord,* he thought. *She's going to fall.*

Sara felt herself falling but it was too late. The ground was rushing up to meet her, as she anticipated the pain of a hard landing. She squeezed her eyes shut. To her relief, instead of the cold hard ground, she felt strong arms enveloping her and breaking her fall. John had made it to her just in time. He caught her and they both tumbled to the ground.

"Sara, are you okay?" John asked as he helped her up.

She turned in his arms. They were so close. As she looked into his eyes, she saw his concern for her, or was it desire? She hoped it was desire.

Gazing down at her, all John could think about was how much he wanted to kiss this woman right now and how right now was so *not* the right time. From the way she was looking at him, he had the feeling that she wanted to kiss him too. The voices of the teens and the other chaperones asking if Sara was all right interrupted them, just in time. Embarrassed that she had been so careless, Sara stepped back and began frantically brushing dirt off her pants.

"Whoa, you're attacking that dirt like it's alive," John observed. Sara stopped, looked at him for a second and then walked away.

John caught up to her. "Where are you going?"

"Back to the bus, I want to change my clothes."

"You brought a change of clothes?"

"Yes."

When Sara turned to look at him, he had stopped following her. He stood perfectly still, looking at her with his mouth open and a look of utter disbelief on his face. He shook it off and walked back towards the teens and the apple trees.

Their group was boarding a wagon for the hayride when John saw Sara several minutes later. She had on a pair of dark colored corduroys with a matching sweater and scarf. She looked like she was going to a fashion photo shoot.

You have obviously never been on a hayride before John said, trying not to laugh.

Why do you say that?

You put on new clothes to sit on a bed of hay with a bunch of kids that have been working in dirt and rolling around in piles of leaves.

Don't remind me. I'm here mostly to keep them in order and on task.

There is some room for them to fun isn't there?

I suppose.

He took her hand and guided her toward the stables on the property.

I've got a surprise for you. We're going to ride horses.

It was her turn to look at him in utter disbelief.

John had secured two horses for himself and Sara so they could ride behind the truck on horseback. After much coaxing, Sara had agreed to ride and allowed him to help her up on the horse. They listened to some brief instructions on riding, and then started off. It was late in the afternoon and the air had become cool. They rode along in silence for a while, and then John stated to speak. "Sara, Your reaction to getting your clothes dirty seemed, well, kind of intense. What's that about?

Sara ran her hand through her hair and adjusted the scarf that hung around her neck. She sat up straighter in the saddle and carefully began to explain.

"My mother was a single parent to me and my two older brothers. She worked two jobs and at times, we felt abandoned. Understandably, she was too tired to do housework or cook when she got home. My brothers were always filthy. I sometimes thought it was on purpose, to show their anger at our situation. I had friends, but was ashamed to let them come over and see how we lived."

Raised voices and laughter drifted back from the wagon. Sara did a quick visual check of the teens, and everything seemed okay. She continued with her story.

"One day I showed Mother my report card. My grades in my required subjects landed me on the honor roll. She noticed that in one of my elective modules that I got an E. It was in Home Economics; cooking, sewing, home organization. I told her the E was for excellent, then she said, "Excellent, we could use some of that around here, a little excellence." From that day forward, I took over our household chores. I went to war against dirt. I cleaned up after my brothers, even if it caused a fight. I cooked our meals and did the laundry. I was on a mission to bring my mother excellence. It worked; the more I did, the more she praised me. I controlled our environment, kept it clean and organized. I did it to get my Mother's attention and her love.

She looked so vulnerable just then, John wanted to reach over and give her a hug. She'd adjusted easily to riding. He had thought that she would. The horses were well-trained. Knowing the trail, they would stay on it faithfully, something Sara could appreciate.

Her posture had relaxed and she was watching the sunset. He thought it best to finish the ride the way it had begun, in silence.

The wagon arrived back at the stables and the chaperones were herding the group toward the campfire for the marshmallow roast. Sara's mood was somber and John felt he was the blame for it, for pushing her to share her story. It was dark now and much colder. He helped her down from her horse. Her hair brushed against his neck, and he felt her shiver a little.

"Hey, if you sit next to me at the campfire I promise to guard you from any rogue dirt that might try to attack you Sara."

Thankfully, she began to laugh. "I'll sit next you, but don't make promises you can't keep."

A few nights later, John was leaving his session with Daniel when he spotted Sara in the in the church hallway. He called her name and she turned. She started toward him with a big smile on her face.

"You're here late. Don't you have an 8 to 5 shift?" John inquired.

Sara shrugged her shoulders. "I do, but with the harvest festival, the cookbook launch, and my regular duties, I'm working double-time."

"If you're ready to leave, would you like to have dinner with me?"

She was hungry, and it would be nice to spend some time with John. She could sit across from him and look into his velvety brown eyes.

I'd love to, but I have to make a stop first. I need to get Maddie Booker's medications to her before she goes to bed. She lives just across the street.

I don't mind going with you.

Maddie Booker was a pleasant woman who was delighted to see them. It was before 8:00 but Maddie was already dressed for bed. She thanked them for bringing the medicine.

"Sara, I'm so glad you've met a young man to date. I have a good feeling about him. He makes you smile."

Okay, now she was completely embarrassed. She looked over at John. He was inching closer to the door, like he wanted to escape.

"Well Maddie we need to be going. You have a peaceful rest tonight."

After they left Maddie's John said, "That was a nice thing you did. She seemed really appreciative.

Sara explained, Maddie is so special to us at True Light, and she's like a grandmother to me. She had started to forget to order and pick-up her medications. I found out about it and I made a schedule for her, of all her meds, the dosages, and refill date. I call in her refills, pick them up and deliver them. All she has to do is notate on the schedule what medications she takes and when. That way I can be sure she hasn't forgotten to take them.

"Not only do you have the church business organized, you have the members' affairs in order.

"It's not like that, I enjoy being with them and letting them know someone still cares."

They decided to eat at an Italian restaurant a few blocks from the Church. After they ordered, John asked. "How did you become the pastor's administrative assistant?"

"Six years ago, True Light Church burned to the ground.

"I remember reading about that in the newspaper."

"Our congregation was devastated. The church had been on that site for more than thirty years. I got an idea to contact long-time members and get copies of any photographs taken of the church. I also interviewed members to collect an oral history of the church. I got together with Will to video the interviews; put them with the photographs on a CD. We sold them to raise funds for rebuilding.

John was impressed. "You did that without being asked?"

"Yes, and it caught Pastor Thompson's attention. He invited a group of members, including me and Will, to pray with him for guidance on how to rebuild the church. He asked if we would all pick an hour of the day to pray so that someone would be praying for the church twenty-four hours a day. He asked us for a forty day commitment.

During that time he offered me the administrative assistant position at True Light and I accepted. The salary was small, but I felt better coming to work at the church where I was needed than being a nobody in the big corporation where I had been working."

"I can't imagine you being a *nobody* no matter where you were," said John. That made Sara smile.

"After forty days of prayer, blessings and miracles started to happen. The pastor was offered some free airtime on one of the local cable stations to broadcast weekly, and quickly became syndicated nationally. The following year he wrote, of all things, a faith-based novel that was released by a major publishing company and hit the bestseller lists. The following year, it was optioned as a movie. It didn't make him rich, but he earned enough to purchase land to rebuild the church on and cover construction costs without a mortgage."

"Sara, you believe God did that because you all prayed for forty days? So if I pray for a car for forty days, one will appear in my driveway on day forty one?"

"No, John, it's not some magic formula, but it does help you to focus, to build your faith. You stop looking at all the obstacles and look toward your goal. You start to get ideas, plans and resources to obtain your goal. Pastor didn't get a check in the mail on day forty-one but he received an opportunity that led to an income that allowed him to reach his goals. It was faith and hard work. Faith without work is dead or unproductive."

As John drove home, he started to think about his own situation. When he voiced his burning need to change his life, he was presented with the opportunity to join Daniel's group and learn skills and make goals. Because he did the assignments Daniel gave him, he was in a position to work on a major IT project that could lead to his goal of a promotion at work. In one of his sessions, Daniel told him that sometimes your family, friends, and co-workers can't see you as a leader. You're the same to them no matter what you do. He talked about how Jesus wasn't recognized as a prophet in his hometown, He was just that carpenter's son, the one with the family drama surrounding his birth. He'd had to leave town and gain his reputation elsewhere to get recognized by those who knew him before.

Now John was doing that, running a project in the community that would give him a new image at work. He remembered that after he first saw Sara, he had said a prayer. He wanted her; he now had the opportunity to win her heart, and he was working hard to reach that goal.

After a training session with his Computer Geek Team, John met Sara for dinner. She gave him the biggest smile when she saw him approaching. *God, you really do care about me*, he said to himself. *She is the best, and I want to be the best for her.*

As they enjoyed dinner, he told her about meeting with the teens and finalizing plans for the festival booth, on time, he added. The booth would feature a gadget petting zoo and download stations so people could purchase the cookbook at the festival.

"Look at the T-shirts we're going to wear." He pulled a shirt out and showed her. "Andrew, one of our team members, designed it and everyone agreed on his graphics"

The look on Sara's face was not exactly what he was expecting; she looked annoyed. "John, T-shirts are acceptable for the kids, but you need to reflect a business image. You're selling a product, and people need to see you as a leader in control."

"Okay. What do you suggest I wear black tie and tails?"

"No, a traditional suit, shirt and tie will do. I know you don't wear that type of formal business wear at the library, but you should at this event."

The last time he'd worn a suit was at a relative's funeral and he hadn't even brought it with him when he moved to Aurora.

"Do you have time to go with me to pick out a suit?"

The gleam was back in her eye. "I'd love to," she replied.

The suit shopping that started the night before, had now extended into the next day. Unbelievable! John only had one day off for during weekend and he had spent it shopping with Sara. Store after store, shirts, shoes, ties. Sara was like a drill sergeant. "Try this on. That's a bad color for you. "Not that one, it's too casual" Sara would bark. When he would be just about ready to tell her he'd had enough, she would turn that sweet smile on him. He would relent and head back into the dressing room. Besides, he didn't want her to know much he hated wearing suits.

By noon Sara was finally satisfied that he would be properly attired. John was ready to head home, put his feet up and watch some television.

As they walked to his car, Sara asked "can we make one more stop?

"John groaned loudly. Sara please, no more shopping.

"Well" she said hesitantly, "it's not clothes shopping. I need to get some groceries. I want to stop at the co-op on Jericho Road. I go there every week to buy fresh produce for a few of the seniors citizens that attend True Light."

"That's a nice thing to do. No wonder everyone at the church speaks so highly of you."

"I enjoy doing it. The co-op is pretty far away from some of them. I know how important a good diet is to their health."

Sara though back to when she first learned her mother had diabetes. She tried to get her to eat better, so she wouldn't suffer so many complications. More times than not her efforts failed.

They arrived at the co-op and went inside. John was impressed. It reminded him of some of the markets in his hometown.

"I didn't even know this place existed" he said as he placed some items in a shopping cart.

"Where do you usually shop?" Sara inquired?

He hesitated, but answered honestly. "Walgreens and CVS".

"What!" She spoke so loudly that other shoppers turned around to see what was going on. "How do you stay in such good shape? Those stores on have processed foods on the shelves." "Not true, they have canned fruits and vegetables, which I've read are almost as good as fresh. Besides, when I go visit my parents, my Mom sends me back with enough food to stock my freezer for months. She's a great cook."

"You have to think about your long-term health John."

"I do. I work out at the gym faithfully at least four days a week."

"I'll make you a meal plan and put you on my route. The next time I come here to stock up I'll drop a bag of groceries by your place on my way home."

John turned quickly into the next aisle, hoping Sara didn't see the panicked look on his face. She could not come to his apartment. If she saw the pigsty he lived in, he would be lucky if she drove by his place and threw him the groceries out her car window.

Monday morning workers arrived at the church to install the internet upgrade. Sara paced back and forth holding her cell phone to her ear.

She'd called John at his cell number three times, no answer. She left a message for him three times, no return call. She dialed again, it went straight to voicemail.

"John, this is Sara. The internet installers are at the church and need some questions answered before they begin their work. I tried to contact Will to come in but I can't reach him either. Please call me as soon as you get this message.

"This is so inefficient," she muttered. "You'd think they would have anticipated this and made sure one of them was here when the installers arrived. I'm going to the library and insist John take care of this."

At the library, John was losing patience with a patron on the phone. Two staff members had called in sick, one of the pages was a no show, and the library catalog kept going down. He'd planned to go to lunch early so he could meet the installers at the church. He could still make it if he could get this guy off the phone.

"I'm trying to find a book I started reading. I was really enjoying it," the caller said.

"Sure, what's the title?" John asked

"I don't remember."

"Okay, what about the authors' name, do you recall that?"

"No, not really."

"Well, what was the book about?"

"Something about a father who moves his family from place to place. I think during the Oklahoma dust bowl."

"Alright, was it a novel or non-fiction?"

"I don't know. I didn't think you could find it. I'll just Google it."

His hand tightened around the receiver and he took a deep breath. "Sir, bear with me."

John asked the man some more questions, made a few educated guesses and finally, found the correct title.

"Wow, just like magic! You people are awesome!"

"Thank you, always glad to help."

John slammed the receiver down, mumbling, "He calls thirty minutes of searching the library catalog, the internet and my brain *"magic."*

Angie approached the desk. "I'm here, and it sounds like you need a break."

"You don't know the half of it. I've got to go—

"Wait! The branch manager was looking for you. She said you had a visitor and she was showing her to your cube.

Great. Probably a vendor meeting he'd forgotten about. He'd forgotten a lot this morning, especially his professional facade. He'd awakened late. Instead of his dress shirt and pants, he had grabbed a polo shirt that had a faded library logo on it, a more wrinkled than pressed pair of khakis off the laundry pile on the couch, and then stuck his feet in some loafers and ran to work.

He had to get to the church. Sara would be livid by now. As the words went through his mind, realization struck him. Sara was the visitor.

Sara looked around at the *jumble* that was John's work area. Piles of books, comics, and papers occupied the corners. There were empty candy wrappers, super hero figurines, and DVD cases on top of the desk. His inbox looked like it hadn't been emptied for months.

"Oh my God, are those really Christmas cards mixed in there?" Sara exclaimed. Underneath the desk sat containers filled with keyboards, gadgets, and cords. There was no order, no sense of decency. The person she had come to know would not maintain a space like this. She had to get out of here. She left the office and headed for the reference desk.

When he saw Sara coming toward him, he felt like an animal being exposed in his natural habitat. She surveyed him from head to toe. Sara had a bead on him like a hunter and she was not letting him out of her sights. She was going to fire on him, and she was not going to miss. Just as he was preparing for the blast, a thought came to him, the words that Daniel had spoken about taking the initiative in a conversation, saying what you wanted to say, getting out of your head and making the outcome the one you want. Granted, Daniel was probably not talking about a situation like this, but John needed to improvise.

He stood up and came around the front of the desk to meet her. Before Sara could speak, he said, "Hi Sara, it's been a very busy morning here, I was headed over to the church, but I could give you a quick tour of the library and introduce you to some of my co-workers if you'd like."

If looks could kill, there would be a big hole in front of the reference desk where his body hit the floor. He had to get her out of there so he could explain. What could he say? His body was taken over by aliens? When they were outside the doors, John started to speak, but Sara threw up her hand to stop him. She turned her back on him and walked away.

When Sara got back to True Light she marched straight to Daniel's office.

He laid down the files he was working on and listened while Sara filled him on John's "*deception*"

"No one is perfect Sara, which includes you.

You polished, cleaned and organized to give yourself the feeling self-control thinking that all your excellence would hide the unworthy person you think you are. You thought perfection would bring acceptance and love. You were working hard to achieve something you already had.

Sara started to tear up. "You're saying that nothing I did mattered."

"No I'm not. The ministry staff appreciates how you keep this church in running order. What I'm saying is that we love you for who you are, not what you do. We've all seen how much kindness you've shown to the elderly and lonely members of True Light. You made sure they had food, and someone to talk to"

"I really like helping."

"And it shows, but there are others who help people that don't get the response you do. The members you help know your generosity is from the heart. You truly care about people. "Daniel, I worry that if don't stay on top of things, if I let one thing slip, my life will get out of hand, I'll be just like…" Sara's voice faded."Just like who?"

"Just like my mother."

John finally made it to the church and took care of the installation problems. As he was leaving he ran into Daniel. His posture spoke volumes.

"You look like a defeated man. Sara told me what happened. Want to give me your version?

John nodded. He gave mostly the same account as Sara had about the situation.

"I wanted to be the perfect guy for her. I was in love from the first time I saw her. It's killing me that I ruined my chance with her."

Daniel thought carefully before responding. "You both have been hurt by rejection and you each responded to it in different ways. Sara tried to be perfect and control everything and you withdrew from communication and relationships with people. John, now is not the time to shrink back and be quiet. If you love her, confront her. Let her know who you are and what you have to offer in a relationship. Help her too see what's important."

After a sleepless night, John was determined to confront Sara. He went to the church in the evening hoping to catch her before she left for the day. He spotted her car in the church parking lot. She was still there, he hurried inside the building. He entered her office without knocking and immediately smelled could smell the disinfectant in the air; if it was possible, the room was more sterile than before. Sara stiffened at the sight of him.

"Did I forget a meeting?" she asked.

The coldness in her words made him take a step back. "We need to talk about your reaction at the library yesterday. We're more alike than you want to admit. We both seek outside approval. You are fanatical about order and cleanliness. Just like when you were a child and you worked to gain you Mother's approval. I think part of your choice to work in a church is to get approval from God.

"Obviously my fanatical cleaning habits haven't rubbed off on you."

"No they haven't."

"A few weeks in counseling and you have it all figured out. "You don't know me, she bit out. "How can you stand there and tell me what I think about God. You don't even believe in God, she raged. "You came to True Light to solve your own problems, not mine."

This was not going the very well, but he wasn't going to turn back now. He stepped closer to her desk and looked her in the eyes. "It's clear that we don't have the same priorities. I'd like to spend my time helping people learn something or find the perfect gadget, rather than meticulously cleaning and straightening a desk in a cubicle I hardly ever use. When I'm answering questions, mentoring a lonely teen or and catching you falling off a ladder, does it matter if my desk is clean, my pants pressed or my bed made?"

"I may be obsessed with ordering my surroundings but at least I don't deceive people."

John could not deny the truth of her words.

"I admit, I always believed, but I believed that God sided with all the people who were against me. It hurt too much to have faith in a God that didn't like me. "True, it's only been a short time, but I don't see God as an enemy anymore.

John dared to sit in the seat right beside her desk. Sara looked down at the items laying on her desk, as if assuring herself that they were still in place. She straightened her back and continued to glare at him. With complete sincerity in his voice, he told her the truth.

"For the first time in my life, I spoke to God from my heart, told him my desires, and He showed me the path to fulfill them, a path to you. I know now that he loves me. He must, because He let me find you. Sara, I love you, but if you can only see my clothes and my untidiness, you're missing the best part of me. I know I wasn't completely honest with you, but a messy office shouldn't make you this angry."

Sara seemed to deflate right in front of him. She sat down, her head bent, looking at her hands in her lap. "When I was ten years old, my father died in a car crash. He was drunk, and he killed a nineteen-year-old boy who lived a few blocks away from us. Instead of the neighbors supporting us in our time of grief, we were shunned. Some people hated our father and took it out on us, especially on my older brothers. Most people just ignored us. My mother had to go back to work. She now had three children to support and the legal problems that came as a result of the accident.

John pulled up a chair and sat down closer to Sara as he listened to her explain.

"She had to sell our lovely home and move us into an apartment in a more affordable neighborhood. My mother ended up with two jobs, two resentful sons, and one very needy daughter. She felt cheated because of my father's actions and she withdrew from us.

"I'm not your father Sara", John interjected.

"My Father was an alcoholic. My Mother loved him and tried to get him to stop drinking. His lack of self-control caused a tragedy that reflected badly on our family. People looked down on us because of his actions. As far as they were concerned, we were just as bad as him."

"My issues are not as severe as alcoholism."

"My dad's problems didn't start with his drinking. First, he started withdrawing from us. He would ignore me and my brothers. He began staying late at work, and stopping off to drink with co-workers before coming home. Eventually, he started staying away from home for days at a time. My mother would make excuses for him. She begged him to get some help. She kept hoping, believing he would change. He couldn't control himself and my mother couldn't do anything about it. I can't live with someone who can't control their habits. That's my deal breaker in a relationship. It may not be important to you, but it is to me."

The weekend of the Harvest Festival arrived, but John was no longer excited about participating. He looked in his closet at the new business clothes Sara had chosen for him to wear. A stark white collared shirt, dark gray dress pants, and a gold print tie. He could wear those clothes and measure up to her standard of excellence, and lose himself in the process.

He wanted to please Sara, but measuring up to her idea of excellence was not his goal today. What was important was working with his team to meet their sales goal to fund the church technology project. Dressing like an insurance salesman at a casual event was not going to attract people to his booth. Once again it was time to dress for where he wanted to go. John pulled the T-shirt the kids had designed out of his dresser drawer, found a pair of jeans in the clean laundry pile, and got dressed. He said a quick prayer for the festival's success and left.

It was controlled chaos in the True Light Church gym. The decorating committee had done an amazing job. The room had been transformed into a farm with an apple orchard. The backdrops on the wall were painted with apple trees, barn doors, and pasture scenes. White picket fences and hay bales enclosed the food and game booths. Sara began checking attendance to make sure all the stations were staffed. From across the room, she eyed the most important station of the festival—the electronic petting zoo and cookbook ordering area manned by John and his Geek Team.

After her blow-up with John the day before, she hadn't spoken to him again. Her heart had leaped inside her when he said he loved her. But how could she have a life with him? His measure of excellence was far different from hers. John was not the man she pictured as a husband. *Could that picture change? Could he be just what I need? Am I too rigid and controlling? Does John need me? Do I love him?*

Sara refocused on the task at hand, being ready to open the doors to the Harvest Festival on time and raising enough money to fund the church's technology plan. As she approached his booth, John turned toward her.

Seriously? She scowled. *He's not wearing the outfit I picked out for him? He's totally casual. What business person shows up looking like that? He's selling a product. Who's going to take him seriously? You know what, I was right—he's not the one. I'll acknowledge his contributions to the project, but on a personal level, we're done.* Without a word to John, Sara stalked away.

As the afternoon progressed, John had one of the teens at his booth deliver Sara a copy of the sales numbers. The cookbook sales were better than projected. Looking at the report, she was very pleased. The webpage and download links worked, for which she had John to thank. Throughout the evening she had noticed John and his team actively engage people to visit the technology booth. She thought she caught him looking her way a few times, but after the way she spoke to him…it was doubtful.

Sarah looked around the gym. Children ran around with chocolate smeared on their cheeks, licking fingers sticky with caramel from taffy apples. Families that participated in the apple bobbing constant were drying their hair with towels and laughing. Men, women, families—messy, disordered, but happy. Order had its place, but not now, not here. Several people came up to her and complimented her on the event. No one cared about the perfectly creased, spotless cream colored outfit she wore. In fact, she looked out of place.

Looking over at John's booth, she saw him helping people download the cookbook to their devices. There were people of all ages gathered around and learning to use the displayed gadgets. People were listening to him, smiling, and thanking him and his crew for explaining how to use the items. He looked happy, confident, in his element. Her words came back to her. *He looks like he's attending a festival, not like a business person selling a product. People feel at ease with him and are willing to go outside of their comfort zone and try something new.*

Wasn't that what he did for her? He had stepped out of his comfort zone. He'd tried to be the picture she had in her head of an excellent man. Her mistake was putting too much weight on outward appearances and housekeeping and not enough on the inside, on the heart. He was participating in a way that showed he was a part of the church and enjoying it.

She looked deliberately at John, then at the table where the pie eating contest was about to begin. She knew what she had to do.

John watched her in disbelief as Sara took the last spot at the pie eating table. He excused himself from the booth and stood in front of the table. Sara motioned for one of the teen girls to come over to her. They exchanged a few words, then the girl took the hair tie off her ponytail and gave it to Sara. She tied her hair back, placed a large plastic contestant's bib around her neck, pushed up her sleeves, and put her head down right over the pie, waiting. John heard, "Ready, set, go!"

Shockingly, Sara did a face plant into the pie and began to devour it, crust and filling, lightning fast. John laughed out loud as he quickly realized that even in her haste, she had an ordered plan to her attack. The stop whistle sounded. Sara raised her head from the pie tin. She was covered forehead to chin with pie filling and crust. The judges passed by for the inspection on the contestants' tins. One judge went to the microphone to announce the winners. "Third place—Murphy King; second place—Robert Johnson; and the first place winner is Sara..."

The cheers and applause drowned out her last name. Sara, who had been trying to clean her face with napkins, made her way to the podium. As she reached for the trophy, she noticed that her hands still had pie filling on them. She shrugged, and then wiped her hands on her immaculately clean pants before grabbing the trophy and doing a victory dance.

John make his way over to her and wrapped her in a warm embrace.

"Lady, I don't know who you are, but when Sara sees what you did to her pants, you're toast" He began to laugh again.

"You know," she said, "Sara needs to get a life. I recommend enjoying a big, gooey, sweet, slice of calorie-laden old-fashioned apple pie."

Seeing her expression grow serious, John took Sara's hand and pulled her into an empty meeting room in the hallway. Taking her in his arms, he looked down at her while she spoke.

"I only looked at the outside, how neat my apartment was, how efficient I was at work, when I should have placed value on what was inside me. What I am is more important than what I do. I'm excellent because of Him, because of the way *God* made me. John, the way you help people, the patience and attention you've shown, the way you made me open my heart…. those things are more excellent than a starched shirt or a tidy office. I measured excellence by the wrong standard. Thank you for confronting me and setting me straight."

"Does that mean I can return those new *professional* clothes to the store?" John inquired.

"No. It means you don't have to pretend to like them."

As he continued to hold her, he looked into her eyes. "This is who I am and what I have to offer. I'll never be a color-coordinated, lettuce eating, appointment book driven type of guy. I don't own an iron or have a 'style'. I'll always have too many gadgets, but I'll keep them out of your way. I'll support your healthy living and eating agenda. I won't get angry when you *organize* me, I won't ignore you, and I won't ever stop loving you. And, when you look up the word happy in the dictionary, you'll find a picture of us cheek to cheek with smiling faces."

"That's a picture I want to look at every day."

"Every day for the rest of your life?"

Sara started to melt, but answered him, "Yes, every day for the rest of my life."

Then, he kissed her.

Weeks later, Sara spoke with John on the phone. "What's your family's favorite dessert? I want to make something that will remind them of home during their visit.

Thoughtfully, he replied, "My Granny Gene's pound cake was always around during the holidays. I'll ask my mom for the recipe."

"No, let me call her myself. I want to get to know her better and maybe collect a few embarrassing stories from your childhood."

"Forget it. We'll just buy a Sara Lee dessert."

Thanksgiving came quickly, but they were ready, thanks to Sara's master planning skills. Sara did the shopping and called him in for the fetching and carrying. The two of them plus Sara's mother and brothers and John's parents would be a tight fit in the condo's dining room. John spent the day before Thanksgiving helping her get the leaves put in the dining table and transporting folding chairs from the church storage. To his surprise, she had him put foam cushions on the chair seats and then she wrapped the entire chair with fabric secured by a bow in back. Who knew? Comfortable, portable, and presentable.

John had insisted on researching the best way to cook a turkey and they settled on smoking it on the patio. John bought a used kettle grill off a bargain finder website, downloaded an instructional video, and convinced Sara to trust him. She did trust him, really, but her practical side swayed her to buy a decent size turkey breast that she roasted and hid in the fridge, just in case.

They would have the traditional side dishes along with a healthy green vegetable and a fruit salad. Sara also experimented with baking some gluten free rolls.

This was their first *couple project*, and as he promised, he didn't get angry when she kept him on schedule. John would gladly change into the outfit she picked for him to wear so he wouldn't smell like charcoal and wood chips at the dinner table. He would have never thought of that.

On Thanksgiving Day, John was exhausted but also feeling hopeful. The food part of the plan was on target. He and Sara had prayed together that the families would enjoy the afternoon and be supportive of their engagement, maybe even want to help with the wedding plans. John had just finished changing out of his smoke infused jeans and sweatshirt when Sara called him into the living room.

Sara was holding a gift wrapped box. Oh no! John stiffened. Did he miss a memo? When did people start exchanging Thanksgiving gifts? Sara recognized his distressed look and reassured him.

"I got an idea and I couldn't resist."

He took the box from her and opened it. Inside the box was a picture in an engraved frame that read "The Definition of Happiness". Next to the wording was the picture of him and Sara at the Harvest Festival, a selfie he'd snapped right after Sara won the pie eating contest. They stood cheek to cheek, grinning from ear to ear, John's hair in a mess, Sara with pie filling stuck to her face. They were beaming into the camera, totally happy.

"Well, John, we have enough information, and we just wanted to bring you in to make you the offer in person. You're the perfect choice to be promoted to the position of Head of Technology Projects for the library."

Laughter filtered down the corridor as John was escorted to the elevator by the library's Assistant Director and the Director of Network Support. After one quick stop at the branch to tell Angie the good news, John was off to spend the evening celebrating with Sara.

Granny Gene's Pound Cake

3/4 sticks of Butter (Room Temperature)

3 cups of Sugar

6 eggs (Room Temperature)

4 cups of flour

1/4 tsp. Salt

2/3 cups of Milk

2 Tbsp. Vanilla Extract

1 tsp. Lemon Extract

1 tsp. Almond Extract

Non-stick loaf pan

In a large mixing bowl use an electric mixer to cream the butter and sugar together.

Crack open eggs and place them in a dish (not beaten).

Pour the eggs one at a time to the butter/sugar mixture while beating the mixture.

Add the Vanilla, Lemon and Almond extracts to the milk.

Add half of the flour and half of the milk to the mixing bowl and mix on a slow speed.

Continue mixing at a slow speed

Add the remaining flour and milk.

Mix until creamy.

Pour batter into loaf pan

Bake at 350 degrees for 1 hour and 15 minutes. The center should spring back when touched.

Sweet Cupids

By CJ Warrant

CJ **Warrant** is an award-winning writer for dark romantic suspense and thrillers that pulls at your heart, makes you shiver with fear and hope for a happy ending. A lover of coffee, baking and family, but not in that order— She's a wife, a mother of three and a cosmetologist by trade. Her stories stirs dark rich plots, with addictive flawed characters you will fall in love with. She's a member of Romance Writers of America and belongs to Windy City, Chicago-North, Contemporary Romance and Kiss of Death chapters. She is also affiliated with Sisters in Crime and International Thriller Writers.

Chapter 1

At first, Beth Monroe through it was a joke when she got a call from the bank saying that her business partner, Hannah Larson, had emptied out their business account.

Not believing for one moment that her friend of seven years could betray her, Beth tried numerous times to contact Hannah that day, but her cell phone went right to voice mail. Worried that it could be foul play—that someone actually forced her to do it, Beth contacted the police. If there was foul play involved, she hoped Hannah was still alive and safe. Money could be replaced, but not a friend.

Beth trusted her partner wholeheartedly and never thought she'd do something so terrible. They'd each put their heart and sweat into Sweet Cupids, a bake shop they'd opened up in the South Loop of Chicago three years ago; they were equally passionate about the bakery.

Or so she thought until the cops confirmed that Hannah acted on her own accord. After the police ran through the security cameras and checked Hannah's apartment, which was empty with nearly all the furniture gone, the realization broke Beth's heart. Her friend stole twelve thousand dollars and fled without a word as to why.

After Beth filed the police report, she opened a new account at a bank down the street from the shop. She transferred some money from her personal account to cover the bills and deposited what the weekend had brought in, but it wasn't enough.

Rent was due, plus the upcoming expenses of supplies and employees salaries had to be paid, leaving only a few hundred dollars for Beth's personal needs. What was worse, Christmas was less than two weeks away. She wouldn't have enough money to cover their needs through the New Year if they didn't sell more baked goods.

Damn you, Hannah.

Beth assumed their friendship was tight. They'd known each other since their NIU days. How could she know of, or see through Hannah's treachery? Her parents were right. Hannah wasn't to be trusted. Admitting

George and Mary's keen perception about her partner grated at Beth's nerves. Their phone call hadn't helped either. Berating her choice was the last thing she needed to hear. They sneered at the news and said, '*We told you so*'.

She wanted—no, needed Sweet Cupids to survive. Her livelihood depended on it. No way was she going to ask her parents for help. Beth had to just suck it up and deal.

It had been four days since Hannah split, and every night Beth worried the shop earned enough revenue to stay afloat.

Beth leaned against the black marble frosting bar in the back of her bakery and wiped a runaway tear from her cheek. What the hell was she going to do?

"No more blubbering," Beth scolded herself while wiping away tears with her not-so-clean, floured apron.

Get a grip. You know you can do it.

A chime from the front door caught Beth off guard. *Crap.* She'd forgotten to lock it.

Beth quickly straightened and walked from the back room. "Sorry, we're closed. We'll be opened tomor…" Beth's words faltered the second she locked eyes with Bryce Landry.

Oh. My. God. Her breath hitched in her throat and her heart thrashed against her chest so hard that it hurt to breathe. Her college love stood just inside the doorway with a tentative smile across his handsome face. Even more attractive than when he left for Harvard, Bryce was the one who got away.

Sun-kissed blond hair, combed back as though he'd used his fingers. Beth always loved that disheveled look on him. His strong, squared jaw showed a five-o'clock shadow. And oh, his beautiful full lips, still very much kissable. She had dreamed many times of his mouth bearing down on her, on her body, and oh! The sex! That vision nearly made her moan right then and there. Of course, she stifled it.

"Hey, Bethie." Those two words pulled her out of her revelry. How she hated him calling her that.

However, his voice was just as deep and hypnotic as ever. His glorious blue eyes instantly woke the side of her she had hidden—no, packed up with duct tape and thrown into the deepest recesses of her mind.

Besides, it had been seven years, and she was over him. Well, maybe not quite so over him. Though enough that his charms weren't going to affect her. Anyway, it wasn't like they dated. They were only friends.

Yeah right, keep telling yourself that lie!

"Hi Bryce," she said in a rush, pushing her brown hair away from her face. "W-what are you doing here?" Beth barely got out the words, hoping he didn't catch the hesitation and the slight lust in her voice. Thank God the display counter sat between them.

How messed up crazy was this? From crying over her woes dealing with Hannah, to wanting to rip off her clothes and do him right on the floor. Beth clung to the hurt she had moments before to regroup herself.

Remember? He slept with your roommate Andrea? Beth's inner voice spoke up and jabbed at her. *Let's not add another log to the forest fire.*

"It's nice to see you too," he said smoothly, but there was a hint of bitterness in his tone. Bryce walked over to her while glancing around the shop. "Nice place. Very eclectic taste. I like the Beatles memorabilia."

What, more sarcasm? So what if she had a Beatles fetish. "Thanks. What are you doing here?" Her voice was slightly strained this time. Beth reached into her memory of their last night, which had filled her with ire and disappointment.

For a brief moment, Beth considered what had she done to deserve more torture in her life. She wanted to scream. Instead, she looked at Bryce's face, and saw exhaustion with a hint of worry. Her anger immediately defused. "Sorry. What can I do for you?"

The intensity in his baby blues studied right back into her muted brown eyes. "I heard about this fabulous place called Sweet Cupids from a colleague of mine. He raves about how good the desserts are here. So, I thought I should check the place out for myself because you know how much I love sweets. So I swung by and *saw you*," he said with a big smile. "How have you been?"

Beth swallowed hard at his sincerity. "I'm...good." *What a liar!*

"Okay." There were seconds of awkward silence before Bryce asked, "Are there any sweets left?" He pointed to the display case.

He knew damn well there were baked good left over. A blind man could see them, or smell them.

Clearing her throat, Beth walked behind the counter and pasted on the best smile she could muster. "Well, I do have a few mini caramel eclairs, three mascarpone brownies, and four of our decadent chocolate cupcakes left." She peered over at Bryce as he leaned closer to the glass case, eyes wide and needing a sugar fix.

"Ooh, chocolate cupcakes. Mmm. They all look good," he said, his eyes bouncing from Beth to the desserts. In that moment, his beautiful sculpted face still displayed a hint of his boyish charms. Just the way she remembered him.

Be professional, Beth. Kill him with your kindness!

His blazing eyes still produced that spellbinding effect, turning her core pulse hot and needy. Yet, her heart broke a little bit more as she admired his handsomeness. Most definitely, she wasn't over him.

It was bad enough that Hannah took off with all their money; now Fate struck again.

Here stood the man she had loved so many years ago, the man who had broken her heart. Beth had never really gotten over that—maybe never would.

She turned away and concentrated on the bake goods, so as not to burst her over inflated

emotional bubble.

What the hell was she doing to herself? She'd turn into a pathetic loser— a blubbery

mess—if she didn't get herself in check.

"Then what would you like?" she asked steadily, although her insides were a balled up mess of nervousness.

As Beth focused on the cupcakes, she remembered how they had first met in a coffee shop near campus, fighting over the last chocolate cupcake in the case. They ended up splitting it, while spending that afternoon laughing, talking, and getting to know each other. Oh God, how she missed him.

The way he quirked his brows when he was in deep thought. How he used to tap his index finger when he was nervous. Or when he got mad, especially at his brother, his blue eyes turned intense. And, oh how he smiled his impish grin at her whenever he'd stolen her cookies. Oh yeah, and he would take a lot. However, she always found money shoved in her Hello Kitty wallet—which she had always kept empty.

Beth missed him more than she could say. Though, when he walked off and screwed Andrea, she wanted nothing to do with him. The memory of that night sparked in her mind like a fuse. She had to tap the anger down. Yet, angry wasn't the word that best described Beth's reaction. No, she was downright fucking pissed. Hannah had stopped her from rushing into the room and beat the hell out of Andrea and Bryce. Even though Beth would have had great pleasure pummeling her roommate, she knew she'd regret it later. Instead, she left.

Even after seven years her traitorous body wanted Bryce.

Don't think about it. He didn't want you then and he doesn't want you now.

"I'll take all of it," he said, pulling her out of her sobering thoughts.

"What?" Beth swept a glance to his face, and froze. Bryce reached forward to brush something off her cheek. His fingers were so warm. A tingle fluttered across her skin, spreading fast through her body, causing her bones to melt.

"Flour," Bryce uttered with a chuckle. He dropped his hand but never looked away.

Thank God for the counter dividing them, or she would have thrown herself right into his arms and kissed him. Damn, he smelled so good—too good and even better than the sweets in front of her.

"What?" Beth shook her head to clear her damaged brain of Bryce.

"Flour on your cheek?"

"Oh, yes. I bake. I'm the baker." Beth closed her eyes. *You're babbling now.* "I'm mean—what do you want again?"

"I said I'd take it all." His voice dropped to a sexy whisper.

"Oh, okay." Beth sputtered out the words before quickly walking away. She needed a reprieve from the masculine scent drowning her senses. But when she returned with two boxes and began placing brownies and eclairs into the one of them, his mouthwatering spice began to mess with her brain again. Too late; she was drunk from the rich sandalwood, the same smell he'd had in college. There was no aroma on earth more intoxicating than the innate smell of Bryce. She slowly breathed in air and let it fill her lungs. Beth swallowed hard while her hands shook slightly at her appalling reaction to his cologne.

Get a grip!

Beth opened the other box and began filling it with the cupcakes. Her focus stayed on packaging the goodies so she wouldn't have to look at him.

Damn. Beth couldn't help it. She had to sneak a peek. When his lips bowed into a beautiful smile, she wondered if they were as tasty as they looked.

He's here for the desserts, not for you.

Hell, Beth wanted to slap her conscience's face for disrupting her wayward thoughts, but knew that reasoning to be true. She remained quiet while emptying the case.

"So…" He didn't finish the sentence. All he did was stare at her.

Was that all he could say? 'So'? The last time she saw him was the day he left for law school. She'd looked at him with utter anguish and walked away when he approached her. Beth never talked to him again, never asked why he slept with that slut.

"So," she echoed back.

"How long have you been open?" Bryce asked, he looked down and tapped his finger against the glass.

He was nervous. Why? And what's with the polite conversation? Okay. She could do that. "Three years."

"By yourself?"

She hesitated, shot him a hard stare, but said, "No. Remember Hannah Larson?"

"The tall redhead?" he asked with a furrowed brow. Bryce never liked her.

"Yes. We're partners." *Not anymore.*

"It's great to have friends you can count on, Beth." Bryce hesitated for a second before he continued. "You've come a long way from selling your cookies to owning your own bakery."

Friends? Look where she'd gotten to by trusting *friends*.

"Yeah. Great." Beth tried to keep the vehemence out of her voice, but a bit slipped out. She folded the box lids down, taped them carefully with gold oval Cupid's bow stickers, and slid them across to him.

"That will be twenty-five dollars even, please." The sooner he left, the better Beth could breathe.

"Really? That's it?" Bryce took the boxes, and handed her his black Amex card in return.

"It's the end of the day. So let's call it 'a friend's discount'," Beth said with a thin smile. Her gut twisted tight when she used the word *friend* in association with him. It was like telling a lie.

"Are you all right, Beth? I didn't want to ask, but when I walked in, you looked upset, like you've been crying."

Now he's asking me if I'm having a bad day? Men.

She swiped the card and handed it back to him. "No, I'm good. Really," she lied, again.

Her pasted smile slipped from her face. Of course she wasn't all right. From losing a so-called-friend who stole from their company and a so-called-friend who broke her heart all in one week, she was lucky her place hadn't burned down.

"I'm simply great." Far from great, but he didn't need to know that.

Beth slid a pen and the receipt over to him to sign. Bryce quickly scribbled his signature and passed it back. He reached inside his coat pocket and took out a card. "This is my business card. On the back is my cell number. Maybe we can have lunch some time, or even dinner."

Beth took a slight step back from the counter and stared down at the card as though it was kryptonite. She noticed the logo, *Landry & Associates*.

She knew the name well. Bryce's family owned the law office since the forties when his grandfather opened the firm. However, she had never thought Bryce would ever work with his family. Working for his family meant that he would have to be serious, like his father and his brother Mark. The pressure would be too much for Bryce to handle. He had emphasized that fact repeatedly in college. She guessed things had changed with him. Lots of things had changed.

"You went to work with your family? Mark, too?

A dark glaze of hurt ran across his face when she mentioned Bryce's twin brother, Mark.

"No." The word came as cold as the frigid winds outside.

Okay. "Oh." It was all she could say.

"So lunch or dinner?" His tone shifted back to light.

"Sure." *No way in hell, buddy, am I going anywhere with you.*

Bryce smiled, but this time it was weak and hadn't reached his eyes. He picked up the boxes and walked to the door. Just before he stepped outside into the cold December winter, he turned and said, "It was really good seeing you again, Bethie. And think about dinner. Please. We have way too much to talk about." He strode out, without another backward glance.

Beth raced to the door and locked it with shaky hands. She turned off the rest of the lights, trudged teary-eyed to her secluded office with the knowledge that her life truly sucked.

Chapter 2

Beth woke up about six a.m. the following morning with a hell of a headache. Tossing and turning all night, thinking about Bryce didn't help the cause. At least she wasn't thinking about Hannah anymore.

After popping two aspirins, she showered, drowned herself with a quick shot of espresso, and headed out to do her errands before going to Sweet Cupids.

Once she finished her shopping at the baking supply store, she dropped off the deposit at the bank and drove straight to the shop.

As she walked in, Gina Reynolds and Freddy Zamora, Beth's baking assistants, ran over and pulled her into the office. The two were talking to her at the same time.

Beth raised a hand up. "Wait. One at a time." She scanned the back room and interrupting them. "Who's watching the front?"

"Renee," Gina quickly replied.

Beth dumped her Vera Bradley purse bag onto the desk and sat down. "Do we have enough carrot cheesecake out in the display?" she asked while pulling off her red sheep skinned boots and tossed them in the corner of the room to dry.

Freddy nodded, but looked worried. Beth doesn't think it was about the cheesecake.

Gina waved fax sheets in her before she spoke, grabbing Beth's attention. "Do you see this? It's a new order for six dozen of each of our mini decadent chocolate cupcakes, mini caramel eclairs, and the bite size mascarpone brownies. And all by this Saturday." Gina took a squeaky breath and continued. "And six dozen of *Beth's cookies*. What are *Beth's cookies?*"

Beth choked on her own spit when Gina said Beth's cookies. *Bryce? No way!* "Who placed the order?"

"Landry and Associates," Gina replied with hesitancy.

"What are Beth's cookies? I didn't see that on our menu," said Freddy, his brows knit tighter. "Is it new?"

"No," Beth uttered, her heart was palpitating hard against her ribcage. She pushed herself off the chair, grabbed her Crocs, slipped them on and sat back down. She was having a hard time breathing.

"Are you okay, chica?" Freddy bent down and asked. He rubbed her shoulder. Beth loved Freddy to death. He was the gay friend all females need in their lives.

Beth gave a small nod, but she wasn't okay. Far from okay. How was she going to fill all these orders without killing herself? Plus, he wanted her cookies, too. She hadn't made them in many years, not since he left for Harvard.

"Breathe." Gina ordered.

"I'm okay. Let me see that fax." Beth grabbed the sheet out of her assistant's hand and scanned through the list. At the bottom of the list was Bryce's signature. "No way," she whispered in denial, shaking her head.

"Where is this place? Can we fill this order?" Freddy asked reading over Beth's shoulder.

"I think it's the large law firm off of Randolph," Gina explained.

"It is." Her stomach began to ache as an acrid taste slowly burned the back of her throat. Filling this order was near impossible—not with all the other orders she had to fill for the holidays. However, it would be great if she could. That meant she'd be able to pay off the suppliers and her employees without selling off her soul. But adding those damned cookies...she had to bake twenty-four hours straight to do it.

"Honey, are we going to be able to do this by Saturday? And what are Beth's cookies? How come we don't know about them?

Beth looked up at the two bewildered assistants and shook off her stupor. "Those were cookies I made in college and sold for extra money," she muttered, still in disbelief.

"Then why aren't they on the menu?" Gina asked.

"I don't want them on the menu." Beth bit out the words, but was instantly sorry. She stood and hugged Gina.

Freddy reached around and hugged them both. "I feel the love."

Beth laughed and pulled back. "I'm sorry for snapping at you, Gina. This is just so much."

Gina's light golden eyes behind her black-rimmed glasses glistened with tears. "I know."

"Okay. Now, what about the orders? Can we do it?" Freddy chimed in while he took the fax sheet out of Beth's hand and studied the list.

"We don't have a choice, do we?" Beth said with conviction. "It will help cover some of the loss of what..." Beth choked back Hannah's name. She wiped away the wetness stinging her eyes. "We have to do it."

"That's only giving us three days to put together five big orders, and one is for a wedding. And with only the three of us—"

"Shh," Freddy silenced Gina. "Beth, we can do this, but do we have enough supplies?"

"If we can get tomorrow's two orders out, the money we make will cover all the expenses for this weekend."

"Then we better shake our little culos fast," Freddy said, laughing while shaking his own rear. Beth adored Freddy's positive attitude. She needed it, especially today.

As much as she wanted to stay away from Bryce, he had inadvertently saved her ass by placing a large order. Saved it at least for the coming month.

For the rest of the day, Beth's mind strayed on and off Bryce, while Hannah's deceptions remained in the forefront as a reminder on why she had to hustle. It was quite crazy, and exhilarating at the same time. When she baked, the time spent mixing all the ingredients together always put her at ease—no matter the circumstances or how bad something turned out.

By the time Beth locked the front door, she could barely move her feet or arms. Her back felt strained, and her legs ached as she headed back toward the office. Halfway across the room, she heard something knocking on the glass. She paused, and her body tightened into a rigid pole. *I'm so not in the mood.*

Beth peered through the window and spotted Bryce with a beautiful smile on his face.

"Damn it," she groaned. Why was he here? Seeing him once was bad enough, but two nights in a row was going to drive her insane.

Reluctantly, Beth shuffled to the front door and opened it. "Come in," she said with a stale tone. She wasn't in the mood and didn't have the strength to debate whether she had time to talk to him. After he stepped inside, she locked the door and headed straight to the back, Bryce following her.

"I don't have anything left to sell you, Bryce." Beth uttered the words with a yawn. Her body hurt when she talked. She threw herself into her chair and leaned back.

"I'm not here to buy anything," he said in a chipper tone.

I hate you right now. Could he be any happier? If she had the strength, she'd smack the smile off his face. "Then why are you here?"

"Can't I come and visit my old friend?"

Beth raised a brow.

"Okay. Did you get my order for this Saturday's party?" He grabbed a chair from the corner and placed it in front of Beth.

"Short notice." Beth couldn't move, but her mouth still enough energy.

"I'm sorry, but once I tasted your cupcakes, I knew you were the only one I want to handle the sweet catering for our holiday party." He gave her another outstanding smile and his eyes sparked with mischief.

What had him so damned happy? Couldn't he see she was hurting?

"Thanks." Beth winced when she straightened in her chair. "Yes, we did receive the fax. I confirmed it with your secretary. So you should have asked her instead of wasting your time coming all the way here."

"I did." Bryce rubbed at his jaw before he spoke again. "I want to apologize for last night, too."

"What about?"

"When I asked you about your partner, I...um, didn't know about Hannah until this afternoon."

Beth shot him a incredulous look. "How did you find out about Hannah?"

"Mr. Robin Doyle."

Damn. One of her patrons. She'd asked him for legal counsel concerning dissolving her partnership. Beth had to go through all the details about the theft. "Mr. Doyle," she said with disappointment.

"Don't be mad at the man. He only wanted to help."

"So he came to you." No matter. Eventually, everyone was going to know what she had done. Beth sucked in a small breath before she answered. "That's fine. It's not your fault Hannah stole all the money and took off." Beth shook her head and began riffling through her pile of papers on the desk. It didn't matter how hard she tried to ignore him, Bryce's scent filled every corner of the small space. Besides, the office was way too tiny for Beth's liking. If her feet hadn't hurt so badly, she would have gotten up and walked out in a heartbeat.

Bryce's hand touched her knee and squeezed. "Beth, I don't want to pry, but how are you going to handle this situation?"

Beth glared at his hand, which he removed quickly. "Why? This doesn't concern you." God, she hated the fact that he knew her business. She didn't need Bryce adding to her emotional baggage.

Bryce straightened and gave her a devilish grin. "The same old Beth. Always on the defensive. I'm here to help you. As a friend, it's my right. You would do it for me."

"Are you sure about that?"

He leaned in, he brow cocked to one side. Oh, so gorgeous.

"Bryce. Thank you for thinking of me but there is nothing you can do for me." Beth folded her arms across her chest. At that moment, she was glad the chair had wheels because she was able to glide backwards away from him.

"Are you going to dissolve your partnership with Hannah?" He lost his smile, his eyes lost the sparkle. They turned hard with a hint of censure glazing them.

Beth leaned further back in the chair and dropped her eyes from his face. "Yes."

"Then you'll need my help," he said with certainty.

"I can't afford you," Beth blurted out and tried to salvage what she confessed. "I-I mean, l have a lawyer in the works." *Too late, Monroe. Bryce wasn't going to buy that.*

"You can't lie, Bethie. Your beautiful brown eyes show the truth."

Did he say beautiful? Holy crap. That luscious smile was back on his face, and his blue eye twinkled with absolute knowledge. How she wished she could reach out and kiss that man senseless and then kick him out for sticking his nose in her business.

No, Beth wouldn't or couldn't afford it, no matter how bad she wanted to kick him out. It wasn't in her nature to be mean. Yes, she could be a bitch, if she mustered enough courage. Though, at the moment bitchiness took too much energy and right now she barely had enough to finish totaling up tonight's receipts. How could she tell him she was barely getting by without degrading herself. Adding lawyer's fees would only drown her in more debt.

"I have a proposal," Bryce said with earnest, pulling papers out of his briefcase and placing them it front of her.

"What do you have in mind, Landry?" she asked, staring at a contract in front of her. Beth shifted her gaze from Bryce to the papers. "What is this?"

"We have some pro-bono work coming. I think you are the perfect candidate for it."

Beth paused, looked at him wide-eyed, and said, "Pro-bono?"

"Free, Bethie," Bryce explained sarcastically.

"Stop calling me that! And I know what pro-bono means," Beth bit back. "Why me?"

"Why not?"

"I'm sure there are people there who need it more than I do," Beth countered. She turned away from his rooted stare. *Focus on the receipts and not his gorgeous eyes!*

"Right now, I only see you, needing it more. Come on, Beth. Don't be so stubborn. Take the offer."

His words were like salvation to her ears, but something inside her made her skittish. "What else do you want?" Knowing full well how Bryce's mind worked, he had more to gain from this.

Bryce gave a chuckle. "You know me well."

"I guess I do." She gifted him a smile, though her stomach flipped as he drew near her.

"One dinner. I told you we have a lot to talk about."

Beth sat up straight, her face mere inches from his. "One dinner? That's it?" How brazen can she get? Initially she hadn't meant to get so close but once she locked eyes with his, she lost her control to think. "Bryce, there is nothing to talk about." Oh God. That came out breathy and wanting.

He inched closer. "Yes, there is a lot to talk about, Beth. One dinner and that pro-bono will be yours." She could feel his hot breath on her cheek, which made her nipples tighten into peaks. "Just one dinner, Beth," Bryce repeated in a rough and begging rasp.

The plea in his blue eyes was like a siren's call. The air surrounding them charged with desire. Her skin tingled, and from the way Bryce's pupils enlarged, he felt it too.

Beth's heart galloped, and her mouth went dry. How could she refuse the man she had loved so many years ago? If one dinner would get her the help she needed, then why not? One dinner with sexy Bryce Landry wasn't going to kill her. It might overload her with sexual frustration, but it was for a good reason.

"Fine. One dinner."

Chapter 3

Three days flew by so fast that Beth didn't have a chance to take a normal breath. At the end of each day, Bryce would come, buy up whatever she had left, which wasn't much, and stay late. He talked until she kicked him out.

It was annoying as hell, but at the same time, Beth enjoyed his company. Truly missed it.

Bryce did most of the talking. About Harvard and how it sucked being away from things that were familiar to him. He also talked about his grandfather, and how before he passed away, made Bryce promise to keep the traditions and help run the firm with his father with whom he butted heads constantly. What a sad choice, to sacrifice what you want for a promise.

However, Beth kept quiet on her opinions about Bryce's decision.

He briefly brought up about their friendship, but Beth quickly squashed it by asking about the holiday party on Saturday. He hadn't mentioned it again; he must have gotten the hint. Though deep down, she was disappointed that he hadn't pushed. Although, that night he had her attention when Bryce got so close, that if she had the guts, she'd lean in and kiss him. No, she hadn't had the guts to do it.

Disheartened by her own lack of courage, Beth focused on being friends again. Maybe she could learn to get forget the past. *Maybe.*

Beth wondered if he'd show tonight, what would happen. Probably nothing.

Bryce hadn't showed. It was a relief and a let down. Deep down, she was actually looking forward to seeing him. Yet, she knew nothing good would come from getting her hopes up, or the possibility of something *more*. What she might have felt back in college was just a strong now, but there would never be anything between them.

Still, with so much to do for Saturday, Beth needed to stay on task. If Bryce came, by the time she finished baking with the last batch of cookies, he would have eaten most of it.

Saturday came in a flurry, with the dusting of snow on the ground. The powder made driving dangerous, and those idiots that never took weather warnings to heart, skidded on the side of the road or against someone's bumper.

Driving from Hyde Park to the South Loop should have only taken fifteen minutes. Nonetheless, with the snow and the idiots, it added another twenty.

Once Beth arrived at the shop, Freddy and Gina were at her side, ready to start the morning off right. The shop itself was busy. With two additional helpers working the front, Beth and her assistants divvied up the baking and packaging duties. They were able to complete four orders with a few hours to spare.

While Freddy and Gina delivered the two big wedding orders in Naperville and Englewood, Beth sent one of the helpers with a hired driver to deliver the two large office party orders in the city. It was worth the hundred and fifty bucks. And if he returned before her assistants, she'd throw in another hundred to deliver Bryce's order. She hoped Freddy and Gina came back first. It would save her that hundred, and she trusted them to set up the table without her.

Envisioning Bryce all decked out was the last thing she wanted. If he got close to her, Beth wasn't sure if she had enough courage to walk away from him. He was simply irresistible, dressed in a three piece suit.

Damn! Beth still couldn't believe she'd agreed to Bryce's one dinner proposal. She wondered when he was going to ask her out. It was kind of driving her crazy.

Nevertheless, if going to dinner with him was the most painful event of the year, then she'd pull herself together with a smile on her face and go. No matter, she was still dreading it.

Suck it up, buttercup! Hannah's words echoed off Beth's brain. Why, out of the all people she knew, would Hannah's chortled voice ring in her head? What had she done in this life for this crap to happen to her? Maybe just being Beth Monroe, third child—a misfit, and a loner.

Stop feeling sorry for yourself, and do what you do best! Beth shook off her pessimistic musing and concentrated on wrapping the rest of the desserts for the Bryce's party.

After filling up the last box, Beth got a call from the delivery driver. Unfortunately, he'd gotten into a car accident on the way back to the shop and wouldn't be able to make back in time take the last order.

Holy Crap. She had to do it.

Dreading the fact that she might bump into Bryce, she sucked back the discord in her mind and loaded up her minivan to drive to Wells, where DiNucci's restaurant was located. After she left a voice message on both assistants' phones to hurry, she locked up the shop and headed out.

With the shitty evening traffic, it took nearly forty-five minutes to get there. Thank God, the snow melted or she'd be late.

At least one thing went Beth's way. She found a close parking spot and immediately took it. She had about an hour to set up the dessert table. Beth hoped Freddy and Gina would arrive soon, or it was going to be nearly impossible to finish on time.

So why was she dawdling in the car? Fear of Bryce Landry? Most definitely.

Beth was beginning to hate herself for feeling all those boxed up emotions she had stowed away for so long. Why hadn't she told him how he had hurt her for sleeping with slutty Andrea on his last night of school? He was supposed to be with her.

She took a couple deep breaths to calm rush of anxiety pushing back into her head.

This was only a job. She had to look at it that way to keep her sanity.

Furthermore, the thought of seeing Bryce in his element made a shiver raced up her spine. *Damn.* More unwanted emotions flooded her as she tried to push down the longing that had wrapped around her as tightly as a constricting boa.

A knock on the car window scared the crap out of her. Beth looked up and saw Gina and Freddy standing there. A thunderous relief rushed through her as she hopped out of the car and hugged the two in a hard arm lock. "I love you guys. Thanks for getting here quickly," she said in a teary voice.

"We got here as fast as we could," Gina said while he pulled away. "Freddy tried to call you, but you didn't answer your phone."

"Crap." Beth released her hold and began to laugh. A level of calm seeped into her, she was able to think clearly. "I rushed out and left the phone on the back bar."

"Again." Freddy shook his head. Long strands of black hair fell forward into his face; he quickly pushed them back with both hands.

"Lets not ponder on that now. We have less than an hour to set up."

"No problem, boss," Gina said jokingly. She walked around the back of the vehicle, with Freddy close behind her, and opened the trunk. They each picked up several boxes of baked goods. Beth grabbed the last four boxes and made her way inside, with her assistants following right behind. After the hostess led them into the main dining room, they started setting up the dessert tables.

With only the last few boxes left to open, Freddy called to Beth. "Beth's cookies?" He lifted a large, thick chocolate chip cookie between his fingers.

Beth could feel the heat rush up to her cheeks. "Yes."

"They're only chocolate chip, right?" Gina asked speculatively. She took the cookie out of Freddy's hand and split in half. She gave him one half while she took a bite out of the other.

Freddy bit into his and said with adoration, "Oh, Dios mio. Chocolate chips. Yum. You need to add this to our menu, chica."

Gina narrowed her eyes at Beth. "I want the story, Beth." The real one." She called out loudly.

Beth looked around and waved her hands to quiet down Gina. "I'll explain later. Right now let us finish this and get the hell out of here before the guests arrive. All right?"

Gina and Freddy looked at each other, then to her and nodded in agreement.

With five minutes to spare, they finished. The tables now bore a smorgasbord of delectable treats.

While Beth's assistants cleaned up and put their equipment back into the minivan, she made sure everything was in the right place. The holiday colors of the decorative desserts coordinated with the party's theme. Bright greens, ruby reds, and glistening silvery white adorned every corner of the hall. The desserts would be just as memorable as the room itself.

Taking a few steps back to admire her display, Beth heard a deep raspy voice call her name. She didn't have to be told it was Bryce entering the room from behind her. She straightened her shoulders, gathered up her courage, and turned. Much to her dismay, he looked more delicious than any dessert at her display.

Bryce walked up to her in a stylish black suit and blood red tie, took her hand, and kissed it.

"You smell delectable," he whispered. He wiggled his brows at her and smiled. She tried to pull away but instead, he pulled at her gently and led her to a couple standing a few feet behind him. "Mom. Dad. This is my dear friend from college, Beth Monroe. She made all the desserts for the party."

Dear friend? Beth guessed at one time they were, but not now. Not really. Seven years apart, and a sleeping with a slut had ended their friendship.

Every second she stood there, more people were entering the spacious, decorated room. Women dressed in elegant gowns and men in suits, and what was she wearing? Her baking wear. White baggy pants with matching lapelled top, partially buttoned of course. And her brown hair scrunched up into a messy bun on the top of her head. Beth stuck out like a well ripen banana amongst the pristine fruit.

"It's nice to meat you, Mr. and Mrs. Landry." She wiped her hand on her shirt before she shook their hands. She caught their adverse looks on their faces and continued. "Have a wonderful evening and I hope you enjoy the desserts." Beth tried to slip away before Bryce tried talking her into staying. Yes, she was way out of her element.

"Don't leave," Bryce urged, grabbing her hand.

"I don't belong here." She pulled her hand out of his, stepping away from him.

"Yes, you do."

The sincerity in his voice made Beth shiver. "I wish I could, but I can't. I'm not dressed for the occasion." *Good excuse, Monroe.* She turned away, her feet closing the gap to the door.

"Wait, I have to pay you," Bryce called out. He followed her outside.

"Beth? Beth Monroe?" A man called out from a royal blue Lexus GS F.

Beth looked up and saw Mark Landry coming out of the luxury car. He was still as handsome as ever, but not nearly as gorgeous as Bryce.

"Mark," Beth said with a smile. She stepped out into the cold and met him half way.

Mark walked up, wrapped his arm around Beth, and gave her a fierce hug. He loosened his arm but kept his left arm around her waist.

"Beth Monroe. How the hell are you? Still as beautiful as ever," he flirted with his eyes, perusing her body from head to toe. Beth caught onto his game in college and made it perfectly clear she didn't want to play.

"Good. How about you, Mark?" she asked, craning her neck up at him. He was at least a head and neck taller than her, but only few inches taller than Bryce.

Bryce and Mark weren't identical twins. Where Bryce had dark blonde hair with blue eyes, Mark had rich brown hair with green eyes. They were almost polar opposites in attitude, too. Mark was the serious one in college, where Bryce had a carefree demeanor...until his father pressured him to go to Harvard. They both had one thing in common. Terrible tempers.

"So far so—"

"Let her go, Mark," Bryce growled. He carried his hands in fists at his sides and his complexion reddened with anger—no, absolute fury.

Whoa. Beth hadn't seen Bryce's fiery anger in such a long time that it made her immediately nervous. "What's wrong, Bryce?" she asked, trying to step back from his brother. But Mark held her tight.

"Hey, bro," Mark responded smoothly, albeit with a hint of trepidation in his tone. "Let's keep it cool. At least for tonight."

"I said, let her go." Bryce took a step forward. His eyes became blue steel.

Mark released Beth, urging her to the side, and stood directly in front of his brother. His smile faltered. "I don't want to do this here, Bryce."

"Bryce, what is going on?" Beth demanded. She took another step back and waited for either one of the brothers to answer. But neither did. The anger from Bryce rolled off him with palpable intensity; his disposition scared the crap out of her.

"Go, Beth," Bryce hissed out. "I'll call you tomorrow." He looked at her for a split second and returned his attention back to Mark. "We need to talk," he said lethally.

"If *talking* is what you want, then yes, I'll talk," Mark countered. "But if you want to fight, here and now isn't the time for it."

Beth wanted to stop whatever was going on between the brothers, looking at Bryce and Mark's hardened faces, she decided against it. Against her better judgment, she listened to Bryce and turned around and rushed to the minivan.

Freddy and Gina were hiding behind the vehicle. Her voice dropped to a whisper. "I'll talk to you two later." She ushered them to go, clicked the lock and hopped in and left without looking back.

The whole time, worry filled her. The brothers were not all right. Not knowing the root of Bryce's anger aimed toward Mark, Beth hoped they didn't end up fighting and ruining the party their parents had set up for the company. Back in college, they had each other's backs. But now, Bryce was ready to rip Mark's head off. Oh God, she hoped it wouldn't come down to that.

Beth took in a deep breath as she slid into traffic on the Kennedy. It wasn't her business why the brothers were fighting. She had enough garbage going on her life. But as she tried to push aside the needless worry, she also hoped Bryce would be all right. She wanted to pick up her cell phone and call him, but remembered she'd left the phone back at the shop. *Idiot.*

Why was she worrying about Bryce so much anyway? He was a grown man and could take care of himself. While trying to put the image of Bryce getting thrashed out of her mind, she pulled up behind the shop and saw the back door wide open.

Chapter 4

Beth wanted to dial nine-one-one, but her scattered brain finally cleared enough to remind her the cell phone was in the shop. Next time she was going to buy a cell phone with Velcro attachments.

Looking around the minivan, she eyed the long black flashlight on the floorboards on the passenger side. Hannah had made her buy it a few years back for protection. It wasn't much use as a flashlight since the batteries went out on it a year ago, but...it was heavy enough to crack any intruder's skull.

Holding it with a firm grip in her right hand, Beth quietly got out of the van and slowly made her way inside. All the lights were off, except for her office. The sound of papers rustling made Beth question what kind of robber would look through paperwork. There was enough equipment around her to pawn off for some decent cash. There was nothing valuable in the office—not even the four-year old computer with a cracked keyboard sitting on her desk.

Eyeing her cell phone at the other end of the counter, Beth slowly glided by the office, then stopped suddenly when she saw a mop of red hair bobbing over the computer screen.

Hannah.

Crap. All the anger that had built up in the past two weeks surged forward and channeled itself onto the redhead. Tightening her grip on the flashlight, Beth charged into the office and screamed, "What the hell are you doing here!"

Hannah stumbled back, knocking her head against the wall. "Ouch," she sputtered as she rubbed her left temple. "You scared the shit out of me, Beth!"

"How did you get in here?" Beth shouted while pointing the flashlight at her ex-friend.

"With my key," Hannah yelled back. "Now stop screaming at me, Beth. I have a headache now. And will you lower that flashlight before you decide to bash my face in." A great idea. Yet, Beth would never do something so horrid and pushed that thought out of her head.

"Your key?" she said incredulously. *Oh Crap.* With all the things she had to deal with, it was the last thing she thought about. "Why are you here, Hannah? There's no money left for you to steal," Beth barked out but with little less bite.

"I'm not here for money." Hannah dropped down into the chair and stared at Beth. "I am looking for my mother's bracelet and ring. I left them here a month ago on this desk." Beth heard condescension in her voice as she pointed at her. Hannah had no right to be bitchy to her. "Where did you put them?"

Was she accusing Beth of stealing the jewelry?

"I don't know what you're talking about. I know for a fact there is no jewelry here. So why don't you tell me the truth, Hannah."

Hannah slumped back in the chair, pulled out one of the side drawer and gasped. "What the fuck is this?" In her grasp was a sandwich bag with a gold bracelet and a ruby ring inside it.

The second Hannah had the clear plastic bag in her hand, Beth remembered Gina was in the office having lunch about a month ago and found them lying on the floor.

"You should thank Gina for that. She was the one who put them there for safe keeping," Beth bit out. She settled against the door and exhaled.

"Why are you here? You could have called. Instead, you come here—sneaking around—I could have called the cops."

"No you wouldn't. You left your cell phone on the counter," Hannah answered with a self righteous smirk on her face. "Well, since you're here, we should talk."

"What about?" Oh, how you stole all of our hard earned cash and then took off without a word?" Beth straightened and took a step toward Hannah and pointed the flashlight at her. "I trusted you, with everything. What made you do this?"

"You." It came out sharp, like a honed knife. "I wanted out of this business two years ago, but I was afraid to hurt your feelings."

"Poor fucking excuse. My feelings had nothing to do this, so try again." Beth snapped back. She wasn't about to back down. Hannah had always been selfish, but now she knew just how much.

Knowing full well Hannah wasn't a threat, Beth put the flashlight down on the desk but kept it close, just in case she was wrong.

Hannah straightened and cleared her throat. "Seriously, Beth. This is your livelihood, not mine. I only went along with it hoping to be a silent partner, and recoup my cash fast until you can buy me out. God, three fucking years, Beth, and the shop is still going strong and more demanding." She raked her fingers through her hair. "I knew I had to help, but you expect so much more out of me than I was willing to give. But I'm your friend, so I went along with it until I couldn't stand it any longer."

"Then why didn't you come talk to me. I would have bought you out. Of course, I couldn't give you all of the money right away, but in a year or so, we would have been even."

"I tried many times to talk to you, but you're so busy that the few times I did, you brushed me off. 'We'll talk later'. Well, it's later Beth, and I'm done."

From the moment they had opened up the shop, Sweet Cupids began growing fast, building a great reputation for servicing parties and events with their delectable desserts. Had she known her friend wanted out, Beth would have found away to do it. She was her friend after all. Or at least she thought she was.

"Hell yeah, I was super busy—still am. Baking early morning—all times of the day. I also sort and packaged up the desserts. But I can't believe that you couldn't grab my full attention?" Beth would never intentionally ignore Hannah. "If it was that important to you, I would have listened."

"Well, you didn't, and I wanted all the cash owed to me." Hannah wouldn't look at her.

"So, you didn't want to settle for payments." Beth wasn't going to beat around the bush.

Hannah stared down at the floor and stayed quiet. Beth knew she hit the mark. "I'm sorry it had to come to this, but Beth, I need the money. Trent and I are getting married. With the cash from the shop, we'll be able to move to California and start a new life."

"Hannah, there were better ways to get my attention. Stealing the money and taking off isn't right choice. I was worried for your life, thinking someone had you at gunpoint and made you do it."

"I'm fine."

"I see that. Why didn't you just drag me out of whatever I was doing and yell and scream at me?"

Hannah shook her head. "I'm tired of discussing this, Beth."

Beth's clarity about their friendship and partnership stung hard and sharp like a swarm of wasps. She was nothing to Hannah, and that was how she had to handle this situation.

Beth's spine stiffened and took an even breath before she spoke. "Okay. Now that I know your true feelings about the business, the money you took will make up two-thirds of what I owe you. With that, I will pay back the six thousand within one year, on a monthly basis." She raised her hand to stop Hannah from interrupting. "I know it's less than the cost you brought into the partnership, but for the hassle you brought to Sweet Cupids, you'll take the offer. And, I won't bring charges against you for stealing the money."

"You can't do that. I'm part owner," Hannah stood up and hissed in her face.

"Remember Hannah, we are an LLC. We are employees of Sweet Cupids. You stole from the company," Beth countered right back in her face.

The realization hit the redhead fast. Hannah's bloodshot, green eyes widened. "Oh, shit. Beth…" Her words trailed off in a choked cry. "You filed charges against me?"

"Like I said, I will drop the charges if you agree to my demands. It's more than fair."

"Fine," Hannah countered through clenched teeth.

"Good. I'll have the papers drawn up in a few days. Where can I reach you to sign them?"

"Just call my cell. I'm staying with Trent until we leave for California next week."

Beth stepped back, and gave Hannah room to leave. "Fine." Beth said, extending her hand. Hannah looked at it for a second with a pinched frown and went to shake it, but Beth shook her head and uttered, "Key."

With a single nod of understanding, Hannah pulled out her key and handed it over to Beth. "I'll hear from you in a few days?" There was a note of resolved admission in her question.

"Yup." Beth folded her arms at her chest and watched her ex-friend and partner clutching the plastic bag to her chest and walk out of the shop.

With resounding relief and a bit of scorched sadness settling over her, Beth collapsed against the desk and huffed out a few deep breaths. Even though Hannah's reason for stealing the money was somewhat asinine, Beth couldn't blame her any more than she could blame herself for being a careless partner. They both should've handled things differently. Admittedly, she would miss Hannah. After all the outlandish things they done in college and opening Sweet Cupids, it was sad their friendship was over.

However, Beth couldn't wait until Hannah signed the agreement and finalize the dissolution of their partnership. Once done, Hannah would be out of her life for good.

After Beth got her bearings back, she noted to herself to get a locksmith as soon as possible to change all the locks. She straightened up her desk, grabbed her cell phone and Bryce's number, locked up and left.

In the car, Beth flipped open the phone and noticed no calls came in. Worry began to seep into her as she debated on call Bryce, or wait to call him tomorrow.

Exhausted, she decided to wait.

On the ride home, Beth wondered what he was doing? Was he okay? The look on his face had been a bit scary. She had seen him mad, but never to the point of fury blazing in his eyes and directed in such deadly manner at Mark.

As Beth pulled up to her flat on Paulina Street, her headlights flashed across the stairs and she spotted Bryce. He was hunched over on the top steps.

How long had he been waiting for her? The overhead light cast an eerie glow over his face when he looked up.

One look at his face and panic filled her.

Chapter 5

What the hell? Beth quickly parked and ran to his side. "Bryce, what happened?" she frantically asked as she lifted his chin. A nervous shudder went through her as she examined his beaten face. Pain, deep and enraged reflected in his blue eyes.

A closer look, his left eye was swollen, with black and blue bruising extending to the temple and a small laceration cutting through his left brow. His top lip was split, and the knuckles on his right hand were all bloody.

"Who did this to you?"

"Mark," he growled. He pulled away from her touch and let out a groan.

"Oh, Bryce," Beth muttered with regret. She shouldn't have left them alone. Deep down, she knew this would happen. "Come on." She pulled at his arm, helped him up and led him to her apartment on the top floor.

Beth quickly opened the door and urged Bryce to the blue couch. She ran into the bathroom and retrieved her green fix-all box. It had bandaids of all sorts and sizes, ointments, disinfectant cleansers, and an assortment of pain pills. Hey, a girl had to be prepared for anything, and Beth always was.

After Beth moistened a washcloth, she headed back to Bryce, who was still standing. She nudged him to sit down on the sofa and began cleaning his wounds.

"You have a lot of Beatles crap." Bryce winced when she wiped at his jaw. "Shit, that hurts."

"I barely touched you," she said incredulously. "And beside, that's what you get for saying my Beatles collection is crap." She gave him a frown, but couldn't help smile at the way he bowed his lips.

"Sorry."

"I forgive you, but only this once." She let out a soft chuckle but had to ask why he was fighting with Mark. "Bryce, what happened? Why were you two fighting?"

He pulled away and looked at her. "Mark had no right pawing you." His words were simple, but Beth knew there had to be more. Bryce wouldn't look the way he did, otherwise.

"Bryce—"

"No, Beth. That man-whore will not touch you again." His clipped words demanded no arguments for her. But that wasn't Beth. She'd argue until she got what she wanted.

"Bryce, I know there is more to it than Mark hugging me. So spill it," Beth declared.

He eyed her with a look that only could be described as annoyance. Pulling his hand out of hers, Bryce said, "About a year and a half ago, I was engaged to Brittany Manning. She was the daughter of one of my father's closest friends and business associates." He laughed, got up from the couch with a groan. Pain lanced across his face, he walked over to window and looked out. "Fuck. This wouldn't have happened if I didn't give my word to my grandfather."

"What does your grandfather have to do with your engagement?"

"If I didn't agree to work with my father, I wouldn't have met Brittany, and Mark and I would still…"

"Be close." Beth finished his sentence. A knot formed in his throat when she knew damn well Bryce missed his brother. They were twins. The deep bond between them was broken over a woman, was simply sad.

"Did you know we were supposed to be married six months ago?" Regret coated his question.

"No, I didn't." Beth wanted to run over and wrap her arms around him, but she didn't move. He stood by the window, straight and stiff, his hands touched his face, wiping away any unseen tears.

"I *thought* we loved each other until…one night, I came home and found her fucking another guy."

The tortured strain in his voice made Beth tear up. Her heart hurt like a dull knife was plunged right through it. She had felt a similar agony herself once, seven years ago when Bryce slept with Andrea. However, she wasn't going to mention that, and it wasn't on the same level as his betrayal.

"What happened?" Beth asked, as she walked over to him and touched his forearm.

Bryce slowly turned around, his broad shoulders slumped and his eyes glistening with tears. Beth hated to see a grown man cry. She reached up and touched his cheeks.

He covered her hand with his, leaned slightly into her touch, and pulled away.

"I was supposed to work late that night, but luckily…" Bryce took a deep breath and continued. "I got done with a client and left the office a few hours earlier than what I had told Brittany. We had a place on Waldon, not too far from work. That time of the evening, it took me about twenty minutes to get to the condo." He stopped talking, shook his head, and faced Beth fully.

He looked right at her—or right through her.

Beth knew what he was going to say. She said for him. "The guy you found with Brittany was Mark."

Bryce huffed out a laugh. "Oh yeah. And in my bed too, of all the fucking places." He pinched his eyes closed, as though to push the image away from his mind. He opened them and said, "Do you know what that bastard said to me right before I kicked his ass?" He didn't let Beth answer. "That asshole had the audacity to tell me that Brittany seduced him—like that makes a big fucking difference. He's my brother. He should have pushed her away—walked away—something." His voice strained with hatred. "And this was the kicker, my father wanted me to forgive Brittany and take her back."

"Seriously?" Beth couldn't believe it.

"I told him, if he wanted to be in bed with the Manning group, then he should sleep with Brittany. I'm sure she wouldn't turn him away."

"I'm so sorry, Bryce." It was all Beth could say as he tried to collect himself. Love sucked. And they both knew it. "So what did your father say?"

"He threatened to fire me. And I told him to go ahead—Fuck!" He raked his hair back and paced the floor. "But do you know what was more surprising about all this shit? Yes, their betrayal hurts like a son-of-bitch—still does, when it comes to dealing with my brother. But I realized I never loved Brittany—not the way I should. She was beautiful, charming, and had the right connections my father liked. And I have to admit, we had chemistry in the bedroom. But outside the bedroom, there was nothing. We had nothing in common. I knew deep down it would have never worked for us. We didn't have the connection, like how you and I had."

He got close. Maybe a little to close that she couldn't think straight. Beth swallowed hard at his admission. She didn't know how to react or what to say.

He started to laugh, stepped back and wiped his eyes. "Shit, I'm crying." He ran both hands over his face and combed his fingers back through his hair. "Why did you stop talking to me seven years ago? What did I do to piss you off?"

Bryce's question threw Beth off guard. "What?" Stunned, she felt her eyes go wide.

He leaned in, mere inches touching her and said, "The day I left for Harvard, I knew you were pissed at me. I want to know why?"

Beth backed away, almost stumbling over the grey ottoman. "You did nothing. I was…just upset you were leaving, and I couldn't face you." The lie sounded good when the words came out. Her throat hurt like hell, though when she spoke.

"You're lying, Beth. You know I can tell." Bryce reached up and touched her cheek, caressing her heated skin with his thumb. "Tell me, please."

Oh God, she wanted to lean into his touch and envelope herself in his warmth. Instead, she side stepped the ottoman and settled herself on the couch.

The small knot in her chest grew into a boulder. It hurt to breath, but she barely managed. Would telling him the truth be worth digging up her heartbreak? No. It wasn't worth the pain.

And looking back, she'd been down right ridiculous about how she reacted. The petty jealousy came from the insecurities of a girl who loved a boy who had no clue about her feelings for him. Her spite ruined a wonderful relationship with Bryce and now that he was back in her life, Beth didn't want to lose his friendship. Beth lost one friend, and she didn't want to lose another. Her heart couldn't take another crushing blow from his rejection.

Besides, nothing good came from dredging up the past.

"It was nothing, Bryce. I was being petty. Childish and stupid."

"I care for you, Beth. I always have. Now, tell me why you were angry?"

He cared for her? Maybe as a friend. Although, her heart leapt a little at his affirmation.

Bryce had no clue how much she loved him—still loved him. She had to tell him the truth or it would eat her inside out. *Here goes.* "I wanted to spend more time with you that last night before you left for Harvard. I...I wanted to give one piece of me that I hadn't shared with anyone else. And when I saw you leave with Andrea, I...I got mad." She felt a tear trailing down her cheek. "Really mad." She couldn't look at him when he reached her side. The memory and the hurt flooded her like acid, and melted deep into her bones.

Bryce traced the tear with his thumb, which sent tiny shivers of want through Beth, but she tampered it down.

"What were you going to give me?" he asked in a choked whisper. He knew damn well what she was talking about. They were best friends. He knew all her secrets.

Beth couldn't talk for a moment, afraid that what would come out of her mouth would sound right, but shook off the panic. "Doesn't matter anymore. I don't have it to give. Anyway, it was too late. You slept with Andrea and I have to get over that."

His eyes went wide. "Where did you get the idea that I slept with Andrea?"

"She was mauling you on the couch and then you left with her." Beth's voice cracked in response.

Bryce gave her a level stare and drew into her, molding their bodies together. Oh crap, he had her right where she always wanted to be. Beth's heart felt like it was racing right out of her chest. *Don't look into his eyes. You will lose.*

"What are you doing?" Beth tried to pull away, but his fingers locked behind her back and wouldn't let go.

"So you saw me leave with Andrea and assumed that I slept with her?" His lips brushed along her ear. His words came out soft with an underlying note of anger disbelief. "You know what assuming makes a person."

Beth pushed at his chest. "I know damn well what an ass I have been, but…" Beth's trailed as her splayed fingers rubbed against his hard pectorals. Damn. The contact generated so much heat that her body was consumed with fire. "I…I—"

"Answer me, Beth. Where did you get that conclusion? "There was no denying this man. The gentle grasp of his hands around her body made her melt, but his heard words made her spine stiffen.

"Well, didn't you?" Beth blasted back. This time she pushed him away, out of his reach. She glared at him. His beautiful sexy grin had Beth thinking twice about her anger. Damn it. She was letting her fears of getting hurt rule her actions again. She took a breath and closed the gap between them. "I'm sorry. I shouldn't have shoved you like that, especially since you got beat up."

"First things first, I didn't get beat up, I did the ass beating. Second, don't say sorry for how you feel. I'm the one who should say sorry."

Did he mean that? Beth wasn't sure because of the way his wicked gleam in his eyes said something totally different. Oh man, she was in trouble.

"Since we are telling truths…Honestly, it was my intentions that night, until I saw you." He paused and reached for Beth's hand. He brought it to his lips, locking eyes with hers and kissed her palm. He had her breathless again. A surge of electricity zapped through her hand, up her arm, and spread through her body charging every nerve ending.

"When did you see me?" Beth could help sounding breathy. Those handsome blue eyes of his had her hypnotized. Her panties became wet and her sex thrummed for his touch. She was afraid to move.

Bryce lowered her hand, but kept a hold of it. Never taking his somber eyes from her face, he said, "I was drunk, and Andrea suggested we head up to her room for some fun. About half way there, in the hallway, I saw a picture of you and me wrapped together, arm and arm at Lincoln Park. Remember that day?"

"Yeah. It was the summer going into our senior year. You came for a visit, and we went to lunch at Lou's and walked around the zoo," Beth remembered that day as though it happened yesterday. It was one of the best day of her life.

"And the guy who took our pictures didn't know how to use the camera on your phone." Bryce laughed. "Beth, you never told me you printed that picture."

Slight guilt filtered in her, washing more of her fear away. "That picture is my favorite." She was barely audible.

He gave her smile and finished. "Well, I saw that picture and it stopped me. I couldn't help but stare at you. Your smile and your beautiful sparkling brown eyes were focused on me while I stared at the goofy Chinese man. And I knew in that moment if I slept with Andrea, our friendship would be over. So I told her no. But, apparently I lost you anyway." He released her hand and stood back.

He thought her eyes were beautiful? Beth was going to cry again by his confession—by all of his confession. "So…you didn't sleep with slutty

Andrea that night?"

"Slutty Andrea?" He laughed again. "Nope," he said with a sensual lilt. His eyes had a beguiling gleam with a hint of mischief in them. She couldn't help but laugh also.

Beth also couldn't help ogling his kissable lips. Oh, how she wished she could feel them on her skin.

"So, why did you assume I slept with slutty Andrea?" he asked, pulling her out of her naughty thoughts.

Beth pinched her lips for a second and said, "Hannah said she saw you leaving Andrea's room the following morning..." Beth's words trailed off. "Hannah lied to me, didn't she?" There was even more contempt for her ex-friend. "I should have know—I knew she liked you too, but I never thought she would stoop this far to screw me over. First you, and then Sweet Cupids."

Bryce closed the gap, leaving a scant of space between them. "I looked for you that night, but Hannah told me you left with some guy. She'd tried on several occasions to kiss me too, but I pushed her away. I never really liked her. She always used you, Beth." Bryce paused for a second and said, "So who was the guy?"

"There was no guy, except..." Beth smiled in amusement. "She was probably talking about the taxicab driver. Hannah had called a cab for me and he drove me to the Marriott down the street."

"I think Hannah was jealous of you," Bryce declared.

"I doubt that. But you know what? Right after I left you tonight, I headed back to the shop to retrieve my cell phone, and I found the back door open."

"Hannah? Did you call the cops?" Bryce took her hands and led her to the couch. He sat down next to her. His touch jumpstart her heart into a frantic race. Her head was spinning with growing need.

"Yes and no. No cell phone," she muttered ruefully.

"What happened?" Bryce asked, pushing the loose strands of her hair behind her ears. She loved the slight sizzle from his touch on her lobe.

"I scared her when I caught her rifling through my office. Then she started to give me a load of crap about why she was there, and finally, after not backing down—and by the way, you would have been proud of me, Hannah spilled about how she only went into business for a quick buck. And of course, she blamed me for not listening. So if you can, like by Tuesday, have the papers drawn up saying whatever Hannah had taken from the account and a third more will be her final payment one year from now."

"Are you sure you don't want to press charges?"

"No. I just want her out of my life," Beth said wholeheartedly.

"Okay. I will modify the dissolution of the partnership and make sure she can't come back for more."

"Thank you," Beth whispered as her thoughts began to drift to their connected hands.

"Well, Beth. Now that that's settled, we've come to another dilemma of our own," Bryce said, wrapping his arms around her waist and pulling her closer.

She let out a ragged breath. "What's that?" His lips were mere inches from hers.

"How many times am I going to make love to you?"

Chapter 6

Did she hear him correctly? "What?"

He leaned in and kissed her, tasting every inch of her mouth. Oh God. His lips were soft, warm, and slightly hesitant. Beth couldn't help but let out a yearning moan. She leaned in and deepened the kiss.

"Bryce." His name slipped out of her mouth like a vow.

"Beth, I want you—I've always wanted you." Bryce's hands stroked her arms, caressing them up and down and then shifting to her back, pulling her in for a long, drugged kiss that left her dizzy and wanting.

The gentleness of his hands on her body made her lean into him. His mouth—tongue sent delicious tremors through her to the point of near climax. She'd wanted this man for so long, and now he was here—right in front of her, kissing and touching her like it was his calling.

"Say yes." The words barely came out audible.

Beth pulled back and looked up at him. She knew exactly what he wanted from her. "Yes."

He didn't hesitate and claimed her mouth again with a carnal, almost desperate declaration. His tongue swept inside her mouth, ravenous and needy, so visceral.

She was desperate for his touch. Without hesitation, their mouths still connected, they stripped out of their clothes in a frenzied rush until Beth could only feel skin. Bryce fell back onto the sofa, bring Beth with him.

Chest to chest, Beth savored the heat of his skin. She ran her fingers through the crisp hairs on his chest, which also tickled the tight buds of her nipples.

Beth hungered for a taste of his skin. She trailed kisses along his throat, collarbone, and down to his chest. His nipples drew tight as she suckled them one at a time, all the while gliding her hands down to the base of his enormous shaft.

Her fingers wrapped tight around his length and moved in a slow, even rhythm.

Bryce hissed out with pleasure. "You're going to kill me if I don't get inside you now."

He pulled her hand away, pressed his rigid erection up against her pelvis, and rocked back and forth. "I want you to taste me." His voice went rough and guttural, like he was in pain.

Beth couldn't help but grin. She made him feel this way, crazy and lustful. Satisfaction flowed through her, knowing she was the source of his pleasure.

Feeling even more daring, she slid down his body while grazing her breasts against his hot skin, feeding off the friction of electricity between them. Bryce let out a low moan as she slid her tongue down his chest, his hard abs, laving her way to the junction of his thighs.

When Beth got to her knees, between Bryce's legs, she focused on the object she most desired. With a gentle grip around his erection, she dipped down and kissed the head. A milky pearl drop of fluid formed on the tip that Beth licked it up and savored his salty taste.

"Oh Beth, take all of me."

And Beth did just that. With each stroke of her hand, her lips tightened and sucked until his body began to tremble.

"I love you. Oh God, Beth, I always have."

His declaration was like a symphony. Tears welled up in her eyes, but she was on a mission. Beth wanted to show him how much she loved him right back. As she took him deep into her mouth, Bryce jerked back and stood up while pulling her to her feet.

Without missing a step, Bryce picked her up and carried her to the bed.

He hovered over her until they locked eyes. "My turn," he said with a salacious grin, and began kissing down her body until he reached her breasts, giving them equal measure. Sucking her peaked buds into his mouth as though they were his nourishment. Bryce continued his lavish attention down to the apex of her sex.

Hot and wet, the torturous pleasure ran through her body with urgency. She clung to him as he ravaged her with his tongue, teeth and fingers until she writhed and cried out his name in a loud rapture.

As her climax began to settle, Bryce slid up her body and nestled himself between her legs.

"Condom," Beth whispered, pointing to the nightstand.

Bryce quirked a brow, but didn't ask why she had condom in the nightstand. He kissed her, reached over, and grabbed the closed wrapper. He sat up, ripped it open and rolled it on.

Bryce wasted no time and pulled Beth's legs up and slipped inside of her wet heat. "Oh fuck. Beth, you feel so damn good."

"Don't talk," Beth pleaded.

"As you wish." At first, Bryce moved in a slow rhythm.

"Faster." Beth grinded her hips up until he sped up the pace. Skin slapping against skin until their bodies melted into one, feverish and greedy.

Faster and faster, Bryce moved into her until he grated out her name between his teeth.

Beth's core tightened with each hard thrust, she called out his name at the same time. Three deep hard thrusts, and they both came in a climatic surge. Euphoric and exhausted, all her strength vanished, leaving her a molten mess.

Bryce collapsed on top of her with heavy breaths against her sweat-dampened skin.

"Bryce..." She couldn't finish.

He slipped out, breaking contact, and fell next to her. After he pulled off the condom, and dropped it in the wastebasket next to the bed, Bryce pulled Beth against him and kissed her shoulder and neck.

"Are you okay? I didn't hurt you, did I?" he asked, his right hand caressing her stomach and between her breasts.

"Yes," she said with a slight giggle. His fingers were doing delicious things to her skin.

"Why are you laughing?" He popped his head up to look at her face.

She turned around and looked at him. *Truth.* "Because I'm happy."

Bryce leaned in and kissed her with such adoration, Beth knew his words of love were real.

She pulled back. "Bryce?"

"Yes, Bethie?" She loved it when he called her that.

"I love you, too." There was no hesitation, no need to be afraid to get her heart broken. She told him how she had always loved him. "Always did. Always will."

"I love you always." Bryce wrapped his arms around her and they clung together with utter love and passion.

Epilogue

Holidays, especially New Year's Day were always about togetherness and new beginnings, especially in Beth's family. Yet, this year, Beth had passed on her parents' invitation for Christmas and New Years. It had always been an obligation, never a choice. This year, she'd let her brother and sister deal with their parents badgering and incessant bullying about Beth's choices she had made.

Apart from listening to her parents' complain, it wasn't a warm holiday welcome anyway. Beth realized that they were never going to be happy for her, and she accepted that. All her life she dealt with them, but not anymore. After the whole ordeal with Hannah, and now Bryce in Beth's life, there was no way she wanted negativity from her parents in her new life anymore.

Beth told them that she wasn't coming, and if they couldn't handle her decisions, and be happy for her, then they wouldn't have to worry about seeing or hearing from her again. Of course, they'd argued that their behavior was because they cared. They apologized, but were they really sorry? Beth knew, no matter how much sorry one person—or her parents said, she wouldn't believe them until they showed her.

Besides, she had so much work to do with Sweet Cupids.

The flurry of craziness during the Christmas season had turned out to be wonderful. The shop profited and pulled in plenty of money to cover all her expenses. What was even better?

Hannah signed all the proper papers Bryce drew up, with one stipulation he insisted; he would loan Beth the money to pay back Hannah, and in turn will pay him without any interest.

Beth knew not to argue with Bryce, and agreed to the terms but with interest. He agreed, and she in turn became the sole owner of Sweet Cupids.

Everything was going well, even her relationship with Bryce. They had spent every day together from the moment they made love. There was still a needle of worry that their relationship was moving too fast, but she just pushed the doubt aside and tried to focus on the good things they shared and the possible future they would have.

So, with the Yuletide done, Beth relaxed on the couch, waiting for the new year. As she worked on some numbers and went over the new menu—she'd added 'Beth's cookies' to the yummy list, the doorbell buzzed.

Bryce.

He'd called a few hours ago, saying he needed to drop something off before heading to his parents' house for a party.

He had invited her to attend, but she graciously declined. As much as she loved being with him, seeing his family—especially his father, didn't bode well with her. She wasn't sure if she could hold her tongue about how he pressured his son into marrying someone he never loved just to strengthen the family's firm.

With Mark, Bryce explained that his brother took off right after they called a truce. Still, she didn't think Bryce would ever get over his brother's betrayal. No amount of apologies would heal those wounds. Wherever Mark went, Beth hoped he'd fix his philandering ways.

Beth ran to the door, opened it and stood there in surprise. Unexpectedly, Bryce walked in with a large bag of food, namely Chang's Chinese take out—her favorite by the way.

"What are you doing?" Beth asked while shutting the door. She couldn't keep a wide smile off her face when the salivating aroma coming out of the brown paper bag made her want to drool. Or could it be simply brought on by the way Bryce was dressed.

He had on a pair of Lucky Brand jeans and a nicely form-fitting but worn out Pink Floyd t-shirt. Oh my God. He she loved the way he dressed down. She bit her lower lip to keep from groaning. A surge of need was rising, but she had to tamper it down or they'd make love and he'd be late to the party.

"New Year's Eve dinner for two." Bryce lifted a bottle of Cristal champagne from out of the bag. His devilish grin hinted that he had more in store for her.

"What about your parents' party?" Beth asked with excitement.

"Nope. I want to share this time with you and you only. We've been separated for too long, and I'm not going to let you spend another moment without me." He leaned in and kissed her. "Now, woman, I'm hungry. Stop asking so many damn questions and let's eat."

Beth let out a haughty laugh, but did as he asked. She grabbed two sets of her ladybug-embellished plates and matching highball glasses, and placed them on the rectangular coffee table.

Eating kung pao chicken, pot stickers, and sweet and sour pork, they shared their first home meal in a beautiful and loving way. To Beth, it was the best meal she had ever eaten.

"Since you brought dinner, I'll make dessert." She wiggled her brows at him.

Bryce's eyes went wide with delight. "Something chocolate?"

"Okay." Beth tapped her finger on her cheek and thought of something fast and easy to make. "How about a coffee cup chocolate cake?"

"Can I watch?" Bryce asked, rubbing his hands together as he got to his feet.

"Only if you don't share my secret recipe." She eyeballed him with a serious frown, but quickly grinned when he smiled like a little kid ready to lick a spoon full of batter.

"He raised two fingers and said, "Scouts honor."

Beth snorted. "Bryce, you are far from an honorable boy scout. Remember, I know your secrets." She got up from the couch and headed to the kitchen.

He smacked her on the rear and followed right behind her. "I'll show you later just how this boy scout can use ropes."

She glanced over her shoulder and let out another giggle. The idea of Bryce tying her up sent a sizzle of need right to her core, and the idea of tying him to the bed thriller her even more. Maybe sooner than later, as she tried to remember if she had any rope in her toolbox.

Shaking her head at the naughty thought, Beth concentrated on their dessert.

Within a few minutes Beth had all the ingredients and two large coffee cups in front of her. Once she combined all the ingredients, she had two cups half filled with cake batter. Beth placed one cup into the microwave and set the time for a minute and half. The second it beeped that it was done, she took the hot cup out and replaced it with the second cup with same amount of time.

While the cups cooled, Beth whipped up some vanilla frosting and added a few drops of red and green gel food coloring. With a fork, she carefully stirred without totally mixing the colors together.

The moment the cups cooled to the touch, Beth scooped the frosting and iced the cup-cake. She handed Bryce a spoon and said, "Happy New Year, honey."

"Happy New Year, Bethie." He scooped up the warm chocolate cake with a large dollop of frosting into his mouth and moaned in delight. "I had doubts, but this is good. You should become a baker." He chuckled and then shoved another spoon full into his mouth.

Beth laughed. "Hmm. Maybe you're right." She leaned in and kissed him, then licked the bit of frosting off the corner of his mouth.

Bryce dropped his spoon, grabbed Beth and wrapped his arms around her. "Got any rope?" And before she could answer, he kissed her senseless.

Oh, yeah, life is sweet.

Microwave Cup-Cake recipe

Single serving size/follow ingredients as steps

1 large Coffee Cup-microwavable
1 large Egg-fork whipped
2 Tbsp of melted Butter
2 Tbsp of Milk
1 tsp of Vanilla Extract
1/4th tsp of Sugar-(for sweeter batter add ½ tsp instead)-mix well
6 Tbsp of Self Rising Flour (Or add 1/8th tsp of baking powder to regular flour and sift)
1 tsp of Cocoa Powder
A pinch of Salt- mix well again
1 Tbsp of mini chocolate chips-stir lightly

Cook in microwave- 1 minute and 30 seconds- NO MORE!
Let it cool for five or more minutes. Cup may be still be hot, so need to be careful around children.
Frosting
6 to 8 Tbsp of Powered Sugar
Splash of Vanilla extract
Heavy whipping cream or whole milk- 1 tsp at a time until you get a loose toothpaste consistency.
Ice the Cup-Cakes.
Enjoy!

Made in the USA
Charleston, SC
09 February 2016